DARK FLIGHT

A COLD WAR THRILLER

JAMES BLATCH

VIVIDDOG

Dark Flight by James Blatch published by Vivid Dog Limited, 4a Church Street, Market Harborough, LE16 7AA, UK

ISBN: 978-1-8384894-3-4

Copyright © 2022 by James Blatch

All rights reserved.

No part of this book may be reproduced in any form or by any electronic or mechanical means, including information storage and retrieval systems, without written permission from the author, except for the use of brief quotations in a book review.

For permissions: contact@vivid-dog.com

This is a work of fiction. Names, characters, places, and incidents either are the products of the author's imagination or are used fictitiously. Any resemblance to actual persons, living or dead, businesses, companies, events, or locales is entirely coincidental.

Cover art: Stuart Bache

This book uses English (UK) spelling

PROLOGUE

Rosamond, California
May 21, 1947

The baseball disappeared into the blinding white of the midday sun. Red squinted, and held up his mitt in an attempt to block the light. The ball was smeared in the orange dust of the desert; he should be able to see it.

Instead, something else caught his eye.

High in the cloudless blue sky: a series of rapid bright flashes.

He lowered his arm, staring in wonder at the pulsing light.

"Damn," he muttered under his breath.

Behind him, the baseball thudded to the ground.

"Jesus, Red!" Joe called from the pitcher's mound.

The kid who'd hit the fly ball reached first base and stopped, staring at the distracted fielder.

But Red was on the move.

He threw his mitt to the ground and bolted, glancing up at the twisting, falling shape as he ran.

He reached his bike, scattered with the others on the ground.

"*Goddamn!*" *Joe shouted. "Where you goin', Red?"*

"Joseph. Language!" Mr Brookland admonished him from behind home plate, but Joe, too, was on the move.

"Red Brunson. Joseph Keel. The game's not over." Joe ignored Brookland and reached for his bike, threw himself on, and pedalled furiously after his friend.

With Joe a few yards behind him, Red swept out of the rustic, uneven patch of desert that Mr Brookland laughingly called a baseball field and on to the main road.

The falling shape was nearly down.

They gathered speed; thin, prefabricated homes flashed past on either side.

Amy Goodyear stopped skipping and stared at them.

"Hi, Red," she called with a beaming smile. Red looked and briefly considered pulling over, but he was on a mission.

He snapped his head back to the tumbling aircraft. The nose careened through the air. He knew enough about g-forces to wonder if the pilot could remain conscious.

It was also silent.

Why couldn't they hear it?

The aircraft grew larger.

Then it was there, just a few hundred yards away, filling the sky, until it disappeared behind the water tower.

A beat later, they heard a WHOMP, *and an orange fireball rose high above the light blue tower.*

The boys stamped on their brakes and came to a puncture-risking stop.

Red panted. He looked across at Joe. Without saying a word, they took off again. They turned right onto a path that ran between two of the houses. The lumpy dirt road became a lumpier dirt track.

"Boys! No!" A shout from an unseen adult; they ignored her.

The orange fire had been replaced by a thick plume of black smoke.

They got to the small wire fence that surrounded the faded water tower and dumped their bikes. Red took a running jump, and Joe followed.

They pushed through a thin row of trees and, for the first time, got a clear view of their target.

The wreckage was contained in a small area. A silver fin remained upright. The centre of the fuselage was mangled, the front cockpit area broken and scattered.

Flames licked around the remains of the jet fighter.

Red gulped and walked slowly towards the burning debris.

PART 1

BRANDON DUPONT

CHAPTER ONE

Aircraft Test and Evaluation Center
Edwards Air Force Base, California
June 10, 1965

"I'd like to say I'll be thinking about you all at A-TEC when I'm walking on the moon. But I can't lie to my friends."

Red leaned against the wall at the back of the room and peered past the short haircuts. He picked up a doughnut from a table at the back and took a bite as the farewell speech came to its conclusion.

He'd heard it before. Three times. And apparently there were four last year. So, that was seven men NASA had tempted away from Edwards's various test and experimental units.

He looked at his watch, frowned and tapped it. The military clock on the wall said 1710. His watch was misleading him as usual.

"You persisting with that thing?"

Red turned to find Jay Anderson laughing at him.

"Seriously, Red, you're the only test pilot I know who wears a broken watch. Look at it! It's falling apart."

"It's not broken," Red said, and rolled his sleeve down.

"Well, you must have been issued an IWC like the rest of us. You sold it?" Jay laughed again.

"I prefer this one. Now leave me alone." Red gave his friend a gentle push.

"Not before I have one of these boys," Jay said, as he reached down for a doughnut.

He took a bite and immediately spat into a napkin. "Damn. These things are stale." He threw the debris into a nearby wastebasket. "I bet they don't have stale doughnuts at NASA."

Red looked back at their departing comrade. "So, another one gone to Apollo. We'll be the only ones left soon."

"You can't blame him. Who wouldn't want to walk on the moon?"

"If they ever get there," Red said. "Long shot, if you ask me."

"You're just jealous."

Red shrugged. "Maybe. Even if I had the experience to apply, I'm not sure they'd have me."

Anderson didn't respond, but he gave Red a sympathetic smile.

"You've got the experience, Jay. Why don't you apply?"

"Who said I haven't?"

Red scrutinised him for a second. "Bullshit."

Anderson laughed. "I tried. Two years ago. Didn't make it."

"You never said anything."

"Guess I was embarrassed."

The room broke into applause as the speech ended.

Anderson put his hand on Red's shoulder and leaned into his ear. "They'll take you one day, Red. But you need to spread your wings a bit, buddy."

Red turned. "What do you mean?"

"You're getting a reputation for caution."

"Isn't that good?" Red felt a flush of disappointment that a fellow test pilot felt the need to speak to him like this.

Jay nodded slowly. "It has its place, but we need to press on with some of these projects. You've come back a couple of times having not completed the mission. Fine, you're worried about something or other, but—"

"But?"

"Maybe it's happening a bit too much with you."

Red thought back to his last couple of project flights. "But the B-57 had a shake. A vibration."

"You were testing a new camera housing on the belly. Of course it felt different." Jay stared at him.

Red spoke carefully. "It was getting worse. I curtailed the flight and wrote it up for the engineers. It felt like the right thing to do."

Again, Jay nodded and looked sympathetic, but it was clear he was letting Red know he'd made a mistake.

"You could have taken it to altitude and probably even to limit speed. The vibration measurements would have been a lot more useful."

"Even if I thought it was dangerous?"

"That's the thing, Red. We're test pilots. You want safety, join Pan Am."

Red thought his caution and safety-conscious approach to flying was an advantage. He assumed it was the reason he'd won his place at Pax River.

No-one had spoken to him like this before.

Jay must have seen the hurt look on his face. "Look, it's

fine. You're new to test flying. You're trying hard, but it's probably time to start pushing things more. You're never gonna get to fly the black stuff until you've proved you can handle it. Time for a new start?"

"They'll never let me near an A-12."

"Red!" A bark came across the room. Both men turned to see Colonel Tucker Montgomery pointing at his corner office.

Jay stared. "Uh-oh. Chickens coming home to roost for you so soon?" He gave Red a friendly slap on the back.

"This can't be good," Red said, as he pushed his way through the dispersing crowd.

Two sides of the colonel's office were windows that looked out onto the unit's little corner of Edwards. As the boss shuffled into his seat behind his desk, Red watched as the mechanics pushed the last of the silver machines back into the dark recesses of A-TEC's hangars. Each aircraft was unique at Edwards, and it usually had its own team of engineers.

His eyes rested on two armed guards posted outside the nearest building.

Montgomery followed his gaze, twisting in his chair. He turned back and smiled. "We have some new toys to play with."

"Toys that have their own armed guards?" Red said.

Montgomery studied him. The silence became uncomfortable. After a while, he opened a folder and began reading. "Project Xenon. Camera housing. Flight One curtailed because of excessive vibration. Modified Aim-9 fins. First flight curtailed due to . . ." He squinted at the report. "Unusual drag characteristics. Project completed by Jay

Anderson. I could go on." He looked up. "You've had an interesting first six months as a qualified test pilot."

"I'm sorry, sir. I made the best call I could."

"Those were expensive calls. Each project delay gets my ass kicked from above. The camera on the B-57 was for the National Reconnaissance Office, and believe me, those guys are not used to delays."

Red bowed his head.

Montgomery held his tone. "We're test pilots, son. We need to push the envelope before we give up. If you're gonna make it at Edwards, you need to grow a pair. Understood?"

"Yes, sir."

Montgomery lifted himself from his chair and moved to the front of his desk. "You've had a tough start in life, I know that. It's why I stuck my neck out for you after you graduated from Pax River. I understand why you're scared. Who wouldn't be, with your background? But you gotta pick things up. Start paying me back for the trust I've shown in you. In short, Red, I need you to cut the crap and start flying."

"Yes, sir."

"Yes, well. I've got another problem now."

Red looked up as Montgomery leaned behind him and picked up a phone. He covered the handset for a moment. "We're running out of test pilots." He reacted as his call was answered. "Tell Johnny to get in here with that Mississippi article." He replaced the receiver. "We've lost three to NASA this year, and A-TEC is always last in the pecking order for the new boys from the schools. We're gonna be short for a couple of years. When I explained this to the Nation Reconnaissance Office, well, let's just say they weren't very supportive."

The door opened, and Johnny Clifford, A-TEC's chief test pilot, came in with a newspaper under his arm.

"They've got something big coming down the line," Montgomery said. "Something high-priority big. The NRO know we're stretched, and they're worried. Now, I can't tell you what's coming, not yet, anyway, but it's the type of project this unit was created for." He paused as he opened the newspaper. "So, there's a plan to fill the pilot vacancies. It's a terrible plan, and I want to be clear, it was the NRO's idea." He gave out a long sigh. "But we figure we have no choice. Tell him, Johnny."

Clifford spread the opened newspaper on the table.

"We're going to establish a new role. Utility Test Pilot."

"What does that mean?" Red said.

"The UTPs will do the grunt work. They need to be engineering-minded, of course, to fit in around here. But we're reducing the need for them to have graduated from the test-pilot schools."

"We're gonna take on regular pilots? As test pilots?"

"They'll work alongside the test pilots. They can ferry the aircraft for maintenance and positioning. They can even fly the routine trials. Straight and level, instrument calibration stuff. I hate to say it, but the NRO's right. We send highly qualified TPs on a lot of routine flights."

"You want me to be a Utility Test Pilot?" Red said quietly.

"Of course not," Montgomery barked. "We want you as a reliable, fully qualified test pilot, we can trust."

"You can trust me now, sir."

"Can I?"

The room was quiet for a moment.

The colonel reached forward and tapped the inside spread of the *Mississippi Clarion*. "What do you see?"

Red examined the pages.

A photograph of a man in dungarees standing next to a biplane. Headline: *THE FLYING HILLBILLY.*

A second picture of a crop duster and a middle-aged man with a leather flying cap in the open cockpit.

Red shrugged. "A farmer in a Boeing Stearman."

Clifford and Montgomery exchanged a quick look. "Check again, son," Clifford said.

Red looked closer; the picture quality wasn't great.

But now he saw it.

The wings were swept. The engine was a radial, but not the usual for a Stearman. Actually, lots of small things were different.

"What is this? I don't recognise it."

"That's because he built it," Clifford said. "From parts thrown out by a couple of flying circuses. And when he couldn't find the parts, he milled them from scratch."

Montgomery lit a cigarette and leaned back. "He redesigned the wings. Albert out there reckons he's given the Stearman a shape that is thirty percent more fuel efficient and fifty percent faster. Although how the hell he gets it airborne on a short grass strip is anybody's guess. Maybe he's added rockets."

Red stared at the face of the farmer, who looked back through the grainy image. Serious but unthreatening. A run-of-the-mill advanced aircraft engineer working on a backwater farm in the Deep South.

"Raw talent," Montgomery said, waving his cigarette in the air. "He was an unremarkable USAF jet pilot. Flew Sabres in Korea but came out when he got back, to run the family farm."

"Jet experience and an eye for aerodynamics and engineering," Clifford added. "These guys are rare. We want him recruited."

Red finished studying the pictures and looked up. Both senior men stared at him.

"We've written to him," Montgomery said. "Eventually got him to agree to a meeting. But he was a no-show. Red, we want you to take a shot at it. Let's recruit Brandon Dupont as our first UTP." Montgomery had a smile on his face.

Red looked between the two men. "Me? Sir, you want me to recruit him? With the greatest respect, I think my best role here is as a pilot. I'm not sure I'll—"

"Son, you're on thin ice with me and Johnny. You know that, right? You're costing us budget, and you could end up costing us an entire project. But we need you. Not just to fill a seat, but to excel in your role as an experimental aircraft pilot. You need to learn to push that safety-first thing down a notch." Another wave of the cigarette from Montgomery. "And we think this little job might help broaden your horizons a bit. And give you some time to think. Take you out of the cosy little world you seem to inhabit."

It was little more than an admin task. And Montgomery's concerns about Red's abilities were unnerving him.

"Think of it as a punishment for bailing on two major projects, if you like," Johnny Clifford added.

Red stared back at the picture. The farmer's face gave nothing away. Where would he start?

"Fly down to Shitsville, Mississippi, and bring me this farmer." Montgomery paused and waited until Red looked up. "Then we can talk about the NRO project."

Montgomery's looked expectantly at Red.

"You want to talk to me about the NRO project?"

He noticed a quick exchange of looks between the colonel and Johnny Clifford.

"That's way we're going to do it. Johnny will take the lead, and we'll assign a junior test pilot alongside him. That could be you."

Red looked down to the newspaper. "If I recruit this guy?"

"We need to know we can rely on you. We'll start with this little task." He tapped the newspaper. "Sign up Brandon Dupont, then we'll talk."

Red wasn't sure if Montgomery was being completely serious. But he thought better of challenging the notion that he needed to recruit a farmer to work at A-TEC before he was assigned to a major project.

He was gonna have to suck it up and head across America.

Clifford stood up. "One other thing. We're up against the Defense Intelligence Agency on this one. They issue the security clearances, and they hate the plan almost as much as we do. So, some DIA guy's gonna hold your hand. We can't sign Dupont without the clearance, so you'll need to be very persuasive."

"Don't piss him off," added Montgomery.

CHAPTER TWO

THE T-38 TALON sat gleaming on the line outside the A-TEC hangar, factory fresh, like a Mustang straight off the line. Ready to purr.

Red climbed up the ladder and laid his helmet and charts on the seat, before climbing back down to walk around, as a technician strapped his holdall into the vacant rear seat.

Minutes later, he climbed away from the California desert and set his heading due east. He allowed the jet to settle at thirty thousand feet and three hundred knots indicated. As he passed over Barstow, he reached forward and activated the timer built into the panel.

It was the least challenging navigation exercise he could think of. A straight line east to a refuelling stop at Kirtland, New Mexico, and then a further hop east on to Columbus Air Force Base, Mississippi.

Five hours in a small cockpit with no one to talk to.

He had his notes on Brandon Dupont tucked into his flight suit, but they were sparse. Dupont was unreachable by telephone, and pretty much unheard of since he'd left the air force.

Below, the shades of brown gave way to green tinges as he crossed into Arizona. The jet was trimmed nicely; he took his hand off the stick and relaxed.

He rolled up his sleeve and inspected his watch, running a finger along the curved outline of the Omega. Each irregular dent and scratch was as familiar as the lines on his own hand.

As the T-38 passed over Flagstaff, he looked out to the left. In the distance was an area of forest with a distinct tear in the earth beyond.

He exhaled at the sight of the Grand Canyon.

"Would you look at that?" he said to no one.

A couple of hours later, he began a descent to his refuelling stop.

Landing at Kirtland was an interesting experience. The air base shared its runway with a civilian airport, and Red had to hold ten miles west of the field. He quickly leafed through the charts to find holding pattern "Zulu."

Once on the ground, he had to work hard again to take the correct taxi route to the refuelling area.

He stepped onto the apron and stretched his legs. It was warm.

As two men emerged from a fuel truck, Red headed off to find a telephone. He needed the latest weather.

On his return, he was disappointed to see the refuelling operation was still ongoing. Tutting to himself, he climbed up to the rear seat of the T-38 and unzipped his holdall.

He took out a small wad of briefing notes and passed the time by familiarising himself with what would greet him in Mississippi.

The Defense Intelligence Agency guy he was to meet at

Columbus was called Leo Rodriguez. Durden Creek Yard was the address they had for Dupont. Red looked at an overhead photograph of the place: a small collection of rundown farm buildings, a few pieces of rusting machinery. These folks were poor.

The only thing that stood out was the landing strip that ran close to the farm. It looked neat and well maintained, just about the only thing that was.

"You're good to go, sir," came the call from one of the refuelers.

"Thanks. Is the huffer nearby? I've got some bad weather coming in to my destination."

The kid looked confused.

"The huffer? The air blower to start the jet?"

"Ah! On its way, sir," he said, but Red couldn't see it anywhere close.

He stretched one more time then climbed back in, tucking his paperwork into the gap between the canopy and the panels. Ten frustrating minutes later, the ground crew finally arrived with the huffer, connecting the hoses to give him the pressurised air he needed for the start.

Air Traffic were helpful, and he went through the start, taxi, and line-up procedure in five minutes. A moment later, he accelerated the Talon back into the clear sky.

Just another nine hundred miles.

Ninety minutes later, the earth changed again. From the flat, featureless deserts of west Texas, the land became green at Oklahoma City. By the time he crossed into Arkansas, Red was mesmerised by the swirling rivers and forests.

As he passed into east Mississippi, the clouds began to build. Out to the south, he saw a collection of ominous Cb. Cumulonimbus. Thunderstorm clouds that would eat a small airplane like the T-38 for breakfast.

He plotted the path of the cloud build-up and realised he needed to get down quickly.

Edging the throttle forward, he increased his cruise to four hundred twenty knots, keeping an eye on his reserve fuel. He needed to land with thirty minutes in the tank. Unit rules.

He got on the radio with Columbus as soon as he could, and they cleared him in for a straight approach to runway 13.

Red adjusted his heading to take him northeast, calculating the minimum turn he could make to get the jet on the ground. Clouds began to gather beneath him. He chose a gap and dived the T-38. At five thousand feet, the ride became bumpy, just below the lowest layer of thick cumulus.

He crossed a wide river about two miles from the threshold and looked up to see his first lightning strike, around five miles south of the field.

"This is going to be tight."

After five hours sitting on an ejection seat, he really did not want to divert. But the desire to press on had killed many before him.

He made the finals turn, careful to keep enough power on through the buffet the Talon was famous for. He dropped the flaps and gear as he rounded out and held the jet at one hundred fifty-five knots.

Another lightning strike to the south.

Concentrate, buddy . . .

Red held the nose up, and the aircraft came down firmly. He stepped on the wheel brakes and held the stick back, killing the speed as efficiently as he could.

Turning off the runway, the tower told him he had about two minutes before they were shutting the airfield down, so he'd better make this bit quick.

He parked but didn't wait for the chocks to be in place before setting the throttles to cutoff and quickly shutting the Talon down.

The rain started as the stairs were pushed alongside, and by the time the crew chief released his holdall from the rear seat, it was torrential.

He left the chief to close the jet up and ran across the flight line, diving into the nearest building, pursued by another strike of lightning.

As he signed the visitors' log, an airman handed him a telephone message from Leo Rodriguez. An order from the agent to check into a motel eight miles south of the base.

Red climbed into his air force-allocated Chevrolet Nova and drove out into the apocalyptic rain. Water seeped in on the driver's-side window.

The motel was small: about ten years old, and already down on its luck.

Behind the counter, a middle-aged woman with a cigarette hanging from her lips stared at a small TV set. As Red arrived, she pushed a registration form towards him. He filled it in, passed her eight bucks for the room and incurred her disdain by asking for an invoice.

"Sorry, ma'am, but I'll be darned if I'm going to pay for this."

"Quite right" came a voice from behind.

Red swung around. A short, balding man sat on a small couch. He wore round spectacles and clutched a briefcase.

The man stood up. "Captain Brunson, I presume?"

Red nodded. "Leo Rodriguez?"

Rodriguez held out a hand, and Red shook it.

The DIA agent caught the look of surprise on Red's face.

"You were expecting me, Captain?"

"Yes. Sorry. It's just . . . your name. I was expecting someone different."

The agent leaned closer and whispered, "We don't always use our real names."

"Of course. Sorry."

"No problem. And I hope you don't mind me dragging you away from the base? We prefer to operate away from the crowds."

"Well, I was looking forward to a steak in the Columbus O Club. But I'm sure we'll find somewhere better."

Rodriguez smiled. "Not on my allowance, we won't."

Red dropped his bags in the room, peeled off his flight suit, and stepped under the weak shower.

Thirty minutes later, dressed in his civilian clothes, he walked out to meet Rodriguez, the humidity hitting him full in the face. The rain had stopped, and the sun had reappeared. Steam rose from the ground as the moisture quickly condensed.

Rodriguez waved from the parking lot, standing next to a gleaming Chevy Impala.

"There's a diner a couple of miles that way." Rodriguez pointed at the highway.

"Good with me." Red ran a hand over the car, admiring the sleek lines. "You travel from Washington in this, Leo?"

"Yes, sir. They do look after us at the agency."

"Apart from the food and accommodation?"

Rodriguez glanced at him. "Like I say, in our jobs, it doesn't do to become too familiar."

Figures from all the agencies turned up at Edwards from time to time, but this was Red's first close encounter with a bona fide field agent. A spy? Is that what they were? He didn't want to sound stupid, so didn't ask.

They pulled up to a diner: a single-storey, powder-blue building set back from the main road. Rodriguez parked and Red peered out his window, wincing at the puddles of water in the parking lot.

As the NSA agent got out, Red nodded to a large stain that ran across both seats. "You gonna get billed for that?"

Rodriguez turned around and looked back. "Stupid milkshake. Went all over me. I'll hand the car back with seat covers. They'll never know." He laughed.

Inside, they both ordered burgers and lemonade.

The agent looked out the window, and Red felt awkward. Leo Rodriguez clearly wasn't much of a conversationalist.

"So, the Defense Intelligence Agency, right?" Red said eventually.

"That's right." Rodriguez replied but didn't elaborate.

"Hmm. I get confused by all the different agencies up there in DC."

"It's easy. The National Security Agency has nothing to do with security, and the Defense Intelligence Agency has nothing to do with intelligence. The important thing to understand is that no one talks to anyone else, and we all hate each other."

"I see." Red replied, unsure if he was supposed to laugh.

To his relief, Rodriguez smiled.

"Anyway, you're not here for a lesson in government departments, Captain Brunson. You want me to clear your farmer to work at Edwards?"

"Yes, please."

They stopped talking as the food and drinks arrived. Once the waitress was beyond listening range, Rodriguez stuck a fork into a pile of fries and held them briefly in front of his mouth.

"I don't think we're gonna be able to clear him. Sorry." He ate the forkful.

Red put his own cutlery down. "I've flown a thousand miles for nothing?"

"Like I say, sorry if it's a waste of your time."

"What's the issue? My boss is pretty excited about him."

Rodriguez tapped his briefcase and rested it on the bench.

"I've done as much as I can. There's nothing on him, outside his service career. He has no civilian background to check. He started in the army, somehow got a college degree out of them before transferring to the air force. Right time, right place. He was fast-tracked onto jets. Converted onto the F-86 Sabre and shipped to Korea. But then, that's it. He came back, got out as fast as he could, and disappeared. We have his Social Security number, but he hasn't popped up on government paperwork for five years."

"So, what's the problem?"

Rodriguez shrugged. "The agency likes to know who we're dealing with. Clearing someone to work at Edwards and Groom Lake is a big deal. We're not comfortable that this guy is outside the usual career path."

"So, what do we do?" Red tucked into his own burger and took a slurp of the cool lemonade. Rodriguez had a calmness and a straightforwardness about him; he'd expected more mystery and distance.

"We go see him tomorrow, it's only ninety miles, although the roads get pretty poor the further you get from here. We talk." Rodriguez shrugged. "He might not want to join, anyway."

"And if he does? That leaves me with a big problem. I can't go back empty-handed."

Rodriguez toyed with his fork. "I'll do my best to fill in

the blanks on his resumé. After that, I can make a call. But don't get your hopes up. It doesn't look great at the moment. And I'm at the end of three-week road trip, so I'm going home after tomorrow either way."

The car jumped, and Red woke with a start.

"Good nap, flyboy?" Rodriguez was laughing at him.

"Where are we?" Red looked out on the rough dirt road. Trees, fields, nothing else.

"We're about ten miles north of Coffeeville, which is in the middle of nowhere, so we're beyond that point."

"Hicksville, USA."

"You got that right."

Red leaned forward and rubbed his lower back. "You weren't joking about these roads."

Progress was slow, but as they rounded a sharp bend in the road, they were greeted by the sight of a large barn, two smaller farm buildings, and a ramshackle wooden house with most windows boarded up. Rusting machinery littered a wooded area to the left of the house. The place looked abandoned, nothing like a viable farm.

But standing out from the ruins was a gleaming airplane. A big, beautiful Stearman-like biplane. Significantly more striking in real life than in those grainy newspaper pictures.

Red whistled, and his eyes went to the wings. They were quite something: swept and beautifully engineered. "Hey, stop the car a second."

They drew to a halt, and Red got out. The cicadas were in full voice, and it was about ten degrees hotter than Columbus.

He undid a button on his shirt—strictly against regulations—and walked over to the biplane, resting on its tail wheel.

The wings had been machined to perfection. They were definitely narrower than a regular Stearman. He ducked under and ran his hand over a strange line set back from the leading edge. A break in the surface a few inches from the leading edge. Metal rods ran from two hinges.

"This thing has slats," he said to himself.

A strong southern accent called out. "Can I help you, son?" Red sprang up.

A tall man in his early forties walked towards him. His hair was neatly parted to the side and slick with something. Otherwise, he looked like a poor southern farmer: oil-stained pants, a blue check shirt, and worn leather boots that may have seen service in the war.

"I was just admiring your airplane."

Red glanced at Rodriguez, standing by his car. Watching, evaluating.

He stuck his hand out. "I'm Captain Red Brunson of the United States Air Force. And I'm guessing you're Mr Dupont?"

Brandon Dupont nodded, but didn't step any closer.

Red withdrew his hand. "Mind if I call you Brandon?"

"Okay, sir."

"Please, call me Red." He turned to the aircraft. "Hey, Brandon, does this thing have slats?"

Dupont moved slowly around to the front of the modified Stearman; Red followed. The older man ran his hand along the hinged break in the wing. Through the yellow frame of the aircraft, Red noticed an elderly man in dungarees standing in the gloom of the doorway of the house. He might have been anywhere between sixty-five and one hundred years old.

Noticing Red's gaze, Dupont turned around. "It's all right, Pappy. Go on in." The farmer turned back to the aircraft. "Flaps on the front, if that's what you mean by slats. They create drag and lift. Enough to see her up safely from the strip and not get dragged down by the trees over yonder."

Dupont motioned to the start of the grass runway about fifty yards away. Red studied the ground; it looked the best-maintained piece of land on the farm. Red guessed he had four hundred feet of usable strip, followed by a ditch, some undergrowth, and then at maybe eight hundred feet, a small cluster of trees. It looked tight.

He looked back at the slats. The hinge was lubricated with shiny metallic parts and a tight wire, exposed over the top of the wing, trailing back to the cockpit.

"Did you make these yourself?" Red asked.

"Yup. Built them in the shop here. She was okay until I put the new wings on. Smaller, faster in the air, but longer takeoff roll. I learned the scary way she'd outgrown the strip." Dupont laughed.

"I can imagine. And so, this was your solution. Brandon, you invented a leading-edge, high-lift device, presumably without knowing what it was."

Dupont shrugged. "I knew what it was. Never understood why the Sabres didn't have something similar. We used a whole lotta runway getting those in the air."

"Korea?"

"Yep."

Red looked over the rest of the aircraft. An additional strut seemed to have been added to the landing gear on each side. Again, beautifully engineered.

"You got a lathe somewhere?" Red said, while crouched under the wing.

"Got some old forge tools."

Red shook his head at the thought of this man hand-crafting precision aero parts in a rustic blacksmith's shed in Mississippi.

He looked back; Dupont was staring at him.

Red took a step closer. "Brandon, you're probably wondering why we're here?" The farmer didn't respond. "Well, I work for a very special unit based in California. And I've got something very exciting to offer you."

Again, Dupont, didn't move or respond. Red stayed silent, returning the stare.

Eventually, the farmer nodded slowly. "Uh-huh."

"We need people like you."

"People like me? Farmers?"

"No, Brandon. We need aeronautical engineers who can fly."

The farmer's expression didn't change. "How much do you weigh?"

"I'm sorry, what?"

"How much do you weigh, Captain?"

"About one sixty."

Dupont moved to the aircraft and reached into the cockpit, retrieving a leather helmet. He turned back to Red with a wide grin.

"Wanna go for a ride?"

Red studied the aircraft and considered the offer. He knew Dupont might invite him up, and he'd dismissed the idea of flying in an aircraft built in someone's backyard. But now that he saw it in the flesh, it was clear this machine was a labour of love. The machining was precise; the engineering looked sound.

And there was something deliberate and methodical

about Dupont himself. If that's how he approached flying, it was going to be a safe ride.

"Okay."

Red helped push the biplane around until it was clear of the barn and facing into the gentle breeze. Dupont handed him the battered leather helmet.

He looked across at Rodriguez and gave him a wave. The DIA man shook his head, but Red ignored him and climbed into the front cockpit.

As he strapped himself in, he checked the anchor points. They looked secure, possibly original from Boeing.

Dupont appeared on the wing next to him, crouched down, and pulled on his straps to ensure they were tight.

He had to admit, the man knew what he was doing.

"There ain't no flying controls in the front, so it'll be up to me if we get in trouble. Sit tight. I'll get her down. Once we stop, get out quick as you can. She's full of gas."

Red nodded at the ad hoc emergency brief. "Got it."

"Well, all right."

Dupont climbed into the rear cockpit, and Red listened to the sound of pulleys and wheels being pulled and turned. Moments later, the engine turned over twice and burst into life. The air buffeted above the plexiglass as the engine noise increased and they started to move.

The ground was smooth for the short journey to the cut landing strip. With the aircraft sitting on its rear wheel, Red had to stretch up in his straps to see the tress ahead.

He was about to find out if Dupont's makeshift high-lift actually worked.

A sheet tied to a metal pole flapped gently at one side of the strip. Wind sock. Slight cross breeze.

Before they entered the runway, Dupont turned into the wind and wound the engine up a notch. He was doing his power checks, another sign that his military flying training was embedded in his routine.

The leading edge of the lower wing was on the move. Red imagined Dupont winding a handle for his improvised slats.

They dropped down by maybe twenty degrees; it was clear that they would add considerable lift.

Dupont moved the Stearman until it faced down the strip. The engine wound up to full power, and they began to roll.

The aircraft pitched forward as the tail wheel came up and, almost immediately, they floated into the air.

"Jesus, this thing wants to fly."

They swept over the trees with plenty of clearance and continued to climb. Dupont put them in a gentle left bank, and Red watched the slats winding back in, followed by the flaps.

They continued the bank and climbed higher. At five thousand feet, in the cool air, they cleared a large lake south of the farm. Dupont began his show.

There were no comms between them, and Red found it difficult to twist in the harness to look back. He figured he was along for the ride and that was that.

The nose pitched up, and Dupont led the aircraft into a smooth and accurate barrel roll. All the way through, Red felt an even 1g holding him in his seat. If he had been an examiner, he would be extremely happy with his student.

The nose dipped, power came on, and Red felt the grunt from the modified engine. Dupont heaved her up into a three-sixty-degree loop. This time Red felt pushed into the seat, impressed at the energy the aircraft sustained.

Between each manoeuvre, Dupont climbed back up to five thousand feet, ensuring a good margin. This was no cowboy pilot.

The demonstration grew progressively more complex and included a vertical stall. Dupont them pitched down, gathered energy, and then pulled them into a steep climb, raising the nose until it was more or less straight up. The energy fell off quickly. For a second they hung in the air high above the Mississippi farmland, before the home-built Stearman began to fall backwards.

This was the sort of position an aircraft could fail to recover from in the wrong hands. But Dupont had the aircraft just offset from the vertical, and with full deflected rudder, she smoothly fell through one eighty degrees into a nose-down attitude for a perfect recovery.

It was an alarming manoeuvre for a passenger, but Red had to admit, the farmer had the skills.

As they descended, Red looked at the smooth rivets in the airframe; he ran a finger over the bright silver buttons, not a scratch, shard or notch to be seen.

Pilot skills and engineering proficiency. He could see why Montgomery wanted him at Edwards.

The aircraft descended and gathered speed. The wind became a roar over the small windshield as they reached the treetops.

Red tried to estimate their speed. One hundred seventy-five knots?

He held on to the sides of the airframe as the modified Stearman began to buffet.

"Jesus." He breathed into the tornado of air crashing into them.

His stomach went south as Dupont pulled them up through what Red figured was around 5G.

Off the top of the pull-up, the Stearman fell around into a curved approach. Dupont touched down with a firm thud and rolled them out on the grass before killing the engine as the aircraft drifted to a halt.

Red removed his leather flying helmet and straps and stood on the seat, holding out his hand.

Dupont looked surprised, but shook it all the same. "Glad you enjoyed it, son."

"I did, very much, thank you. Now, Brandon Dupont. How about that chat?"

The house was dingy and smelled of rotting timber. Gaps in the boarded-up windows let in only the odd shaft of sunlight, illuminating swirls of dust.

A discoloured mirror hung over the fireplace. No photographs, no paintings, no ornaments. Nothing that said it was a home to anyone.

Pappy sat in a rocking chair, in the shade at the back of the room. Dupont stood in the centre, with folded arms.

"So, what do y'all wanna say?"

Red looked around at the old sofa and chair and thought better of trying to sit on either.

He pointed to a dining table behind the sofa. "Could we sit down?"

The three men took their seats, but not before Red and Rodriguez tested the rickety chairs with a quick prod.

Dupont sat at an angle with an arm resting on the table.

Before Red could say anything, Rodriguez fired off his first question.

"Why'd you leave the air force, Brandon?"

The farmer didn't flinch at the directness. Instead, he studied Rodriguez.

"Done my time."

Rodriguez waited, but clearly no further illumination was coming. He made a note. "You have a pilot's license for that thing?"

"*That thing* has its own license. Yes, sir. From the FAA. I have my own license, too. That what this is about? You come to ground me?"

"No, Brandon," Red said quickly. "Quite the opposite."

"You have any other relatives alive?" Rodriguez said.

Dupont shook his head. "Just me and Pappy now."

Rodriguez studied his notes and opened a brown file. "Says here you served in Korea. In Kunsan?"

Dupont nodded.

"But you didn't want to stay in and keep flying?"

"Ma died. Jo died. I had the farm to look after."

"Jo?" Red asked.

"My sister. Died of fever in '53."

"I'm sorry," Red added.

Dupont looked at Red and smiled. "Thank you, Red."

Red felt the warmth in his sympathy. The older pilot had a deep maturity and calmness about him.

Flying experience and a little worldly wisdom. Wasted out here.

He glanced at Rodriguez. The agent was leafing through his notes. Red turned back to their host. "Brandon, I want to make you an offer."

On the edge of his vision, he saw Pappy turn his head very slightly.

"You're exactly what we're looking for at Edwards Air Force Base in California. Have you heard of Edwards? Chuck Yeager? It's where he broke the sound barrier, in an X-15."

"Damn nearly killed him," Dupont said, and leaned

back in his chair. "They didn't understand the pressure wave."

Red laughed. "That's right, they didn't. But they modified the wing and controls, and they got there. And that's what we do. We test and revise until things work. Now, you wouldn't be a qualified test pilot, but we would get you fully certified as an engineer and a commercial pilot. You'd be a key part of the team, moving aircraft and helping the qualified TPs like me with our workload. You'd have a nice house, access to the base facilities, including a medical centre. You and your father would be well looked after."

"Uh-huh . . ."

"Uh-huh, yes?"

Dupont lowered his gaze.

"This is an incredible offer, Mr Dupont," Rodriguez said. "Why aren't you biting his hand off?"

More silence from the farmer.

"And you know what?" Red said. "We have a great time. Lots of parties. And the flying? Well it's the best in the world. Of course, you'd have to pass the clearance process from Mr Rodriguez here, and there'd be a refresher course to pass in the T-38. But even that would be quite something. I can tell you, the Talon is a helluva ride."

"Them that fly out of Columbus?"

"That's right. We have a few just for us pilots to get around. It'd be your regular jet. It's supersonic, Brandon. Beats an old biplane any day of the week."

No answer, but a hint of a smile.

Red glanced at Pappy, who remained as still as a shop dummy.

Rodriguez lifted his briefcase onto the table. "Son, can I ask you a couple of more questions?"

"Uh-huh."

33

The DIA agent lifted out a small wad of papers and took the lid off a fountain pen.

"Did you go to school?"

"Sorta. Miss Honeybeach teached us for a couple of years. Then I had to pull my shifts here."

"Ok, so you didn't go to college."

"Not until I joined the army. They sent me."

Rodriguez looked down at his forms. "Did you ever apply for anything after you left the air force? Are you registered with a doctor?"

"Doc comes here to see Pappy, but we don't pay. He does it for free."

Red smiled to himself at this family living in the nineteenth century in the middle of modern America, like pioneers arriving in the West. He pictured bath night once a week in front of the stove.

Yet, somehow, he was perfect for them. A natural engineer and pilot, and so confident, assured. The army gave him an education, found his potential, lifted him up. Now he was falling back down. Red wanted him to join A-TEC, not just because it was a waste leaving him on the farm, but because he was good. He couldn't imagine him ever getting flustered in the air.

"Brandon." Red put his palm on the table. "Whaddya think? You want to move to California and work with the latest flying technology in the world?"

For the first time, Dupont looked across at Pappy. "Well, that's mighty kind of you, and I sure do 'preciate you comin' all this way. But I don't think I can just leave here. With or without Pappy. We got four fields now. I do most of it by myself." He shrugged as if that was that.

Red sat back in his chair. His chance of progressing to the NRO project had hit a wall of obstinance.

Rodriguez shuffled his papers and leaned forward. "Son, I don't think you fully understand what's on offer here. This is a once-in-a-lifetime opportunity. You'll never get a chance like this again."

There was a movement to the side, and Red looked around to see Pappy stand up and leave the room. Maybe this was his chance to hear what Dupont really thought.

"You and me flying together in California," Red said. "You want to say yes!"

Dupont looked down at his shoes and scratched the table with his dirty fingernails. "I'd better say no, sir. But like I say, I sure do 'preciate the offer."

"C'mon, man. This is silly. You worried about the fields and whose gonna farm them? You'll be on a government salary of . . . Leo, what's the salary?"

Rodriguez scanned a document in the papers on the table.

"Four thousand two hundred twelve dollars. That's nearly three hundred fifty dollars a month, son."

"He said no."

Red whipped his head around to see Pappy standing in the middle of the room with a shotgun aimed at them.

"Shit," Red said.

"Pappy . . ." Dupont spoke in a tone someone would use to gently chastise a cat. "No need for that. These people were just leaving."

Rodriguez leaped to his feet. "Sir, please put the gun down. We're here on official government business. You're committing a felony."

Red stood up slowly, keeping his eyes on the old man.

Pappy took a step forward and kept the gun levelled at them. "He said no. Now get out."

35

Rodriguez looked panicked. He stuffed his paperwork into his briefcase.

But Red slowly turned back to Dupont and whispered, "Is this what you want, man?"

"Now!" Pappy shouted.

Dupont avoided Red's eye, as he followed Rodriguez past the snarling father and into the brightness outside.

It took a second for Red's eyes to adjust to the bright sunlight. He paused, but felt a prod in the back. Pappy was an inch behind him.

Protecting his son from a better life.

Refusing to show any fear, Red walked slowly to the car. Rodriguez was already stuffing his case into the back before climbing in.

As they pulled away, Red glanced back to see Pappy standing steadfast in the yard. In the shadow of the doorway behind him, he could just about make out the figure of Brandon Dupont.

They stopped at a diner in Coffeeville. The adrenaline burst prompted by the sight of a levelled 12-gauge had subsided, and Red felt tired.

Rodriguez looked pale. How much time had this pudgy guy actually spent in the field?

"What do we do now?" Red asked.

"I'm tempted to report him to the locals," Rodriguez said. He stirred his coffee and looked lost in thought.

"But you're not going to?" Red asked, prompting him.

Rodriguez exhaled. "I doubt they'd do anything. This probably counts as normal behaviour around here. In any case, that would be the end of it for Brandon Dupont."

"So you think it's not over? There's still a chance?" Red was surprised.

Rodriguez shook his head. "No. We're done." He stopped stirring and looked directly at Red. "It's a damn shame, but that's that."

The food arrived. Red's mind was turning over. "I don't think we should give up so easily."

"We don't have a choice, Red. The old man chased us off with a shotgun. I'm not going back there, that's for sure."

"But you saw Dupont. He's a genius, living in a cow field. He could be at Edwards, at the centre of it all. A pilot among the best in the world."

Rodriguez stuck a fork into his hash browns. "You can't save everyone you meet, Red Brunson."

Back at the motel parking lot, Rodriguez shook Red's hand as he climbed into his car.

"You heading back north?"

Rodriguez tapped his briefcase "I've gotta little paperwork to do, then I'll get on the road. I prefer to drive overnight." He gave a weak smile. "I'm sorry it didn't work out for you, Captain."

"Yeah. Me, too." Red heaved his overnight bag from the trunk.

"Where will you be tonight?" Rodriguez asked.

"In the Bachelor Officer Quarters at Columbus."

"Sleep well and safe flight tomorrow."

Rodriguez disappeared towards the motel.

At the base Red was happy to be allocated a good-sized room. He lay on the bed, closed his eyes, and tried to nap.

It was hard to shift the image of Dupont from his mind. The man with so much promise, left to rot in the fields.

It didn't feel right. There was a connection there.

He drifted off eventually and was woken by a sharp rap on the door.

Red swivelled off the bed, noticing it was dark outside.

On the other side of the door was an airman.

"Arrived at the main gate for you, sir."

Red looked down to see a large, brown government file.

"Thank you."

He rubbed his eyes and sat on the bed. Inside the cover was a handwritten note.

Just in case . . .
  Leo.

He realised he was holding one hundred pages of completed and signed security clearance for Brandon Dupont.

The O Club was filled with young lieutenants on their advanced jet training, drinking and laughing. Red could only dwell on what Brandon Dupont had given up.

A lieutenant colonel approached his table. Red sprang to his feet and stood to attention, but the senior officer waved him to sit down.

"No luck today, huh, Brunson?"

"No, sir."

"I'm Bill Ryman. I head up training here. Agent Rodriguez called me. Said we're to provide any support we can, but I guess you're going back empty-handed?"

"I'm afraid so, sir."

"Too bad. Sorry we couldn't have been of more service. I used to fly with Tucker Montgomery. So you give that old bastard a kick from me."

Red smiled. "I might not kick him, sir, but I'll pass on your regards."

"You do that, son. See you in the morning. Your jet will be on the line and full of fuel."

The clanging alarm clock once again intruded on Red's attempt at a full night's sleep.

He silenced it and picked up his watch, winding it carefully.

After breakfast, he entered the training squadron close to the flight line. In his case was Dupont's security clearance to work at Edwards. But with no Brandon Dupont to go along with it, the trip had been an expensive waste of time and money.

The squadron was a busy, bustling place. To one side was a large, open locker area with men who looked like boys changing into flight gear, nervously glancing at their brief for the day's sortie.

Red went to the ops desk ready to file his flight plan and grab the latest weather. Another refuelling stop in New Mexico and another straight line across the continent.

As he read through the notices for his route, he heard T-38s firing up outside. The noises and smells brought back his own days at Columbus. Sometimes two sorties a day, each filled with a series of tasks. Mistakes were allowed, but only once. A failed sortie meant a recheck. Two failures and you were in front of the review board. Often, that was it for dreams of being a fighter pilot.

For all the glamour and excitement, jet training was a physical and mental grind like no other.

And yet Red missed it. The camaraderie that comes with navigating an ordeal. Making bonds that will last for life. Plus, the T-38 is an awesome jet, every child's dream idea of what a fast airplane looked like. Sleek and purposeful.

If only he could get Brandon Dupont up in one.

Red paused his form filling, put his pen down, and looked around the unit. He tapped the table, mind turning over.

He looked up to the admin officer on the other side of the sign-out desk.

"Excuse me. Is Lieutenant Colonel Ryman in today?"

The officer pointed at a corridor that ran down to Red's left. He wandered down until he found Ryman's name on a door. It was ajar.

He gingerly leaned into the room. Ryman was at his desk, in flight suit.

"Brunson? You off?"

"Actually, sir, I've had an idea."

Minutes later, he was in his flight suit, walking to his fuelled and ready Talon.

As he ran through the start-up procedures, Red pulled out some notes he'd made from the T-38 flight manual. He committed the slow flight parameters to heart.

Climbing out of Columbus he headed southeast and made a climbing right hand turn until he captured the reciprocal heading, aiming the nose at Coffeeville.

He kept the speed at a slow two hundred knots, but still, he was approaching Coffeeville in less than twenty minutes. His first task was to find the farm.

He spied the two large grain towers that marked the edge of the land, and lowered the nose, feeding in more power. In the distance, he spotted the small grass strip, surrounded by crumbling buildings. The yellow Stearman sat right where Dupont left it the day before.

Red lowered the nose a little more. Scanning the forward view for cables or high trees, he let the aircraft sink to one hundred fifty feet. The earth flashed past him, and the T-38 ate up the mile or so left to run.

A final nudge on the throttles; he didn't want anyone to miss this.

He flashed directly overhead the house with the engines at full power. He must have been within one hundred feet of the roof.

He pulled up and banked over as the Talon screamed into the sky.

Looking back over his shoulder, he saw a figure run from the house.

Bingo.

He swept back around in a wide arc, pulling the throttles back to idle. The speed bled away quickly, and as he rolled out with the farm two miles away on the nose, he dropped his flaps and landing gear.

The jet slowed to one hundred forty-five knots, and he fed in a good handful of throttle, with a little allowance for how slowly the engines spooled back up from idle.

He found himself with a distinct nose-up attitude, but the aircraft held its height.

Red crept closer to the farm, engines howling to keep the metal jet airborne.

He gave himself a small adjustment so he could see the buildings below. Dupont was there, smiling and shouting.

"You gotta follow me up, old man. *C'mon.*"

He made sure he passed all the way over the farm at one hundred forty-five knots before feeding in the last inch of throttle he had to spare. The Talon responded with a gentle climb, and as the needle swept through one hundred sixty knots, he raised the gear, followed by the flaps, and entered the same pattern as before.

Sweeping around a second time, he was disappointed to see the Stearman still on the ground.

"Don't you get it? I'm flying like this so you can join me."

He set the jet up for another slow pass. Everything down and dirty.

This time he allowed the Talon to sink even lower. He gave the jet the gentlest of nudges to ensure he flew between the house and barn. Straight over the strip.

There was no way he could put down on the grass and expect to get up again, but he could come close.

Seventy-five feet as he crossed the property boundary.

Finally, Dupont was on the move. Running towards the strip.

Red brought his concentration back inside. He descended to just fifty feet before pushing the throttles to max again. A slight lag as the engines wound up. He nudged the nose down to tease the airspeed up. The cockpit view filled with trees as the jet continued to sink, but eventually the needle moved, and he raised the nose as much as he dared.

With what must have been a deafening roar below him, the T-38 pulled up into a spectacular climb.

As the speed picked up to something normal again, he banked and looked over his shoulder.

The Stearman's prop was turning.

"Ha ha. Let's go!"

As Red flashed across the farm, Pappy emerged from the

house and stared up. Red was relieved to see no gun in his hands.

He set up an orbit a couple of miles north and waited.

"Come on . . ." he urged Dupont under his breath.

A burst of yellow appeared, climbing above the trees. Red smiled under his oxygen mask and studied the hastily written notes on his kneepad.

He reckoned the Stearman's top speed was about one hundred twenty-five knots, but Montgomery told him they estimated Dupont's modified wing gave him a fifty percent increase in top speed.

"Well, let's see about that."

He continued in the orbit as the Stearman approached from the east, slowing the aircraft to one hundred fifty-five knots, which was the basic approach speed for a fuel-light Talon. It gave him good enough manoeuvrability, and he rolled out, facing southeast, and looked over his shoulder. Sure enough, the farmer was coming up on him. Just a few knots in it, but enough to close up.

Red kept the jet steady and straight. The Stearman got closer, and eventually, a yellow shape appeared in Red's side vision.

He looked across to see Dupont giving him a wave in the back seat.

Red gestured forward with his hand, hoping Dupont would recognise it as a *follow me* sign.

They stayed in loose formation, and Red called up Columbus to warn them that the Stearman had no radio and the pilot might act unpredictably.

For twenty-five minutes they travelled in a rare formation of aircraft separated by thirty years and what felt like a century of innovation.

As they approached the air force base, he turned gently,

giving Dupont plenty of space and time to follow. He lined up the T-38 just offset from runway 13, allowing Dupont the extended centreline. He lowered his gear and went to full flap extension.

Looking across, he pointed down for Dupont, indicating they were going to land.

He led the farmer down the glide slope, and was pleased to see Dupont's trademark leading edge slats winding out.

As they crossed the threshold, Red banked gently away and let Dupont land and roll out as he came around for his own landing. By the time he brought the jet to taxi speed, Dupont was shutting down outside the squadron.

Red taxied in as the squadron boss and two other pilots greeted Dupont. Instructors, he assumed.

He brought his Talon to a stop and scribbled the times on his kneepad. By the time he climbed out, Dupont was already on the tarmac surrounded by a small team, which included Lieutenant Colonel Ryman.

Red observed from a few yards away, listening to the farmer explaining his new wing and leading-edge modification over the distant whine of jet engines. Dupont's confidence was striking.

"You seen this, Red?" Ryman called him over.

"Quite something, isn't it?" Red replied.

He watched as Ryman completed a tour of the Stearman, and he made a note to let Montgomery know just how useful he was being.

Eventually, they emerged back at the nose of the prop aircraft.

"Colonel, do you think we have flight gear that would fit this young man?" Red said.

Ryman smiled and looked at Dupont. "How about it? Want to get back in a jet?"

. . .

Inside the locker room, an equipment specialist appeared, tape measure in hand. He checked Dupont's head, thigh length, and weight. He gave Red and Colonel Ryman a subtle nod. Dupont was good for the ejection seat, heavy enough to arm it and thighs short enough to ensure he wasn't kneecapped in the event of an emergency exit.

After fifteen minutes of pulling on increasingly heavy layers of flying clothing, Dupont began the transformation from farmer to fighter pilot. He settled his helmet's inner ear cups like a pro before strapping his oxygen mask over his mouth and nose, and checking for leaks. He was confident and efficient.

Ryman slapped him on the back. "Well, go enjoy yourselves and listen carefully to Captain Brunson. He's one of our best."

Red led Dupont out to the jet, where a marshaller had lined up a fresh set of steps with the rear cockpit. He ushered Dupont up and told him to step on the ejection seat, before watching him lower himself into the cockpit. The farmer immediately started to run his fingers over the instrument panel, quickly identifying the main dials and controls. Red took him through some systems he might not be familiar with.

"F-86 Korea, wasn't it?" Red asked.

"Yeah."

"Well, the Talon's a little more up to date. I think you'll enjoy it."

Red helped him with the straps, pulling them tightly over his shoulders so he wouldn't lose Dupont through the canopy when they inverted.

Finally, he plugged the farmer into the aircraft—oxygen,

air for the g-suit, and communications—and took him through the procedure for arming the ejection seat.

He gave him a friendly pat on the shoulder before disappearing down the stairs and up into the front cockpit.

Red lowered the canopy and signalled for the pressurised air from the huffer. He waited patiently, watching the revolutions rise on a small dial, before moving the throttle an inch or so forward, firing fuel into the engine. It caught and he set the throttle to idle. The ground crewman diverted the flow into the second engine. It was now about a hundred degrees in the aircraft, and Red quickly selected a blast of cool air before he had to shut the air conditioning off again for the takeoff.

"You secure?" Red asked.

"Yup."

"Okay then, I need you to look to your left. You'll see a metal pin with a red label dangling."

"Got it."

"Remove it—"

"—you want to remove both, then set the seat live?" Dupont asked, interrupting him.

"Ha. Yeah. You've not been gone that long, have you?"

Red noticed a ground-crew member give a thumbs-up to Dupont behind him. Clearly he'd held up the pins to be counted. A good safety drill.

Red then worked methodically through the checklist, despite his familiarity with it. A lot had gone into this flight, and Red was conscious of having senior officers such as Colonel Ryman doing his bidding.

No mistakes now.

In his small mirrors, he watched as Dupont checked out his surroundings. The farmer had slipped back into the unique world of the military jet pilot, with ease.

"You ready?"

"Yes, sir" came a drawl from behind him.

Red taxied them out, lined up on RWY 13 and stood on the brakes, while bringing the engines up to a scream. After waiting for the instruments to stabilise, he released the brakes and pushed the throttles into afterburner. The jet jumped forward before accelerating hard as the burners kicked in.

He raised the nose, allowed the aircraft to creep into the air. As the airspeed needle swept past one hundred fifty knots, he raised the gear, quickly followed by the flaps. Red held the nose around three degrees as the speed wound up. When it got to three hundred knots, he snapped the stick back, pulling 5g on the Talon as the rocketed skyward.

Dupont let out a "Yee-haw!" over the intercom.

Red watched the speed carefully; he lost a lot of energy in the pull-up but judged he had enough left to get them all the way over. Once inverted and facing back the way they came, he rolled them upright to let the aircraft accelerate through three hundred knots again, hoping he wouldn't get in trouble for busting the T-38's limit below ten thousand feet. Once at three fifty, he performed a second zoom climb, this one slightly shallower but no less impressive. He glanced over his shoulder and saw Columbus growing smaller. As the speed got down to two hundred knots, he used the last of the energy to perform an aileron roll, turning them upside down, before levelling out, building speed once more.

Dupont made more whooping noises from behind.

"You enjoy that?"

"You bet! Pretty smooth through the range. No buffet?"

Red shook his head at the farmer's need to analyse the T-38's aerodynamics.

"It's a great jet. You wanna have a fly?"

For the next ten minutes, Dupont took the controls. Red observed as he got used to the throttles and engine response, the aircraft's handling, and even the buffet close to the stall.

As with any new student, Red covered the controls with his hands, ready to take control. But there was a proficiency to Dupont's flying that gave him confidence the jet was in good hands.

He talked him through the procedure for landing, and they carried out a three-hundred-knot join in the overhead, breaking into the pattern with a seventy-degree roll. The farmer flew it okay, but he needed prompting. They would have to effectively put him through flight school to bring him up to scratch and issue his military licenses.

Red kept hold of the stick and throttles as Dupont attempted to set the T-38 up for an approach. It was tricky without experience; the aircraft required some amount of anticipation. But he got there in the end, and it was a safe and satisfying plonk onto the runway at Columbus.

After taxiing to a stop, Red shut the aircraft down and popped the canopy up. He made his seat safe, unstrapped, and stood up, looking down on his smiling passenger.

"Okay, farmer. Time to make your mind up. You wanna be paid to fly the latest military aircraft? Or do you want to grow soybeans for the rest of your life?"

Dupont was still strapped in, his arms resting on the rim of the fuselage. He looked around just as two T-38s took off as a pair on the main runway. After the noise subsided, he turned back to Red.

"Three fifty a month, you said?"

CHAPTER THREE

RED WAS WOKEN by an urgent hammering on the door.

"Jesus, what time is it?" He tried to focus on the alarm clock.

0645.

He staggered out of bed, aching from the long trip home in a cramped cockpit.

"Captain Brunson?"

A man in a white shirt and tie stood on the other side of his screen door.

"Yes?"

The man held out a government ID badge. It had his photograph and a seal Red didn't immediately recognise.

"I'm Agent David McInery from the Federal Bureau of Investigation. Sir, may I come in?"

He led the man into the kitchen and offered him coffee. McInery looked around doubtfully at the empty kitchen.

"Actually, I have only water," Red clarified.

"I'll pass. Thank you, son." The agent placed some papers and forms on the breakfast bar. "You met with a

Defense Intelligence agent called Leonard Rodriguez the day before yesterday?"

"Yes, sir, in Mississippi."

"Mississippi. That's right," McInery said, opening a notepad. "And when exactly did you last see him?"

"Late afternoon. In a Motel America near Columbus Air Force Base."

The agent nodded and made a note. "You see anyone else around?"

"Um, I mean, there were other cars in the parking lot, but I can't recall anyone in particular. Mind telling me what's going on?"

"Agent Rodriguez is dead. Murdered."

"What?"

"His body was found close to a rest area off I-75. Couple of miles north of Chattanooga."

"Jesus." Red pulled a chair out from his small kitchen table and sat down. "When?"

"Yesterday, morning. But, the body was pretty badly burned, and they don't know exactly when he was killed. So, they're keen to know his precise movements."

Red shook his head slowly. "I can't believe it."

"When he left you, where did Agent Rodriguez say he was heading?"

"Said he was going straight back to DC. He wanted to drive overnight."

The agent nodded and made more notes. "That would fit with his route."

"Poor Leo. Was he married?"

"Yes, sir. Two boys."

"Damn."

"Son, was there anything unusual at all about your time

with Agent Rodriguez. Did you get the feeling you were being followed, for instance?"

Only one image popped into Red's mind.

"Not followed, no. But someone did pull a gun on us."

McInery stood up straight and stared at him. "What did you say?"

"Actually, it wasn't that big a deal. It was this elderly hick farmer in Coffeeville."

"Where the hell's that?"

"Nowhere, is where it is. About a hundred miles south of Memphis."

"What exactly happened?"

Red pinched the bridge of his nose. "He basically chased us off his land for having the audacity to offer his son a job."

"He threatened you with a gun? An actual weapon?"

"An old twelve-gauge, I think. Probably wasn't even loaded."

"You don't think he was serious? That he couldn't have come after Leo later?"

Red shook his head. "No. This was just some crazy old man on a farm in the middle of nowhere who wanted to keep his son by his side. Besides, how the hell would he have known where Leo was?"

"He didn't follow you?"

"Definitely not."

"How can you be so sure?"

"We drove out on a dirt road for about two miles. There's no way he was behind us, believe me. Plus . . ."

"Plus?"

Red hesitated. "Plus, I saw him the next day."

"You went back?"

"Not exactly. I flew over, in a T-38. I saw him outside the house."

"What's a T-38?"

"It's a military jet. It's a long story, but I flew over around ten thirty. He was definitely on the farm then. I doubt he ever leaves it."

McInery made a note. "You're sure of the time?"

"Yes, sir."

"I guess that makes it impossible it was him, then."

A horrible thought came into Red's mind.

"Agent Rodriguez gave me the signed security clearance for the guy we met. Is that still valid?"

The FBI man riffled through his papers. "Brandon Dupont?"

"Yeah."

The man shrugged. "That's not part of my investigation. Rodriguez was at the end of a long road trip. I understand this was a small job added on at the last minute."

Red wrote the location of the Duponts' farm in McInery's notepad and showed him to the door. "What do you think happened, Agent McInery?"

"Local cops think he was taking a nap in a rest area and was jumped."

"Christ. Poor Leo. He probably didn't see them coming."

"Lucky for them he didn't. He would have torn them limb from limb."

Red smiled politely.

CHAPTER FOUR

RED MADE the drive into Edwards and turned onto the dusty outer road to the A-TEC offices. He'd stepped into the pilots' planning room just in time to be summoned to the boss's office.

"This is becoming a habit," he said as he dropped his car keys on a desk.

Montgomery sat at his round meeting table with Johnny Clifford, across from two men in short sleeves and neckties.

"Congratulations."

"Thank you, sir."

"The T-38 trick worked, then?"

"It did. I got a lot of help from Colonel Ryman, sir."

"Good. We're not out of the woods yet, though. He'll have to get through advance training at Columbus. But it sounds like you've made an ally in Ryman. That should help. Well done."

"Thank you, sir."

There was a pause. Red looked uncertainly at the two men sitting opposite. They were motionless, apparently waiting for their turn to speak.

He turned back to Montgomery. "Sir, I've told Agent McInery everything I know."

"This isn't about Agent Rodriguez. Red, this is Brad Walker and David Gomez from the National Reconnaissance Office. Gentlemen, this is Captain Red Brunson."

Red nodded a hello.

"Good to meet you, Captain Brunson," said Walker. "We worked with Leo Rodriguez back at the start of the U-2 project. Damn shame what happened."

"Yes, sir."

As he took his seat, Johnny Clifford pushed a paper file towards him.

He looked at the cover.

N A T I O N A L R E C O N N A I S S A N C E O F F I C E
Classification: Top Secret
Operation Falling Star
NRO Trial #971004-066
Phase 1a—High Altitude Power Transition
Assignation: Aircraft Test and Evaluation Center, Groom Lake
Vehicle: Lockheed A-12

"Open it," Clifford instructed with his usual curtness.

The first thing that caught Red's eye was a schematic diagram of the fastest aircraft on earth and one of the United States's most closely guarded secrets: the A-12.

He looked straight at Montgomery.

"My side of the deal, son. But I tell you now, this won't be a picnic. In fact, you better buckle up. It's gonna be one helluva ride. You up for this?"

Red felt Johnny Clifford's eyes on him. He knew Montgomery liked him, but Clifford gave nothing away. If he had to guess, he'd say the chief test pilot actively disliked him.

"Yes, sir."

He looked back at the drawing of the A-12. It was in the form of a breakout diagram, and he now realised it was displaying an unusual modification: pylons on top of the wings, and what looked like missiles.

Gomez spoke up. "We need to evaluate very high flight levels with the aircraft transitioning from traditional jet power to rocket power. We've chosen A-TEC."

"Rocket power? So, these aren't missiles?" Red said, pointing at the objects above the pylons.

"No." Clifford took over. "They're small solid rocket boosters. SRBs. The aircraft will take off under normal jet-powered conditions and climb until just before the jet engines flame out."

"About eighty thousand feet," Montgomery said.

Red whistled.

Clifford continued. "At that point, with momentum still taking the A-12 upwards, we'll ignite the SRBs and begin the second phase of flight to a new maximum altitude, before coming back in a parabolic arc and landing under conventional power. Unfortunately, the jet engines could be damaged if they're running at the high Mach levels, so we'll need to shut them down before ignition and relight them on the way back down."

Clifford spoke in a matter-of-fact way, as if he were telling Red how to treat his Buick.

"It's the same principle as the early X-Planes," Montgomery said. "Only they used a B-52 to get up high before igniting their firework. But make no mistake, shutting down a jet engine and relighting it, is highly unorthodox and not something we'd normally choose to do."

"Okay" was all Red could manage. His mouth felt dry.

"Flying with the SRBs is the tricky bit," Clifford said, sounding much more serious. "A firework is exactly what an SRB is. Once lit, there's no switching off. You're strapped in for the ride. They won't have much fuel in them at first, but that'll gradually increase, until we find the limits."

Red was trying to make sense of everything he was being told. He felt bombarded. The A-12 could fly to eighty thousand feet? That was the sort of top-secret information that only a few people in the world knew.

He was now one of them.

Then he thought about the second phase, and how dangerous and unstable it sounded.

He tried to calm himself down and concentrate on the details.

"How does the relight procedure work?" He looked up at Johnny Clifford.

"Onboard compressor for engine one, with valves to divert from engine one to two. As a backup we use the airflow, if we're low enough and still orientated correctly. But let's not test that."

Montgomery tapped the table. "Each part of this trial requires expert handling. We think you're up to it. Don't prove us wrong."

Montgomery stood up, and Clifford pointed at the folder.

"It's all in there, Red. You'll have to familiarise yourself with the project thoroughly. You start your A-12 conversion tomorrow night."

"Tomorrow night?"

"It should go without saying," said Gomez, "that this

entire exercise is top secret. All flying will be completed after dark out at Groom Lake."

"Must be why I've never actually seen an A-12," Red said.

"Exactly. But you'll be sitting in one tomorrow night." Montgomery winked at him.

Red picked up the folder and checked the title of the project again. *Falling Star*. "What's this all for? Just testing the limits, or is there a purpose behind it?"

The men exchanged glances.

"That's the sort of question you don't ask," Montgomery said.

Red and Clifford left the room together.

"Read that folder today," said Clifford. "Go to bed late tonight and get up late tomorrow morning. I don't want to see you in here before eleven-hundred. You're gonna need all your energy for the first A-12 flight."

Red gave up on sleep around 0730.

After a shower, he sat at his small kitchen table and made notes on a blank pad. He copied out the A-12 airborne procedures he had memorised the night before, to ensure they stuck. One of the problems with flying a supersecret aircraft was that you weren't allowed to remove any of the paperwork, not even the checklists. The public knew the A-12 existed, but that was about all they did know.

The unveiling to Red of the A-12's full spec came with a tightly bound aircraft bible Johnny Clifford had thrown at him. Top recorded speed so far: 1,922 knots.

He scribbled on a scrap of paper to convert it. 2,112 mph. Approaching Mach 3. "If my pop had seen this...," he whispered to himself, "he wouldn't have believed it."

And he and Johnny Clifford were tasked with taking it faster. Much faster.

He could scarcely believe he was one of the two pilots who would do that.

Actually, part of him didn't believe it. Something would go wrong. He'd be found out long before they were due to light the solid rocket boosters.

Once in the office, Clifford placed him in front of a blackboard with the A-12's panel crudely sketched out. It was crazy that the first time Red would see and sit in the jet, he would be flying it.

He made him recite the airborne procedures by heart. He was allowed to read off a list for the prestart and shutdown.

Then they began the emergency checklists. Red was dismayed to feel the weight of the flip-book.

He opened it and scanned the contents.

Engine fire.
  Abandoning the aircraft.
  Brake, steering, or tire failure.
  Engine failure.
  Double engine failure.
  Emergency gear retraction.
  Fire warning—Takeoff Refused.
  Drag Chute Failure.

And so it went on.

Maybe thirty separate emergency procedures.

Each heading had a page or more of instructions.

"You need to memorise them all by tonight. There's a lot

of commonality with the bigger jets we fly, but look for the differences," Clifford said. "You can't take these home, so I'll leave you alone for a bit."

The chief test pilot left the room, and Red pulled out a sheet of paper and pen.

Feeling as if he were in the foothills of Mount Everest, he began the process of committing a small book to memory.

In the afternoon, he was fitted with a space suit.

It wasn't exactly what the NASA astronauts were wearing. It was a dirty orange colour and had stitched seams, but it was heavy duty and sealed with a plastic covering on the inside. As he pulled it on, he felt nervous for the first time.

There was no two-seat version of the A-12 available, so Red's first flight would be solo.

His world became increasingly isolated as two technicians zipped the suit up around him. They pumped the oxygen and sealed the helmet over his head. He wasn't connected to an intercom, so hand signals were his best method of communication.

The men fumbled with the apparatus, and Red stood in his own quiet world listening to his breathing, trying to settle his anxiety.

An image of Brandon Dupont's biplane floated into his mind. In thirty years, they'd gone from that to the A-12.

He closed his eyes as sweat trickled down his forehead.

There was a sudden whoosh.

The helmet came off, and cool air hit his face.

"All done."

He opened his eyes as one of the technicians spoke to him.

"We'll be at Groom to suit you up for the flight. We look after the equipment."

Red armed his seat in the back of a T-38 while Clifford whistled through the checklists. A few minutes later, they lifted off into the early-evening Mojave sky.

"You know, when I began advanced training, I was scared of this plane," Red said. "It was my first supersonic aircraft. Now it's just a taxi service on my way to fly an A-12."

But Clifford didn't respond. Was the intercom broken? He listened carefully and heard the major breathing. Clearly, he wasn't a man for small talk.

The sun was falling quickly as they turned onto short final. Groom Lake was the vampire of airfields—passive in the light, alive in the night.

A small army had assembled on the tarmac. This was an aircraft that required a hundred men to get in the air.

An armed guard stood outside a modest hangar that opened out directly onto a large apron that led to the taxiways.

The main hangar doors were shut, but Clifford led him around to a small side entrance.

They stepped into a gloomy interior.

Feeble lights did their best to illuminate the jet, but its matte-black finish was designed to swallow light particles.

Red ran his hand along the thin outer edge of the fuselage and wings. Even within the Edwards test-pilot community, this was a hidden gem.

Clifford switched on a flashlight. "You'll need this." He pointed at the steps that led up to the cockpit.

Red climbed up, and Clifford showed him how to open the canopy from the outside. "Don't worry about remembering much of this. There'll be a ground team to see you off."

He shone the flashlight into the cockpit.

"Looks like any other aircraft we fly," Red said, taking in the familiar dials and controls.

"It's built out of titanium and has two engines that produce fifty thousand pounds of thrust. This is nothing like any aircraft you've flown. You better not forget that. Get in."

Red lowered himself onto the seat.

He closed his eyes and ran his fingers over the key controls. An old habit.

Clifford appeared next to him on the ladder and made him recite the emergency procedures out loud.

The J-58 engines required special handling. They worked in two different ways below and above Mach 2, but in Red's first few flights, he'd keep to Mach 1.5.

"I hope you're ready for this," Clifford said, as he backed down the ladder. "Let's go get something to eat. When we come back, it'll be time to suit up." The chief test pilot disappeared out the hangar, leaving Red alone with the A-12. He took a few breaths and lifted himself out.

The Groom Lake canteen was busy.

"I guess this counts as breakfast time for a nocturnal base," Red said, as they found a table. "Any idea what this is all about?"

Clifford didn't look up from his food. "Believe it or not, I have the same security clearance as you."

They ate on in silence. Eventually, Clifford looked up and took a drink of water. "Something's coming , though."

"Really?"

"Yeah. I've seen this pattern before. Something's coming."

"Another aircraft?"

"Another aircraft. Another missile. Who knows? But, this isn't about the A-12. At least I don't think it is. We're not the right people, this is a CIA toy. I think they've got something in the shadows." He paused and looked directly at Red. "They're testing us as well as the SRBs. Don't forget that. You've been given this ride, but don't think they can't dismiss you just as easily."

Red finished his last forkful of chilli, preferring the silence to Clifford's unhelpful observations.

He glanced at the clock over the door. In a few hours, he would join a tiny group of men who'd got to fly a secret spy plane.

At 2100, the Lockheed aircraft was towed from its lair.

Red worked through the flight profile one last time, sitting in his space suit without helmet, before waddling across the apron, supported by a small team of suit technicians.

Clifford gave him some final instructions. "Treat her gently. The faster you go, the gentler you need to be. This thing has no g-tolerance to speak of, so turns need planning and plenty of space. The outbound VOR will come up faster than you think, and we don't want you overshooting or turning late. Don't blow this project open by appearing in the sky over Vegas. And watch your speed. She will get away from you quickly. Remember, you're supersonic only in the designated box. That's one hundred miles from here and no lower than forty thousand feet. Got it?"

Red nodded, but was sure he looked uncertain. Clifford

regarded him for a few seconds. "If something goes wrong, fly the plane first, work the problem using the checklists. If that doesn't work, remember the ejection procedures. This thing needs to hit the ground nose-first and full speed in an area devoid of humans."

Two technicians arrived with Red's helmet.

"We fit it in the cockpit once you're connected to oxygen," one said, and they led him to a golf cart for the short journey to the flight line.

The A-12 was out in the open, bathed in floodlights.

For the first time, Red noticed most of the support staff were gone. "Where is everyone?"

"Canteen," one of the technicians answered. "They're sent inside when the bird's out in the open."

"They want as few eyes as possible on this thing," the other man added.

The aircraft looked every bit as mysterious outside as in the shadows, a schoolboy's idea of a flying machine from the year 2000.

The ball of anxiety in his stomach weighed a ton. He tried to regulate his breathing, but wasn't looking forward to the helmet going on again.

Before he mounted the first step, he got a tap on the shoulder. Turning around, he saw a photographer.

"For our records only," a voice said from the dark.

There was a blinding flash. Red felt giddy and disorientated as someone turned him around to face the steps.

"Come on up," said a male voice.

"Give me a second, dammit."

"You okay?"

Red turned to see Brad Walker from the NRO. The customer.

He nodded and tried to smile. "Yes. Fine. Just don't want to rush."

Walker stepped back and waited for Red to climb the steps.

It was tight, squeezing into the cockpit wearing a space suit.

One of the techs appeared at the top of the ladder and fiddled with the hose and equipment connectors. He disappeared back down the ladder, before reappearing a moment later, helmet in hand.

Red took a final gulp of cool air before the tech lowered and locked the helmet.

The man seemed to take ages checking the seals.

Eventually, he gave him a thumbs-up and disappeared.

The steps were withdrawn.

Red got to work bringing the jet to life. He worked through the checklist until he got to the canopy-lowering point. He operated the lever and, as it came down around him, he realised he hadn't tried this in the hangar.

It wasn't a great view: ironwork in front and small windows to the side.

The ground power connected, and the air bleed kicked in. He fired up the first J-58. The noise seeped through the closed canopy and into the sealed helmet. This thing was loud.

By the time the second engine was hot, the machine was vibrating.

Every part of the aircraft: straining, pulsing, breathing.

He looked out and moved his head around to ensure he got a good look around. Everyone had melted into the shadows beyond the floodlights.

This must be how a pitcher feels in a packed night game.

How did they do it? Perform with all eyes on them?

His call sign was Transport 1, a deliberately innocuous phrase.

He began the taxi and dabbed the wheel brakes to ensure they were operational.

As he taxied, he regressed further into a world that included only him and the aircraft. The lights disappeared behind him; only darkness lay ahead.

He went through the Aborted Takeoff procedure and then the Engine Failure After Takeoff list.

Lined up at the end of the runway, Red stared at the tower and waited. Eventually, he saw a green flare. Radio silence compelled the tower to use a simpler method to convey clearance.

Red took a deep breath and advanced the throttles to the intermediate slot. This would give him full military power. As the A-12 leaped from its position, he pushed the throttles to the second stop, and the burners kicked in.

He felt the shove and watched the speed needle respond.

There was only a light breeze, but Red found himself fighting the rudders more than he expected.

A hundred knots on the dial already.

The needle was moving fast.

One hundred sixty knots. The aircraft thundered.

This was the fastest he'd been along the ground in his life.

The A-12 plunged into the darkness as Groom Lake receded behind him.

He edged back the stick and held it. The aircraft lifted gently and beautifully into the air.

Seconds later, the runway threshold flashed beneath him, and Red marvelled at how much tarmac this thing had used, and how quickly it had used it.

He tucked the gear up and at five hundred feet made the first gentle turn onto a northeast heading. Raising the nose slightly, he took her out of afterburner and let her climb at three hundred fifty knots.

Something felt different. This was the big boys' world now. Behind him on the ground was a group of people who, somehow, entrusted him with the world's fastest airplane.

It was supposed to feel good. Instead, he was nauseated.

The space suit made him claustrophobic, and even a basic instrument scan was a laboured process.

He managed the throttles to climb at four hundred fifty knots.

Thirty thousand feet came up quickly.

He checked his navigation aid. The VOR at Butte, Montana, was fast approaching. Red reengaged the burners and allowed the A-12 to climb farther to forty thousand feet. As he lowered the nose, he kept the burners on, and the aircraft slid into supersonic with barely a murmur.

His first turn was upon him. He rolled gently, with Johnny Clifford's warnings echoing around his head.

He was within two miles.

He'd left it too late.

"Come on, come on . . ." Red urged the A-12, but didn't dare put any significant g-force on.

The numbers counting down to the VOR began counting up, and he was still forty degrees off his target heading.

"Shit."

Finally, he rolled out on the new course, then added ten degrees to merge with the correct track to the next waypoint.

"Christ, this thing is fast."

In level supersonic flight, the A-12 kept smooth and stable.

His second turn was in Wyoming, and he began the hundred-degree change in direction two and a half miles out. Even then, he overshot the beacon, but he was getting closer.

Clifford hadn't been exaggerating when he'd warned him not to appear in the sky over Vegas by accident. Any lapse in concentration, and he'd be halfway across the country.

On the penultimate leg, towards Nevada, he began a thirty-five-degree roll nearly three miles out.

Red checked the stopwatch and carried out his pre-descent checks. He pulled the throttle back and let the speed sink below the Mach 1 point on the dial.

One hundred twelve miles from Edwards, he began to let down.

He focused on the ground track, double-checking the bright lights of Las Vegas were well to his south.

What would the drunks and revellers make of it, if he had overflown? He imagined headlines screaming about a UFO.

By ten thousand feet, Red entered an extended long final for Groom's main runway. He checked the rate of descent and ensured he was on the glide slope. No ground beacons could help him here; this had all been calculated with pen and paper ahead of time.

Seeing the approach was good, and he shuffled in his seat as he always did. No matter what you flew or where you were, the landing was always the bit that took up most of your attention. He liked to feel comfortable, relaxed.

The runway lights blinked on in the distance. Red sat upright and checked their position in his canopy. He was a little high. He let off some power and lowered the nose. Gradually, the runway moved up into a position about two inches from the bottom strut of the frame. He fed the power back in and raised the nose to capture the new position.

At one mile, he concluded the prelanding checks, and the gear unfolded beneath him.

The airfield raced towards him; the A-12 had a hell of a landing speed.

As he got to half a mile, he realised he was high again.

"*Shit.*"

Red pulled the throttle back, and the rate of descent increased. He quickly fed it back in, wary of an undershoot that could severely damage the jet, and him.

He hadn't done enough. His touchdown point was way past the piano keys.

He had to throw this one away.

"Transport One going around," he called into the radio, and then immediately regretted it. He wasn't supposed to call anything unless it was an emergency.

Another failure for Johnny Clifford to note.

He pushed the throttles into afterburner and selected gear up.

The black aircraft growled back into the dark sky.

Red's heart pounded. He was annoyed with himself.

The worst-case scenario was being binned after just one flight, and he'd just taken a step closer to that.

The turn onto downwind was agonisingly slow. The A-12's circuit was wide, and performed at five thousand feet for secrecy.

Vegas twinkled in the distance, as he established himself on the southwesterly track in opposition to the runway.

Keep away from the slots, Red.

He began his giant one-eighty turn glancing out his right-hand window, desperate to get a visual on Groom. He couldn't see anything, just blackness.

Red checked the beacon. He should be correct.

Damn. Where is it?

Just fly the plane, Red.

Too many aviators had found themselves in a hole in the ground because they'd become distracted with everything but flying.

As he rolled out on the runway heading, the runway lights came back on. He'd missed that in the procedures. Now he knew they kept the lights on for the bare minimum of time during A-12 operations.

Man, they make this difficult.

This time the approach felt better. Small adjustments. Speed held nicely at one hundred sixty knots. He lost the last five knots at one mile and set the aircraft slightly nose up.

He saw the touchdown point, aligned with a rivet on a canopy strut. He used it as his reference, riding the throttle and nose pitch with small inputs, to keep it in the same place.

The secret aircraft crossed the threshold, and he felt the ground effect of the air cushion under the wings. But she sank through that, and the main wheels came down with a satisfying bump.

He set the throttle to idle, lowered the nose, and pulled a handle to stream the braking parachutes.

Red had to remind himself not to brake. But it was hard, as the jet streaked down the tarmac. Eventually, the second chute took over, and the aircraft slowed to fifty-five knots, at which point he could assist with the wheel brakes.

The A-12 came to a crawl with about five hundred yards of runway left. He pulled the chute-release lever before the aircraft came to a halt.

For a moment, Red just sat there, steadying his breathing.

With reluctance, he pushed the throttles forward again and shifted the A-12 off its moorings, swinging it round towards his reception party.

As soon as the second engine was winding down, the marshallers ushered the A-12 back into the dark recesses of the hangar.

Red gathered his papers.

After a little help unstrapping and backing onto the ladder, he hit terra firma. A technician removed his helmet, and he exited through the main doors as they were being closed.

"Congratulations, son." Colonel Montgomery handed him a cold bottle of beer. He hadn't realised the boss would be there.

His hand was shaking, but he took a swig and savoured the cold drink as it slid down his overheating insides.

Clifford wasn't drinking and looked more serious. "First approach?"

Red shook his head. "Too high. I adjusted twice but couldn't seem to capture a good profile, so I threw it away."

Clifford winced. "We won't always have the fuel for a go-around in the future. You need to get that right. How about the turns? And don't bullshit me. We'll have the radar track soon."

"I started two miles out for the first one and still overshot—"

"By how much?"

"Two miles, maybe."

Clifford shook his head. "Too shallow with your bank.

Treat her gently, yes, but if you under-bank at those speeds, you go off track, and we can't have that. Try again tomorrow." He glanced at his watch. "Tonight, in fact."

Clifford walked off.

Montgomery gave Red a sympathetic smile. "Listen to Johnny and work on what you need to work on, but well done. You've joined a small, select group."

"Thank you, sir."

The colonel fished a sheet of paper from his pocket, unfolded it, and handed it to Red.

It was a pilot assessment note.

Exceptional natural ability. Quiet determination. Responds well to instructions. No repeated failures, so far. Difficulty in conforming to airborne procedures. Doesn't blend well socially. Taking some adjustment, but happy to continue.

Red was taken aback. "*Doesn't blend well socially?* What does that mean, sir? With all due respect, I take part after hours as much as anyone."

Montgomery laughed at him. "This isn't about you, Red. This is Brandon Dupont. I asked Ryman for a frank assessment. Your farmer's doing okay."

Red looked again at the note. The farmer *had* done well.

CHAPTER FIVE

RED AND JOHNNY CLIFFORD touched down at Groom Lake at 2200. Red had barely slept, and by the time Clifford returned with the A-12 from his own familiarisation flight, he was struggling to keep his eyes open. He stamped his feet and tried to shake himself awake. Should he declare fatigue? No pilot should be expected to fly anything in this state, let alone the world's fastest aircraft.

But what would that say about him? That he wasn't coping with the schedule, after just twenty-four hours.

An admission such as that would be fatal to his place on the project. And, with Red's record, it could be the end of his brief time as a test pilot.

"Brunson!" A shout came up from behind. The suiting-up team were ready for him.

He stood like a mannequin while two technicians pulled the orange space suit over his regular coveralls.

The A-12 was on the ground nearby and being turned around by a small army. Refuelers completed their work, while men from A-TEC removed instruments from apertures on the other side of the fuselage. The forces on the aircraft were carefully recorded for each flight. Any over-G would be discovered quickly.

Clifford's warning about under-banking ran through his mind.

And on top of all of that, he wasn't fit to fly.

"You ready?" Clifford marched over.

"Yes." Red mustered as much energy as he could.

"Good. Get the turns right tonight. We need to be trying out the shutdown and relight tomorrow." He glanced at his watch. "Well, later today."

Once Red was in the aircraft, helmet on and canopy down, adrenaline kicked in and pushed the fatigue to one side; at least for the time being. Hopefully, it would last long enough for him to get back down in one piece.

For the second night, he took the A-12 on a rare track over land, to make use of the radio beacons. After this, all their flights would be out over the Pacific.

Two miles out from his first turn, at Mach 1.5, Red rolled the A-12 seven degrees. It felt like a more positive manoeuvre. He realised he'd spent his first flight trying to nudge the jet around the turns, hence the overshoots.

He rolled out, feeling the small allowance of g-force subside.

On track. No adjustment needed.

His mood lifted.

He had eight minutes before he needed to initiate his next turn. For the first time in the A-12, he had some room to breathe.

Instinctively he glanced at his wrist, but his old Omega was buried under the sealed space suit.

He'd flown more precisely tonight. Yesterday was ragged, rushed, and imprecise.

Red thought about his battered watched. Ragged and imprecise.

He wondered if Jay Anderson was right. He should upgrade to a new DoD-issued timepiece?

Start looking the part.

But Red knew, he would never do that.

The next two turns were also well within the parameters Clifford had set.

Forty-eight minutes later, having covered four states, he lined up on long final, and the Groom Lake approach lights blinked into existence.

After landing, he brought the jet to a halt, as directed by the marshaller, in front of the purpose-built hangar. He shut the engines down, and the ground handlers attached the tug. Just like the previous night, he sat in the aircraft as they pushed it into hiding.

He glanced up at the night sky, just visible through the top of the windshield. Did any Soviet satellites get lucky tonight? Could they even see in the dark?

He knew better than to ask the NRO guys those sorts of questions.

Out of the jet, Red quickly shed his space suit. He was exhausted. The adrenaline had worked for only so long. Now came the crash.

Clifford was nowhere to be seen. In fact, no one was there to ask him how it went.

Red gathered his kit. He looked across the flight line and saw the chief test pilot by the T-38.

"Mind flying back? I'm exhausted," Clifford said as Red arrived at the steps.

"Fine."

Clifford was already climbing into the rear cockpit, making it clear it wasn't really a request.

Red hesitated at the top of the steps. "It went well tonight. All the turns."

Clifford pulled the thick straps over his shoulders and didn't look up. "I know. They traced you on the radar."

Red waited a moment longer, but Clifford continued to busy himself with strapping in.

It was all he could to fly straight and level back to Edwards.

When they landed, he stared at the pad on his knee and tried to remember what he was supposed to record. He was so tired; his brain was slowing down to almost zero. Eventually, he came up with the landing time and durations for the aircraft and engines.

"Christ, this is ridiculous."

Clifford was waiting for him at the bottom of the steps. "Tonight, we shut down and relight. Memorise the procedures before you go home and get in early enough to go through them again before we fly to Groom. You need to be on your A game."

An hour later, Red collapsed onto his bed. He'd tried to read the procedures, but nothing was going in. He'd try again tomorrow.

Or maybe just admit to Clifford and Montgomery that he wasn't good enough for this.

The only bright spot from a relentless day was that Red slept for nine hours.

He was woken by his phone.

"Brunson," he answered with a croak.

"Change of plan." It was Clifford. "We're not flying tonight. The bird's gone back to the shop to have the SRB pylons fitted. But get in here. They want to brief us on the next phase."

The two NRO agents were back in Montgomery's office. The same briefing paper sat on the table, and Red refamiliarised himself with the strange modification the A-12 was about to undergo: a small solid rocket booster mounted on a heavy pylon, on top of each wing.

As he waited for the meeting to start, he tried to imagine what it would be like lighting those things. He couldn't. They would be turning an aerodynamic airplane into a rocket at eighty thousand feet. He would then have to somehow hold on for the ride as the rockets threw him into a ballistic arc, peaking at one hundred fifty thousand feet.

Space.

The aircraft would then slowly cede its height to the grip of gravity and begin its gentle descent, nose down. Hopefully.

He and Clifford would have to be patient; wait for the thickening air to bring the speed under control until the aircraft was no faster than Mach 2.1, at which point the relight procedure would be viable.

Who the hell deliberately shuts down his engines and then tries to relight them, ten miles up?

As he thought it through, Red gave the operation a thirty percent chance of success. And somewhere in the list of possible failures were scenarios in which he wouldn't get out alive.

His biggest fear was losing complete control in the thin

upper atmosphere, a rarefied place where an airplane had no business. Wisps of air. Nothing for the wings to bite. It was those dangerous minutes between rocket power and the relight that worried Red. Tales of previous X-Planes tumbling out of control, or skipping on the top of the atmosphere, filled his mind.

The pilots easily lost consciousness under those forces. And that was that.

He was glad Clifford was down to the fly the procedure first.

"Gentlemen, good job on the workup." Montgomery began the meeting. "The bird's back at the shop for the modifications. But we think it's worth briefing you two on the third phase of Project Dark Strike." He looked at the NRO guys. "Gentlemen, if you'd be so kind."

Brad Walker, the agent who seemed to do most of the talking, produced another document from his briefcase and set it on the table.

"You should know our technological race with the Russians has moved to space. Both sides have developed missiles that travel six hundred miles up and fall within a mile's accuracy onto a city. And both of us are developing satellites that can read a newspaper in a man's hand. Now, when it comes to Russian satellites passing overhead, what can we do about it?"

Red didn't think it was his place to say anything, but he knew what the answer was. Everyone did.

"Nothing," Clifford replied.

Brad Walker continued. "We're about to change that."

"You wanna fly the A-12 into space to take on Soviet satellites?" Clifford asked.

"The A-12's an aircraft, not a spacecraft. This project isn't about the A-12. This project is about an aircraft called the XS-81."

Red wondered if he'd missed a briefing somewhere; he'd never heard of it.

"The what?" asked Clifford.

Walker opened his folder and pulled out a schematic diagram of a new aircraft. He turned it around to face him and Clifford.

"What d'ya see?" asked Montgomery, smiling at Clifford.

Red scanned the line drawing and read the numbers that ran along the bottom of the page.

Clifford read the numbers as well. "She's a beast. Two hundred eight feet long? Twice the size of the A-12." He ran his finger over the diagram. "Four engines." He pointed at the midpoint of the wings. "What are these? J-58s?"

"J-59s," replied Walker. As far as Red knew, there was no such thing as a J-59. The reveals kept coming.

"Okay, and these?" Clifford pointed to two large cylinder shapes that ran along the bottom of the fuselage. "Missiles?"

"SRBs."

Red puffed his cheeks. "They're huge."

"They need to be," Montgomery replied. "See anything else?"

Clifford shook his head. "This? Radar?"

He pointed at a bulge underneath the cockpit. From the way the diagram had been presented, it looked as if it were clamped beneath the SRBs.

Red scrutinised the diagram. "Is that a third SRB?"

Walker turned the page and presented a new view of the XS-81. From side on, they could see the SRBs were set apart, with pylons running down the centre of the fuselage.

A missile sat next to the aircraft diagram. Long, wide,

and with a bulge at the nose. Once again, this was a new piece of US material.

"That's a big missile for an aircraft to carry," Clifford said.

"Launching this thing is the objective we're working towards. It's part SRB, part missile, part spacecraft. The radar at the front can lock onto and track an orbiting object. It can accelerate from Mach 8 to escape velocity, but it has very limited manoeuvrability in space."

Montgomery tapped the desk in front of him. "It's a satellite killer, boys."

A prickly heat climbed up Red's back. Things were moving too fast.

He wasn't good enough for this. He'd screw it up and kill himself. Maybe take others with him in a blaze of incompetence.

"You okay, son?" Montgomery said.

Red snapped back into the room. "Yes, sir."

Walker was still talking. ". . . We've been trying to convert existing ICBMs into something that can knock a satellite out for five years. But it can't be done. The accuracy's not there. Two years ago, this project began. We started with the missile, code-named Icarus. We've got it to where we believe it can complete the intercept, but it needs a lot of help to be in precisely the right piece of sky, at the right speed, at the right time. This task is all about precision. The radar's useful only as a proximity fuse. The missile needs to be launched already on its interception track. Luckily, satellites are predictable."

"Did you say Mach 8?" Clifford asked.

"Yes, it needs a head start."

"But Mach 8?" Clifford leaned back in his chair and

turned his palms up. "Can this thing really get to that sort of speed? And stay in one piece?"

"We got the X-15 to Mach 7. This aircraft has twice the rocket power, albeit for a shorter period."

"How would we even control it?" Clifford asked, and he pulled the diagrams closer.

"We're learning a lot from Apollo for this."

Clifford looked up at the agents. "You've built this thing already? We haven't even tested the small SRBs on the A-12. What if it's not controllable?"

"You'll have to find a way to control it. We're open to any modifications you suggest."

Red stared at the men around the table. He felt as if he were at the movies, watching some science-fiction film.

He was in over his head. About to be found out.

Or about to die.

Did Clifford feel the same way? He'd made it clear he was surprised by the revelation of the XS-81, and even sceptical. But was he scared, too?

The chief test pilot leaned forward and tapped the diagram. "Mr Walker, you're speaking in a matter-of-fact voice about an incredibly dangerous and unknown flight profile. You're not about to send us to our deaths in the name of a research project."

"Easy now, Johnny," Montgomery said. "That's what the A-12 flights are about. They're your opportunity to build up to the XS-81. If it's not going to work, you'll find out along the way, and no one needs to go on a suicide mission. But, you should know, the president is aware of this project. He's been told the '81 is on its way."

The NRO men exchanged a glance.

"Exactly. And we're relying on A-TEC to deliver, Colonel," Walker said.

"If the concept doesn't work, it doesn't work. We can't perform miracles. Even Johnson should understand that," Clifford said, protesting.

"They're staking a lot on this," Gomez said. "A lot."

"We'll give it our best shot," Clifford said, leaning back in his chair. "But we won't knowingly kill ourselves. That won't serve anyone."

"Fine," Gomez said. "One more thing. This is currently our most secret project. The US government has made certain undertakings to the United Nations about weapons in space. We're currently negotiating a treaty to cover it, but the lawyers think this is very likely a breach of what we've promised. The Soviets cannot know the true nature of this project. All XS-81 flights will be carried out at Groom Lake at night. It's need-to-know, so the details are kept inside A-TEC. Any breach of the security will be treated as a crime against the state and dealt with accordingly. So, if you talk in your sleep, don't share a room. If you get chatty when you're drunk, stay off the booze. If you find yourself in a bar and a woman suddenly wants to fuck you, report her to the CIA. The Soviets *will* be watching and waiting for someone to mess up. If it's you, you'll go to prison for a long time. Understood?"

The men nodded, including Montgomery. It was clear how the hierarchy worked when it came to state secrets.

The meeting broke up.

Red stayed in his place, not trusting his legs to work.

Clifford glanced at him. "Take the rest of the day off. You look beat."

"Before you go, Brunson," Montgomery said, "I need a word."

. . .

With just the two of them left in the room, Montgomery handed Red a folder.

"Your farmer's arriving Monday."

Red checked out the title on the file: *Edwards Multi Unit Ferry Pilot.*

"Ferry pilot?"

Montgomery waved a hand. "It's the job title. Base commander wants a clear line between the test pilots and these guys. They're here to do the routine and keep you guys free for, well, the other stuff. Anyway, gotta be a step up from dusting crops, right?"

"Definitely."

"Good. So, look after him for a couple of weeks while we wait for the A-12 to come back. Do some flying and make sure he's all over the procedures here. Then show him the bars and brothels. That should settle him in."

Red stared at him for a moment. "Is that a joke?"

Montgomery shrugged. "Just make sure he's settled."

It was hard to keep the July desert sun out of his bedroom. Red hung a couple of towels over the drapes, but it had little cooling effect.

Lying on his back, he tried to settle his anxiety.

Everything was coming at him too fast.

The A-12 flights had already stretched him. He felt he'd found his limit, but was about to be pushed over the edge.

The edge of space.

He closed his eyes. An unwanted vision filled his mind.

The smell, the twisted remains.

PART 2

DARK STRIKE

PROLOGUE

Rosamond, California
May 21, 1947

THE HEAT HIT their faces like an invisible wall.

Red and Joe moved slowly around the flaming remains of the silver fighter jet.

As they reached the far side, Red's eyes were drawn to an awkward shape, on the edge of the mess of metal and fire.

A shape that did not fit the sharp-angled lines of twisted wreckage.

A shape that could be only one thing.

The man had been thrown from his cockpit, arm outstretched as if in a final desperate bid to climb free from his death pit.

They walked around, keeping back from the ferocious heat.

Until they were a few feet from the body.

The legs twisted, ungainly, no longer fitting the human form.

The arm reaching forward, out of the remains.

A silver helmet, turned towards them. Lifeless eyes below a blood-scarred forehead.

Red snapped his head away, reeling from what he saw.

His friend Joe stared at him, mouth open, waiting for Red to say it.

CHAPTER SIX

EDWARDS AIR FORCE BASE, California
September 1965

Brandon Dupont was virtually unrecognisable. His
unkempt hair had been cut to a cropped military style. He
wore a smart white shirt and black pants with a crease, and
clean new shoes. He looked younger, closer to his forty-two
years.

He stood in the guardroom by the main gate with a large
bag in his hands, beaming at Red.

"Captain Brunson. How are you?"

"Very good, thank you, Mr Dupont."

Red looked him up and down. "So, where's the farmer I
met?"

Dupont laughed. "Well, you know a shave and a shower
can change a man."

Red tapped on the guardroom admin office window and
spent the next forty-five minutes in a sea of paperwork,

eventually extracting Dupont's passes for Edwards and A-TEC.

As they walked from the guardroom, Red regarded the transformed Dupont. His demeanour was natural. He stood straight, walked confidently. He even seemed to have lost some of his southern twang.

Dupont must have caught the expression. "What? You didn't think I'd make it here?"

Red shook his head at the confidence on display. "Where's Pappy?" he asked, half expecting the old man to be lurking in the shadows, shotgun in hand.

"He's stayed back home."

"He'll be okay?"

"Uh-huh. He'll be fine. Now, how about you, Red? How are you holding up?" Dupont gave him a sympathetic smile.

"Why do you ask?"

Dupont shrugged. "You look a little tired."

"I'm fine. But thank you for asking."

After a short drive into the mass of brown and fawn government buildings, Red pulled up in front of a two-storey apartment block.

"Second floor, room thirteen." He pushed a key into the front door.

"I'm sharing?"

"No. You have your own apartment."

Up the stairs, Red opened the door. "One bedroom. Who wouldn't want to be without a US government couch and drapes?"

Dupont dropped his holdall on the floor. "Thanks. I didn't realise they'd pay me *and* give me somewhere to live."

After Dupont hung up his neatly pressed civilian

clothes, Red drove him around Edwards, pointing out the various organisations that shared the base. Eventually, they arrived at A-TEC.

They walked into the pilots' office, and Red introduced him around.

"This is our chief test pilot, Johnny Clifford. He's my boss, and that makes him your big boss."

Clifford stuck out a hand. "Welcome. We need all the help we can get. You designed that wing on the Stearman?"

"Yes, sir." Dupont didn't elaborate; there was an awkward pause.

"Okay, well, Red here will show you the ropes. It's important you understand the local procedures. We share this facility with some pretty important organisations, and we try not to piss them off."

"Yes, sir."

They spent the rest of the day filling out more forms. The security instructions for members of A-TEC were contained in a fourteen-page, closely typed document. It took Dupont an hour to read it, initial each page, and sign the back of his personal copy.

At 1700, Red tapped him on the shoulder. "Wanna beer?"

"We're not gonna go flyin'?"

Red laughed. "You have a mother lode of paperwork to get through first. You'll fly Friday, I promise."

Maggie's Grill was where the A-TEC officers and men hung out. A wooden, single-level building on the edge of Rosamond, twenty minutes west of the base.

Pilots used the bar to line up a run and break over the main runway, causing the liquor bottles to rattle a tune on their wooden shelves. But no one ever turned his or her head. Another test pilot letting his drinking colleagues know that some of them were still working.

Red pushed open the door. Three men stood at the bar, drinks in hand. It was otherwise empty, understandable for a Monday evening.

"It's the Red Baron!" Maggie called as she lifted an engraved glass off a hook above her.

"This your dad?" she joked, looking at Dupont as they approached the bar.

"This is Brandon," Red replied. "He's going to be flying with us."

Maggie took in the newcomer and nodded slowly. "So, this is the farmer."

"Uh-huh," Red said.

She turned back to Red. "You okay?"

"Yeah."

She didn't look convinced. "You wanna be careful with that job of yours, Red. You're getting old before your time."

Maggie, thin, sun-baked, and of indeterminate age herself, poured the beers.

Two men at the bar turned and checked Dupont out before going back to their beers.

"You got a call sign, mister?" Maggie asked.

"Hooker," Dupont said, and the men around laughed.

"I don't wanna know why they called you that. Anyway, the glass is four dollars. I'll engrave it, and it stays on the hooks here until you leave." She motioned to a row of hooks that ran in a line above the bar.

But Dupont's eyes went to a set of seven similarly engraved glass tankards on a shelf in front of a large Southern Comfort mirror behind the bar. The shelf was labelled *Pancho's Boys*.

Maggie turned her head and looked back at him. "They didn't get to leave."

Red and the other men silently raised their drinks.

Dupont joined them, before Red set a five-dollar bill on the bar. "I'll get the this. My welcome gift."

The door opened; Jay Anderson appeared with three other test pilots from A-TEC.

Red hurriedly picked up the glasses. "Quick. We'll be stung for their drinks as well if we wait here."

They moved to a table in the corner. The room was hot, even with the windows open and two fans doing their best to get some circulation going.

"By the way, we don't use personal call signs at A-TEC. Montgomery thinks it alienates the civilians. But you can't put your real name on a glass behind the bar."

"Fair enough. Not hugely fond of Hooker, anyway."

"I bet. Now, tell me about Columbus. We heard you did pretty good?"

"They started me on the Texan, but for only two weeks. Then the T-38." He drank some beer, then looked at Red with a smile. "It's a pretty neat jet."

"Sure is."

"Has its limitations, though."

"And I'm sure you found them. They certainly have confidence in you. I saw the reports. You know, a couple of years here and we could get you through one of the schools."

"You think?" Dupont said, but he didn't look excited about the idea. "You went to Patuxent?"

"Pax River? Yep. I'm air force, but the schools like to mix it up a bit, so I was assigned to the navy school. The air force school's here at Edwards, and the Brits have one, too."

Anderson and the others joined them, and Red did some

more introductions. Anderson settled next to Red and leaned in closely.

"You okay?"

Red nodded. "Sure. Why does everyone keep asking me that?"

"Just checking."

Red fixed him with a confident gaze. "I'm fine. Thanks, Jay."

He leaned back and caught Dupont observing him over the rim of his beer glass.

For the next couple of days, Red kept his new charge busy with the mountain of operating procedures for A-TEC and Edwards. By Friday morning, he was ready to fly.

At 1000, he had Dupont in the front seat of a T-38, taxiing to the runway hold.

They listened on the radio as a B-52 with an engine out was vectored onto the extended centreline.

"Only seven engines," Red noted.

Dupont laughed into his oxygen mask. "That thing needs all the power it can get."

Eventually, the bomber's shadow flashed over them as it descended over the threshold and made an unremarkable landing.

"What was that thing in the belly?" Dupont asked, and Red glanced back at the jet. He had some sort of pylon, but it was now too far away to make anything out.

"Dunno."

Dupont made the radio calls and got them airborne.

From the back seat, Red directed a tour of the local area. He started with the landmarks they used for visual orientation: Maggie's, various crossroads, and Leuhman Ridge, a small outcrop of rocks to the east.

"You navigate using rocks?" Dupont asked.

"The desert goes on forever and looks the same. It's easy to get disorientated, so learn the rocks. And remember you'll be flying a variety of aircraft. Not all of them have navaids."

Red showed Dupont how to avoid the congested airspace around LA before directing him back east.

After twelve minutes, they reached an imaginary line in the sky, and Red had Dupont set up an orbit.

"This is the outer limit of Groom Lake. You cross into that without permission and expect a court-martial, if you're lucky."

"And if you're unlucky?"

"They'll shoot you down. But don't worry. I'll choose good songs for your funeral."

"Thanks. And I suppose I can't ask what goes on at Groom Lake?"

"Nope. Now, your first test. Get us to China Lake."

For a full two minutes, they sat in the orbit. Red could just see Dupont turning a chart over in his hands while presumably keeping the Talon level with his knees. He laughed.

"Got it," Dupont finally called out.

"Hallelujah!"

The farmer banked them and rolled out west. After a couple of minutes, he banked again and ran north. Red looked out his window and down at the brown, desolate earth beneath them. He laughed again when he realised Dupont was navigating using Highway 395.

As they approached, Red told him to carry out a full-stop

landing at the Navy Weapons School. He remained quiet in the back and let Dupont contact the tower at China, then watched as he used the chart to position them for a run and break, one thousand feet above the pattern height. He braced himself in the back as they rolled into a one-eighty-degree bank, Dupont using it to lose speed and height. He initiated a perfect curved turn onto a short final, before touching down between the oblong white lines that marked the ideal spot.

He was good.

They parked as directed on a corner of the large apron. Various navy jets were dotted around them.

The canopy whirred open. It was searingly hot. Fall was yet to arrive in the Mojave. Red loosened his flight suit and stripped away unnecessary clothing, leaving them with his helmet and g-suit on the seat in the T-38.

"What's that?" Dupont asked, looking at a single-engine fighter. Red recognised the F-8 Crusader, but wasn't sure what was attached to the front of it. A bulbous dome, presumably housing some new radar.

He put a hand on Dupont's shoulder.

"You're gonna have to stop asking this sort of question. Seriously. These places are need-to-know."

"Okay. I was just interested."

Red laughed. "I know, but curiosity can get you in a heap of trouble around here."

They went into the navy evaluation unit.

"You're gonna be ferrying aircraft around the Mojave," Red said. "So, today is about familiarisation."

"Sure."

On the short one hundred thirty-mile hop back to Edwards, Red announced that Dupont was ready for his first task.

"Okay," Dupont replied from the front.

"It's a simple one. This jet is due a two-hundred-hour inspection. That happens down at Nellis. So, after lunch we'd like you to run her down. They'll service it while you drink coffee. Takes about three hours. Then bring her back. Okay?"

Dupont orientated the chart again.

"You can plan on the ground this time."

On the ground, Red paced as Dupont used a grease pencil to mark up a local area chart. They were about to let a farmer from the Deep South fly a million-dollar jet to Las Vegas.

He didn't think for one second that Dupont wasn't trustworthy and reliable. But he was still getting used to the idea that this was the same person he'd met in Mississippi.

"He good to go?" Colonel Montgomery had appeared by Red's side.

"Yes, sir. I think so."

"Well, all right then." Montgomery wandered off.

Jay Anderson appeared and leaned over Dupont's charts. "You can't miss Nellis. Head for the casinos rising out of the desert and land before you reach them."

A couple of the guys around laughed. Dupont gave him a weak smile.

"You'll be fine," Red said. "Don't sweat it. Just enjoy the freedom."

Dupont picked up his paperwork, and Red gave him a friendly slap on the back as he headed off to the locker room.

"If he doesn't come back with that jet, they'll take it out of your salary, Red," Anderson said and laughed at his own joke.

Before Red could respond, Johnny Clifford appeared by his side and handed him a folder.

"We have only four pairs of SRBs," he said quietly, "so each burn needs to count. These are the profiles for next week. I'll handle Flight One, which will be inert. I'll carry out handling checks for any aerodynamic changes we need to be aware of. If there are no new issues, you'll be flying Burn One immediately afterwards, okay?"

Red felt a surge of anxiety, but he nodded and opened the folder as Clifford walked away.

For Burn One, the SRBs would have just ten percent fuel capacity. It was expected to accelerate the A-12 to Mach 3 and ninety-five thousand feet.

Provided there were no unexpected handling issues, Burn Two would be twenty-five percent fuel, with an expected height of one hundred twenty thousand feet and Mach 4.5 achieved.

Burns Three and Four would both have fifty percent fuel with no estimates for height or speed. Into the unknown on Thursday and Friday.

If he survived the first burn on Monday.

Red had been reading about the dangers of skipping across the top of the atmosphere. A few pilots had got themselves into trouble in the X-Planes a decade before. Just another thing that would reach up and grab you if you weren't on your game.

After each flight, readings would be taken from a range of instruments attached to the body of the aircraft.

There would be nowhere to hide if he messed up. Even if he recovered.

It was nearly 1700, and no one had heard from Dupont.

Red nervously tapped the desk.

"Looks like him," a voice called from a window at the far side of the room. Red got up and looked out, in time to see a T-38 turning onto the A-TEC flight line. Relief swept over him.

A few minutes later, the farmer appeared. He was sweaty, with hair matted to his head.

"How'd it go?" Red asked. Dupont shrugged in reply.

"Fine."

"Well, you better get home and shower, because it's Rosababes night."

A few cheers went up from around the office.

Dupont raised an eyebrow.

"Friday night at Maggie's. It's the closest we get to the bright lights around here. I'll pick you up at eighteen hundred."

Dupont jumped over the side of the car and landed on the back seat of Jay Anderson's red Ford Falcon.

Red yelped as he sat on his hand. "Easy, tiger."

"Sorry, Red."

"Forget about it. Brandon, you know Jay already. We stay friends with him 'cause he has the best car." He patted the driver on the shoulder. "And this is Micky Luciano, known to the world as Luch." He turned to the man squeezed into the back on his right. "Honestly, I have no idea why we stay friends with him."

Luch leaned forward. "'Cause I'm the best looking, and the girls flock to me."

"Is that what you think?" Red said. "You sad, deluded little man."

General laughter as they set out. Pilots from Edwards on Friday night patrol.

The low car scrapped its way along the straight desert approach roads leading from the airfield. After they'd driven through the southern airfield security, they didn't pass a single other vehicle.

"This place really is the middle of nowhere," Dupont said.

"Really?" Red replied. "From you? The man from Nowhere, Mississippi. This is a metropolis by comparison."

Anderson turned to Dupont. "Don't listen to him. I came from Nebraska, and this place is even less populated, believe me."

"Ah, but not on a Friday night at Maggie's."

"Maggie's? It's pretty quiet there, isn't it?" Dupont asked.

"Not on a Friday," Red said. "The music is provided by a fat cowboy called Roger, and the fried chicken is best avoided if you want to function normally on Saturday. But it seems to be the main attraction for the sweet, innocent girls of Rosamond, the Rosababes, and their wiser, more experienced cousins in Lancaster—"

"And they're all hoping to bag a pilot," Anderson said. "So be on your guard."

"I think I'm a little too old for any of that."

Twenty minutes later, they pulled into Maggie's dusty lot, to the muffled sound of music. Next over was a gas station with a single pump and an ancient man in an old wooden chair.

The air was only marginally cooler inside Maggie's than it was outside.

Red surveyed the scene. The place was busy, with tables filling up.

"About three-to-one female-to-male ratio, I'd say."

"Hey, Red!"

A girl appeared in front of them. She had auburn hair and was wearing a gingham summer dress and a beaming smile with two rows of gleaming white teeth.

"Hey, Sarah. How y'doing?"

She put her hand on Red's chest. "Fine, now you're all here." Her eyes flicked to Dupont. "Well, hello-ee. You got a new boss, Red?"

"Sarah, this here is Brandon Dupont. He's joined the team."

"Well, welcome to nowhere, Brandon. I hope you live long enough to enjoy some of the unique sights we offer."

"Don't talk like that, Sarah," Red said.

She withdrew her hand and turned back to Red. "Well, you know what I mean."

"You wanna drink, Sarah?" Red asked, lightening the mood.

"Sure, we're all over there." She pointed to a group of girls sitting in a large booth against the far side of the building.

"What was that about?" Dupont asked, as Sarah headed back to her group.

Red paused. "She's made some unlucky choices in who to go out with."

"Unlucky?"

"We do dangerous work. But you'll be protected from the worst of it." He looked over his shoulder. "She's a sweet gal, actually. She could do with catching a break."

Anderson appeared with a tray of beers, and they made their way to the girls. Roger the Cowboy began a rendition of "Ring of Fire" at least an octave higher than Johnny Cash. Red winced, and let the beer numb the assault on his ears.

They got chatting, but Dupont stayed quiet as friends around him caught up on the week's events.

He seemed content not to initiate any conversations.

To Red's relief, Sarah made her way over.

"Scooch!" She said to Anderson. "I need to speak to the new boy."

Anderson shifted along the red cushioned bench, allowing Sarah to squeeze between him and Dupont.

Red couldn't hear all the conversation, but he got the impression Dupont was irritated at the attention from Sarah.

The beers continued to arrive, and the next time Red looked up, Sarah had her back turned to Dupont, while he was chatting to Luch and the others.

Sarah caught him staring and gave him a quizzical look.

He raised his bottle to her, and she flashed a smile.

The sunlight streamed in through the shutters, illuminating Sarah's smooth skin. The top two buttons on her dress were undone, and Red caught the pattern of light freckles on her upper chest.

Her smile lingered.

A crash of a bottle on the table.

"Eww!" one of the other girls shouted as she sprung up from her seat.

"I'm so sorry, ma'am," Dupont said with a slur. "I slipped."

Sarah quickly set the upturned bottle back on its base and helped brush her friend down.

"It's hardly anything, Maureen. Don't fuss."

Red glanced at Dupont, who was suddenly looking tipsy and remorseful.

"Let me buy you a drink," Dupont said.

Maureen smiled at him. "Why, sure!"

She moved from the table, and the men gave Dupont some space as he slowly extricated himself from his seat.

"Go easy there, tiger," Red said. "Something tells me it's been awhile since you had a beer or two."

"I'm fine, son," Dupont said, and he followed his new friend to the bar.

Red watched them for a moment, then shuffled in next to Sarah. "What do you make of him?"

"I don't think he likes me."

"What? Why d'you think that?"

"I dunno. It just didn't feel as if he wanted to be talking to me."

"I think he's shy. He's a long way from where he came from. Plus, he's probably scared. You are frightening, after all." He poked her in the shoulder.

"Well, I guess I scared *you* off, Captain Brunson."

Her look lingered for a second before Red laughed it off.

Maureen and Dupont reappeared. Maureen retook her seat, and Dupont went back to where he was sitting, three people away from her.

More beers arrived, and soon the talk turned to the usual topic: flying.

"His fighter-pilot curved approaches are a thing of beauty," Red said, motioning to Dupont.

Dupont smiled and closed his eyes. "It's all in the lake curve . . ." he slurred.

"The what?"

"We had a lake. I used shore to guide the outer edge of the wing. It brought me round perfect. Every time. Easy." He finished the sentence with a small belch.

"Where was that?" Anderson asked.

Dupont's eyes flicked open. He looked as if he'd just woken. "Oh, can't remember."

"You can't remember?"

"Down south somewhere."

The other pilot persisted. "MacDill? Eglin?"

Dupont thought for a moment. "Actually, maybe it was . . . Korea."

"Korea?"

Red laughed. "He's drunk. Leave him alone."

"Bit weird, though, to forget an entire air base."

"Jay, let it go."

They stayed another hour. Shots arrived. Dupont tried to refuse but gave in to a chorus of encouragement.

When it came time to leave, Red helped the farmer to his feet.

"Is he okay?" Sarah asked.

"Sure!" Red responded. "Well, maybe."

The men sang in the car as the cool wind washed over them. Anderson drove straight past the turn for Edwards.

"Hey. Isn't that where I live?" Dupont said and hiccupped.

Red put his arm around him. "You don't wanna spend a lonely night in that shitty building. Back to mine for a night-cap, and you can sleep on the couch."

They drove on for a while. Dupont glazed over and put his hand to his mouth.

"Stop the car!" Red yelled, and Anderson obeyed with a screech of brakes. Dust flew up as Red got Dupont's head over the side of the vehicle. Just in time. His spew hit the ground in an ungainly splatter.

When he was finished, they hauled him back and drove on to Red's. He helped Dupont from the vehicle.

"Sorry, boss," Dupont said, bowing his head to Red.

"I'm not your boss. And I don't give a rat's ass what you do in the evening. We all need to blow off a little steam."

Behind them, Anderson spun his wheels on the desert dust and disappeared into the night.

Dupont wobbled, but remained upright. Red looked across to the old water tower.

"Hey, Brandon, wanna climb the tower?"

Dupont stumbled again, and Red immediately knew that was a potentially fatal suggestion. "Maybe another time."

"You go up there?" Dupont said, reaching out with his hand to prop himself up on the side of the house.

Red looked at the bulbous top of the tower. "Used to. But don't tell my pa."

"I thought your pa was dead?" Dupont said.

Red turned back and stared at him.

Silence passed. Dupont stumbled into the house.

"I guess I'll put you to bed," Red said, more to himself.

He got Dupont to lie down on the couch and found him a blanket to keep the night chill out.

"There's a john by the front door and water in the faucet."

Dupont lifted his hand in appreciation. "Thank you, son."

Red paused for a moment and sat down next to him.

"I think you would have liked my pa. He was a pretty cool customer, like you. Never seemed ruffled by anything. Except when Mrs Emmanuel told him about me and Joe up the water tower. He was pissed that day!"

Red looked down, unsure if Dupont was still conscious.

"How did you know about my father, Brandon?"

The man from Mississippi started snoring.

CHAPTER SEVEN

RED ARRIVED at A-TEC at 1100. It was a strange feeling starting four hours after most of his colleagues on a Monday morning.

"Afternoon," Jay Anderson said, mocking him.

"You're so funny," Red responded. "Where's Brandon?"

"Up with Clifford, learning to fly the B-57."

"Really? Big-boy stuff. That thing's a death trap."

"I hope he's sobered up."

"He slept it off on Saturday and was gone when I got back with some lunch. He probably slept the rest of the weekend."

Red found an empty side office, secure enough for him to open classified documents. He sat at a desk and opened the NRO project briefing.

In the first flights, they had engaged the secondary afterburners at flight level four hundred, otherwise known as forty thousand feet. But that was routine for the A-12. Lighting freshly mounted solid rocket boosters would be a whole new ball game.

An unknown game. Suitable for only the sharpest of the bunch.

Why did they think that was him?

He read through the notes on the SRBs. They'd apparently fired them several times on the ground, but they could only estimate the impact the sudden extra thrust would have on the flight profile. The worst aspect for Red was that they couldn't be shut down or jettisoned. They were fireworks. Once lit, you were along for the ride.

Jay Anderson opened the door to the side office and stuck his head in. Instinctively, Red closed the manuals.

"So, I'm to be your cabdriver!" he announced.

Red was confused.

"The old man's put me on C-130 duty with Cofferr. We're flying your millions of ground crew and engineers to the air base that shall not be named. Every night!"

"I see."

"Meanwhile, you get to arrive in style in a T-38 with Johnny. I don't know how you pulled that one, Brunson."

Red shook his head. "Me, neither. I'm surprised they've spared you."

"Me, too. I think your NRO guys are calling the shots."

Red thought for a second. "It's because I'm junior, of course."

"What?"

"The reason I'm partnered with Johnny is because I'm the office junior. You're too valuable."

"Well, now I'm a taxi driver for you, so that didn't work out well for me."

Anderson left the room, and Red wasn't entirely sure how serious he was being. Was he upset? Jealous of Red's place on a secret project.

He was welcome to take over.

Red packed away the flight manuals and procedure books and headed to the locker room. They had a T-38 to take out to Groom. Clifford had asked him to look after the flight.

He stood staring at his g-suit, distracted by his thoughts.

Clifford and Dupont appeared from the airfield. Red quickly lifted the outer clothing off the hook and began to dress.

He glanced up to see Dupont looking nonchalant as he removed his flying gear.

"How'd it go?" Red asked as Clifford passed by.

"He's good." The chief test pilot then headed off to the planning room.

Red continued to dress in silence. In his peripheral vision, he noticed Dupont had stopped changing and look over.

"Thanks for Friday night, Red. I appreciate it."

"I got us some lunch, but you were gone."

"Didn't want to impose on you."

"No problem."

Red went back to his clothing, pulling on his jacket.

Dupont stayed where he was.

"Everything all right, Brandon?"

"Sure. But you're anxious, I think? I hope you don't mind me saying so?"

Red paused and turned to face him. "I guess. Big flight tonight. And I'm on my own, so a little anxious. But that's all right."

Dupont walked over and put his hand on Red's shoulder. "Anxiety can be good, but it can also get in the way."

Red considered this for a moment. "I'll be all right in the cockpit, I think."

"I'm sure you will. Just concentrate on the details. That's

what I do. Make yourself too busy to worry about anything else."

Red flew over Death Valley and tried to pick out Groom Lake in the late-afternoon sun. It was impossible. The whole area looked flat and brown, like the rest of the Mojave Desert. He glanced at the stopwatch, keeping the T-38 on the heading he'd calculated. Two minutes and twenty seconds into the last leg, and he saw the telltale lines in the sand. As he descended and carried out a run and break over the top of the spartan field, he spotted a crowd of men beavering around a trolley.

The SRBs had arrived.

After rolling out on the wide expanse of flat desert floor, Red lined up behind an airfield truck with a large *FOLLOW ME* sign on its roof.

The last rays of sun were falling below the horizon. Red swung his jet onto the apron, facing the A-12 hangar, just as the black aircraft was pulled from its lair.

A few minutes later, he and Clifford climbed down the steel steps that had been pushed up to the T-38. Another small team clambered over the sleek, hypersonic aircraft. Next to the jet was a digger, with the first of the boosters in its raised bucket. It was around fifty feet long, maybe half the length of the aircraft.

The men around the jet wore masks. Odd. The rockets were supposed to be inert for Clifford's first flight.

"Gentlemen." A shout carried on the wind.

The NRO guys, Walker and Gomez, marched towards them.

"Small change of plan," Gomez said. "We want to light

the rockets on Flight One. We're short on time for this workup, and we've streamlined."

"What about flight-testing them first?" Clifford said. "Do we know how they'll affect lift and drag?"

"We're basically combining the flight test with the first burn. If there are any handling issues, you can abandon and come back early, of course."

"And land with two highly explosive fireworks on the wings?" Clifford said.

Red's eyes flicked over to the A-12 and the SRBs. They were volatile; that was the point. Built for burning only in the upper atmosphere but lethal in the thicker surface air.

"The engineers are confident there'll be no issues with the aerodynamics," Walker said.

"Are they? Maybe they'd like to fly then?" Clifford stared at Walker and Gomez.

Gomez rubbed his eyes, trying to dislodge some sand. Walker looked down at his clipboard, then looked up at Red and Clifford. "Look, the project is being accelerated."

"Accelerated?" Clifford said. "We haven't flown the first flight. Does Colonel Montgomery know about this?"

Walker raised a hand. "The National Reconnaissance Office is running this project. We don't have to consult Montgomery. Orders from above, I'm afraid."

"High above," Gomez added.

Clifford shook his head. "Listen, we do things in an orderly manner. Why the damn rush?"

A ground handler appeared and started to attach a tow bar to the T-38.

"Son, can you give us a moment, please?" Walker called above the breeze. The young man didn't need telling twice, and he disappeared into a yellow tractor.

David Gomez took a step forward. "The XS-81 is ready to

fly. We need to get the initial SRB tests done by the end of this week. You'll take over the '81 from the company test pilots next week. We need to be ready for an operation on October thirtieth."

Red and Clifford looked at each other; Clifford turned back and spoke first. "Operation? You mean we're going to take out a Soviet satellite?"

Walker took over. "There's a dead Soviet satellite on its way down. It'll enter the atmosphere on the thirty-first, and when it does, it becomes unpredictable. It could come down in the middle of the Arctic or the middle of Oslo. Who the hell knows? The Soviets clearly don't give a damn, but we do, and this is the perfect opportunity to demonstrate our new ability without triggering World War Three. But we have a window of a few hours on the thirtieth. That's the last day the satellite path will be predictable."

"It's a perfect situation for us," Gomez added. "We can legitimately take it out, because it poses a threat to civilians. The missile will reduce it to smaller pieces that'll burn up on reentry. All done in the name of safety. The Soviets will know we've done it, but they'll have no idea how."

Brad Walker smiled. "We'll reveal our capability without giving anything away. Or breaking any United Nations commitments. Like I say, it's a perfect opportunity. Johnson wants it to happen. He believes this will make the Russians think twice about what they put into space above us."

The men stood in silence for a moment.

"We've a helluva long way to go before we're ready to fire this thing," Clifford said. "Who knows if it'll work?"

"We have faith in A-TEC," Gomez said.

The desert wind chose that moment to pick up, carrying sand, the perennial issue for mechanics at Groom Lake. The men covered their eyes.

"But one more thing," Walker shouted. "This all fails if word gets out. For now, this is the USA's most valuable secret, and we expect to keep it that way. Flights between 0200 and no later than one hour before sunrise. We also limit who's on the project to the absolute essentials. Understood?"

The men nodded.

"October thirtieth?" Red said, his voice croaking as the dry wind caught his throat.

"We have one shot," Gomez said as he made notes on his clipboard. "We need to release the missile under the satellite track and well away from prying eyes, so you'll be launching from the northern tip of Alaska."

"In six weeks?" Clifford whistled. "That's tough. Can we work up a flight profile in that time?"

"You have only five sets of SRBs for the '81, and we need one for the mission. So that's four full dress rehearsals. You'll have plenty of time."

Red turned to look at the A-12, which was looking ready for the first test of the smaller SRBs. "Christ."

Clifford turned to him. "I hope you're up for this, Brunson."

Red sat on the running board of a brown military wagon, away from any aircraft or volatile rockets, and lit a cigarette. He tried to process what he'd just been told, but he just didn't have the space in his head.

He would pilot Flight Two an hour after Johnny Clifford landed, assuming they had enough darkness left. The one good thing: he would now be Burn Two, and not the first to light the boosters. All being well, Clifford would be doing that about now, high over the Pacific Ocean.

They had no direct contact with the A-12, just a hand-held radio they used to communicate with the tower. In any case, the flights were flown in radio silence, as far as possible.

Red tried to imagine what Clifford was going through. He glanced at his watch, figuring the SRBs were due for lighting just before 0230.

What would it be like? Would the A-12 be controllable?

He mused to himself that in test-flying, there was always something that could go wrong, but every flight in this project seemed to him to have a much higher chance than normal of failure, possibly with tragic consequences.

Time went slowly. Red tried not to stare at his watch, but as the minutes ticked past 0315, by his calculations, Johnny Clifford was overdue.

He didn't say anything.

A couple of the engineers were chatting in low voices, but no one seemed unduly worried.

Red stood up and stared into the night sky. The orange lights dousing the apron meant the stars were hidden; they would likely hear the A-12 before they saw it.

As long as it was on its way back, and not at the bottom of the Pacific.

The handheld radio burst into life.

"He's inbound. Twelve minutes."

Red exhaled and sat back down.

"Long final" came the next call.

Moments later, he could just make out the shape of the dark jet as it crossed the fence about a mile from where they stood.

It came to halt on the flight line, and the recovery team stood up, waiting for Clifford to shut down the howling J-58s.

Red looked at the two small missiles on the wing. They were blackened. The ground guys set up the stairs, and Johnny Clifford gingerly backed out of the cockpit and climbed down onto the concrete hardstanding.

Red approached him. "How was it?"

Clifford looked serious. "A lot of vibrations. They'll need to check the airframe. Got to seventy-seven, six hundred and tipped over. Descent profile was nominal."

"The relight?"

"Nominal." Clifford walked off. "You better be ready, Brunson. It's a helluva ride."

Gomez appeared by his side. "We're out of time for tonight. You'll be first up tomorrow."

Red was both relieved and immediately anxious about the next night. Clifford flew them back, and he drove home to attempt sleep.

Red's house was little more than four prefabricated walls loosely joined and covered, pretty useless at keeping heat out and warmth in.

By 0800, the day's heat was on the rise and he lay motionless, staring at the ceiling, eyes open with no chance of further slumber.

Clifford had insisted he stay home and rest until at least 1300; he had five hours of nothing but worry ahead of him.

On a whim, he went for a drive.

He turned his Ford Galaxie onto a track that ran to the south of Edwards. At the point closest to the main runway, he pulled over, got out, lit a Lucky Strike, and stared into the empty approach lanes.

All was quiet save for the distant whistle of a jet engine somewhere on the base.

He drew on the tab and inhaled deeply.

Edwards could be an odd place. The centre of the world when it came to aircraft development, but sometimes it resembled one of those abandoned mining towns—nothing but tumbleweeds.

There was no Officers' Club to speak of. The men, officers, and civilians rubbed shoulders with little regard for rank. They drank off base, lived off base, but spent most waking hours working.

The distant noise grew louder, and he turned to see a B-57 taxiing towards the southern threshold.

Dupont. His second day of conversion to the lumbering British jet.

Red imagined him in the cramped cockpit, head poking into the plexiglass bubble. It wasn't an exciting aircraft to fly, but it was an important one to master. They used it a lot for photography and instrumentation.

Dupont would be put through his paces today. Engine failures in the B-57 had a habit of killing the unwary.

The aircraft turned into wind. Black smoke thickened from the back of the engines before he heard them spool up.

Red followed the jet as it flew straight into the pattern around Edwards.

Dupont flew the turn onto runway 04R with precision, rounding out with no noticeable corrections needed. The shadow flashed across him as the Canberra briefly blotted out the sun and came in for a solid landing.

On the next circuit, the aircraft was out of balance, the left wing edging ahead of the right. Practise engine failure. This was the gotcha scenario for the B-57. Whoever was instructing Dupont would be watching, hawkeyed for the quick and correct actions required to keep the aircraft in the air.

The B-57 passed over him for a second time, expertly lined up, even while flying out of balance.

They'd struck lucky in Shitsville, Mississippi.

Red ate alone in the commissary and headed into the office, spending the afternoon studying his notes. He wanted to speak to Johnny Clifford about his experience, but he resisted, fearing the chief test pilot would sense his jitters.

Dupont was there, nose deep into another set of pilots' notes. Before Red could catch up with him, he was out of his seat, having a quick word with Clifford, and heading out the door, car keys in hand.

"Where's he off to?" Red asked.

Clifford appeared distracted, with a pile of paperwork in front of him. "Uh, dunno. Something about moving."

"Moving? Moving where?"

"Dunno, Red. He's your pal, isn't he?"

Clifford flew the T-38 to Groom this time, leaving Red to stare out the window at the darkening desert. Sporadic pools of lights formed on the ground. After a few minutes of flying away from Edwards, even those died out. Groom Lake really was hidden in the shadows.

Just the way the National Reconnaissance Office liked it.

It took two hours for them to ready the A-12 and the SRBs, which were heavier than the previous night, with more fuel.

Suited and booted, Red closed the canopy.

These were the moments he hated. Alone inside the cockpit while all eyes outside were on him.

Waiting for a mistake.

A few taxiway lights showed the way to the main runway, and as he turned onto the wide tarmac strip, the main lights came on.

He looked to the tower and waited for the signal; he was under strict instruction to make no unnecessary radio calls. A green flare appeared, arching into the air. Red took a deep breath and advanced the throttles slowly. The A-12 required careful handling when you had highly explosive rockets on your wings.

Thirty seconds later, he nudged the powerful jet off the runway and into the black. Behind him, he imagined the runway lights already switched off.

An unregistered flight from an airfield that appeared on no maps.

A thought suddenly occurred. If he crashed, what would his superiors even say?

Would they make up some story about a road accident?

He continued to accelerate the A-12 turning towards the Pacific coast. He was quickly at twenty-five thousand feet and Mach 0.85. To his south, he could see the bloom of lights that marked Los Angeles and the sudden end to civilisation where the Pacific started.

Ten minutes out to sea, he began his climb to the ignition point for the SRBs. He punched through the sound barrier with the merest shudder that ran down the length of the jet.

At sixty-seven thousand feet, with full afterburners, he prepared to light the fireworks.

Red's heart beat hard in his chest as he held the stick lightly and made sure the nose was exactly twelve degrees up and the wings level.

He had second thoughts about his grip, and tightened it with his left hand—the wrong hand in normal circumstances—while his right moved down to the SRB ignition switches, installed next to the radio.

He armed the igniter for both SRBs and brought his thumb to the single switch that would light both, hopefully. If only one lit, he would have to eject in a matter of seconds, before the g-forces tore the aircraft apart.

He took one more deep breath and pushed his thumb down.

There was a loud, deep bang, and he was slammed back in his seat. The nose of the jet rose rapidly, and he quickly brought his right hand back to the stick, pushing it down, fighting to keep twelve degrees of angle.

The whole aircraft vibrated like a speeding train that had come off the rails and smashed over large wooden sleepers. His hands shook through the stick; holding the attitude was a struggle. He had just a few seconds to shut the jet engines down or risk having the turbine blades ripped off.

He moved his left hand to the throttle and slammed it closed, before trying to locate the fuel cock valves, but he was shaking so much he couldn't focus on the labels. Had he got the right ones?

"Jesus wept! This thing's gonna shake itself apart." Was this normal? Clifford said it was a "helluva ride," but it felt as if the jet was about to break into several pieces one hundred twenty thousand feet over the ocean.

His chances of rescue were low, even if he survived the ejection.

The roar of the SRBs drowned out everything, and so Red had no idea if the engines had shut down. He tried to read the N1 gauges, but everything was blurry.

He concentrated on keeping the nose at the predetermined attitude, bringing both hands onto the stick.

The aircraft seemed to settle into a pattern of vibration, like a pneumatic drill hammering into a road surface.

Around one minute after he'd lit the fireworks, they ran out of fuel and whimpered out with a few deep *whomp* sounds.

Sudden silence.

He looked out at the orange glow on the western horizon. Hours after the sun had set at ground level, its rays folded over the curve of the planet.

Cleared of the vibration-induced blurriness, Red scanned the instruments, again. One hundred forty thousand feet. It felt as if he were in space, although several thousand miles an hour short of being able to leave the planet's grip. And so, as Isaac Newton predicted, the aircraft began to descend.

The trick now was to keep the A-12 upright and ready for the thicker air as it fell back to Earth. The danger of tumbling was very real and probably not survivable.

Red kept a light touch on the stick, gently pushing the nose down when he felt the first signs of buffet.

The altimeter started to accelerate as it wound down. At one hundred thirty thousand feet, the buffet became more pronounced.

Another loud bang startled Red, and he tightened his grip on the stick, only to feel the aircraft pitching, nose up. It must have been a pocket of thicker air, disturbing the gentle glide.

The nose continued to rise, and Red pushed on the stick. The air was watery thin, and it left the A-12 unresponsive.

"Shit."

If the nose continued up, the aircraft would slip into a tailspin.

And that wouldn't be good.

He glanced at the checklist on his wrist.

RELIGHT—ONE HUNDRED TWENTY THOUSAND.

He was still ten thousand feet too high for the jet engines, but the nose was steadfast in its decision to rise. The buffet became more pronounced, the stick useless in the thin wisps of atmosphere.

Speed was bleeding away.

He had no choice.

Red reached down to his left to relight the engines, his hands gliding across the cocks, valves, and compressor switches.

The bespoke onboard compressor wound up the left J-58 while he held his thumb on the ignition. The nose continued to climb, pressing Red down in his seat. He was now seconds away from the aircraft rolling onto its back.

There would be no recovery possible, just a black, unwelcoming Pacific Ocean to receive him. He briefly imagined his insignificant pink body in a vast sea of sharks and God knows what else.

Fear of that watery grave began to overwhelm him.

He froze.

For a moment, Red stared ahead, taking in the last views of the world he would ever have.

Another jolt shook the aircraft.

It seemed to wake him up.

He shook his head. It wasn't over. He had to keep working.

Go down swinging, at least.

He brought his eyes back to the engine dials; the starboard engine had caught. He inched the throttle up to about twenty-five percent and got busy diverting the bleed air to the left jet engine.

The A-12 began to roll, slowly, but noticeable. This was it.

No coming back.

Heart thumping in his chest, still at over one hundred twenty thousand feet, he tried full rudder deflection and advanced the left side throttle to max, desperate to get control back.

The aircraft lurched back to the right and he compensated with left stick, willing the wings to find some bite in the almost nonexistent airflow. It was like trying to push a piece of thin paper underwater. His eyes darted over the left engine dials.

"Come on, come on . . ."

It became dark outside again, and he stared at the artificial horizon, willing it to come down.

Nothing happened. But it wasn't getting worse.

The A-12 had stabilised.

The left engine was now firing, and he went to full afterburner on both.

"Come on, baby!"

The aircraft started to respond, as it fell through one hundred fifteen thousand feet, and Red could finally nudge the nose down.

By one hundred ten thousand, it felt positively twitchy, and the nose settled at five degrees below the horizon.

He brought the engines back to dry power, conscious of the thirsty nature of the afterburners.

Gradually, the A-12 transitioned back to jet-borne flying, and at ninety-five thousand feet, he could coax her around to head southeast and back to land.

He exhaled and closed his eyes.

He'd almost lost it, and it terrified him. His first major trial as a test pilot had nearly been his last.

And there was more to come tomorrow night. More fuel, more speed, and even higher into the airless upper atmosphere.

He shivered at the prospect, then shook his head and focused on the task at hand.

What was it Dupont had said? *Concentrate on the details. Become too busy to remember you're scared.*

He ran through the TACAN procedures that would set him on a wide rejoin for Groom.

The altimeter unwound until he was down to thirty thousand feet. He cross-checked the TACAN with his chart. It was essential he kept to a narrow, preselected corridor, lest he appear in the busy Californian controlled airspace and attract unwanted attention.

The Mach indicator showed him still supersonic as he approached the coast. As discussed with Clifford during the procedure workup, he carried out an orbit over the sea until the energy bled away.

It took just twelve minutes to cross over Edwards and set himself up for a long final into Groom.

It was an approach carried out on nothing but faith in the navaids until the runway lights blinked into existence at one mile.

He rolled the jet out and taxied in. In the moment of solitude after shutdown, before the stairs appeared at his side, Red tried to gather his thoughts.

After a moment, the canopy motored open and a technician appeared, helping him remove his clunky space helmet.

"Enjoy the ride?" the man said, beaming at him.

"Something like that."

On the ground, Clifford looked at him expectantly.

Red took a deep breath and forced a wide grin. "One helluva ride! Just like you said."

Clifford eyed him suspiciously. "Good."

The NRO men stood close by, making notes as usual.

Red gathered his papers, from his kneepad. He felt the solidity of the earth beneath his feet, and a large part of him didn't want to leave the ground again.

"Project meeting tomorrow," Clifford shouted across wind. "Midday. Full debrief before we proceed."

Brad Walker raised a hand to object, but Clifford had turned his back on him and headed towards the T-38 and their ride home.

Red spent an uneasy few hours in bed, reliving the nightmarish scenario.

Somehow, sleep eventually arrived.

By 0900 he was in the shower; by 1000 he was queuing for breakfast in the commissary, along with Edwards's night-shift workers.

He picked up his plate of pancakes and eggs, and spotted Dupont at a table, poring over two large books.

"Looks like some heavy reading," Red said, glancing at the open pages of engine schematics as he sat down.

"Yeah. Just tryin' to learn more about these modern jets. Theys a long way from the F-86."

Dupont looked up, his expression serious. "You okay, Red?"

Red pushed a piece of pancake into a dollop of syrup and shrugged. "Does it seem weird to you?"

"What?"

"That one moment we're flying at stupid speeds, seconds away from sudden death, and the next we're eating pancakes, getting ready to do it all again? As if this sort of thing is normal?"

Dupont closed his schematic book. "This is normal for a test pilot, isn't it?"

Red nodded. "What was it like in Korea?"

"Same, I guess."

Red studied him for a moment. "I'm jealous of you, Brandon."

"Jealous? Of me?"

"You make it look so easy. I watched you yesterday. You've mastered the B-57 in what, two flights?"

Dupont waved it away. "It's not that hard. And I'm not done yet. More engine failure practise with Jay to come, apparently." He tapped at the books. "They're a handful for me or anyone."

"But there's something about your attitude. You have this calmness and control. I wish I had it."

"Sure you do."

"No. I'm a mess up there. I feel as if I'm just tearing around, waiting for it all to suddenly end."

Dupont took a slow sip of his coffee and replaced the mug on the table. "Something happen last night, Red?"

He hesitated.

"You know we're not supposed to discuss the projects."

"But?"

"I don't know . . . I had a bad trip. But I couldn't talk to Clifford."

"You were in a single seat?"

"Yeah."

"Okay. Well, do you think you should have said something?"

"I think it was my fault, not the aircraft's. So, what's the point in telling him? I'll just get thrown off the project." He looked up. "Maybe that would be a good thing. Truth is, I nearly bought it."

Dupont frowned at him, the way a father might look disappointed with his son.

"You think I should have said something?" Red said.

Dupont nodded. "Of course. That's what you do here, isn't it? Fly and report what happened. Look, I could tell something's up, even before you went last night. So can everyone else, by the way. You don't want to do this alone, Red. You've got to have those conversations, even if you don't feel you want to."

Red dropped his cutlery onto the plate. "I guess I screwed up, huh?"

"Go easy on yourself."

"But it was my fault. I didn't handle it properly. Didn't anticipate."

Dupont leaned back on his chair, and Red caught his appraising look. "Well, Red, if you're going to navigate this thing without showing all your cards to Johnny Clifford, maybe you need a little backroom help. Wanna fill me in on what happened?"

Red looked around the room again. No one was close to them. But he shook his head. "I can't, I'm afraid."

"Okay. But I might be able to help the project." He winked. "I see you all disappear in the evening. Jay Anderson flies the Hercules. You and Clifford in the T-38, all heading east. Only one place out there, I know of. Let me guess. You're flying the A-12?"

Red couldn't stop a hint of a smile. He tapped his fork for a second, before leaning across the table. "Obviously, this stays between us."

"Of course."

"We're flying the A-12."

"You surprise me." Dupont laughed.

"Man, it's amazing. It's a Mach 3 capable. Two phase engines. Big engines. But we're taking it higher using solid rocket boosters."

"Christ. A rocket plane? Like the X-15?"

"Yes, but no need for a lift from a B-52."

"So, what was it like?" Dupont asked.

Red puffed out his cheeks. "Terrifying. Johnny described it as a wild ride—it was more like a death rattle for me. The damn airframe nearly shook itself to pieces, but the worst part was keeping a usable attitude when the burners flamed out before I could start the engines."

"How high?"

"One hundred forty thousand feet?"

"Christ!" Dupont looked impressed. "And you'd shut down the jet engines? So you had no propulsion for a few minutes at the top of the climb?"

"Yeah."

Dupont burst out laughing.

"What's so funny? I wasn't laughing a few hours ago, I can promise you."

Dupont took Red's pencil from his hand and began marking up the crude sketch of the A-12. "Man, you think you're scared. You're not scared enough. This thing has not been thought through."

Below the aircraft outline, he drew several horizontal parallel lines and then used the pencil to point at the gaps between them.

"So, this is your thick air. Good for big wings and slow flight. My Stearman loves it." Red nodded as Dupont pointed at the area above the bottom line. "As we get faster and higher, we need the smaller wing surface, thin leading edges. I guess that thing you fly is at home down here. But then, you fly her up high, where literally all of that is useless. So you use rockets. And what? You *hope* she stays upright? I mean that's some crazy shit right there. Stupid, actually."

"Well," Red began, feeling he needed to defend the project methodology.

Dupont cut him off with a wave of the pencil. "But that's not all. You then need to transit back down to the atmosphere using . . . nothing? I mean, there's nothing on this aircraft. Sorry, spacecraft. Seriously, Red. What are you thinking?"

"When you put it like that, it does seem to rely on a little hope."

"What do spacecraft have?" Dupont asked.

Red thought about the Apollo machinery currently being flight-tested from Florida. "They use fins and gimbals to change the thrust of the rocket engines in the air. We have some fins in place, but the SRBs aren't rocket engines. They're fireworks, and we can't control them."

Dupont nodded. "That's in the air. But what do these Apollo craft use in space? Isn't it some sort of vent?"

"Yeah. Blasts of compressed air from vents all over the craft. Thinking about it, the X-15 had reaction control jets. Even more powerful."

Dupont leaned back.

Red stared at the sketch then looked up. "You think we need control jets on the A-12?"

Dupont smiled.

Red went for a long walk around the base until it was time to report to A-TEC. He arrived around thirty seconds before the scheduled project meeting with the NRO men. He was the last to take his seat in Colonel Montgomery's corner office.

"Nice of you to join us," Walker said and tapped his watch.

"Am I late?"

Walker ignored him and opened the agenda. "Before we present the XS-81 notes, do you gentlemen have any observations about the flights so far?"

"It's not great above a hundred thousand," Clifford said. "A bitch, actually. The issue is control in the upper atmosphere with no means of propulsion. It's dangerous and ill-equipped."

"I thought it was just me," Red said.

Clifford shot him a look. "You didn't report anything."

"Can you be a little more technical?" Gomez said.

"There's no air up there," Clifford said, "and she's an airplane. See the problem? Getting her to stay upright is like fighting with no weapons."

"Any suggestions?"

"Reaction control jets," Red said. The men around the table looked at him. "I mean, that's what the X-15 used, isn't it? And Apollo uses gas vents, right?"

Gomez and Walker both smiled.

"Sorry. I shouldn't have said that," Red said, immediately doubting the usefulness of his conversations with Dupont.

"That's some smart thinking, Captain Brunson. And we're way ahead of you. The XS-81 has a full set of powerful reaction jets and compressed gas vents for when the engines are shut down."

Red exhaled with relief and noticed the smallest nod of approval from Clifford. But the chief test pilot then turned to Walker. "In the meantime, you're sending us up in the A-12 with no means of control?"

"The engineers didn't expect issues until you got well above one hundred fifty thousand."

"Well, there are issues," Clifford replied. "And for the record, we lost good men in exactly these circumstances."

"Fine," Gomez said. "We think we've learned enough from the A-12, anyway. It was only ever a proof of concept. You've both done a burn and relight."

"So, we abandon it?" Red asked.

Gomez tapped a pencil on his folder. "We'll jump to the XS-81." He looked up at the two pilots. "Like we said, it's equipped for the thin air. We've learned a lot from the space programs. But there's a lot to learn about the handling up there. You're limited by the reserve of compressed air. It's all in the notes."

"Has it flown?" Clifford asked.

"Of course," Walker said. "The Lockheed guys have air-tested it."

"Up to forty-five thousand, subsonic," Gomez added. "You can create your own workup program. Add in the time we'd allocated for the remaining A-12 flights. But no more."

"Are you two happy with that?" Colonel Montgomery asked.

Johnny Clifford gave a curt nod.

He didn't seem to need Red's response.

"I need to talk about personnel." Montgomery aimed himself at the NRO men. "I lose two test pilots every night to haul the ground team out to Groom in the C-130. That puts them out of action for the next morning. I know the boys need maximum workup flights, but no more than necessary. This project is causing a backlog headache for me."

"With respect, boss," Clifford said, "we don't know what we're dealing with here. We can't rush this."

"I have full confidence in your ability to tame her and get service ready, in good time."

Montgomery rose, signalling the meeting was over.

"What about the Utility pilots?" Red said.

"They're not cleared for this," Gomez snapped.

"But it's just a ferry flight, right? We wouldn't be asking them to fly the XS-81."

"But they'd see it," Walker added. "And we can't have that."

The coffee was lukewarm, but it would have to do. Red poured himself and Clifford a mug. They settled down in their adopted side office and read through the official handling notes and flight manual for the XS-81.

"She's a beast," Clifford said. "No doubt about that."

"One hundred sixty-eight feet! It'll be like flying a Greyhound bus," Red observed.

Clifford shook his head. "Not with four engines producing forty thousand pounds of thrust each. She'll be like a sled on rails. And that's before we light the fireworks." He opened up a schematic. The four engines were clustered together, with the four internally mounted SRBs clamped below. The aircraft stood on elongated landing gear. "Sure is an ugly bitch."

Clifford pointed at several small openings on the underside of the fuselage. "Control jets. Just like you predicted." He looked at Red. "That was impressive. I'm not sure it would have occurred to me."

Red hesitated. "Actually, it wasn't my suggestion." Clifford raised an eyebrow as Red leaned back in his chair. "I know we're not supposed to discuss it outside of the project, but I've found it useful to talk things through with Brandon. The jets were his idea."

Red held his breath for a moment.

"You crossed a line, Brunson. Don't do that again."

Across the office, men leaped to their feet. Red and Clifford also jumped up. They left the office to see faces pressed against the windows; both men joined their colleagues as shouts went up.

Over the heads of the men, Red could see the black plume of smoke. His heart started thumping.

Dupont was due to be flying.

"It's one of ours. The B-57," someone confirmed.

"Holy fuck," Red said.

Clifford slowly turned to him. "That your farmer? Sorry, son."

Events unfolded in a depressingly familiar pattern.

The men could only watch as fire trucks screamed across the airfield to the crash site.

Montgomery came out his office and stood quietly behind them.

"Look!" someone shouted.

Red pressed himself up against the glass. A figure walked from the direction of the threshold. An ejectee. Alive.

But there was no way of telling whether it was Anderson or Dupont from this distance.

He stared intently, squinting, trying to make out what was what and who was who.

The Canberra was a smoking wreck. Foam spilled out a fire truck and doused the flames.

Still only one figure had been seen. Firefighters moved around the wreck, pointing.

Fifteen minutes later, they learned who had survived

when Banrdon Dupont stepped unsteadily into the A-TEC office. His face was drawn and streaked in black soot.

Men looked at him expectantly. Dupont shook his head slowly.

A couple of the pilots turned away. Red caught a flash of anger on the face of Jimmy Cofferr, and others. The disquiet about using non-test pilots at A-TEC had suddenly come to a head. He sensed immediately that Red would be blamed for Jay Anderson's death.

Montgomery appeared and walked up to Dupont. Red had never seen him look so serious.

"What happened?" Montgomery said.

"Jay's dead."

"What happened?"

"He was demonstrating the practise engine failure."

"Anderson was flying?"

"Yes, sir. He dropped the throttle back while we were still downwind. I'd not seen that before. Major Clifford used to do it only when we were on final. So Jay demonstrated it to me. But he left the turn late. I warned him about the over-bank, but he ignored me. The tail seemed to stall first and started a sort of cartwheel."

"A cartwheel? In the air?"

"Yeah, it was a weird stall. I've experienced nothing like it."

"Fin stall," Red said. "It can happen on the Canberra."

Dupont shook his head. "We had no height, and we was rolling fast. I pulled the handle. There was no option."

"And Anderson?"

"I don't know. I blacked out. But they found him in the wreck."

. . .

Maggie's Grill quickly filled up.

There was no ceremony, but after hearing the news, Maggie lifted Jay's glass from its hook, and placed it at the end of the line in front of the mirror.

Unusually, Johnny Clifford joined them.

The group of twenty or so men stood in a loose circle and silently toasted their friend with bourbon.

As Red replaced his glass on the bar, Sarah arrived, her eyes bloodshot.

She came to him, her features cracking as she wrapped her arms around him.

They didn't say anything. Her hug lingered; other pilots moved away.

Sarah withdrew and wiped her eyes. "I don't know how you handle it," she said as she retrieved a tissue from a pocket.

"Who says we handle it?"

Red looked across to see Dupont standing with the group of A-TEC pilots and aircrew. The news that Anderson was the flying pilot seemed to have taken the pressure off him. Especially once the full story came out. Jimmy Cofferr admitted that Anderson had tried this stunt before in the Canberra and nearly lost it.

There would be an enquiry. The manual would be modified to ban such a manoeuvre, no doubt. But that was for tomorrow.

The bourbon flowed.

At one point, Red found himself next to Clifford. "Is it too early to talk about who'll replace Jay in the C-130?"

Clifford shook his head. "No, but it's not our decision." The chief test pilot looked across the group towards Dupont. "Why are you standing up for him, anyway?"

"He's good. Useful."

. . .

Later in the evening, they sat around a couple of tables that had been pushed together. Red allowed the alcohol to ease his anxiety. The adrenaline from watching the events unfold was subsiding. He leaned back and stared at Sarah, sitting on a stool at the end of the bar chatting with Maggie as she dried glasses.

Sarah turned, and their eyes met. She gave him a quizzical look and he smiled back, admiring the way the late sun caught her hair. A couple of buttons were undone on Sarah's shirt.

He looked down at the empty glasses and bottles. "I'll get these. If we wait for the staff to serve us, it'll be Saturday."

Red walked slowly, watching Sarah as she crossed her legs, laughing and leaning forward. He felt the blood start to move.

She raised an eyebrow as he approached. "How you doing?"

"Okay."

"A mix of whiskey and beer for the table, please, Maggie." Red handed over the empty Bud bottles and bourbon glasses.

Red picked up Maggie's pen on the bar and fiddled with it while he waited.

"It's easier for you," Sarah said.

"What do you mean?"

She shrugged. "You have each other."

In that moment, Red realised Sarah had become a part of A-TEC, and yet she was on the outside. So here she was, sitting at the end of the bar by herself, having lost a friend.

"Jay asked you out once, right?"

Sarah laughed. "Last year, I think."

"But you said no?"

"I had eyes for someone else back then, Red."

Maggie reappeared with his drinks and he felt the silence between them, like a radio call with no response.

As he picked up the tray, he thought he caught a look of disappointment in Sarah's face.

Red let a slip of paper drop from his fingers. She looked down to retrieve it, and he headed back to the boys.

As Red sat down, he stole a quick glance behind him.

Sarah's face lit up as she studied the note.

"Absolutely not." Walker spoke first. Gomez immediately went back to his papers.

"I'm running out of men." Montgomery spoke quietly.

Walker looked annoyed. "Who the hell is Brandon Dupont, anyway? He's not even on your staff list."

"He's new and like I say, he's a Utility pilot. And can I remind you, the scheme was your idea to fix exactly this sort of problem. To stop us using highly qualified TPs for low-skilled flying."

"But we agreed, ferry pilots would not be cleared for this sort of project." Walker shook his head. "It's too risky."

"You don't need a qualified TP to run a limo service in a C-130 out to Groom every night. Look, I don't know the guy well, but Red trusts him."

Walker looked at Red, who was sitting opposite him across Montgomery's office table.

"Where's he even come from? Does he have full clearance?"

"He has the same clearance as every one of my pilots. He's from Mississippi. Air force jet jockey. Got burned out after Korea and went back to the farm. We handpicked him. He's good."

"How long have you known him?"

Red shook his head. "Not long, but he's good."

"Sorry, son. We need some history before we let people through the dark curtain." Walker turned back to his paperwork.

"He's not a Communist spy, I can promise you." Red found himself laughing at the idea.

"You think that's funny?" Walker said. "It's not about him working for the Russians. He could be a homosexual, for all you know. Open to blackmail."

"He's not a homosexual."

"You know that?" Gomez asked with a raised eyebrow.

"He was cleared by Leo Rodriguez, remember?"

Gomez and Walker paused.

"Rodriguez was a good man." Walker turned to Red and asked, "Did he interview him, or just fill out some forms based on your information?"

"I went with him to the family farm. They spoke. He asked the questions and gave me his clearance papers personally. Brandon's spent the best part of three months in refresher training at Columbus. No alarm bells. No homosexuality."

Walker looked at Gomez, and Red sensed the mood shift.

"And you can vouch for him?" Gomez asked.

"Absolutely. He'll be useful to have around."

The NRO agent tapped his pencil. "And Rodriguez spoke to him in person? And was satisfied?"

"Absolutely."

Walker looked at Montgomery. "If I say yes, will this get you off our backs?"

. . .

Outside in the main A-TEC office, the mood was subdued. Red thought better of talking with Dupont about his new role, lest it be greeted by a grin and a handshake in front of the others.

Instead, he settled in a side office with Clifford and buried himself in the XS-81 notes. Next to him, the chief test pilot drew up a flying program for the next week at Groom.

They would be flying together, side by side, in the roomier cockpit. But it was essential they both knew everything that needed to be done.

And there was a helluva lot of things to be done.

"Just handling this thing will take every bit of concentration we have," Clifford said. "And then we have to work out how to get it to Mach 6 at three hundred thousand feet in precisely the right place."

Red couldn't conceive how the hell they would ever get to that stage.

"One thing at a time," Clifford said, and he went back to his draft schedule.

At lunchtime, Red wandered out into the office. "Is Brandon around?"

"Not until tomorrow," the admin officer said. "Night stop in Hurlburt. Coming back with a shiny new C-130."

At home, Red showered and changed into a freshly ironed shirt. He drove to the edge of Rosamond and a small row of single-storey prefabs. As he pulled up, a screen door opened. Sarah, dressed in a red tartan shirt and pale slacks, stepped into the early-evening sun.

"Howdy!" she shouted as he got out of the car.

"Ready?"

"You're early. A girl has to prepare."

"You look great."

She disappeared back into the house and Red leaned on the car, allowing the last rays of the day warm his face.

When he opened his eyes, Sarah was in front of him.

"Where are we going?"

He opened the car door for her. "I thought we'd try Maggie's." He walked around and got in behind the wheel.

"Hmm. I've heard great things about it."

Red laughed.

They drove on in silence for a minute or so before Red felt the need to fill the gap.

"Good day?"

"Well, you know it can be quite taxing on the register at the BX, but somehow I raised my game and met the challenge." She put a hand on his shoulder. "How's the team?"

"We're good." He wound down the window and let some air in. "It's not our first rodeo."

At Maggie's, they settled into a booth at the far end of the large bar area, and Maggie brought them a couple of beers. Red noticed an exchange of smiles between her and Sarah.

"So, big man," Sarah said when Maggie left, "is this a date, or something else?"

"Well, I think it's a date."

"You think?" She smiled. "Let me know when you've decided."

Red laughed. "It's definitely a date."

"I see." She toyed with her bottle and poured the beer into a glass. "You've changed your mind since you told me it wasn't going to work?"

"Always straight to the point."

Sarah shrugged. "A girl likes to know where she stands."

"I enjoy talking to you," Red said.

Sarah looked at him, biting on her bottom lip. "I guess that's a good start. So what was it before? Why'd you break it off?"

Red exhaled. "You want the truth?"

"Of course."

"I thought you wanted to marry. I thought you saw me as your ticket out of Rosamond. All I wanted back then was a date."

"We *were* just dating."

"I know, but . . . it just felt like the longer I stayed, the more I got your hopes up that you'd found your way out, and that at some point I'd let you down. So, I guess I just did that sooner rather than later."

Sarah took in the answer.

He put his hand on hers. "Sorry . . ."

"It's fine. Of course I saw you as a ticket out of here. Who wouldn't? But I'm not stupid. I knew we were just dating. If it happened, it happened. But if it didn't, then fine. I wasn't trying to trap you."

"I guess I just panicked."

"Panicked?" Sarah furrowed her brow.

Red held her eye. "Maybe I was the one who started to think it was more than just dating."

Sarah's eyes widened. She blinked, then moved forward and kissed him. He rested his hand on the back of her head. She tasted sweet, and he felt a rush of nerves in the pit of his stomach.

Behind them, a noise erupted from the entrance. They broke off and looked around to see several of the A-TEC boys spilling loudly into the bar.

"Great," Red said. "I thought after last night, they'd take this evening off." He looked at his battered Omega watch and frowned. The hands showed 1110. He tutted and tapped the face, then took it off his wrist and wound it.

Sarah reached over and took it from him. Instinctively, he went to grab it back, but stopped himself.

"Easy there, Red, I was just looking."

He watched anxiously as she examined it. The cracks in the glass and the heavily scratched metal were exposed by the sunlight streaming in through an open shutter.

"I don't know why you carry this thing around. It never works."

Red took it back. "I don't like the new ones they give out to pilots, and I can't afford to replace it." He put it back on his wrist, latching the buckle on the leather strap. "It's fine. I just forgot to wind it."

Behind them, the other group of pilots laughed loudly at something.

Sarah leaned around the booth to steal a glance. "No Brandon tonight? Do they blame him for what happened?"

"No. I don't think so. He's off collecting an aircraft down south. Back tomorrow."

"Well, he owes me a set of keys. Can you get them off him when you see him?"

Red looked at her, trying to work out if she was making some obscure joke. "A set of keys?"

She looked surprised. "Yeah. The spare set to the house."

"Sarah, what are you talking about?"

"He didn't tell you?"

"Tell me what? Are you two moving in together?"

She laughed. "He's renting my folks' old house on Sierra. I can't believe he didn't tell you."

Red shook his head. "He didn't say a thing. When did this happen?"

"Last week. I told him I wasn't sure what to do with it, since Pa died, and he offered to pay rent and I accepted." She took a swig of her beer. "Thing is, he has both sets of keys. Says he needed someone to help him move in. I guess that wasn't you."

"It definitely wasn't me."

They sat in silence for a moment.

"I told you he was odd," she said, eventually.

"Well, at least you two are getting on now. Remember when you thought he didn't like you?"

She shrugged. "I don't think he does. This was all business." She paused. "Maybe he's one of them?" She laughed.

"One of them?"

"You know? He likes men? They say they're everywhere. We just don't know it."

"A homosexual? Don't be ridiculous."

"I was just joking. It's fine by me, by the way. I don't care."

Red shook his head. "Sorry. It's just . . . that kind of talk can cost a man around here."

After a chicken dinner, Red paid the check and drove Sarah through the dark, dusty street to her small house at the edge of town.

"Friday night with the boys tomorrow, but how about we go somewhere Saturday? Maybe the lake at Castaic? And . . ."

"Yes?"

"I think maybe we should ask Brandon to come along."

"Really? Three of us?"

"Yesterday must have been tough. And what else is he going to do? Sit in his new house alone?"

She didn't look convinced. "I guess."

"It'll give you two a chance to get to know each other."

"Fine. But I'm working until noon."

Before Sarah got out, she leaned over, and they kissed again.

Red smiled at her. "I think it's all the conversations we've had since we broke up."

"What d'you mean?"

"I think that's when I started to fall again. Honestly, I don't talk to anyone the way we talk."

"Fall where?" Sarah said, smiling.

But Red didn't answer. He leaned in for one more kiss.

"I'll pick you up at one on Saturday."

"Sure." She climbed out the car and then leaned back in. "Don't forget to wind your watch, Captain."

CHAPTER EIGHT

"THERE IT IS AGAIN," Red said as he pushed an open folder across the desk. *"The Max Q issue."*

It was the second time he and Clifford had seen reference to some sort of problem, presumably to do with the sound barrier on the XS-81. Despite several enquiries through Walker and Gomez, they'd heard nothing back from the company pilots who carried out the first flights.

"It can't be anything significant," Clifford said, barely looking up. "They haven't even taken her through Mach 1."

"Maybe that's why," Red said. "Do you think this is being rushed?"

The chief test pilot didn't reply.

Red puffed out his cheeks. "I need a break."

The two of them had been stuck in their side room for three days now; he thought he could recite most of the operations notes for the XS-81 from memory. Mostly it was procedures, with precious little hard data on how it would handle. He stood and stretched, looking into the main office. Dupont was back.

"Shall we tell the farmer about his new job?" Red said.

Clifford looked up from his own note-taking. "He's your man. You tell him."

Red wandered out, to find Dupont filling in his logbook.

"Hey, buddy. How was Florida?"

"Beautiful from the air. Saw little of it from the ground. Just some burger joint on Hurlburt."

Red looked around the room. Too many eavesdroppers, close by. "Wanna go for a walk?"

Dupont finished his logbook entry. "Everything all right, Red?"

"Sure. Just thought you might like to talk."

Dupont paused before closing his logbook, putting down his pen and standing up. "Okay."

They left A-TEC and walked along the airfield fence, which was dotted with buildings of various sizes.

"Sarah tells me you've moved into her folks' old house."

Dupont winced. "Oh, yeah. I meant to tell you."

"Didn't like the government couch?"

"It's nice to have a little more space."

They arrived at a gap between hangars. Red led them to a spot where they could see the main field.

A noisy B-52 fired up its eight engines on the far side of a taxiway. A long orange object was slung underneath. Red squinted; he'd heard something about a runway denial weapon being evaluated by a neighbouring unit.

"So, what was it like? The ejection?"

"Same as last time."

"You've ejected before?"

"Yep. Blacked out both times." Dupont kicked the ground. "I remember the run-up clearly. I knew Anderson was losing it, but he was pretty sure of himself, and I found it difficult to intervene. He's got a lot more experience than me. Sorry, he *had* a lot more experience than me."

"Have they spoken to you?"

"There's an investigation, but the bird was pretty beaten up. So, it's just interviews. Next week, I think."

"That's standard. You'll be fine. They sent you flying again pretty quickly. That's a good sign. And there's another good sign for you."

"Yeah?"

"I told you about the A-12, in confidence."

He held up both hands. "Hey, Red. I didn't say anything to anyone."

"I know, I know. But with Jay gone, there's a gap in the team." Dupont turned to face Red directly. "That got your interest. Now, before I say anything else, this will not be flying anything experimental or fast. In fact, you'll be crewing the C-130 with Jimmy Cofferr. Your job will be to take ground crew and equipment to Groom Lake every evening next week and probably beyond. It's a night shift, I'm afraid."

Dupont beamed. "The A-12?"

Red bit his lip. He should have checked what he could say, in advance. But he figured Dupont was coming with them, so he surely had to know.

"And there's another aircraft. I can't say too much. It's an X-Plane. XS-81."

Dupont shook his head. "Never heard of it."

"No, you haven't. But you'll see it on the flightline next week."

"More edge-of-space stuff?"

Red laughed. "You'll be glad to know it's equipped with reaction control jets."

Dupont's eyes were wide. "Glad to hear it. Red, did you get me onto this project?"

Red lifted his shoulders. "You deserve it. You're helping

me and the project already. And, you've been through a lot. I feel bad speaking ill of Jay, but he should never have put the aircraft and you in that position."

The B-52 throttled up a quarter of a mile away; the noise was still deafening. The men moved back beyond the buildings that lined the western side of the airfield.

"What are you doing tomorrow, Brandon?"

"Fixing up the house."

"To hell with that."

CHAPTER NINE

SARAH WAS late out the BX.

"Come on!" Red called as she walked slowly across the lot towards the car.

She ignored him and continued at her own pace. "I'm not your dog, Captain Brunson."

He laughed as she slid onto the Ford Galaxie bench seat.

"No aches and pains from the ejection?" Sarah said, turning to Dupont on the back seat.

"No, ma'am."

"Good. By the way, do you have my spare keys?"

"Oh. Sorry. I left them locked in the house."

She scowled. "Okay. Well, can you drop them off at my house later?"

"Sure."

Sarah turned back to the front as Red pulled out of Edwards. "Red, when's Jay's funeral?"

"It's today, actually. In Utah. It's a long way for us all to go. Colonel Montgomery is there."

"Sure," she said, after a while.

"I wonder if his brother got back?" Dupont said from the back.

"Where's he?" Sarah said.

"Flying F-8s in Tonkin," Dupont replied. "Vietnam."

"Christ. His poor parents. I don't know how you do it." She rummaged in a purse and found a lipstick. "I don't think I can take another one. You know, I've been hanging out with the A-TEC guys for four years. Jay was the fifth we lost." She opened the lipstick and turned to Red. "No more. So, look after yourself. You, too, Brandon." She adjusted the mirror and applied a layer of red.

The road was typically desert shaped, long and straight. Red had hoped the trip would be a distraction. But in the car's quiet, all he could think about was Monday, and their first flight into the unknown. Hints of problems in the manufacturer notes had not settled him. Clifford's unresponsive and uninviting presence made it worse.

He readjusted the mirror and glimpsed Dupont: eyes closed, warm air rushing over his face from an open rear window.

He needed some of that. It wasn't heroics or bravery; it was having ice in your veins. Cool as you like. Orderly, precise. That's what would keep him alive. He was glad Dupont would be there at Groom.

It took ninety minutes to arrive at the oasis of Castaic Lake. The water shimmered blue, in vivid contrast to the reddish brown of the surrounding desert.

They parked above a fishing jetty, and Red climbed out and took in the view. The lake had a distinct V shape, and they stood at the bottom point of the V, with vistas either side.

High above, a noisy commercial airliner climbed out of LA.

"What do we do now?" Sarah said as she joined him.

He moved to the trunk and opened it. Two bags of sandwiches, beer, and snacks were pushed against his wheel jack.

He smiled. "Picnic?"

"I think you might be the perfect man."

The three of them hiked along a gentle ridge for close to an hour. Red and Dupont carried the food; Sarah took the blanket.

"This'll do," Sarah said as they came to a flattish part of the rock. "These shoes weren't meant for climbing."

They set up camp and tucked into the ham and pickles.

"This anything like your fighter-curve lake, Brandon?" Red asked.

Dupont took a bite of his sandwich. "Nah. Hey, Red, where's a good place to buy a car?"

"Hector's," Sarah and Red said at the same time and then laughed.

"Hector's is farther down Sierra towards Oban," Red said. "It was Sarah's pa's place until he sold it."

"Hector was your dad?"

"Yep. You're living in my childhood home, believe it or not."

The breeze got up a little, but it was still warm. Red finished his food. He looked at Dupont. "Wanna go for a little walk, pal?"

"I'll guard the paper bags, shall I?" Sarah said.

"Oh, you can come, too."

"No, it's fine. I'll doze."

Red and Dupont set off, climbing the steeper rocks

above. Dupont was nimble and overtook Red, who picked his way carefully.

"You an expert rock climber?" Red said, puffing.

"Ha. No. Just need to blow off a little energy, I guess."

They reached a plateau but found it too windy, so Dupont led them down a hundred yards or so, where they sat on a couple of large rocks. The far end of the lake was just about visible, although it got hazy at its extremity.

"One of those summer days that looks perfect until you get into the smog at two thousand," Red said.

"You always think about flying?"

"Don't you?"

They sat in silence for a while. Red watched a couple of birds diving on the water.

"D'you know much about birds, Brandon?" He shook his head. "Well, can you name anything you see here?"

Dupont looked around. "I can't see any."

Red laughed. "A pair of grebes on the lake, way down there. A small flock of Canada geese flew over a couple of minutes ago. I think I saw some sort of wren on the way up. And they're crows." He pointed at a collection of black birds two hundred yards to their right, foraging around the rocks. "Surely you recognise them? You must have them on the farm?"

Dupont looked bemused. "Did you bring me out here to talk about birds?"

"No, I guess not."

"You want to talk about next week. The X-Plane. You worried?"

"Do I look worried?"

"Yes."

Red picked up a couple of pebbles, tossing one of them

down the hillside. "We've read everything there is to read. But . . ."

"But?"

"Well, it's had only half-a-dozen shakedown flights from the factory. We don't think it's gone supersonic. So, there are a lot of unknowns."

Dupont nodded slowly. "That's unusual, isn't it? Doesn't it normally take a year or two before the company releases it to the customer?"

"Not the X-Planes. We work alongside them through the development. It's not like this is going into proper service." Red threw the second pebble. "Actually, it might not even get past next week. Who knows what issues it's got?"

When Red looked up, he saw that appraising look again from Dupont. It was unnerving, sometimes, the way he looked at him. Not staring, just a look as if he's trying to puzzle him out.

"What?" Red asked eventually.

"Tell me about the camera pod test on the B-57," Dupont said.

Red fiddled with another pebble. "You know about that?"

"Jay told me you came back early on a couple of trials, and that was one of them."

"Yeah, well, I picked up vibration almost straightaway, as we climbed out. I had a navigator, and we both felt it. When I increased to three hundred fifty knots, it became more pronounced."

"So you scrubbed the test?"

Red shrugged. "I didn't want the thing to rip off. I thought it was the right thing to do."

Dupont nodded slowly. "But they weren't pleased?"

"No one said anything at the time."

Dupont looked around the lake and then back to Red. "You made that decision because you weren't expecting the vibration and you had no reference point."

"What do you mean?"

"What I mean is, in flying, we make our decisions on the ground. In the air, we execute them. We don't want to be thinking, 'I've never seen this before, what shall I do?' when we're actually flying. What we want is 'oh, *A* has happened, so I'm going to do *B*.'"

Red turned his palms up. "How would I have known?"

"What happened in the wind-tunnel tests? How strong are the bolts or whatever attaches it to the pylon? What sort of vibration can it sustain? When will the camera become damaged? What will the vibration sound and feel like? When is it too much? These are all the questions you needed to ask the engineers on the ground. And more. Anything you can anticipate."

Red shook his head. "What if they don't know the answers?"

"Did you ask?"

"No. I guess not."

"Imagine having had reassurance, for instance, that this thing shakes like a machine in a Laundromat, but it's strong and stays in place. Then you would have anticipated the vibration and pressed through the higher speed part of the trial. We make our decisions on the ground, so we don't have to think in the air."

Red smiled. "You make it sound easy."

"I'm a strong believer in making complex things easy by breaking them down."

"You learned all this from building a Stearman?" Red asked.

"When your life depends on something, it helps concentrate the mind! So next week, just remember to break everything down. Learn as much by heart as possible and work the problems methodically in the air. Like you're following a decision chart, not having to second-guess anything. And remember, I'll be there. We can debrief and talk through everything, so each time you fly you'll have a plan. Think of me as you own personal backroom support crew."

"Thank you."

"You bet. You're a good pilot, you just need to modify your approach a bit to become a good test pilot."

Red nodded. He couldn't disagree.

The breeze made a gentle whistling noise through the sparse vegetation around them.

"You know what's odd about you, Brandon?"

"There's something odd about me?"

Red laughed. "Not like that. But your file, I mean I didn't see it, but the DIA agent did, and he said you were, and I quote, 'an unremarkable pilot' during your air force career. And yet, here, I honestly think you might be the best pilot in the unit."

Dupont shook his head. "I know I'm not. Anyway, I just did what I had to do in the air force."

"You wanted to get back to the farm?"

"Yeah."

"And yet you gave that all up after one flight in a T-38?"

Dupont rested his back on the rock. "I did try to say no, remember?"

"Your pappy said no for you. With a twelve-gauge."

"Yeah, sorry about that. He just needed a little time to get used to the idea. Once he knew my salary would bring in more than the farm, he dropped his tone."

"And dropped the gun?"

"Well, I'm here, aren't I?"

Red smiled and stood up. "Shall we head back down?"

They sped up their descent, turning it into a race, Red being a little less expert on the loose rocks than his farmer friend.

When they were getting close to the dozing Sarah, Red caught up with Dupont.

"Thanks for the advice, man."

"Sure. And, I tell you what, why don't I come over tonight and we can go through your procedures again?"

"Thanks, I'd like that."

"No problem, Red. We're in it together. I appreciate being on the project."

Sarah rose from her nap.

"Have fun, boys?"

"He's nimble for an old man." Red laughed.

Sarah smiled and picked up the picnic rug.

They walked back to the car. Sarah put an arm around Red, and they moved ahead of Dupont.

"Maggie's for dinner tonight, just the two of us?"

"Well, actually I was going to get some takeout."

"Oh, okay, that's fine."

"Brandon's coming over," he said and checked her for any sign of disappointment. She didn't look thrilled.

"I see. You know there's an expression, 'Three's a crowd,' right?"

Red picked his words carefully. "Actually, it'll just be me and Brandon."

She raised both eyebrows. "Really?"

"Yeah, sorry, it's a work thing, and we can't discuss in front of—"

"—a nobody like me?" she said, interrupting.

"That's not what I meant. We can't discuss it in front of

anyone." They walked on in silence, approaching the car. "You understand, don't you?" he added.

"Uh-huh."

Back at Red's, Dupont made him write out everything he could remember from the procedures.

One by one, they discussed each list, Dupont constantly asking questions, prodding and poking to ensure Red had considered every eventuality and thought through his responses.

It was late when the farmer stood up quickly.

"Getting good rest should be on a checklist," he announced and made his way to the door. "See you later, buddy."

Red looked down at the copious notes they'd produced. All against the rules, of course, outside the confines of A-TEC. But he knew his performance on the project depended on this level of revision, and he couldn't spend twenty-four hours a day at Edwards. It was a breach of security done with good intentions. He was giving the project the best chance of success.

And it was good to have a partner. Someone backing him, dedicated to his own performance.

Even Muhammad Ali had a cornerman.

CHAPTER TEN

RED COULDN'T STOP STARING.

The XS-81 was twice the size of the A-12, with sleek, curved black lines—so black that light got lost in it, making it hard to read its true shape. The aircraft stood high on its ungainly landing gear, absorbing the floodlight on the pan.

Engineers poked into various apertures, particularly on the underside and at the trailing edge of the wings.

He walked around to view the beast from the front. For all the world, this looked like an illustration on the cover of a science-fiction magazine. He couldn't believe he was the one who would climb into its electrical cockpit and take her to the edge of space.

"Daedalus," a voice said from behind. Red turned to see Johnny Clifford with the two NRO men and two others he didn't recognise, wearing grey flight suits.

"What do you think of the name?" one of the men in a flight suit asked.

"We don't have to call it anything," Brad Walker said, interrupting. "The agency prefers Experimental Designation XS-81."

"Snappy," said the man. He stuck out his hand. "Troy Cipriano. We flew the Daedalus in, about an hour ago."

Red shook his hand. "You did the first test flights?"

"Sure did."

Clifford appeared. "Great. We have some questions."

Cipriano laughed. "I bet you do. But I warn you now, we don't have many answers. We carried out one hundred landings, about seventy-five hours in total."

"Mach 1?" Clifford asked.

"Not part of our trial. But I can tell you she gets rough at the higher numbers. We reported everything back. But that's it for us . . . in fact, we've been told once we leave here in ten minutes, we'll never see her again."

Clifford raised an eyebrow. "So, no supersonic transition? No ceiling? No SRB burns? No relights?"

Brad Walker stepped in. "These gentlemen are not cleared for the full operational specification of the XS-81."

"We know you want to shut her down and relight," Cipriano said. "Although God knows why. Everything's built in to help you, and our backroom team has worked out procedures. Most you have already. The rest are in the cockpit."

"Better late than never," Clifford said. He didn't look happy.

"Major, this is not our circus. That much has been made abundantly clear. But good luck."

With that, the two pilots left the group. For the first time, Red noticed two other men standing nearby. They looked like agents of some sort, possibly DIA. As the pilots left, the other two followed. A personal escort away from Groom Lake.

This really was a secret. Presumably the engineers and

designers understood the full spec, but the actual company pilots were kept in the dark.

"What does it mean?" Red asked.

"What?" Walker said.

"Daedalus?"

"It's Greek. Apollo was taken, so I guess they chose Daedalus. You don't have to use it."

"The XS-81 Daedalus," Red said, looking back at the aircraft. "Something from the future."

"Your farmer's showing a lot of interest," Walker said, nodding at Dupont, who walked around the back of the jet, running his hands over the black surface.

"He's good. Useful." Red said.

"Get him away," Brad Walker ordered.

Red watched as guards rounded up all but those necessary for flying operations, and that included Dupont.

He did not look happy, and at one point he looked pleadingly at Red.

Red shook his head and watched as they were ushered onto a bus, which drove them towards the buildings on the other side of the airfield.

He and Clifford went to the front of the hangar to meet the suit-up teams. Fifteen minutes later they waddled to the entry hatch underneath the Daedalus fuselage.

A technician in white overalls with a clipboard opened it and pulled down a yellow ladder. Clifford went up first, Red followed him into the belly of the beast.

The cockpit was smaller than he expected. He had to wait for Clifford to manoeuvre himself into his seat before he could step onto the right-hand position and slide in. He fumbled with the levers and moved forward until his feet were comfortable on the rudder pedals. It was a strange feeling to know only he would ever sit here.

He rested his right hand on the stick and his left on the centre throttles. The cockpit was well designed. Sitting upright, he got a good view forward, although it was restricted to about forty degrees either side unless he craned his neck.

A wad of papers sat on Clifford's lap. More procedures. He shared them out, and they got reading.

It was overwhelming, how much they had to learn. The flight tonight would involve a fraction of the process—just the usual airborne checks—but once they got higher and into the more complex flight profiles, it would be a full-time occupation keeping on top of the lists.

They rehearsed the main checks, then looked for the dials and switches mentioned in the advanced lists.

Clifford was curt, and his hands moved almost too quickly for Red to follow.

He thought of Jay Anderson. Anderson full of confidence, not really listening to any concerns from Dupont in the B-57. Would Clifford be the same if they got into trouble?

He looked down to the yellow-and-black handle between his legs, then examined the canopy above them. He could just make out the joints where the roof would separate. *Hopefully.* Nothing about this thing was fully tested, least of all the ejection system.

The longer he stayed in the inert XS-81, the more the ominous feeling grew in his stomach.

A voice whispered to him. *This is where you die, Red.*

Time passed slowly. Red tried to distract himself with the notes and lists they carried on board.

He looked out the window, trying to work out what the delay was. Men stood to the side of the aircraft in conversation.

He wanted to know the time, but getting to his watch

was impossible. Clifford said nothing as usual, and Red hesitated to start any conversation lest it annoyed him.

Eventually, Red muttered. "That must be an hour now?"

Clifford shrugged.

Red thought about trying to doze, but he didn't want to start the flight feeling groggy.

"Come on!" he said.

"Take it easy, Red. This is new to them as well," Clifford said. Red glanced at him and saw that his eyes were closed. Lucky him.

Some minutes later, maybe twenty, the hatch behind them opened.

Red did his best to shift himself around in his seat, just about able to see an engineer, waving his fingers across his throat.

"Scrubbed!" he mouthed.

Red felt a wave of relief. *Alive for one more day.*

After being briefed about a complex issue to do with fuelling, Red and Clifford desuited and once in their regular flight suits, made their way back to the T-38.

Clifford made his way up the steps as Red heard a shout from behind. He waited while Dupont ran over from the C-130.

"Everything okay?" Red said.

"Didn't particularly enjoy being stuck in the canteen."

Red looked across at the ground crew, which had emerged after the Daedalus was pushed back into the hangar.

"It's how they operate."

"Maybe I'd be better off doing something else."

Red felt a stab of panic. "No. I mean, give it a chance."

"Can you ask them?"

"They're pretty jumpy about it." Red looked over to the NRO guys, who were heading towards the C-130. For the first time, he spotted a couple of armed guards near the hangar.

Dupont backed away towards the Hercules. "Well. I dunno, Red. It's not much fun for me." He turned and broke into a trot.

The alarm clock clattered at 1000. Red had slept well, but as soon as he woke, he felt the nerves of what would surely be the first flight for them in the Daedalus tonight.

The fact they couldn't even follow the fuelling procedure wasn't a great start. But then he'd seen somewhere in the reams of papers on the jet that fuelling was a high-pressure process. The jet leaked on the ground and so could be fuelled only a few minutes before engine start and taxi.

The office was quiet. Red sat down at a desk and copied out the checklists once more, to help commit them to memory. He didn't want to be fumbling about up there, with Clifford snapping his fingers.

He looked with dismay at the sheer volume of lines of notes and procedures.

Dupont appeared next to him. "You okay?"

Instinctively, Red covered his notes, but then remembered the farmer was part of the team. Sort of.

"Trying to make sense of it all. I can't believe we're going to fly this thing tonight. I can't even remember the after-takeoff drill. And half this stuff is new to us. We got it only yesterday."

Dupont smiled at him and leaned over, looking at the

notes. He whistled. "Man, you've got bad handwriting." He laughed.

"That doesn't help," Red said.

Dupont stood back up and looked around, before surprising Red by picking up his pad and the wad of official documents. He headed off.

"Where you going?"

"Follow me."

Dupont led him to a side office, closed the door, and scrawled 'Daedalus Flight Prep' across the top of the blackboard.

"Let's break it down."

Over the next hour, they dissected the nonstandard procedures Red and Johnny Clifford would have to carry out at the various stages of flight.

The blackboard became full; Dupont stepped back and wiped everything clean.

Red protested, but then the farmer divided the board into new sections. He made new lists, referring to the paper-work. Red watched as the clump of procedures became an ordered pattern, associated with various phases of flight and priority.

He watched in awe as Dupont brought a startling simplicity to a complex set of tasks.

Each list was subdivided, with double circles around supporting checklists.

Dupont turned back to Red, who was already nodding.

"The airborne checks you think I need to memorise?"

"Exactly." Dupont looked back at his work. "I figure you'll have time to refer to the sheets for most of this. Especially as there are two of you. But Daedalus is gonna keep you busy during these phases." He pointed to the pre- and post-SRB lighting procedures and the main engine relight lists. "These you'll be far better memorising. It'll free you up to concentrate on the aircraft attitude, which I think will be critical."

Red studied the double-circled areas. "Actually, there's not that much to commit to memory."

"Nope. Not when you look at it like this. Want to take it down?"

Red grabbed a fresh pad and transferred Dupont's handiwork across two sheets. When he'd finished, he ensured Dupont wiped the board completely clean and headed back to his desk, with his new, simplified aide memoir in hand.

He memorised the key lists, closing his eyes to recite them every few seconds, grateful with every moment, that Dupont had helped simplify them down to just a few batches of procedure.

When he looked up, it was getting dark outside. Time to go to work.

The white-coated technicians helped him onto the ladder that led into the underside of the XS-81. Red had a mild fear of heights, and the top of the ladder was fifteen feet off the ground. He felt awkward and cumbersome in his space suit, his hands gripping the rungs tightly until he was inside and stepping onto the small space behind the pilots' ejection seats.

The technician sealed the hatch behind as he clambered into his position.

Johnny Clifford was already strapping into to the left-hand seat.

They sat, without straps, while the fuelling took place. It took twenty-five minutes.

Eventually, they got the signal and strapped in.

The five-point harness was familiar enough. Red slotted everything in and tightened the shoulders. He donned his helmet and plugged in his personal equipment connector.

A few pops and whines sounded in the headphones built into the helmet as Clifford followed a written checklist and flicked a switch to Run.

The auxiliary power unit in the tail fired up.

"Intercom check," Clifford said.

"Check," replied Red.

Clifford moved on to the prestart list; Red flipped over his pages, trying to keep up.

A few moments later, he took over reading out the actions while Clifford flicked the switches.

The four main engines fired up one by one.

As Red shuffled his notes, he referred to the two-page diagram of checks Dupont had helped create. It gave him a visual guide to where he needed to be and when memorised checks would be needed.

After ten minutes of laborious diagnostics and a few exchanges with the technicians on a ground loop plugged into the aircraft below, they were ready to roll.

The men in white coveralls walked away.

Visibility was not ideal for taxiing. They relied on the marshaller in front of them to ensure everyone was clear. A kid with two paddles in his hand was handed two chocks, which he held up for the pilots to see.

Clifford advanced the throttles on the world's most secret aircraft. The Daedalus shifted from its moorings, and he immediately dabbed the wheel brakes before settling into a steady taxi out towards the darkened runway.

As they trundled away from the apron lights, he handed over control so that Red could test his brakes and rudder steering.

Clifford took back control for Flight One.

Once lined up, the runway lights came on. In radio silence, having completed the takeoff checks, Clifford advanced the throttles to 40 percent.

The jet roared.

Vibrations came in waves down the airframe. Was that normal?

"She's flown before," Clifford said into the intercom as if reading his mind. He released the brakes and pushed the throttles into reheat.

The airspeed indicator moved off its resting position. Red watched and called out "V1" as it reached 180 knots.

"VR rotate," he shouted a moment later, and Clifford eased the stick back.

The XS-81 seemed stuck to the runway. Red looked back at the needle—210 knots, they should be airborne. The end of the runway couldn't be far away, although it was hard to see in the dark.

Just before he said anything, he felt the familiar feeling in his stomach as the aircraft lifted into the air.

"Like a seabird stepping off a cliff into a stiff wind," Clifford said, in a rare moment of poetry.

The XS-81 raced away from Earth.

"Wow!" Clifford said. Red exhaled as he tucked up the gear and completed the after-takeoff checks from memory.

Twenty-two minutes later, over the Pacific, in the dead of night at thirty thousand feet, Red took control.

The dial showed Mach 0.88.

"Time to go supersonic," Clifford said.

With the nose level, Red advanced the four throttles using two grouping levers.

They took a familiar kick in the backs as Daedalus accelerated up through the high subsonic Mach numbers.

A vibration like the one they felt on the takeoff roll began to build, shuddering forward from the nose.

The aircraft oscillated up and down. Small, rhythmic vibrations.

"Approaching Max Q," Clifford said.

"I don't like it," Red said. "It's fighting me." His hands gripped the throttle quadrant.

"Leave the throttles! Continue."

The vibration reached the rear half of the fuselage, and the aircraft began to seriously shake.

Red's vision became blurred. "We've got to stop!"

"Keep going!" Clifford shouted over the howl. "We're test pilots, dammit."

Red could barely read the needle, but the Mach meter still showed a zero; they hadn't got through the wave yet.

Two loud bangs came from behind them.

Red scanned the instruments. "Shit! What was that?"

The Mach meter now showed 1.1.

The vibrations eased. Red kept the burners on until they got to 2.0. The flying was smoother, but his heart was still beating hard from the punch through Mach 1.

He eased back the throttles and allowed Daedalus to slow back down the numbers.

"I thought she was going to break up on us," he said, croaking.

Clifford took over for the recovery. "Every inch of this thing needs to be inspected. Let's hope it gets us home."

Red sat in shock. They shouldn't have pushed it.

He concentrated on deep, rhythmic breaths as they followed the landing procedure. In the thicker air at low level, the flutter began again, but less violent than before. He had to remember to make notes in between reading out the checks.

On finals, at two miles, the runway lights at Groom came on.

"Come on, baby," Clifford said as he held Daedalus on a precise descent on the extended centreline.

Red clenched his fists as they crossed the threshold. Clifford dropped her onto the runway at two hundred ten knots, Red let out a long exhale.

The NRO boys did not take the news well.

"It's probably nothing," Walker said. "Let's see how she is in Flight Two."

Red glared at him. "Nothing? We heard it through our helmets at Mach 1. It wasn't *nothing*. It could have been the main spar, for all we know."

"I'm sure it wasn't—"

"You can't be sure of shit until you've checked it over," Clifford said. "Thoroughly." He walked off. Red followed him to repeat the process of desuiting and climbing back into their regular flight gear for the trip home.

As they walked out to the T-38, Red looked around for Dupont. But the props were already turning on the C-130.

Back at Edwards, Red waited for the A-TEC Hercules to arrive.

Dupont was the last into the building; most of the others had left.

Red got up.

"Hey," Brandon said, looking surprised.

"Can we have a chat?"

"Sure."

Red led him into the side office and closed the door. "There's something very wrong with the Daedalus. I don't think I can fly it again." His voice cracked slightly, and he immediately cleared his throat. *Test pilots don't cry.*

"What are you talking about? Of course, you can."

"At the Mach 1 point, she almost shook to bits. We heard two loud bangs. I thought that was it. I thought the aircraft was breaking up. She was shaking so badly. We shouldn't have continued. By myself, I would have pulled the throttles and gone home."

"But Clifford pushed you on?"

"I was terrified. I don't think I can go through this again. I'm going to quit."

"If you quit this project, they'll throw you out of A-TEC, won't they?"

Red sat down; Dupont pulled up a chair across the table from him. Piles of XS-81 related papers sat between them.

"I don't think I'm cut out for this. Until now, it's been fine, more or less. But this stuff . . ." He waved at the papers. "This is suicide."

Dupont looked confused. "Two bangs? Did you feel them?" He leafed through the papers.

"No. Just heard them."

He watched as Dupont located the main schematics.

"Well, I don't think it was the main spar, or anything central to the fuselage. You would have felt it. Not just heard it."

He watched as the farmer studied the diagram, running his finger over the lines of the Daedalus. "Can I have some blank paper?"

Red gave him a couple of sheets. Dupont pulled a pencil from a flight-suit pocket and began to sketch out a copy of the aircraft diagram. He glanced up at Red. "You look like shit."

"Thanks."

"Go home. You need your rest. Let's talk it over in the morning. Promise me you won't speak to anyone first."

Red nodded. "What are you going to do? You need to rest as well."

Dupont shook his head. "Anyone can fly a C-130 and sit in a canteen for four hours. I'm going to go through these until I find the wind-tunnel results. The answer will be in there somewhere."

At 0900, Red's phone rang. It was Clifford to tell him they were grounding the Daedalus for the day to examine it.

"Did they find something broken?" Red asked.

"Dunno."

Red drove slowly into A-TEC. Relieved there would be no flying, but anxious the engineers would report something to Walker and Gomez, only for the NRO men to send them back up.

Dupont was on a bench in the locker room pulling on his flight suit.

"You off somewhere?"

"Delivering a T-33 to China Lake. Apparently, we're not going to Groom tonight?"

Red sat down next to him. "No, they're taking a look at the airframe. Did you find anything?"

"Maybe. I need a bit more time."

"How are you getting back from China Lake? Will you have time?"

Dupont laughed. "Calm down. It'll be fine. Someone will get me back here, and I'll carry on looking into it."

"What did you find?"

"I'll tell you when I get back."

With that, he picked up his gloves and headed off to the equipment store.

Red lifted himself up, went back into the main office, and pretended to do admin for the rest of the day.

Dupont did not reappear.

At 1700, Clifford sent him home.

"Get some rest. We're back at Groom tomorrow night."

"So, they did they find something?"

"We'll find out tomorrow."

The rhythm became routine: Red trying to sleep past 0900 to give him the required rest, but usually giving up around 0800.

He needed to hear from Dupont. He was supposed to be his wingman. Looking out for him.

He didn't want to get to Groom Lake to have a second flight sprung on him, with no progress on finding the issue.

If the NRO men tried that, he had a big decision to make.

He made his way into the base and dumped his flight case on a desk. Dupont appeared immediately, looking as if he hadn't slept.

"What happened to you?" Red asked.

"What do you mean?"

"Yesterday? I never saw you again!"

"Oh, someone drove me back. Took a while, so I went straight home."

Red couldn't hide his disappointment. This didn't feel like the partnership Dupont promised.

"Can we go somewhere quiet to talk?" Dupont said. For the first time, Red noticed the XS-81 flight manual in his hand.

"Sure."

In the side office, Dupont divided the papers into small piles.

"You found something?" Red asked.

"See these wind-tunnel tests? They were buried in the paperwork. But, they don't say anything about issues at Max Q."

"Right." Red sat down. "So they have no idea what the issue is. In which case, I quit. I'm not flying that thing just to find out when the aircraft destroys itself."

"Well, hold on there, friend. You haven't heard me yet. Thing is, as far as I can tell, they didn't wind-tunnel-test what you're actually flying."

"What do you mean?"

Dupont spread the notes out in front of him. "Here. It's just a reference, but they talk about the SRB and missile profile on the model." He looked at Red expectantly.

"I don't get it."

"I think it needs the missile. I think it was designed to pass through the sound barrier fully laden with the SRBs and that missile. And it's large, right? It runs the entire length of the fuselage. It will make a difference."

Red sat up. "So, that's why the company pilots were ordered to keep her subsonic. And why they think we can take her faster—they assumed we would be flying with the missile."

On the ground at Groom, Clifford jumped out the T-38 and left Red to finish the after-flight procedures. By the time Red caught up with the chief test pilot and the NRO men, he could see Clifford was angry.

"You want us to fly the aircraft into an unstable and violent phase of flight so you can study the numbers?"

"We need some more data," Gomez said, as if he were asking for the weather report. Walker, standing next to Gomez as always, shrugged. "You're test pilots, right?"

Clifford shook his head. "Tell me again exactly what your guys found."

"The housing for the SRBs cracked. Two of them. Not serious. Not the main airframe or spar. Look, we're not asking you to push through Max Q. Just get close to it. The additional sensors the engineers have added will pick out exactly where the pressure wave is causing issues."

"I have an idea," Red said. All three men turned to him.

"Let's try flying with the missile in place."

"What difference will that make?" Clifford asked.

"It's just a guess, but it changes the aerodynamics significantly. It could be the issue."

The NRO men looked at each other. "We don't have a missile yet," Walker said.

Clifford shook his head. "It doesn't need to be the real thing. If Red's theory is correct, an inert one will do. Can they wind-tunnel-test this?"

"We can ask, I guess," Gomez said. "But it's going to cause delays, and we don't have much time."

"If we break up over the Pacific," Clifford said, "delays will be the least of your worries." He picked up his T-38 flying helmet and walked away.

Red loitered. "When they do the wind-tunnel tests, tell them to try both with and without the missile."

As Red followed Clifford back to the T-38, he looked back to see Walker draw a hand across his throat at the team around the Daedalus. Supervisors waved their hands in a circle in the air in response, and men sprang into action, pushing the secret aircraft back into the hangar.

Dupont stood near the C-130, clearly receiving the news that the test flight was off. He looked up, and Red gave him a thumbs-up.

Two days later, on Friday afternoon, Dave Gomez tapped on the side office door. Red lifted himself from the manuals and let him in.

"You were right."

"Really?" he said, and he caught an approving look from Johnny Clifford.

"Yeah. Without the missile there's too much pressure on the underside of the fuselage, the landing-gear housings, and the SRB mounts." Gomez looked down at his notes. "Something to do with the shape of the wave. But, with the missile in place, and some fuel in the SRBs, the pressure's dissipated to the outside of the wings, which can flex and absorb."

"Good job, Red," Clifford said. "Very good." He turned to Gomez. "So, we need a missile."

"They can't produce a dummy. You'll have to wait for the actual missile, and that's going to be three weeks minimum."

"So, we're out of time for the launch?"

Gomez shook his head. "No. We'll accelerate. Once the missile is fitted, we move straight to SRB testing. You two need to compress that timetable."

"You mean put everything that was spread over six weeks into three weeks?"

"Two flights a night if necessary. We've got permission to move forward to a midnight start. President Johnson wants this satellite taken out. I don't think he cares about any of us sleeping."

Clifford drummed his fingers for a moment. "We don't even know if the sound-barrier issue is solved with the missile."

"You'll find out on the first flight back. And if it is, you can press on to the SRB." He looked at Red. "Thanks for your help on this."

Gomez left the room. Red hesitated for a moment and then went after him, catching him up near the exit.

"It wasn't me."

"What?" The agent looked confused.

"The theory about the missile. It wasn't me."

"I don't understand."

"I talked it through with Brandon Dupont," Red said, and studied Gomez for the inevitable angry reaction. Instead, Gomez looked around the office, laying eyes on the farmer, who sat at a desk writing a report.

"Uh-huh."

"Yeah. He's good at this stuff. Very good. He just saved us a whole heap of time. He might even have saved the project. I think we could use him better."

Gomez's eyes flicked about. "You know you're not supposed to discuss this with anyone outside the project."

"He's on the project."

"He's a cabdriver, Red. Well done. Wherever it came from, it was useful. But what do you want? There's space for only two pilots."

Red shook his head. "He doesn't need to be a pilot to help us. Just let him in on the pre- and postflight discussions. I promise you, he's good. He'll help." Gomez didn't look convinced. "He could be the magic ingredient. This project is on a knife edge as it is. We need all the help we can get. And . . ."

"And?"

"I need him."

"What does that mean?"

Red hesitated. "He helps me personally. It's scary up there."

Gomez pushed the door open. "You're a big boy, Red. You don't need a farmer's help." He looked back. "And stop talking to people. It's gonna get you in trouble."

The evening lights of Rosamond beckoned as Red drove away from Edwards. His late mornings and night shifts had messed up his perception of day and night, but at least he felt awake now. He had three weeks' reprieve from the sense of danger that seemed to accompany every visit to Groom.

Three weeks of some Sarah time.

He parked and tapped on her door.

"Come in."

The kitchen was empty. "I'll be out in a moment." Sarah's disembodied voice carried from the bedroom.

She emerged in a check dress, with her hair cropped short.

Red gaped.

"You don't like the hair?"

"I love it." He reached forward and pulled her close for a kiss.

"You're just saying that."

"Promise."

They walked to the car. "Shall we pick up Brandon?" Red said.

"Doesn't he have his own friends?" she said as she climbed in.

"Sure."

Red turned the car across the Main Street and pressed on the gas pedal. Two long seconds later, the cumbersome Ford gathered speed.

Sarah shrugged. "Okay, I suppose I could do with getting my damn keys back."

Red turned down Sierra and pulled up outside Sarah's folks' old home. The drapes were drawn, and it was hard to tell if any lights were on inside.

He got out and knocked on the front door. The place felt deserted.

"Are you sure he lives here?" Red shouted back to the car. Sarah got out and leaned against the passenger door.

"Yeah. It always looks like this with him."

No response from the knock. "Guess he's already at Maggie's."

Red walked back and climbed into the driver's seat.

"Oh!" Sarah said.

"What?"

"I just saw the drapes move."

Red looked back at the house. "Really? That's weird. He must have heard me knock."

She climbed back in. "I guess he doesn't want to come out and play. It's because I'm with you."

Red pulled away. "Don't be silly."

"It's true. You don't see how he is with me. *Perfunctory* doesn't describe it. When it's you, he's all friendly."

They drove on in silence for a while.

"And he's still got my spare keys," Sarah muttered.

Maggie's was busy. For the first time, Red and Sarah did not hide their relationship.

"You took him back?" Jimmy Cofferr said. "Poor decision-making, Sarah."

"You leave my lovebirds alone," Maggie said from behind the bar.

A year ago, Red would have been embarrassed. But seeing Sarah's smiling face in the crowd, he felt something different.

Pride.

CHAPTER ELEVEN

THE FIRST WEEK PASSED SLOWLY. Red had given up on the XS-81 manuals and picked up some routine trial work on an F-104. The single-seat jet with a new air-to-air missile fit was enough to occupy him. Each flight required a written report.

By the middle of week two, he wanted to prepare for the return of the XS-81. To help him, he recruited Brandon Dupont.

They set out the remaining tasks and brought a suggested order together.

Late one afternoon, Red called Clifford into the side office.

"What do you think?" he said, pointing at the suggested flights in order on the board.

Clifford nodded. "Good job, I was about to suggest we think about this." He gave Red a friendly slap. "You're ahead of the game."

He then noticed Dupont sitting at a desk in the corner of the room.

"Ah, of course. The farmhand."

"He's got a good eye for procedure."

"Must have been useful during the harvest," Clifford said and shook his head, making for the door. "Good work. Can you get it written up and distributed? Then we need to break down each trip."

"We're on it," Red confirmed.

"I'm sure you both are." Clifford left the room.

Red gathered the sheets they'd used to plot out the schedule.

"Let's go through some of the unknowns before we finish," Dupont suggested.

They talked through any scenario they could think of, making a list. Each topic would need further drills and procedures applied.

At 1900, Red leaned back on his chair and studied the gloomy page of possible failures.

"They won't all be survivable," he observed.

Dupont turned his chair to face him. "Red, can I ask you a question?"

"Sure."

"Are you looking forward to this?"

Red had to think about the answer.

"I'm not sure. Maybe not."

"Listen, buddy, you're an elite test pilot, flying a unique aircraft. One for the record books. Maybe not soon, but at some point, this will even be in the history books, with your name next to it."

"You think I should be enjoying this? What about the risks?" Red waved at the extensive list they'd made, just from the top of their heads.

"Use that fear to ignite your own rockets. Nothing makes you feel alive like facing death."

Dupont got up and gathered the papers.

"Is that your attitude, farm boy?"

The farmer reached the door. "You're not the only one heading into the unknown."

A few days before the resumption of flights at Groom Lake, a group from NASA arrived at the neighbouring unit, and a few of the guys went over to say hello. Red tagged along.

He found himself next to Gus Grissom, who had nearly drowned after splashing down in his Mercury spaceflight.

Short, trim, and wearing his trademark close-cut military hair, Grissom had become something of a hero in the public's eye.

"How do you deal with the fear?" Red asked.

"If it's gonna happen, it's gonna happen," Grissom said. "You just have to do your bit to make sure it doesn't. If I die up there, it'll be someone else's fault. Not that that will be much consolation!" He laughed. "So, what are you flying at the moment, son?"

Red thought for a moment. "Nothing special."

Time sped up.

On Friday, he saw Dupont in the office with the two NRO men. He caught up with him later in the afternoon.

"What was that about?"

"They want me to make sure Groom's ready for the Daedalus to arrive on Monday. Guess I've drawn the short straw from rounding up the right people and making sure they're on the ground."

"I guess they trust you now."

"Thanks to you, Red."

The office emptied out, and Red headed home.

He didn't want to go to Maggie's, but Sarah persuaded him.

He scanned the bar when they arrived. "No Clifford, no Brandon? As usual."

Sarah fished a dollar out of her purse. "Their loss."

"Maybe I shouldn't have too many."

"Why?" Sarah swivelled around. "Think you're drinking too much?"

Red looked down. "Maybe I should be taking a lead from men like Brandon? Maybe he's showing me the way to behave?"

Sarah studied him. "He wasn't that well behaved once, remember?"

"Once."

They joined the group near the bar, but Sarah was quiet, and Red thought he'd put a dampener on the evening.

When they got home, she invited him in.

"Do you mind if I don't?" Red said. "Sorry, baby. I've got a big week coming up, and I need to start shifting my sleep pattern."

She nodded. "That's such a strange excuse, I'll have to believe it."

On Monday, forty-five men made the trip from Edwards to Groom Lake. Dupont carried out his duties diligently, and the C-130 left during daylight hours to ensure the ground team was in place. After dark, Red and Clifford walked out to the T-38.

Under cover of night, a small army was assembling, far from prying eyes, to carry out the most secret of tasks.

Red thought about President Johnson, two and a half thousand miles across the country, in the White House.

He'd never met him, nor was he likely to. All he knew from the news was that he was mired in an escalation in Vietnam. And according to the NRO, eagerly awaiting updates from each flight they carried out.

It must seem simple to him, Red mused. *Shoot down that satellite!*

Clifford flew them. Red stared out into the dark, recalling Grissom's words. *Cover every eventuality. If it goes wrong, make sure it's not you.*

With Dupont's guidance, for the first time, he believed they *had* covered everything. They'd also broken it down into manageable chunks.

Without realising it, Dupont had somehow prepared him in every way for the next stage.

When they climbed down the stairs onto the apron, Red sensed a serious atmosphere.

The solid rocket boosters were not to be toyed with. Smoking was strictly prohibited on the entire site, and Red heard they even searched the ground crew for lighters before allowing them on board the C-130.

"Would you look at that?" Clifford said. Along the entire length of the underside of the fuselage of the XS-81 was the missile.

"It's huge," Red said.

He and Clifford walked into the front of the nearby hangar, which had become their suiting-up zone.

They waddled out, with the men in white coats carrying their helmets behind them.

As they got closer to the XS-81, Red spotted Dupont, papers in hand, crouched under the far end of the aircraft. Brad Walker and Dave Gomez stood above him, leaning in to hear what he had to say.

"I think your farmer's giving Walker and Gomez a lesson

in aerodynamics," Clifford said. "Don't know how you pulled that off. I thought they didn't want him anywhere near the thing."

They strapped in, silently.

Helmets on, Red carried out his copilot duties and took Clifford through the prestart and start checks.

They taxied. The wheel-brake test was extremely gentle, just a soft application to ensure the aircraft would slow down if needed.

"SRBs on board," Clifford said. "No sudden movements."

Moments later, he gently nudged the Daedalus off the tarmac into the black night sky. They punched through a thin layer of cloud at around eight thousand feet and climbed to altitude over the Pacific.

Red took control, as before.

He advanced the throttles to full reheat.

The aircraft kicked, but less violently. More mass, more drag, slower acceleration.

He concentrated on holding the nose slightly up, another idea from Brandon Dupont. Before he had a chance to check the Mach meter, Clifford announced they were through.

"One point one! Didn't feel a thing."

Red looked out the window, leaning forward to see the wingtips. The invisible wave would have washed across them. It was too dark to make anything out, but if there were any issues, they would have felt something.

"Okay, I got her," Clifford said as he took control for the first SRB burn. He engaged the reheat, and they climbed to one hundred thousand feet.

Even from the copilot's seat, Red could feel the jet become sluggish. They were now doing Mach 2.8 and about ten degrees nose up.

Clifford encouraged the nose down to five degrees, the designated attitude for the burn.

But the jet wasn't having any of it.

"She doesn't want to come down."

Red carried on with the preburn checks, using a small flashlight.

Unlike the A-12, the jet engines would be shut down before lighting the SRBs.

With the throttles back and fuel cocks closed, they had only seconds to get their secondary power source lit. If the aircraft slowed too much, they couldn't carry out the burn.

Red reached a crucial phase in the checklist.

"Nose. Five degrees."

He looked up; they were only at nine.

"It's no good," Clifford said. "She's too slow to respond."

"We have a few seconds. Just let her come down in her own time."

But it was no good; the nose was barely moving.

"Control jets?"

"They'd just be compressed gas without the engines, and we're not supposed to need them at this stage. But what the hell . . ."

Clifford's hand went to the small joystick used to direct the vents. The nose moved more rapidly. As it approached eight degrees, he used the stick to give a squirt of opposite force to stabilise. But the Daedalus continued to pitch down.

"Curse it!" Clifford used one more blast to try to get her straight.

Red looked at a small dial with a white needle. "Less than three quarters on the compressed gas now, Johnny."

They should probably scrub the test. It was too risky to try to manoeuvre in the stratosphere without a full tank of air.

Should I say something?

Clifford was on the main stick now, edging the nose through four degrees, just about to capture the target attitude.

Red looked at the Mach meter. It was below two.

They were now well out of parameters for the SRBs. He had to assume Clifford knew this.

"There." Clifford held her steady at five. "Ready to fire. Shame we've blown the airspeed and compressed air. Let's go through the relight. If that's smooth, we can go down to sixty thousand, then try the climb to ignition point again before we go home. Gotta find a way to get the angle right without needing the vents."

"Roger that," Red said with relief.

The engine relight was a single button push, and pleasingly a nonevent. A clever auto-sequencer used bleed air diverts until each engine caught. Red and Clifford simply monitored the dials.

On the second attempt at a climb to SRB ignition, Clifford rotated the nose of Daedalus down to the assigned five degrees much earlier. It slowed the descent a touch, but that was fine; they flew with plenty of jet fuel.

At one hundred thousand feet, they both noted the moment they could have shut down the turbofans and sparked up the SRBs if they'd still had enough vent gas.

"Good enough," Clifford said. "We'll light them tomorrow."

Red took over and turned back to land.

Clifford talked him through the process for achieving the right attitude, and they agreed Red should perfect it himself before they moved forward to the SRB lighting phase.

Landing with the rocket fuel still on board was another

nervy experience, especially as they caught a gust on short final.

"Easy, baby." Red was ready to go around rather than risk a heavy landing, but she smoothed out, and he used the flare to grease the XS-8I onto the tarmac.

Walker and Gomez were not happy. They had wanted to see black scorch marks indicating the SRBs had been fired.

"Each new manoeuvre in the aircraft is a first," Clifford said. "We should expect to discover things along the way that set us back."

Gomez shook his head and wagged his finger at them. "We don't have time for setbacks. We've got eighteen days until we move north. Twenty days until the missile release. You haven't tested the SRBs tonight." He pointed at Red. "And now you want tomorrow night for him to try the first part, and still you're not going to fire them?"

"If we'd fired them tonight," Clifford said, "we'd be coming back down the Mach numbers in an airless atmosphere with no way of keeping her in shape. And I need Red to be proficient before either of us lights them up. If we're not on top of that attitude, she'll slip into a tumble and that'll be that. What use is Daedalus to you at the bottom of the Pacific?"

Walker snorted.

"Look, if Red nails it first time tomorrow, we'll carry out the burn."

Behind them, the hypersonic aircraft was being towed back to the hangar. Dupont sat inside the cockpit, looking after the brakes.

"I guess he's one of us now," Red said.

The team reconvened the following night.

Walker looked agitated.

"For a special agent, he doesn't cope well with stress," Clifford said as they suited up.

"He should try flying this thing," Red said. He looked at Clifford, but he was busy with his suit fitting and didn't respond.

As they emerged onto the apron, Red watched the technicians striding back and forth around Daedalus, preparing for the second attempt at an SRB burn.

Dupont approached them. "They're twenty-five percent fuelled. We'll use tonight as a calibration to predict future flight level and speed, so it's critical to note the top of arc as accurately as possible."

"You in charge now?" Clifford said, fiddling with his space-suit collar.

"No, sir. Just helping out. I think the NRO agents like to have me as a go-between with the engineers."

"Guess you're not going to the canteen tonight, then?" Red said with a wink.

Dupont walked back to the huddle around the aircraft and fell into discussions with the company reps.

The aircraft seemed to have a couple of new panels on the side, since coming back with the missile on board. More sensors. It reminded Red how critical each flight was. The XS-81 bristled with devices that fed a central data recorder, and there would be nowhere to hide if they made a mistake.

Time passed slowly as the refuelling team in protective suits readied themselves. Red and Clifford prepared to reenter the Daedalus.

Gomez met them at the hatch. "We're worried about the timeline."

"We know you are," Clifford replied. "We're doing what we can."

"The long-range forecast isn't great. We're concerned about positioning for the operational flight. We may need to bring it forward to early next week."

"Jesus. We've barely got started."

"That's why we're worried. Remember, there will be a small release window for the missile launch. You might want to start thinking about positioning, as well as height and speed."

Clifford rolled his eyes and stepped onto the ladder underneath the XS-81. "I'll tell you what. Let's see if she doesn't explode or shake apart when we light the rockets first, shall we?" He disappeared into the belly of the aircraft.

"We'll brief you on Alaska tomorrow a.m.!" Gomez called after him.

Red let Gomez back down the ladder before climbing up.

Not being the most stressed person on the project was a novelty he was enjoying.

As he settled down into the right-hand seat, he realised something almost remarkable. He was looking forward to it.

One of the tweaks to the procedures they made when considering what could go wrong meant that they sat with helmets off during refuelling. Less encumbered, should they have to egress fast.

"The NRO boys care about a lot, but they don't care about our lives, do they?" Red said.

"Nope." Clifford didn't look up from his paperwork.

Over the next thirty minutes, the crowd outside thinned out, with nonessential personnel shepherded away to the canteen.

He reread the freshly printed list headed "GROUND FIRE DURING REFUELLING." He chuckled to himself.

"Wouldn't really be a fire, would it?" he said, showing the page to Clifford.

"Huh?"

"It would be an explosion."

"Hmm."

Red looked down at his watch, on an extended strap around the outside of the pressure suit. The familiar cracks. A semibroken device, associated with failure. But it brought him comfort. The adult equivalent of an old teddy bear.

"We do need to start thinking about Alaska," Clifford said. "Walker's right about that."

"We haven't lit the SRBs yet. It seems a long way away."

"It's the end of next week, maybe sooner."

Red decided to put it out of his mind. They had a flight to execute. Dupont would be on hand on the ground to help with the next phase of planning.

He made a mental note to ensure the farmer would be coming up north with them. He'd fight any security objections from the NRO twins.

Eventually, he and Clifford were told to don gloves and helmets and start her up.

The J-59s wound up to a familiar howl, and Clifford taxied them to the main runway.

Once over the ocean, the push to Mach 3 was, again, uneventful. Red managed the attitude carefully.

By the time they reached seventy thousand feet, they were exactly five degrees nose up. Red followed Clifford's calm instructions, and between them, the aircraft floated into the correct attitude and speed for the SRB burn.

Clifford took control as Red went through the engine shutdown and SRB ignition checklists.

Once everything was in place and they'd both checked their straps and pulled them a little tighter, the chief test pilot pressed a single caged button that auto-sequenced the ignition. For a moment, they heard nothing, but felt the vibration running through the fuselage.

Then the rockets came to life with a loud thump that hit them in their backs.

The aircraft was flung forward on a 4G acceleration. Red took a deep breath and strained, forcing blood up to his brain, before releasing, realising the force wasn't affecting him in the way a pull-up would.

The jet kept remarkably stable, with Clifford using both hands on the stick to ensure a precise attitude.

The Mach meter wound up, passing 4.5, and the g-force kept coming. It was wearing, tiring.

They settled into a stable climb and acceleration, the Daedalus frame shaking under the stress.

The needle was just sweeping up to Mach 5 when the SRBs ran out of fuel with a few WHOMPS that shook the aircraft.

Red noted the flight level, one hundred seventy-nine thousand four hundred feet. He held a pencil in the thick space-suit gloves and wrote as best he could on his kneepad clipboard.

Clifford's hand went to a small joystick mounted between them, in front of the two throttles. He nudged it down, and a small cloud of opaque gas fired up from a vent set into the nose.

The aircraft gently pitched down. As it reached about seven degrees below the artificial horizon, Clifford nudged the joystick up to stabilise their new attitude.

The XS-81 had felt solid and controllable in the thin air, far more than the A-12.

With the correct attitude, Red finished his note-taking and looked out the window. They were thirty-three miles up, and the curvature of the earth was clear. To the west, as before in the A-12, Red could see the remnants of the day, as the sun's rays crept over the horizon.

It was peaceful.

Two men silently falling back to Earth.

As they approached eighty thousand feet, Red worked through the next checklist: the relight sequence.

Clifford's hands moved across the switches and valves, grateful for the auto-sequencers. Starting each engine manually could create havoc in the little time they had.

Unlike the hands-on A-12, the XS-81 felt like a top-of-the-range Cadillac, with every mod con.

The engines spooled up, and soon they were back to conventional flying for a standard recovery back at Groom Lake.

When they emerged from the underside of the aircraft into the cool desert night, Dupont strolled up to them.

"What was it like?"

"Fine," said Clifford. Brunson has your readings."

"How high did you get?"

"One seventy-nine."

Dupont took a step back and whistled. "On twenty-five percent fuel. Mach number?"

"Five on the nose."

On the way back, Red tried to read his thigh-pad notes in the orange gloom of the instrument panel. He'd actually written the word "smooth."

It all felt very different from the chaotic A-12 flights.

"Start thinking about the release point," Clifford ordered over the intercom. "We'll be using radio beams, but that's about all I know. Getting it to Mach 8 in exactly the right piece of sky, while managing a full SRB burn? It's gonna be busy. Still a long shot, if you ask me."

"We'll break it down," Red said, reassuring his captain.

They flew on in silence before a few brief radio calls and an uneventful landing at Edwards. Somewhere behind them, the C-130 with Dupont and the rest of the ground crew chugged along, keeping the Edwards air traffic controllers from their beds for another hour.

CHAPTER TWELVE

RED TAPPED at the door and listened carefully for sounds of movement.

He looked back down the road; the early-morning sun was causing wisps of water vapour to evaporate from the freshly sprinkled lawns. The town was yet to wake up. He glanced at his watch.

Sarah was also yet to wake up, apparently.

He was about to turn back to his car when he heard footsteps.

The door opened. There she was, nightdress hanging askew across her shoulders, eyes blinking into the light.

"What time is it?" she muttered.

"Pancake time!" Red lifted a brown bag.

Moving slowly, she opened the door and ushered him in, a smile starting to form. "What is it with you air force people? Really, what time is it?"

"It's late. Nearly seven."

"Nearly seven?" Sarah raised one eyebrow. "You mean it's six-something?"

"Did I mention pancakes? I think you're forgetting about the pancakes."

She pushed the door shut. Red found a plate and tipped the pancakes out.

"You got maple syrup?" He turned, and Sarah was standing an inch away. She wrapped her arms around his neck and kissed him, long and deep.

When eventually they disengaged, he pushed his forehead against hers, smelled her skin, and lost himself.

It was moving quickly, and he was enjoying it.

She broke away and fished a plastic tub of maple syrup out of a cupboard.

The two of them ate on high stools at Sarah's small kitchen top, which also served as her dining table.

"So, I'm not going to be around for a bit," Red said.

Sarah stiffened. "Where are you going?"

"We have to move to a different airfield, just for a few days. It means I'll be busy the rest of this week, then away from Monday for a week or so."

Sarah slid the remains of her pancake around the plate, mopping up the last of the syrup.

"Okay," she said quietly.

Was that sadness in her voice? Resignation?

Red stood up and put his hands on Sarah's shoulders, fixing her with a stare. "Now, you listen to me. This is just a week or so, I promise. And yes, Sarah, I will be back."

She smiled weakly. "The time I can cope with. But, Red, I don't think I can go through losing someone again."

"Stop it. I'll be fine. I'll be back. You have a Captain Brunson promise. Plus, I have Brandon watching my back."

"Oh. He's going, too? Are you sure he watches your back?"

"What does that mean?"

She toyed with her food. "He's not exactly one of the team, is he?"

"What do you mean? He's actually becoming an important part of the team."

He kissed Sarah's forehead. She stood up and hugged him, resting her head on his shoulder.

"When did your mom die?" she asked.

"December '51."

"Around four years after your pa?"

"About that. Why?"

"You're an only child, Red. As an adult, as a pilot, you've never had someone who cares for you. Someone waiting for you, worrying about you."

"I don't know what you mean. I like to think a few people at least like me."

"But not the way I do. All I'm saying is, you're not just keeping yourself alive for you."

"How about we try to get some time this weekend before I head out?"

She nodded but didn't look up.

As he left, she headed off to the bedroom, but paused. "Did Dupont hand you my spare keys?"

He shook his head.

"Jesus Christ. What's wrong with him? I've a good mind to break in."

"Don't do that."

"Why? It's my goddamn house."

"I'll speak to him."

Johnny Clifford already had the air charts of Alaska spread out on a large map table.

"This is it. Wainwright," he said, pointing at a tiny dot on the northern coast of the state.

"There's nothing there," Red said.

"The strip's good enough, though. New, in fact. There's a radar station nearby, which is the only reason the place exists, as far as I can see."

Red followed the lines that led from the airfield. About eight hundred miles north, Clifford had marked a complex series of annotations.

"This the release point?" Red asked.

"Yep. The math guys are working on the precise release box. They told me we'll get the window nearer the time. But it's likely to be small for both time and place."

"How small?"

"Around one minute and within thirty or so miles of the datum. Too early or late and the satellite will be out of the missile's envelope."

Clifford stood up straight and stretched out his back.

Red looked across at the lines of longitude. Eighty-two degrees north. "And I'm assuming our compass won't work."

"Correct. Too close to magnetic north. We're gonna be using two radio beams. NRO has a team already up there, installing it all."

"Not much to go wrong, then. I'd give it twenty percent."

"Don't tell Tweedledum and Tweedledee that." Clifford nodded towards Montgomery's office, where Walker and Gomez were meeting with the colonel.

Over the next two hours, Red helped Clifford devise the best possible flight plan. They chose a peninsula tip about one hundred fifty miles east to use as their initial point. They'd be heading on the 345 radio beam from there, powering up into the stratosphere to their hypersonic missile release point.

"Will we even know if we've hit it?" Red said.

Clifford shrugged. "I doubt it."

"Definitely not," Gomez said. The two NRO men had appeared silently by their side. "The impact will be over the horizon, on the other side of the pole. Any debris that makes it through reentry will come down in the Barents Sea."

"And if we miss?" Clifford asked. "Where does it come down?"

"Hard to say." Walker took over. "Once it contacts the upper atmosphere, it will start to break up, but unpredictably. It's a big object, and [or so] we expect some of it to get through—best guess is the biggest piece will come down somewhere in Norway."

"So, missing is not an option," Gomez said.

Clifford leaned back over the map, rolling his eyes. "There's a lot of moving parts here."

"What does that mean?" Walker said.

"I'm just saying there's a lot that can go wrong." Clifford sat up straight and ran his finger over the map. "Look at the size of this area. Think about how precisely we need to position Daedalus. And then think about the relatively tiny target, moving at what? Seventeen thousand knots."

"You're saying you can't do it?" Walker said.

"That's not what I'm saying. I'm simply pointing out that it's not a foregone conclusion."

Walker looked stressed. "We're doing our job. We expect you to do yours."

"Christ, Walker, we're doing everything we can. I'm just trying to keep your ambition in check here. If you've told the president this is a sure thing, that's your problem."

"Fuck's sake, Clifford. *Now* you tell us it won't work—"

"We told you on day one—"

"Easy, gentlemen." Dave Gomez stood up and folded the map. "This is getting us nowhere. We know you're doing your best, and we know there are no guarantees. Johnson knows that, too, doesn't he, Brad?"

Walker puffed out his cheeks. "I'll let you tell him when it fails."

Clifford shook his head and got up; Red followed him back to their side office. They looked through the window to see Dupont scribbling on a blackboard, with two engineers either side of him.

"What's that about?" Red asked Clifford.

"Something to do with the fuelling and starting procedure in the cold. Your farmer's getting his teeth into everything."

Red stared as Dupont sketched out a precise procedure.

"Leave him to it. Best we figure out exactly how we're going to release this damn thing to save those goons' asses."

That evening, Red handled the Daedalus during the second SRB burn. Now filled to fifty percent, the 4G acceleration went on significantly longer. But as they climbed even higher, topping out at two hundred ten thousand feet, the ride was smoother.

As the rockets flamed out with a *WHOMP* noise, he had his first experience with the gas vents.

The nose was riding up. He gave it a good burst, and the movement shifted down.

"Easy!" Clifford warned him, his hands covering the controls, ready to intervene.

Red gave a little nudge on the underside vent to arrest the transition.

It took him several short, stabbing bursts to stabilise.

They were passing one hundred twenty-five thousand feet by the time he'd finished.

"You need to do better at that," Clifford said as he hit command on the sequencer for the engine relight.

The next day, Red arrived to a tense atmosphere.

Clifford greeted him as he entered the project office. "There's a problem. Weather's coming fast."

Red glanced out the window at the blue sky.

"Not here, idiot. Up north. They're worried we won't get in."

Walker and Gomez appeared.

"Snowstorms and winds gusting sixty knots," Clifford said.

Walked nodded. "By the end of tomorrow. It's not too bad in the morning."

"But this weather system is due to hang around all week," Gomez said. "Over the launch window."

Everything these guys had promised the White House was disappearing in a blizzard.

"Right," Clifford said, rereading the bulletin. "So we could get in tomorrow, but then we're snowed in for the actual mission?"

"Dupont doesn't think so," Walker said.

Clifford dropped the paper on the table. "Is he a weatherman now, as well as an engineer?"

"No. He thinks you'll be able to take off in bad weather. You just won't be able to return."

"He's right," Red said. "Getting airborne isn't the issue. As long as we can see the white lines on the runway. That thing is fast on the ground. It won't be too hard to get it up and above the weather. But, yeah, landing with no vis. Out of the question."

Walker folded his arms and faced Clifford. "So, we get you in overnight tonight, ahead of the weather. Then run antisnow ops all week at Wainwright, so you can launch. And we find you somewhere suitable to land after the missile release."

"It's marginal," Clifford said. "And that's an experimental aircraft."

"There's a lot riding on this, Major," Gomez said. "Dupont thinks—"

"Jesus Christ. If I hear one more time that Brandon Dupont thinks we can do something—"

"He's just looking at the performance stats," Gomez added. "We asked him. Look, we'll give you what you need on the ground. They're experts at keeping runways open."

The men stood in silence for a while. But it felt to Red as if the decision had been made.

Another decision that put his life on the line.

"I need to discuss it with Red," Clifford said. There was a pause, before the NRO men realised they were being dismissed.

Clifford closed the door. "I hate rushing. It's how people get killed. And I don't give a damn what Dupont thinks. He'll be flying a C-130. You could land that thing on an iceberg."

They both sat down.

"What do you think, Red? This is your ass as well as mine."

A picture of Sarah popped into his head. She was right. He was an only child, and orphaned from the age of nineteen. He'd never had someone at home waiting, relying on his return. Did he need to say no for her sake?

He pulled the folded map across the table and opened it up. It was a long haul up to the north of Alaska. But then the Daedalus was the fastest aircraft on earth . . .

"We can't land in the dark and in marginal weather," he said. "That's a dangerous combination on a jet with minimal navaids."

Clifford nodded. "Agree. They won't like it, but that can be our red line. What about the divert? You happy with that idea?"

Red looked back at the map. "Where d'you think they'll send us?"

"Greenland? Iceland? Northern Europe? Who knows? Somewhere remote is my only guess."

They called the NRO men back in; Montgomery joined them.

"We'll go tonight, but timed so we land in daylight," Clifford said.

Walker shook his head. "That's strictly against protocols. The Soviet satellites will see us, and then it's game over."

"Then we don't go."

Red looked between the two men. "We can use the clouds to keep reasonably well hidden, and if the weather report's right, we'll be landing under some sort of layers."

Gomez pointed at the map. "Plus, it's in the middle of nowhere. We'd be unlucky if a pass happened to coincide with the arrival. I'll can ask Langley about timings."

Walker tapped his foot. "Okay, then. Plan to arrive at dawn. That way the majority of the flight is dark. I'll get on the horn and try and persuade them in DC."

By 1400, they had a flight profile and authority.

Walker and Gomez wanted them to relocate to Groom to

continue the planning, so the C-130 team needed to get airborne soon. They had a helluva long journey at two hundred eighty knots ahead of them.

"You've got sixty minutes before the Herc leaves with or without your clothes," Clifford said.

Red darted from the office and jumped into his car. He drove straight to the BX.

"Is Sarah here?" he asked a woman on the register.

She looked up at the wall clock. "Not due for another hour."

He ran back to the car and drove too fast down Rosamond highway.

"Come on!" He willed the vehicle to find some extra grunt.

Sarah wasn't home; her car was gone.

He looked at his watch.

Out of time.

CHAPTER THIRTEEN

It was surprisingly clear as they coasted over the southern border of Alaska.

"Civilisation," Clifford said over the intercom as he peered out the small triangle of window on his left.

Red looked out on his side and saw a distant cluster of orange lights ten miles below. He checked his chart using a light on the end of a tube.

"Anchorage. Does that count as civilisation?" He unfolded the paper and looked to the far top of the land mass and their destination. "Still eight hundred miles to run. Let down in about twenty-five minutes."

"Roger that."

A pale glow was forming on the eastern horizon, the first flames of daylight. Twenty minutes later, the clouds began to build thousands of feet below them.

Clifford drew back the jet-engine throttles and lowered Daedalus's nose. By the time they passed ten thousand feet, they'd lost visibility in the grey mass of cumulus.

Occasionally, a gap opened and Red squinted ahead, searching for the distant lights of Wainwright Field.

"They should stand out a mile in this wasteland, if it wasn't for the damn cloud."

"As long as it's broken, we've got a chance," Clifford said.

Red gave him a second course correction. They were down at six thousand feet now.

"This is it. We're going to need some visual soon."

The landing lights of Daedalus created a white halo around the nose. Droplets of water in the wet air glistened and twinkled.

Red leaned forward, putting a hand on the panel. His eyes searched the reflected light, looking for gaps.

Without good sight of the runway, they simply couldn't land.

"There!" Clifford shouted and pointed left of the nose, but as Red looked across, the aircraft swept into more cloud. Clifford turned his eyes back down on the instruments. Red's eyes searched with even greater urgency.

Suddenly, another break, and the lights of Wainwright glittered.

"Tally!" He looked at the approach. There was more cloud about, but it seemed to bottom out about a thousand feet below them.

"Take us down quickly. Three thousand five hundred." Red didn't dare take his eyes off the approach lights.

Even in the orange-tinted sunrise, the field looked grey and dark from a distance. Red could just make out the construction compound for the hastily extended runway.

"Come left two-seven-five," Red added, cross-checking the heading indicator.

Clifford put them in a gentle descending turn to the left.

The approach lights moved left to right across the windshield, occasionally disappearing behind passing cloud.

"Dammit," he said and glanced down at the altitude. "Try two thousand five hundred."

Clifford continued down, but Wainwright was gone from view. Beads of sweat trickled down inside Red's helmet.

As Clifford brought the jet to below two thousand eight hundred, the visibility opened up again, and Red could see the oasis of runway lights once more.

"Visual! Come right . . ." He looked at the heading indicator and came up with a guess. "Three-five-zero."

Clifford complied and levelled at two thousand five hundred feet. Finally, he looked up from the panel.

"Got it! Prelanding, please."

Red found the checklist and read out the list of actions. Clifford had them stable now, with full flaps and gear down. He looked up in time to make the turn onto final. Much closer than they planned.

"One mile," Red said, estimating.

Clifford checked their descent and pulled the throttle back further. Red kept his head still and watched the threshold lights carefully. They remained stable in the same place on the windshield.

"Good job. Hold this."

A few seconds later, they passed over the fence, and Clifford raised the nose further to give Daedalus as smooth an arrival as he could.

The wheels thudded down, maybe a hundred yards short of the ideal touchdown point. Red let out a long breath into his intercom.

"I hear ya," Clifford said.

The cold blast hit Red like sandpaper being rubbed on his face.

Dave Gomez, at the bottom of the aircraft steps, bundled into a giant fur coat, laughed at him. "What were you expecting?"

Red looked across to see the C-130 that had arrived in the night.

"Any trouble getting in?" Brad Walker asked.

"Not at all," Clifford said, and shared a glance with Red.

The sky was now mainly blue. "We should have waited ten minutes," Red said.

Walker looked up at the sky. "Don't be fooled. Weather's coming."

"Can't come soon enough," Gomez said. Red raised an eyebrow. "Soviets launched another satellite twenty-four hours ago. Right now, we want cloud cover."

Red looked back at Daedalus as the ground crew took control. "You really think they have no clue at all?"

Gomez shrugged. "How could they? I mean, sure, they might have got lucky today, the first time she's been out in daylight. But even then, they'll have no idea what they're looking at. Believe me, I wouldn't be in a job if they knew so much as the project name."

The ground crew attached a tractor to Daedalus. A new, purpose-built hangar sat on the edge of the hardstanding about six hundred yards away.

"I've never seen her in the daylight before," Clifford said.

Walker nodded. "Makes us nervous."

The crew pushed her backward, with Dupont in the cockpit, overseeing the repositioning.

"We'll show you around," Walker said. "Not that there's much to see. Then get some rest. We'll brief you on the latest situation over dinner tonight."

. . .

Sarah got in from her late shift at the BX; the house felt cold and quiet.

She toyed with a note, left on her register.

Your pilot friend came looking for you.

She drove past the A-TEC lot and saw his car. But the building was out of bounds for the likes of her.

He was gone. She could feel it.

She slumped on the couch that ran under a window in the kitchen, pulling her legs up and curling into a ball.

Why had she allowed herself back in this situation?

I'm such a fool.

After a few minutes, she felt slightly better. Nothing like a good cry.

The refrigerator was bare, and she thought about sitting at the bar eating chicken and talking with Maggie. It was too tempting, plus the company would be good for her.

As she went to grab her keys, her eyes settled on the empty hook where the spare set to her parents' house should have been.

Clifford and Red had to share a bare converted office room with two makeshift beds. After the flight, they dozed the day away, preparing their body clocks for more nocturnal activity. Red was woken by the sound of wind buffeting the windows.

Next to their room, a staircase led up to the control tower and radar room. Red walked in the opposite direction along a dimly lit corridor. At the far end he passed an armed guard into a large briefing room that had apparently become an ad hoc communal space for eating and passing time.

A map table filled the middle space. Men sat or lay on government couches along the walls.

The NRO men were chatting by themselves, looking at charts.

"Who's the guard?" Red asked quietly.

Gomez looked across to the armed soldier in camo. "Ever heard of the CIA Special Activities Center?"

Red shook his head. "No."

"Good."

Clifford arrived and immediately looked at the charts and maps.

Walker tapped a small pile of papers. "This is your bible for the missile release. You'll find the latest window calculations here." He lifted one of the sheets. "The earliest launch is nineteen-thirteen local the day after tomorrow. The latest you can go is oh-two-one-two. They are the last seven passes when the satellite's track will be predictable. After that, it begins its tumble."

"As discussed at Groom," Gomez said, "it looks like you'll be landing in Europe, and we don't want the asset airborne in the daylight, so we're aiming for the earlier launch." He reached across for a new set of papers. "Here's the forecast for here and the alternative landing sites."

Red took the sheet and squinted. "Snowstorms, gusting forty-five knots. That's marginally better, but still marginal." He glanced across to the windows. Horizontal snow was illuminated by the apron lights.

"There won't be much respite. So you need to plan on an instrument departure."

Clifford shrugged. "Like we said, if we can see the white line on the runway, we can get her up."

"From the alternates, we like Machrihanish," Gomez said, pushing a map forward. The airfield, nestled on the outer reaches of the west coast of Scotland, was circled. "It's remote, and we control it."

"Weather?" Red asked, looking at Clifford, who had the forecast sheet.

"Better than here, but not great for a visual approach at night."

"Where else is there?" Red asked.

"Bardufoss," Clifford said. "Just south of Tromso in Norway. Doesn't look too bad. But still dicey."

"Is that it?" Red asked, looking at the map, with the North Pole at its centre.

"Worst-case scenario is Mildenhall," Walker said, pointing to a circle on the eastern side of the UK. "But it's close to population, and it could compromise the secrecy of the project. We'll transmit the latest weather and make a recommendation once you've released the missile."

Gomez opened a new air chart and placed it over the top of the map. It covered a few thousand square miles showing the Russian coast on one side and Canadian islands on the east. A huge stretch of empty Arctic Ocean sat in the middle. Over the ocean, miles from anywhere, was a rectangular box with a dotted line running through its centre. Each dot was marked with a time.

"Now, for the release itself, we've widened the box to fifty square miles. Your actual release time depends on your precise position."

Red and Clifford leaned over and studied the figures.

"The farthest point from the coast, which we prefer, is here." Walker's finger landed on a cross on the dotted time-line. "Oh-three-thirty-eight and seventeen seconds. That's GMT. Which is an hour and fifteen after the earliest departure from here."

"What's the margin?" Red asked.

Gomez and Walker looked at each other.

"We figure you have about twelve seconds either side and maybe ten miles from the ideal launch spot," Gomez said. "But we can't know for sure. So we'd like you to be as precise as possible."

"Twelve seconds?" Clifford said. "Seriously?"

"The satellite's traveling at seventeen-thousand miles-per-hour. If you shoot early or late, it'll be out of range. You need to give the missile the best chance of an intercept."

The wind chose that moment to gather pace and emit a low howl as it swept across the low roof above them.

After a few moments mulling over her plan, Sarah came to a resolution and headed to the car.

The drive to her parents' old place on Sierra took about ten minutes. Leaving her vehicle on the road, she walked up to the front and opened the screen door.

She peered through a small window. The view was distorted by the curved pattern in the glass, and the image was impossible to resolve.

Stepping on to the porch, she examined the front windows either side of the door. Both had drapes drawn across, as usual.

Sarah walked around the back of the house. It was hard to see anything in the evening dusk.

Drapes were also drawn across the back. But the rear door had only a battered old blind, hanging lopsided. She moved closer and put her hand to the glass.

Between the broken slats, she could see into the rear hall and part of the front room.

She stared for a second before shifting her position to try to see more of the interior of the house.

"What the hell?"

As predicted, the weather continued to worsen as darkness fell.

Red made his way up into the control tower's "glasshouse." It was empty. He took a seat and watched the snowstorm. The wind buffeted the building and caused the odd bang outside. He looked at the large angled windows and figured everything up here was overengineered for the extreme weather. Or at least, he hoped it was.

He could just make out a pair of armed guards huddled next to a building close to the tower, every inch of their bodies covered and protected from the elements. Beyond that, the only movement he could see was the regular sweep of the runway by a snowplough with orange flashing lights.

The idea of launching in weather like this . . .

He heard a noise behind him and turned to find Dupont emerging up the stairs.

"Jesus, you scared me."

"Ah. Sorry, Red. I thought it was empty." He started to head back down.

"It's fine. Come on up."

Dupont paused and then continued up. He was wrapped up in full cold-weather gear.

"You heading out?"

"I left some stuff in the Hercules."

"I would leave it. You'll barely see your hand in front of your face out there." Red turned back to the surrounding glass windows.

Dupont stood next to him. "Why are you in the dark, Red?"

He shrugged. "Just checking the conditions. You think we can get airborne in this?"

Dupont looked out. "Taking off? Yeah. Forget about landing, though. But they've got a helluva snow-clearing operation going on. You'll have a clear strip and hopefully a dip in the wind. You'll get her away."

"I wish I had your confidence, Mr Dupont," Red said, and laughed.

"You'll be surprised what you're capable of, Red."

Red looked at him, the older man's face lit in the sodium glow. "Thank you, Brandon. I wouldn't have got this far without you."

"Forget it."

Red stood up. "Right, I'm going to eat." He made for the stairs but paused after his first step down. "By the way, what are you doing up here?"

"Same as you. Checking on the weather."

Flat plains spread out on either side of Sarah's Jeep Wagoneer as she sped along Rosamond Boulevard. The sun had begun its rapid descent below the horizon, and she flicked on her headlights. Putting her foot down, she chided her dad's old car's lack of power, finally edging it past seventy MPH.

At the Edwards gate, she flashed her base pass.

"Don't you work in the commissary, ma'am?" the guard said, looking across the road to the large store.

"I do. But I have a meeting with Colonel Montgomery at A-TEC."

The guard stepped back and opened the barrier.

After parking and walking to the A-TEC front door, she

paused. It seemed quiet. Most people had long gone, but she knew from experience, the unit operated all hours.

She pushed open the door and for the first time ever, stepped inside.

The main office looked very ordinary. Rows of desks, with a few side rooms scattered around.

"Sarah?" A voice came from behind her.

She turned to see one of the pilots, Jimmy Cofferr, packing his case for the day.

"Jimmy. Is Colonel Montgomery here?"

Cofferr studied her for a moment. "You know you're not supposed to be in here?"

"It's important."

He slowly stopped latching his leather case and walked over to a corner office, obscured by drawn blinds. Sarah watched as he tapped on the door and stiffened his back before entering, closing the door behind him. She stood there, feeling self-conscious in the centre of a secret office she had no right to be in.

A moment later, the door opened, and Cofferr waved her over.

"My dear," Montgomery said, as she entered his office. "How lovely to see you out from behind that cash register."

"Hello, Tucker."

"Take a seat."

As Sarah sat down, she glanced back towards Coffer, loitering by the door.

"Thank you, Jimmy," Montgomery said, and the test pilot withdrew, closing the door behind him.

Sarah looked beyond the colonel to the apron outside his office. Several jets were being towed, presumably away for the night. She never was much good at knowing which aircraft was which, but she recognised the T-38 Talon they often talked about.

Montgomery had a half smile on his face and glanced back to see what she was looking at. "Hopefully there's nothing classified out there. Now, to what do I owe this unexpected pleasure?"

"It's Brandon Dupont. I think you need to see something."

"Okay," he said slowly.

"Not here, in Rosamond."

"You want me to go thirty minutes into town? Come on, Sarah. What's on your mind?"

Sarah shuffled in her seat for a moment. "I've always thought there was something . . . off about him."

"Off?"

"Odd. Like . . . I mean, I don't know exactly how to put it." A hint of impatience crept across Montgomery's face. "It's his house. It's empty."

"Empty?"

"I know he's deployed. Obviously, I don't know where. But I understood it was just a few days."

Montgomery gave a shake of his head. "Sarah, I can't discuss—"

"I know. I'm not here to get any information from you. I just want you to know what I saw."

"An empty house?"

"Completely empty. I mean *bare*. Not a thing left."

Montgomery narrowed his eyes and seemed to be trying to work out what to do with this information.

"Perhaps he lives like that? He's a simple guy."

"Nobody lives like that. Tucker, he's not coming back. I'm sure of it."

. . .

Red and Johnny Clifford ate beef stew with potatoes. The communal room was filling with ground crew, engineers, and agency staff. No one wanted to be outside if it wasn't absolutely necessary.

Some ate, others chatted, a few slept.

Gomez and Walker sat on a bench against the wall.

"You two ever apart?" Red asked.

"Sure. I let him shower alone," Gomez said. Red laughed at Brad Walker's obvious discomfort.

Johnny Clifford got up and headed to a small fridge on the floor near the door. He returned with four bottles of Coors beer.

"Gentlemen," he said as he snapped the tops off.

The four of them clinked bottles.

"To a successful Operation Falling Star," Walker said.

"Amen," Clifford replied.

Red shifted his empty food tray to one side and dropped down on the bench next to Gomez. "So, how does someone end up working for the National Reconnaissance Office on a black project like this?"

Gomez took a swig of his beer. "Brad and I met on the U-2 trials."

"CIA?" Clifford asked.

"Yeah. But after Gary Powers was shot down, they began to wind up the operation. A bunch of us were told to find other work."

"Not quite true," Walker said. "If you remember, we were assigned to the DoD as pen pushers. Sorting clearances for the DIA!"

"Oh, yeah. That's right. They tried to get us to join the mass ranks of office dwellers."

"How'd you get out of that?" Red asked.

"Brad and I had investigated satellites. Even before

Powers, we'd worked out it was the future. And so, we somehow convinced the NRO that we had the type of experience in recon that they would need. Amazingly, it worked."

"Not for everyone," Walker said. "Poor old Leo Rodriguez ended up with a suitcase and necktie, as you well know, Red."

Red winced at the memory. "I hadn't thought about Leo for a while. Did they ever catch the guy who killed him?"

Walker shook his head. "Nope. They think it was a robbery that went wrong." He paused. "We couldn't get over it. How someone the size of Leo could be overpowered by some punk in a rest area."

Red laughed. Walker looked up at him. "You find that funny?"

"Well, sort of. He wasn't exactly an athlete."

"Are you serious?" Gomez said. "What's your idea of an athlete? Six foot three and two hundred pounds is athletic where I come from!"

"He played college football for Memphis State for a season," Walker added. "Pretty decent tight end, apparently."

"I can believe that," Gomez said. The two men clinked their bottles together.

Red stared at them. "Leo Rodriguez? You're talking about the DIA guy who came with me to Columbus?"

"Yeah. You did actually meet him, right?" Walker asked.

Red spoke slowly. "The Leo Rodriguez I met was small, bald, and fat."

There was a sudden hush in the room. All eyes were on Red.

The wind buffeted against the outside walls.

Walker and Gomez slowly rose from their seats.

· · ·

"Government cars go a lot faster than mine," Sarah said, from the back of Tucker Montgomery's Ford Galaxie.

"They do when Bill drives them," Montgomery said.

"Thank you, Colonel," the driver said, accelerating further.

"Thank you for listening to me, Tucker," Sarah said.

"No problem. I was done for the day, anyway. You know, I'm sure there will be an explanation."

"Maybe," Sarah said quietly.

The car entered the outskirts of the town.

"Another two blocks, then make a left," Sarah said.

After the left turn, Bill pulled over. Sarah climbed out and led the colonel to the house.

It was dark, and the dim streetlights did little to penetrate the drapes and blinds. She led Montgomery around the back, and he shouted to the car.

"You got a flashlight, Bill?"

The driver handed over a long, black, government-issue light. Sarah stood to one side as Montgomery shone it inside and pressed his face up against the glass of the back door. The beam swept around as he peered through the gap in the broken blind.

Eventually, he stood up.

"It just, you know, looked odd," Sarah said, suddenly embarrassed to have dragged a four-bird colonel all this way to stare at nothing.

Montgomery stepped away from the door; Sarah's heart sank. But it was only to give him some space. In one sharp movement, Montgomery shoulder barged the door, almost knocking it off its hinges.

Sarah yelped with surprise and stared into the open space.

"Figured we might as well have a proper look around,

now we're here," he said, and trudged in. "The government will pay for the damage."

The lights came on as Montgomery fiddled with a couple of switches on the wall.

The place was indeed empty.

They peered into the back bedroom. The bed didn't even have sheets on it. The kitchen had some clean plates on the top, but no evidence of food.

In the living room, a tatty sofa and two bare chairs were all that remained.

Sarah held her hands up. "Don't you think this is odd? No photographs, no mail? It's like no one ever lived here."

"You sure he did actually live here, Sarah?"

"Yes, Tucker. We called on him." She paused, remembering the occasion. "Not that he opened the door."

The colonel grunted and moved to the hallway between the living room and kitchen. Sarah followed. As he walked past an under-stairs cupboard, he paused, looking down. Sarah noticed it, too. Marks on the edge of a floorboard, with a small fresh splinter of wood.

Montgomery tapped it with his foot. The board was very slightly loose.

He crouched and ran his hands over the bare wood.

"What is it?"

He opened the cupboard door and shone his flashlight, feeling to the end of the plank. He tried to prise it up with his fingers.

"See if there's a knife or something in the kitchen, will you, honey?"

"You need to be clear about this, Red," Walker said, staring at him. "Leo was tall. Your guy was nothing like that?"

"No. Absolutely not."

"You know what this means?"

"What?"

"The real Leo may have been killed before you even met the guy who told you he was Rodriguez. Jesus Christ, he was probably his killer. How could the FBI have been so fucking dumb?"

"So," Gomez said, "if Leo Rodriguez wasn't who he said he was . . ."

"Where is Brandon Dupont?" Walker said, as he withdrew a handgun.

"Easy, Brad," Clifford said. "We don't know anything for sure yet. Let's just ask him a few questions."

"Where is he, Red?" Walker asked again.

Red shook his head. "Last I saw him, he was in the control tower."

Montgomery finally got the floorboard up with the help of a kitchen knife.

He pressed his head to the ground, and with the flashlight, searched the space under the surrounding boards. From what Sarah could see, it was empty.

The colonel reached in and retrieved a small piece of wire. He held it in the beam, turning it over before putting it to one side.

Reaching back in, he swept the area with his hand, stretching as far as he could.

"Doesn't seem to be anything else—" He stopped short.

"What?"

His arm was now as far as it would go, without removing more boards.

"I think there's something way back here." He withdrew

and sat up, grunting with the effort. "I think I just pushed it farther away." He looked around, but the hall and cupboard were empty. "Do you have something long and solid anywhere? A wooden handle or something?"

Sarah went into the kitchen and reemerged with a rolling pin. "This do?"

"Perfect."

Montgomery immediately shoved it into the gap below the floor and anchored it on a beam. Using the rolling pin as a lever, he pushed down on one end and strained to put as much weight on it as possible.

There was a sudden loud crack, and Sarah let out another yelp.

A second floorboard shattered around its nails.

Montgomery swung the flashlight around. Just visible was a dark object that had somehow found its way deep under the existing, nailed-down floorboards. The colonel carefully teased it out and picked it up.

He scrutinised it, squinting as he studied the side. It was about the size of a bag of sugar and had four small dials and a meter.

He passed it to Sarah. "How good are your eyes? Can you read that writing?" He pointed to the characters next to each dial.

She stared at them for a second. And shook her head. "It's not English. It looks . . ." She tailed off.

"What?"

"It looks like it's Russian, Tucker."

Montgomery closed his eyes. "See if the phone's working, would you, dear."

.   .   .

It didn't take long to establish the fact that Brandon Dupont was not in the building. The tower was empty, as were all the side offices.

A phone rang somewhere, but no-one seemed to think answering it was a priority at that moment.

Walker and Gomez, panic written across their faces, bundled themselves into thick fur coats that were hanging on hooks by the door.

One of the guards repeatedly tried to raise the patrols over a handheld walkie-talkie.

"It's no good. They probably can't hear a thing over the wind." He joined the NRO men as they headed outside.

Red and Clifford pulled on the last two coats and followed them.

Visibility was poor. The wind howled around them, clattering against the windows. Red screwed his face up as ice-cold air stung his skin.

"Jesus," he said as the wind caught his breath.

He ran to keep up with Gomez and Walker, hurrying in the direction of the aircraft hangar.

As they rounded the end of the office block, Red could just about make out one of the apron floodlights.

Between the hurrying agents in front of him, he glimpsed a horrible shape on the ground.

He immediately knew what he was looking at.

Walker and Gomez got to the bodies first.

Patches of red spread out in the snow beneath the two dead guards.

Red panted, staring at the macabre scene in disbelief. He shot a look at Johnny Clifford, who held a hand in front of his face to shield him from the onslaught of snow.

The wind noise grew even louder; a roar was building, as if a tornado was arriving to add to their misery.

Red's face ached; he wasn't sure he could stay out much longer.

"Look!" Clifford shouted, and Red followed his outstretched arm in the direction of the runway.

Just visible was a dark shape, moving swiftly left to right, about five hundred yards away.

The roar wasn't a tornado.

Walker started to run, but Red knew it was hopeless. The shape was a fuzzy silhouette in the snowstorm, but there was no doubting what it was.

Daedalus spat out large licks of flame as the after-burners roared into life. The noise became even more deafening as the aircraft thundered away from them.

Red stared for the final few moments of visibility until Daedalus disappeared into the storm.

PART 3

VASIL DEMICHEV

PROLOGUE

Rosamond, California
   May 21, 1947

Red stood and stared.

A dreadful, pained expression had frozen on his father's lifeless face.

Why had they come here? Why had they chased this falling star as if it were a toy to be played with?

He stepped forward, drawn to the outstretched arm.

Just far enough from the flames.

"Red, no!" Joe warned. "What if it blows!"

Distant bells clanged from the base fire service.

Their time here was limited.

Red's last moments with his father.

On the end of the arm: a battered wristwatch.

With one hand shielding his face, Red moved forward again.
Crouching.

He cradled his father's hand.

And quietly slipped off the watch.

223

CHAPTER FOURTEEN

Airborne over Alaska
November 1965

He sat in silent shock, the dark interior of the C-130 matching his mood.

Red couldn't bring himself to look up; he couldn't bear the prospect of making eye contact with the men he'd let down.

The atmosphere in Wainwright had been oppressive once word got around.

The soldiers repacked their equipment for the flight home in virtual silence.

No one had said it to his face. But he knew what they were all thinking.

He'd pushed for Dupont at every stage.

Without him, he wouldn't have even been in Alaska. He never would have been on the project. Never near enough to the country's greatest secret. Never in a position to steal it from under their noses.

225

Red felt his right hand; he was shaking.

The emotions were overwhelming him. But in the mix—along with the anger, betrayal, and shock—was something else.

Sorrow.

The inside of the Hercules was a sombre place. They'd lifted off during a break in the weather.

The initial outburst of fury from the government agents had subsided and been replaced by a glumness, a resignation that they were at the centre of an unforgivable incident. A blight on the United States that would live in intelligence infamy forever more.

Phone calls to DC had left them in no doubt about their predicament.

Red had overheard Walker saying President Johnson was incandescent with rage at the level of incompetence.

He couldn't fathom that the president of the United States was enraged about something he'd done.

His thoughts turned back to one person.

A man whose name he didn't even know.

Apparently, Colonel Montgomery had confirmed "Brandon" had been using a Russian radio from his house in Rosamond. Final clarification, as if they needed it, that the aircraft was headed east.

He had no idea how Montgomery had discovered the radio, but it had been a half hour too late.

They had all been too late. If they'd had that casual conversation about Leo Rodriguez only a few minutes earlier.

Instead, the realisation came just in time to watch Daedalus disappear into the weather.

Wainwright Field was just four hundred miles from the

Soviet border. They estimated the jet had enough fuel in the tanks to give it a subsonic range of fifteen hundred miles.

It was gone. Smuggled away from under their eyes and now resting in the middle of a vast area. Thousands of square miles. Presumably with Soviet aeronautical engineers poring over it.

The most embarrassing episode in United States military history, Walker called it.

Was he seriously comparing it to Pearl Harbor?

Red had asked Gomez if they blamed him, but he waved it off.

A dismissal or a deferral?

"Of course it's your fault," Red said to himself, the words lost in the din of the C-130.

He'd been played by the man purporting to be Rodriguez. And then played by the man purporting to be Dupont.

They had all been played.

But it was Red's naivete that had cost the United States a critical asset.

An asset designed to keep its people safe.

Red closed his eyes and tuned in to the drone of the engines.

They were woken for landing.

Weary-looking men fished around for straps and buckles to ensure they were secure.

On the ground, the ramp opened; daylight filled the musty cargo space. Reluctantly, Red picked up his belongings, following Clifford into the Edwards morning and an uncertain future.

Clouds scattered as far as the horizon. A rare day of rain for the desert.

"Captain Brunson?"

Red turned to see a slim man in a dark suit standing a few yards from the line of men exiting the aircraft.

"Yes."

"This way, please."

He glanced back at Clifford, who gave him a weak smile.

The man ushered him into the rear of a black car. They drove a short distance, towards an area of small buildings on the edge of the airfield. Red had taxied past them many times, assuming they were disused.

"What's going on?" he asked, voice wavering.

The agent in the passenger seat half turned. "Debrief."

They arrived at the collection of huts, set back from the security fence that bordered the airfield. The metal corrugated roofs showed signs of rust and neglect. They looked as if they dated back to the early days of Muroc before the place was called Edwards.

Perhaps Chuck Yeager operated from here?

Famous test pilots with unblemished records . . .

The agent walked ahead and opened the door of the largest hut.

It was murky inside. Dust swirled around the two lights that hung from the ceiling.

Four men stood by a table in the centre of the room. As Red entered, two of the men took seats, while the other two stepped back into the shadows.

The agent showed Red to his chair, facing the two seated agents.

"Captain Brunson, this is a formal debrief of the events

leading up to the disappearance of the XS-81," one of them said.

Red suddenly realised how tired he was. Drained, unable to think clearly.

"What the hell is going on?"

"We're here to question you. It's urgent, I'm afraid. Time is a factor."

The man who spoke wore a white shirt and black tie. His top button was undone, and his sleeves were rolled up. He had a pen in his hand, poised over a pad of yellow paper.

Next to him, a larger, older man in a jacket drew on a cigarette.

It was clear Red had no authority in this room. He was the most junior by some way.

But something made him want to push back.

"Who are you?" he heard himself asking.

The man in the white shirt looked surprised. "We're from the government."

"I guessed that. But isn't it polite to introduce yourself?"

The man turned to look at his colleague, who shook his head.

He turned back to Red. "My name's Ron. As I said, we have some questions. Tell me about your arrival in Mississippi."

Red considered insisting on a proper introduction. But in that moment, he realised something else.

He wanted to talk. He needed to unpack what had happened as much as anyone.

"I flew down."

"Commercial?"

"No, in an A-TEC jet. A T-38."

The man made notes. "Continue," he said, without looking up.

"I intended to stay on base, but Rodriguez asked me to join him at a motel."

"He was there, on base? When you arrived?"

Red shook his head. "No. He left a message."

"You didn't think that was odd?"

"A little. But when I met him, he said agents like him prefer to keep away from the crowds." His interrogator wrote quickly. There were awkward gaps. In the silence, Red thought he was being judged on every word, by every man. "I don't have a lot of experience working with spies," he added.

"You never saw him on base? You only met him alone?"

"Apart from when we were with the Duponts."

As he answered the questions, it started to look obvious. The impostor had made sure he wouldn't run into someone who knew the real Leo Rodriguez. After all, he looked nothing like him. And Red had gone along with the unusual arrangement without protest.

The questions became detailed. What did he wear? What did he sound like?

Red went over his description several times.

"What car did he drive?"

"An Impala. It didn't look like a government car. He said it was his."

After finishing a note, the agent looked up. "It was Rodriguez's. He was killed in it. After he left you, they put his body back inside and torched it."

A chill ran through Red. He'd been at the centre of murderous events, like a clueless schoolboy.

"You didn't notice anything off about him or the car? Beyond the fact he'd dragged you away from Columbus?"

Red did his best to recall the meeting. He was impressed at the vehicle. But there was . . . something. What was it?

"A stain."

The man looked up, eyebrows raised. "What?"

Red spoke slowly as he tried to picture the seat cloth. "There was a stain on the seats. I mentioned it. He said he'd spilled a shake."

There was a pause.

"Rodriguez was stabbed in the neck. I guess that was the only part of the vehicle they couldn't completely clean."

Red bowed his head. All that time in the car, casually chatting with a man who'd been part of an assassination just a few hours before. Sitting on the blood of his victim.

"Captain Brunson?"

Red looked up; the man stared back expectantly.

"I'm sorry. What did you ask?"

Rain pattered on the metal roof.

"Where did you go? That night."

"A diner."

"Describe the conversation."

Tiredness fogged his mind.

"Nothing out of the ordinary. He said he was unlikely to give Brandon the security clearance we needed."

They continued, chronologically. When he got to the Duponts' farm, the questioner pulled out the FBI report into Rodriguez's murder.

Red winced at a black-and-white photograph of a charred body slumped in the burned-out car. The image of his own father's twisted, burning body invaded his mind.

The questioner scanned the FBI notes. "Dupont's father pulled a gun on you?"

"Yes. Was he one of them, as well?" He already knew the answer. This had been a sophisticated trap.

"You didn't detect anything odd about any of the accents?"

Red shook his head. "They had southern accents. I'm from around here, so I'm no expert, but they sounded like what I'd expect in Mississippi."

As Red spoke, a drip of water landed on the desk. The white-shirted man snatched his pad away.

"We need to move," he said.

The jacketed man next to him turned and looked into the shadows.

From against the wall, another agent stepped into the half light.

"We'll take over the A-TEC offices. This is their mess. It's the least they can do."

Fifteen minutes later, Red arrived at A-TEC, along with the team of suited agents.

He stood outside the offices, looking in while two of the men went inside to deliver the news that they were about to commandeer the building.

He watched as Colonel Montgomery stood, hands on hips in the centre of the planning room. He looked indignant.

The two men waved the others in. Clearly, Colonel Montgomery's objections carried no weight.

Red was so tired he could barely function.

He stood against a wall, while the agents found a suitable side office. They chose the room he and Clifford had occupied during the Groom Lake flight-planning sessions.

Montgomery appeared in front of him, looking riled.

"You look like shit, Brunson. Go home and get some sleep, for Chrissake."

Red felt a burst of emotion at the coldness. His eyes teared up.

Montgomery softened his tone. "You've been through a lot, son. Get some rest. They can talk to you tomorrow."

"Will they arrest me?"

"Just go home. Rest. I'll deal with them."

Montgomery headed off to the side office. Red could just about hear the conversation.

"I'm sending him home, and that's that. You can talk to him tomorrow."

Montgomery turned back to him. "Go!"

Red slept fitfully on his return home and woke early.

His watch, unsurprisingly, had stopped.

The kitchen clock told him it was just before 0600. He had no idea what time it was when he'd made it to bed. It was still light, though. For all he knew, he'd just slept for fifteen hours.

A note from Sarah sat on the kitchen top.

Call me.

He didn't want to. Consumed with an issue he couldn't come close to discussing with an outsider, he wanted to be back in A-TEC. He needed to learn his fate.

He was secretly pleased that security meant he could never confirm to Sarah that she was right, that there was something "off" about Brandon Dupont.

He sensed she'd be pleased he was revealed to be an enemy.

Enemy. He toyed with the word. It didn't ring right. Brandon Dupont was a pilot. Accomplished, brilliant.

What would he say to Sarah? Dupont suddenly got reassigned.

As the gate barrier lifted for him, his thoughts came back to the unshakable sense of doom and responsibility.

Government cars littered the lot around the A-TEC. Inside, it was crawling with even more men in dark civilian suits and pressed white shirts. The A-TEC staff were crowded into a corner and the smaller side offices.

The agents huddled in urgent conversations. Walker and Gomez were nowhere to be seen.

As Red passed a desk, he saw a stack of papers marked *SECRET*. He looked down and started to read a list of Russian place names.

One of the suits quickly covered the pile up with a brown folder.

"Authorised eyes only," he said.

"Brunson."

Red turned to see his interrogation team waiting.

Back in his seat, the same arrangement faced him. A slim man in a white shirt made notes. Three others listened, without comment.

"Let's talk about Dupont. How did he fit in?"

Red went through the early days of Dupont's arrival. His quick adaptation to the flying.

"He was . . . a little socially awkward."

"What do you mean?"

Red pictured Dupont at Maggie's. Quiet, never quite in the rhythm of conversation. "Hard to describe. He didn't seem to be comfortable in the bar." The man continued writing down everything Red said. Every now and then, he shook his hand to stave off cramping. "But not everyone's comfortable like that," Red added.

"How was his flying? Did he seem familiar with the US way of operating?"

"He was good. Precise. I think he did have some issues with procedures at Columbus."

"Makes sense," the agent said.

Red had a flash of the B-57 patterns he'd witnessed from the end of the runway. "He was a talented pilot. No doubt about it. Of course, the crash wasn't his fault."

The agent stopped writing and looked up.

"The crash?"

Red looked among the men in the room. "You know he ejected? From a B-57 Canberra."

"No, Captain Brunson." The man next to his questioner spoke for the first time. "We didn't know."

"Jay Anderson was flying. He had this habit of cutting the power for a practise engine failure way early in the pattern. It meant flying a heavy, out-of-balance aircraft through a curved approach. He was demonstrating it when they stalled."

"And they ejected?"

"Brandon got out. Jay was killed."

The agent flicked through a pile of files to his left. Red could see the FBI report from Mississippi and then the files for the Dark Strike. He opened one of them.

"Here. Thought I'd seen his name. Anderson crewed the C-130 that ferried to Groom Lake each night?"

"Yes."

"The job Dupont got?"

A heavy silence filled the room.

"Let me be clear. Anderson dies, Dupont escapes. A-TEC then assigns him to Anderson's role on its most secret project?"

Red's mind reeled, but he stayed motionless. The implication crashed into his consciousness, but he couldn't focus, couldn't make sense of it.

"I don't think so," he said weakly.

"You don't think what?"

Red shook his head, trying to think clearly. "It must have been a coincidence," he whispered.

"Can you speak up, please?" The agent barked.

Red looked directly at him. "You've got this wrong. How could he have crashed deliberately, ensured Jay died, and he somehow survived?" He shook his head. "Choosing to crash a jet and eject? That's insane."

The man in the jacket leaned forward. "Son, you have no idea how far these people will go to get what they want. They don't care about lives. Not even their own."

The rest of the interview went by in a blur. Red got the impression they'd already been debriefed by others, probably Walker and Gomez.

They were particularly interested in the changes Dupont made to the aircraft.

"When did you first discuss the Max Q issue?"

Red shook his head. "I can't recall exactly."

"But how long between you discussing it and him providing the solution?"

He considered the talk on the ground, some of which he wasn't even part of. "A couple of days, I guess."

The man made his notes. Where was he going with this line of questioning? He was missing something.

After two hours, the agent put down his pen. He looked around the room and exchanged nods before turning back to Red. "We're done."

The men stood up quickly.

Red rose and left the room.

Apparently, still a free man.

Clifford was waiting for him outside. "Come on. He wants us."

.   .   .

Montgomery looked exhausted. Worry lines Red had never noticed ran from his eyes.

"How was it?" the boss asked.

"They think he killed Jay Anderson."

"What the hell?" Clifford said. "That's bullshit."

"I told them that," Red said.

"We're looking into it," Montgomery said slowly. "We had only Dupont's description for what happened on board. It's possible, however unlikely, that he sabotaged Jay's seat, then deliberately flew the jet into a stall."

"That's crazy," Red said. "I don't believe it."

Montgomery shook his head. "They've got it in for us. And they're not the only ones. Johnson's in a rage. Bob McNamara wants us shut down and handed over to the CIA."

"Christ," Red said. He felt sick. "They didn't arrest me. Do you think they will?"

Montgomery hesitated. "I don't think so. But if they shut A-TEC down because of this, you, me, Johnny . . . we'll be tainted and unemployable. You better dust off those applications to the airlines."

"With respect, sir, I'm staying here." Clifford looked between Red and Montgomery. "I say we fight back. This was the NRO's idea, right? The Utility Pilot bullshit?"

"It was," said Montgomery, "and we told them we were against it from the beginning."

"Then these fucking G-men need to understand how it works in the military. They order us to take on Jack Nobody from Mississippi, and when he turns out to be a spy, they try to blame us? Fuckers need to take responsibility for their own actions." He looked through the glass panel in the door.

Red had never seen Clifford talk like this.

Montgomery seemed distracted. He drummed his fingers on the desk.

"Well, they outrank me," he said eventually. "So, for the time being, we have to play their game."

"What in the hell are they actually doing, anyway?" Clifford asked. "What is there to do?"

"Containment. First, they want to find Daedalus. But they're staring at maps that cover two million square miles. Second, they want to find the rest of the cell that got Dupont here. Theory is, there's a Soviet handler somewhere. Probably the guy you met, Red. He would have planted the story about Dupont in the newspaper. The real Brandon Dupont is missing, of course. Probably dead, along with his family. They knew we were on the lookout for utility pilots, which means there's someone at Edwards or at the NRO working for them."

"You think they knew about Daedalus and planned all this to steal it?" Red asked.

Montgomery shook his head. "Hell, I didn't know about Daedalus three months ago. No, they were here to steal our secrets. Any secrets. They just got lucky."

Red shook his head. "So, who *was* he? He must have been a test pilot, and with a lot of experience. Think of all those mods he made. He helped Daedalus fly."

"He had that radio, remember? He always came back a day or so later with the ideas. He could have had the entire Tupolev Design Bureau at his disposal."

Red closed his eyes for a moment. "So that's why they were interested in the timing? They wanted to know when Dupont knew about something and when he came up with the solution. It must have been how he was working. It's why he held on to Sarah's spare keys and kept us out of the house."

Montgomery looked up. "Son, keep Sarah's name out of this. They don't need to know."

"Of course," Red said uncertainly. Not sure why the colonel thought he would mention her to anyone.

"I assume the US won't make any public accusations to Russia?" Clifford asked. "Demand they return the Daedalus?"

Montgomery shook his head. "Admit the Soviets stole a jet that's not supposed to exist and that contravenes our international commitments? The Commies aren't stupid. They took it knowing we couldn't protest."

The colonel clasped his hands together and rested his chin.

Clifford shook his head. "So, what do we do? How do we save A-TEC?"

"They'll give up looking for the Daedalus. When they decide it's gone for good, they'll decide who's to blame. Walker and Gomez will be fired, of course. Then me. Then you."

"What if they find Daedalus?" Clifford said.

"Find a jet hidden somewhere in a wilderness that stretches from the Arctic Circle to the Mongolian steppes? Believe me, they're not going to find it."

The two pilots stepped out the office. Red felt his knees might give way.

Clifford scanned the room, taking it all in. He looked full of purpose.

Red leant against the wall for support. "What can we do?" he asked. But Clifford walked away.

The person Red wanted most, the person who'd know what he should do, was now in the Soviet Union.

Without Brandon, he was friendless in A-TEC.

"Come with me," Clifford said, glancing behind him from across the room. Red followed as he strode towards their old office.

Clifford knocked and opened the door.

Three men in white shirts and ties stood around two tables pushed together. They were all smoking, and none of them seemed to look at the large map spread across the table. Red recognised the man who had been sitting next to his interrogator.

There were two other figures, seated in the shadows.

Dave Gomez and Brad Walker.

They sat quietly, looking haggard, expressionless. Red felt sympathy for two more men with the weight of failure on their shoulders.

The condemned.

"Can we help you?" one of the G-men asked.

"Could we take a look?" Clifford said and gestured towards the maps.

"Not a chance."

"We might be able to help."

"You've done enough."

"Jesus, man. It wasn't our fault—"

"We don't need you anymore. And *he* shouldn't be anywhere near here."

Red assumed the man had meant him, but his head was down, staring at the charts.

Somewhere in that vast land mass belonging to the USSR was Brandon Dupont.

A thick black line ran from Wainwright Field all the way to the heart of a mountain range labelled "Verkhoyansk." An arc radiated out either side. This was the extent of Daedalus's range.

"We flew with him," Clifford said. "Maybe we know something."

Red's eyes flicked across the contoured land. The eastern extreme of Russia was littered with areas of brown relief. Not great for airfields, but it also featured wide expanses of plains with dozens of small towns. To the south was a long peninsula that ran hundreds of miles into the Bering Sea. The Daedalus could have made it halfway down.

"If you know something, then you damn well better tell us," the suit said.

Red glanced up to see him taking a step towards Johnny Clifford.

"Are you fucking serious, man?" Clifford said, raising himself to his full five feet nine inches.

Was Johnny defending him?

"Take it easy, for Chrissake" A deeper voice joined the debate from the sides. The man from the interviews. He waved his cigarette. "But he's right. This is way beyond your pay grade now, Major."

Red went back to the map, sensing their time in the room was coming to an end.

"It's a big area, but there's not much in it," he said quietly. "Can't be that many military airfields?"

"And we're done here," the G-man continued. "Thank you, gentlemen."

They were ushered away.

Clifford stood outside the door for a second. Heavy breathing like a bull ready for a fight. He headed across the office back to Montgomery.

. . .

"What do you want me to do, Johnny?" The colonel lifted his hands into the air. "You think I like having these spooks commandeering my unit?"

"They're acting like they own the place. We're trying to help, for Chrissake." Clifford tapped his feet for a moment. "Maybe it's a way out for Red. If we can."

Red stared at Clifford.

"Leave them to it," Montgomery said. "They're pissed at everyone, including their own. It's important that it's their mess to sort out. Not ours." He sat down and pointed at a chair. "Red, sit down. Johnny, can you give us a moment?"

Clifford moved to the door.

"Johnny," Red said, and the chief test pilot turned around. "Thank you."

Clifford nodded and left the room.

Red slumped in the seat and let out a long breath. "I'm ready to go. In fact, I want to."

Montgomery tilted his head and leaned forward on his desk. "If you want."

Red looked out at the airfield. An F-104 from one of Edwards's other units taxied out. A shaft of sunlight reflected brightly off the silver wing. He blinked and looked away.

A sudden memory of a falling silver machine.

Death among the flames. A hand reaching towards him, imploring.

Imploring what, though? *Don't do it, son. Keep your feet on the ground.*

He'd ignored the warning. Choosing instead to continue his boyish fascination with supersonic aircraft and blue skies.

When he thought about it, his time with Dupont was the peak of his flying career. He'd found a partner who could get the best out of him. Finally, he was starting to believe he was capable. A highflier in every sense.

Until it crashed around him.

A very different crash from the twisted metal and burning fuel by the water tower. But a crash, nonetheless.

The blue sky replaced instantly by a battered, dark reality. A world of subterfuge and recrimination.

The 104 turned away, heading towards the long runway.

A voice in his head told him it was over. He'd never again be at the controls.

"How you doing?" Montgomery asked.

Red turned back to the colonel. He was being studied.

"I miss him."

"Dupont?"

Red nodded.

There was that sorrow again. Misplaced grief.

"He killed in cold blood, Red. He may have killed Jay."

Red picked at his fingernails. His mind raced, desperately trying to untangle the lies. There was truth in there, too.

He wanted to find a truth that accommodated his friend.

"Have we considered that Brandon was not acting of his own free will? That he was being threatened?"

"He's Russian. You understand that? Years of voice training and probably undercover work. You don't do all of that with a gun to your head." Montgomery pulled out a thin cigar from his case. "It's over, Red. You need to let him go. And Johnny needs to wind it down a notch, too. I don't want to antagonise these guys."

He lit the cigar.

"It's time to start thinking about you. Your future."

"You think I have one?"

"I think we can help you. Get you out of here quickly."

Red looked up. "Fire me?"

"Transfer you. Out of sight, out of mind. Maybe they'll forget."

He placed a letter on the edge of the desk. Red peered at it. On a DoD masthead, the subject heading read: *TEST PILOT EXCHANGE PROGRAM 1966*. In the letter's body was a list of openings for TPs of at least two years standing.

Patuxent River.

Istres, France.

China Lake.

Boscombe Down, England.

West Porton, England.

Linköping, Sweden.

"Sweden?" Red said, looking at the only destination that was underlined.

"Forget Sweden. It's a damn university. No flying. How about West Porton? A brand-new unit, doing similar work to us." The colonel raised an eyebrow.

"England?"

"We think it's best. Jay Anderson worked hard for this exchange slot. I'd like you to take his place."

Red turned the letter over in his hands. The gist was a two-year exchange to share skills.

"I'm honoured. But two years. That's a long time. A long way from home. Do I have a choice?"

"They have whisky in England. And girls. I can tell you from experience." He winked. "I'll need an application. With my recommendation and Johnny's, we think you'll be in good shape."

Red placed the letter back on the desk. "You're getting rid of me? Because it's my fault? Because I failed here?"

"Stop feeling sorry for yourself. This is the only way out

of here that doesn't result in you flying a puddle jumper for the next thirty years."

The door swung open, and one of the men in suits leant in.

"Do you people ever knock?" Montgomery barked at him.

The man ignored him. "We're gonna need more space. Can you clear out more people, please? Including him." He pointed at Red.

Red gunned the engine and ripped the car out of Edwards. By the time he entered Rosamond, his mood had still not improved.

He winced at the sight of Sarah standing outside his house.

As he got out of the car, she moved in and hugged him tightly.

"I'm sorry," she whispered.

He pulled back. "What for?"

"About Brandon, of course."

He paused. "What do you know?"

She looked quizzical. "Tucker didn't tell you?"

"Tell me what?"

She shook her head. "You boys and your secrets."

At the small kitchen top, Sarah told Red what she'd found and how she and Colonel Montgomery had discovered the Soviet radio.

At one point, she seemed taken aback by his expression. "What?"

"It's just . . . I don't know. I guess I always saw you so

differently from anything that happened at A-TEC. And now here you are suddenly in the middle of it all. It's funny."

"Funny?" she asked, raising an eyebrow.

"I was kinda dreading seeing you."

"Thanks!"

"Not like that. I wasn't looking forward to having to pretend nothing was going on at work. And now I don't. You uncovered Brandon Dupont. I can't believe it."

"You think I'm just a checkout girl?"

"Not anymore."

Sarah went to the sink and poured a cup of water. "What will happen to him?"

"What do you mean?"

"Brandon. Now he's found out. What will they do with him? Jail?" Red stared at her. She suddenly looked panicked. "They haven't hurt him, have they?"

Red steepled his hands and rested his chin on his fingertips.

"Red!"

"No. Nothing like that."

"Then what?" Sarah walked back to the table and sat down. "What is it, Red? Tell me!"

He took a deep breath. "I'm sorry, Sarah. If the colonel hasn't told you, I can't."

"Told me what, Red? You're scaring me. Is Brandon still alive? Please don't tell me they killed him." Her eyes filled with tears and worry. "I can't live with that."

He reached across and grabbed her hands. "It's nothing like that, I promise you. He's alive."

"Then what happened? I expected him to be arrested and to read about it in the papers."

Red shook his head. "You'll read nothing about him in

the papers." He leant back and tapped the table. "And I'm sorry. I can't say any more."

She pulled her hands away. "What?"

"I'm sorry, honey."

She stood up and puffed her cheeks out. "If it wasn't for me . . ."

He tilted his head at her. "You know how it is."

"Yes. I'm not part of your gang. I'm on the outside. You've made that clear. And yet you and Tucker expect me to keep your secrets for you. It would be nice if you'd show me a little more trust."

"I do trust you."

"Clearly you don't."

"Sarah." He felt his voice waver. "Don't be like this. I need you right now." He screwed up his face, embarrassed that he was on the brink of tears. "God, I'm so weak. Sorry."

Sarah sat down and put an arm around him. "What's wrong?"

He shook his head slowly. "It was all my fault."

"What? No. How was it your fault? You were ordered to recruit him, right?"

He stared at the table.

"He wouldn't have been in Alaska if it wasn't for me. I pushed for him at every stage. I trusted him. They trusted me."

"That's a good quality, though. It's not your fault. He duped you, honey."

Red took some breaths and tried to collect himself.

"I think maybe it was because he was my friend. And Johnny, he was so cold the whole time. I needed someone. Brandon was there for me."

Sarah rubbed his shoulder. "Surely you weren't the only one who fell for his routine?"

"They want me out."

"That's awful. And who the hell are 'they,' anyway? Surely not Tucker? He doesn't blame you, does he?"

Red shook his head. "I don't know. He wants to send me to England."

"England?" Sarah's voice was tinged with disappointment. Red had scarcely had time to think about her role in all of this. He'd never be able to take her with him. That was a privilege reserved for only married couples.

She removed her arm, but stayed where she was.

That protective instinct kicking in again.

Here comes the distance.

"What a mess," he said, more to himself.

"So, are you going to tell me what happened in Alaska?" Sarah asked quietly.

"You didn't trust him, did you? All the way through, you had your doubts. I should have listened."

Sarah shook her head. "No, that's not fair. I thought he was weird, a loner. I never for one moment thought he was a goddamn Russian spy. I went to the house because I was angry he hadn't returned my spare keys."

"He couldn't, could he? He couldn't risk you letting yourself in while he wasn't there."

"I guess not. So, Red, where is he?"

Red took a deep breath. "Maybe I could do with a new confidant. Now that the previous one is in the USSR."

She stared at him. "What?"

"Brandon wasn't just spying on us. He stole a secret experimental aircraft. Took it from under our noses. We were right on the northern tip of Alaska. A few hundred miles from the Soviet border."

"He was planning it this whole time?"

"It's scarcely believable, but we think so."

"When did this happen?"

Red looked up at her. "Let's just say if you'd gone to his house thirty minutes earlier, we'd still have the XS-81 and Brandon would be in a cell."

"I can't believe it. Do you know where he is now?"

"Well, that's the million-dollar question. Literally."

"So, what's happening at Edwards? They trying to find him?"

"The place is crawling with men in suits from the agencies. God even knows who they are."

Sarah put her hand back on Red's arm. "And they all blame you?"

They sat in silence.

Eventually, Sarah got up. "I still can't believe it." She crossed to the refrigerator; it was empty. "Wanna grab something at Maggie's? I think we could both do with a drink."

It was quiet in the bar.

They ordered the beef chilli to share and settled into their favourite booth.

Sipping on her beer, Sarah shook her head. "We all sat here the first time I met him. Remember?"

"I know. It's crazy."

They sat in silence for a while, Red constantly thinking back to his time with Dupont, going over every conversation, every walk together. The food arrived and they tucked in, both lost in their own thoughts.

"Have you thought about what you told him?" Sarah said eventually.

"When?"

"Whenever. I mean, you two seemed to get along. How

much does he know about you? They'll have a file in Moscow with your name on it."

Red thought about it. "A bit, I guess. But I don't think that was really what he was after. I think he was more interested in the other stuff."

"And how much do you know about him? I mean, did he ever give anything away?"

Red toyed with his bottle. "I've been through everything with them. I told them he was a bit awkward, but honestly, I didn't think there was much more to know about him. He was Brandon Dupont from Mississippi, who flew Sabres in Korea, worked the farm with his pop, and we persuaded him to give all that up and come here. Nothing else to know. Obviously, I should have done better."

"I guess he was being more guarded than we knew. Maybe he wasn't even drunk that night. Remember?"

"Oh, that night. I'd forgotten about that. Ha! No, I'm pretty sure he was wasted. For a Russian, he didn't seem able to hold his drink."

They finished their food and headed back to Red's, settling on the sofa.

Red stretched out, Sarah tucked in close, her arm draped over him.

"He slept it off on here," Red said. I put him to bed like a child.

Sarah wriggled down and rested her head on his chest.

But Red shifted and sat up.

"What is it?" she asked.

"Hmm."

Sarah stared at him, propping herself up on her elbow. "What?"

"Probably nothing, but when I come to think about that night, there was something odd."

"What d'you mean?"

"Do you remember, he told this cool pilot story about learning to land smoothly? Using a lake. And he seemed to talk about an airfield he knew like the back of his hand. Somewhere he'd flown a thousand patterns."

"Sorta," Sarah said. "He used the curve of the water somehow?"

"Exactly. He lined up his wingtip and hit the same landing spot perfectly every time. Like he'd cheated. It was funny until . . ."

"Until?"

"Until Jay asked him where it was. And Brandon couldn't answer. He couldn't tell us the location of this airfield he knew so well."

"He was drunk, though."

"Yeah, but Jay was right. Who forgets an airfield? I mentioned it again at the lake. I guess I always found it odd. I think he changed the subject. Damn, I completely forgot about it. And now, I'm just wondering . . . why didn't he want us to know?"

"What are you thinking?" Sarah asked.

Red stared at her.

"I'm thinking he made a mistake."

The next morning, Red raced into A-TEC early.

"Are they still here?" he asked as he bustled into the office.

"Who?" Jimmy Cofferr said.

"Them," he said, spying two of the suits in the map office. He marched in.

"You again," said one of the G-men as he folded up the last of the maps and slotted them into a leather briefcase.

"Where are Walker and Gomez?" Red asked.

The man shrugged. "The Labour Exchange?"

Red stared at him. "Put the maps out again."

"We've been through this—"

"Just put them out, for God's sake, and stop being so fucking petty. You want to find Daedalus or not?"

The men stared back. Red stood his ground, blood pumping. Slowly, they turned their attention to a dark corner of the room behind him. He swivelled. A figure he hadn't noticed was sitting cross-legged on a chair. He drew on a cigarette and nodded at his colleagues. That same man again. The monosyllabic agent.

They unpacked the series of charts that covered the eastern end of the USSR.

The man with the cigarette stood up and moved next to Red.

"I'm Special Agent Dick Vinari," he said, offering his hand.

"Finally, an introduction." Red shook it. "You already know who I am, obviously."

"You have some information for us, Captain Brunson?"

Red turned back to the table and leant across the maps. He began a methodical scan starting at the northernmost point.

His eyes darted from side to side, as he used his finger to trace the areas he'd covered.

The two men opposite shuffled their feet. He ignored them. Vinari kept still, chain-smoking next to him.

The land Red stared at was 95 percent empty.

"Where does everyone live?" he said.

"What are you looking for?" one of the men asked.

Red's finger darted from feature to feature, trying to be methodical and not miss any of the vast area.

"Lakes?" Vinari said, following his movements. "Are you looking for lakes?"

Red didn't look up, but continued his hunt. "A very particular arrangement."

"What, exactly?"

He hunted farther down the page, approaching the middle of the charts. "I'll know it when I see it."

Minutes ticked by. Red's eyes were straining. He needed a break. He fished a pen out his top pocket and placed it carefully on the map, then stood up and stretched.

The pen was only a few inches from the bottom of the chart; his heart sank.

Vinari sighed. "Let us in on the secret, Captain Brunson. Maybe we can help."

"Is this accurate?" Red asked.

Vinari looked down at the maps. "For the main geographical features, yes."

"What about the man-made features? The towns. Airfields."

Vinari paused. "We have other imagery, but I'm afraid that's highly classified."

Red furrowed his brow. "I don't understand. You have more up-to-date maps? Why can't I see them?"

"They're not maps. They're images, and they're not allowed out of a building in Maryland."

"But you know of stuff that's not on these maps? Airfields?"

Vinari nodded slowly. "We have a list."

"Can I see that? Can you mark them on the map?"

Vinari didn't respond. He folded his arms and looked at the charts on the table. Red watched as he toyed with his bottom lip.

"I'll ask. Give me a couple of hours."

It took Red a moment to realise he was being dismissed.

At 1100, he got a shout from the side office.

Inside, the maps had been covered by small strips of paper.

Six of them.

"These are airfields?" Red asked.

Vinari nodded. "Try not to make a draft. It took an age placing them."

But Red was already drawn to one small strip of white paper, almost directly in the centre of the land mass.

He leant in closer. "Omolon," he said, jabbing his finger. "But there's already an airfield marked, by the town. It's not what I was looking for."

"There's another airfield," Vinari said. "That's what the paper represents. Almost certainly military. Which is why it's not on the map."

Red looked again at the terrain. He'd seen the lake on his first pass, with its elongated northern shoreline, curving gently. But the town and its airfield were the other side of a river valley. Maybe ten miles from the water. No good.

However, the piece of paper was on the southern side of the river.

"Do you know precisely where this other runway is?" Red asked.

Vinari shook his head. "You want precise? I'll need someone to describe it over the horn. You'll have to leave the room again."

Before he got to the door, Red turned and walked back to the map. He took out his pencil, leant over the lake, and drew a line about one mile north that ran parallel to the shore, ending at the western extent of the water.

He put the pen down, to puzzled looks, and left the room.

Twenty minutes later, they called him back in.

Vinari stood, arms folded, in front of the table, waiting.

"How did you know?"

The atmosphere in A-TEC changed almost immediately.

Urgent meetings took place in every corner, and even outside on the apron. Red stood at the far side of the room in front of windows that looked out to the expanse of Edwards's taxiways and runways.

He wondered where so many men had been hiding.

A C-130 Hercules that didn't belong to A-TEC arrived on the apron.

Vinari seemed to lead the switch from investigation to action, spending an intensive couple of hours on the phone, in the side office. A group of men turned the central area into a makeshift command centre.

Another senior special agent arrived and gave his orders. It was difficult to tell who was in charge.

"Everyone not directly involved, please find somewhere else to work," he shouted.

"Excuse me." Colonel Montgomery emerged from his office. "I'm still the CO around here."

"Colonel, A-TEC is now being directly administered by the CIA—"

"The hell it is! You want to take us over? You better have a signed letter from President Johnson."

"It's okay, Hank." Dick Vinari emerged from the map room.

"Colonel, we appreciate your flexibility. We need a planning room, and we haven't got the time to relocate. So, we're going to have to use this space and some of your facilities. I know it's not ideal. But . . ." He looked around the room, and his eyes settled on Red. "If your boy here is right, we might clear up some of this mess, and I think we'd all benefit from that."

Montgomery surveyed the room, taking his time. "I'm staying here. You keep me informed."

"Fine. But we can't have other people in the office."

"Where the hell am I supposed to move an entire unit?"

"You're going to have to give them a couple of days off," Vinari said. "I'm sure they won't mind."

Montgomery looked over Red's shoulder to the airfield. "We have work—"

"Your other work doesn't matter this week," Vinari said, interrupting. "This is the only thing the White House cares about, believe me. And getting this right is your only hope of survival. Get in our way, and I'm afraid my report up the chain won't be favourable."

Montgomery glared at him. "Goddamn you."

"A-TEC's on the thinnest of ice, Colonel." Vinari softened his tone. "I suggest you lend us your full cooperation."

"Fuck," Montgomery said under his breath. He headed back into his corner office.

Vinari addressed the room. "That's it. If you're not working for us, find somewhere else to be." The staff cleared out, but Red stayed. Vinari looked across. "I'm afraid that includes you, Captain Brunson."

Red walked over to him. "Are you serious? I'm the only reason you've got a shot at this."

"You're also the only reason we're missing a billion-dollar airplane." Vinari spoke gently, but it sounded like a

Mafia man explaining the facts of life to an informer. "You've done your bit. Leave it to us now."

In the brightly lit office, Red got his first proper look at this mysterious man. Presumably CIA. Midforties, maybe. Short, neat brown hair, clean-shaven and a round face. He looked more like an accountant than a spy.

"What will you do?" Red asked.

"Destroy Daedalus. Leave no trace."

"I meant about him."

Vinari's expression didn't change. "Just leave the mission to us, Red. Join your friends. I expect they're in the bar by now."

The BX was quiet. Red walked into the front area that sold yard stuff for kids.

He glanced down the line of four cash registers, but she wasn't there.

"Can I help you?"

He turned. A middle-aged woman with huge hair bore down on him. Over her shoulder, he spotted Sarah, folding clothes onto a table.

"I'm fine, thank you," he said.

Sarah was in her own world, humming as she worked. She looked beautiful. A beautiful spy catcher.

He put his hands on her waist.

She jumped and turned. "Hey!" Sarah smiled, then playfully pushed him away. "You'll get me fired. What are you doing here?"

"An unexpected day off."

"Oh." She hesitated; he stayed next to her.

Slowly, she held up a sweater in her hands. "Well, I have to fold these now. I don't have an unexpected day off."

"I want to talk to you. Is there any way you can get off early?"

She looked at the white clock that hung high over the entrance and shook her head. "We shut at midday."

"I'll wait."

An hour later, Sarah emerged from the store, smiling. But this time it looked forced.

She climbed into the car and leant over to kiss him. "What is it, Red? What's happened?"

He started the engine and drove towards the main gate. "Let's get out of here."

Once they were on the straight road back to Rosamond, Red let out a long breath. "I think they're going to kill Brandon."

"What? Are you serious? Have they found him?"

Red's fingers tapped the steering wheel. "I found him. At least I think I have."

"The lake?"

He nodded.

"And now they're going to kill him?"

He lifted his shoulders and sighed again. "I don't know for sure. But these guys. They're serious. There's something about the way they operate. They're going to destroy the aircraft for sure. But I think they'll hunt for Brandon, too."

"And you think they'll kill him? Why? As a punishment?"

He shook his head. "No. Because he knows too much. Think about everything he learned here. And it would also send a message to the Russians."

Sarah stared out the windshield and slowly shook her

head. "Aren't there rules about that sort of thing. Conventions?"

"Not when it comes to spies. None of that applies."

They drove on in silence for a few minutes. Red blinked and wiped at his eyes.

Sarah put a hand on his shoulder. "Baby. Pull over."

The tears fell, splashing into his lap. He brought the car to a stop and turned to Sarah, falling into her embrace.

"Sorry. I don't know what's wrong with me."

"It's fine, baby. It's fine. It's a lot to deal with."

"I'm not dealing with it, am I?" He sobbed into her sweater.

After a few seconds of letting it out, he felt some composure return, but stayed locked in her arms.

"It's all too much. Everything I do makes things worse. I didn't think about it. I wanted to find Brandon to . . ."

Sarah pulled back and wiped his cheeks with the back of her hand. "To what?"

"Bring him back."

She stared at him.

"I know," Red said quietly, dropping his head. "They would never do that."

She pulled a handkerchief out her bag and set about cleaning up his face. "Baby, you were attached to him. I can see that. But . . ." She hesitated. "But it wasn't *him*, was it? He was playing a part. You don't even know his real name." She shrugged as she put her hankie away. "And let's face it, Red. He betrayed you. He's a traitor."

Red pulled back. "No. No, he wasn't. He was loyal to his country. And he was loyal to me."

"But he duped you. He was being loyal to manipulate you."

He shook his head. "No. Some of it was real. And for the first time in my life, I had someone to look up to."

He felt her hand go down to his wrist, her fingers brushing against the side of his watch.

He pulled his arm away.

"You never liked him."

"That's not fair, Red. I was suspicious. For good reason. You can't blame me for that."

"I'm sorry. It's . . ."

"It's okay." She stroked his hair.

"He doesn't deserve this. And I was the one who led them to him."

Twenty minutes later, they pulled into Rosamond.

They both glanced down Sierra Highway as they crossed it. A couple of long black cars remained at the entrance to the road leading to Dupont's house. What had they told the neighbours about why they were turning the place upside down?

Something caught his eye, a little farther down Sierra. A large collection of cars outside Maggie's. It would normally be closed in the middle of a weekday.

"Looks like they opened the bar," Sarah said. "Come on."

About forty men from the unit were well into their second or third drink. The noise level was rising.

Johnny Clifford spotted them enter and waved them over to the bar. "They thrown you out as well?" He picked up a couple of bottles and handed them over. He paused, looking at Red. "You okay?"

"Sure." Red downed half the Budweiser.

They joined the conversations. There was a holiday atmosphere, triggered by the most unlikely of circumstances.

Red leant into Sarah and whispered, "No one's discussing it. We're all so well behaved."

"You know the rules, Red. And so do I."

As Red downed his fourth, the doors swung open, and a pair of military policemen stepped inside. Some conversations stopped.

The two men walked down the three steps from the door and scanned the room.

"We're not doing anything illegal," someone shouted.

The rest of the conversations stopped; all eyes turned to the intruders.

One of the policemen took another step forward. "Captain Red Brunson?"

Red's back stiffened. "Yes?"

"Come with us, please."

The policemen said little on the drive back to Edwards. As they dropped him off, one of the officers escorted him all the way into the building.

"They must really want me here, huh?" Red said.

"Just doing my job, sir."

The main planning office had been transformed. Most desks had been pushed together to create one large table in the centre of the room, with spare chairs propped against the wall. Some men sat in huddles, hunched over piles of paper.

"He's here," Vinari said to a new man next to him. He was older, with white hair and dark eyes.

"You're Brunson?" the man said, loud enough that the

room quietened.

"Yes, sir."

"First, what makes you so sure he's in Omolon?"

Eyes swivelled back to Red. Men put down their pens.

Red didn't recognise anyone from A-TEC.

A voice piped up behind him. "You wanna have this conversation in private, Mr Doyle?" Colonel Montgomery said.

"No. We make this decision as a team." The man apparently called Doyle turned back to Red. "Why are you so sure, Brunson? Is this just a hunch or actual intel?"

Red took a breath.

"Like I told Mr Vinari, it makes sense."

"Makes sense? I'm gonna need more than that."

"Think about it. He gets airborne in terrible weather. We're too far north for a reliable compass. So, he has to climb above the weather to see the stars. He can then navigate roughly using the pole star. Remember, he's by himself in a cockpit designed for two crew, so he's busy. I'm willing to bet he knows the frequencies for this airfield by heart. So, it's his best bet. Dial them in and try to get close enough to pick something up."

"And you think that's Omolon. Why?"

"It's the one airfield in the world he knows intimately. He described its layout to me. Of course, I didn't realise it was Omolon at the time, but I'm sure that's what he was referring to. He'll know the area well enough. It's like my training base at Columbus. After a year of flying in and out, bashing the pattern, planning nav routes, I could have found my way back without a map from a thousand miles away."

Doyle appeared to be appraising him. "You need to be sure, son. We're about to spend a lot of resources on this mission."

"I know him. And I know this sounds odd, seeing as he stole Daedalus and all, but he's not one to take chances in the air. He would have followed the best option. And I'm willing to bet that was getting it on the ground at Omolon."

Doyle drew in a long breath and exhaled. Vinari whispered something and looked across the table at a small group to Red's left. "Tell me about the convoy, again."

Red watched as a group of three men shuffled papers. One man held up a single sheet with handwritten notes.

"Three low loaders left Neryungri yesterday. Going north."

"North? Isn't Omolon east for them?"

The man took a map and held it up to Doyle. "It checks out. You'd need to go north to hit the main route east. Takes at least two days solid driving. Our best bet is they'll break the airplane into three parts, drive it back on the trucks to Neryungri. Then it's on the train back to civilisation, or what passes for civilisation in Moscow. Probably to the Tupolev plant."

"So, you agree with Brunson?"

The men consulted with one another. The leader glanced to Red and back to Doyle. "Omolon lines up with what we're seeing. That's all we can say."

Vinari leant across and spoke quietly to Doyle again.

It was clear who was in charge; everyone deferred to Doyle.

He slowly looked around the room, then nodded.

"Good enough. We go."

The noise of twenty separate conversations started up again.

Doyle turned back to Vinari and two other senior agents. Behind them in the shadows, Montgomery nodded at Red, before retreating to his office.

Red was left standing alone. Briefly forgotten. The men outside seemed to be moving equipment. He walked up to the window and got a closer look. They were dressed in dark, nondescript military clothing. No units identifiable. On the ground were blankets, and in neat rows they placed guns, ammo, grenades, and equipment Red didn't recognise. Enough to invade a small country.

"Jesus," he said under his breath.

As he watched, they added more material from the back of nearby vehicles.

A man in a black beret seemed to be directing the operation. He looked bald underneath the hat, and he had a bushy black beard. He was also about seven feet tall.

The man pointed at a line of similar-looking guns: curved with a wooden stock. Not American. The weapons had been placed neatly into an open black chest, which the men closed and hauled onto a trolley. Moments later, it was wheeled away to the waiting Hercules.

"I'm guessing you've never been on the inside of one of these operations?"

Red whipped around to find Brad Walker standing next to him.

"You!"

Walker laughed. "Yeah, me. I'm not in Siberia yet." He pulled out a packet of cigarettes and gave one to Red. "Oh, the irony."

"What irony?"

Walker nodded to the soldiers outdoors. "These guys are going to actual Siberia. Mine will be metaphorical." He lit their cigarettes. "I'm guessing some paperwork job back in Maryland."

"But you're still here."

Walker drew heavily on the cigarette and exhaled

towards the window. "They want as much intel as possible. They're nervous. This is a big risk. If they get to Daedalus and . . ." He hesitated. "If they get to Daedalus, all good and well. The Soviets can't complain, or won't complain. But if it goes wrong? If they come down somewhere Daedalus ain't? Well, the Politburo will describe it as an unprovoked invasion by the US. And that's dangerous. They're messing with fire here, based on some pretty flimsy intel."

"And of course, the US would have no way of explaining it away, without admitting we'd built an aircraft to attack their satellites?"

"Exactly. That's the only reason I'm still here. To tell them what I know. I'm guessing that's why they brought you back."

Red turned and faced the room, enjoying the calming effect of the tobacco. He shook his head. "They didn't ask me much. Just wanted to know how I figured Brandon was in Omolon."

"They haven't asked you about being the ID agent yet?"

"The what?"

"They need someone to positively ID Dupont. My advice is to follow my lead and refuse. You don't want to be a part of what happens out there. Not to mention that fact you'll be in a shitstorm of bullets."

Red watched Doyle across the room; Vinari was stuck to his side like glue.

"They'll kill him? Execute him in cold blood?" Red said and looked directly at Walker.

Walker avoided his eye and shrugged. He took another draw on his Marlboro. "Of course."

"And you agree with that?" Red asked.

Walker shuffled his feet, eventually looking back up at Red. "Vasil," he said.

"What does that mean?"

"That's his name. Vasil Demichev. And yes, they're going to kill Vasil Demichev. The Soviet spy."

"Kill a man just for doing his job? He's a test pilot first. Like all of us. He just happened to be on the wrong side. But . . ."

"But? Being on the wrong side is a big deal around here."

"But he's one of us."

"No, he isn't."

"He was, though. He spoke perfect English. He flew brilliantly, contributed to our success. He fits in here," Red said, as earnestly as he could. "Surely, we could bring him back?"

Walker laughed. "Oh, Red. I love your optimism and your sense of humanity, but it's out of place here, buddy. These guys lost good men on the beach in Cuba four years ago. I doubt they're in the mood for handshakes and forgiveness. They're not flying a thousand miles into enemy territory on a recruitment drive. They need to destroy our secrets. And that's not just the airplane. It includes the knowledge he's carrying around."

"Cuba? You mean the Bay of Pigs." Red nodded towards Doyle and Vinari.

"Andrew Doyle is deputy director at Langley. He's in charge. The troops out there are from the Special Activities Center. Also CIA. You're now standing in a room where the DIA and the National Reconnaissance Office are the second- and third-most important organisations. All we need now is for the White House chief of staff to turn up. This operation just got pretty damn big." He finished his cigarette and found an ashtray on the windowsill. "But it needs some big balls and some big authority. Like I say, if they fail to find Daedalus, and Vasil Demichev, this'll make the Bay of Pigs catastrophe look like a typing error."

Walker patted Red on the shoulder and wandered away.

Red stood alone against the window, looking across to the rearranged desks. One pile of papers looked familiar, and he wandered over.

A loose brown sleeve covered up a couple of small notebooks. He opened them and leafed through the pages, immediately recognising Dupont's drawings. Beautiful technical sketches of leading edges, trim tabs, and even a sketch of a panel inside Daedalus, with a recommendation for where an extra control should go.

The lines of the sketches were extraordinarily straight, and the accuracy in the detail was mesmerising.

There was passion and even love in this work.

He thought of the unsuspecting Vasil, sitting at a desk in Omolon, occupied with the latest technical problem, his mind on aerodynamics and thrust ratios. Not bloody Communism. Or Capitalism.

He doubted Vasil had a political bone in his body.

He was a pilot first. Like his friends in Edwards.

But politics was coming for him.

An American aircraft would arrive. A man would find him and put a bullet in his head.

"Brunson!" A shout went up. Red turned to see the bearded soldier inside the room, next to Doyle. It was Vinari calling him.

"This is Gabriel," Vinari said, as Red walked over. The soldier nodded, offering no handshake or surname.

"You have a recent photograph of Demichev?" Gabriel asked, his voice deep and coarse. The voice of a man who shouts for a living.

Red shook his head. "Nope."

"None?" Gabriel looked annoyed.

"We're not allowed cameras on base, and I can't think of

an occasion anyone's brought one out off base."

The men turned back to a folder in Vinari's hands. Red peered over his arm and glimpsed a black-and-white image of a young man in an oversize USSR military hat.

He laughed. "How old is that?"

Vinari showed him the file. It was Dupont, all right, but several years ago. A formal ID picture, Red guessed. The handwriting on the white edge of the photo was in Russian, an alphabet Red couldn't begin to read. But the notes under the picture were in English.

Demichev, Vasil Mikhail. Active c.1963—

"This his CIA file?" Red asked.

"It's pretty bare."

Gabriel took the folder from Vinari's hands. "Is this definitely him?" He directed his question at Red.

"I think so, but that's twenty years old, at least."

"Shit." Gabriel pushed the folder back into Vinari's hands. "You gotta do better than that. We'll need to be sure. Find another picture."

"Before tonight? Forget it."

"You're going tonight?" Red asked.

"Thank you, Captain Brunson," Doyle said. "That will be all. We need to clear the room before the brief."

Vinari turned to Red and looked apologetic. "That's you, then, Red. Thank you for your help." He walked towards the door, beckoning Red to follow.

But Red stood his ground. He looked up at Gabriel. "I'll find him for you."

There was a pause before Vinari stepped back in. "Out of the question. This is a highly classified mission. You are already under orders to deny any knowledge of anything you've seen today. Plus, you're a test pilot. This is a different world. You'd be a liability."

But Gabriel was appraising him. "It's going to get messy," he said, apparently ignoring Vinari's protests.

Vinari swivelled his head between Gabriel, who stared at Red, and Doyle. "You're not serious?"

Doyle didn't respond.

"I can get him back," Red said softly.

Gabriel snorted.

Vinari shook his head. "This is exactly what I'm talking about. This is crazy. You can't take an amateur on a mission like this."

"Amateur?" Red said.

"Yes. When it comes to covert military operations, you, Captain, are an amateur, and you should be as far away from them as possible."

"You have a better way of ensuring a positive ID on the ground in Omolon?" Doyle said.

Vinari waved the folder. "We have a photograph."

"He looks nothing like that now," Red said. "I recognise it's him, but you wouldn't recognise him today based on that."

Gabriel stroked his beard. "This won't be a picnic. Things will be furious on the ground. You'd be there for one reason. To provide a positive ID—"

"I'm not coming to organise his execution," Red said.

He pushed his shoulders back and stood as straight and tall as he could.

Vinari raised his voice, directing it at Doyle. "I told you he'll be a liability."

"We're not fucking around on the ground," Gabriel said, keeping his gaze on Red. "We'll have seconds."

"Son, we do not have permission to kidnap an officer of the Soviet air force," Doyle said to Red.

"But you can kill him?"

"It might sound odd to you, but yes. Under these circumstances, we will get away with that. And that's what we have permission for."

"Then forget it. Mr. Vinari, can you organise a ride out of here for me?"

Vinari placed Demichev's file in a box on the table. "Let's go."

"How?" Gabriel said, his eyes narrowing.

Red studied his face. Pockmarked, with a scar that ran back towards an ear. Had someone tried to cut his throat?

"How what?" Red asked.

"You said you can find him. How?"

"I know him. I know his habits. I'll help you locate him. But I promise you, I can get him to come back, voluntarily. I can sense it. This is where he belongs." He turned to Doyle. "Think what an asset you'd have. A Soviet test pilot. You can put the shoe on the other foot. Turn this disaster into a victory for the president."

Vinari shook his head. "This is crazy. Even talking about this, it's nonsense. Demichev isn't going anywhere. It's been decided."

The four men stood in silence. Gabriel had barely taken his eyes off Red through the whole conversation, but he slowly reached into the box and took another look at the file picture of a young Vasil Demichev.

"Captain Brunson, would you give us a few minutes, please?"

Red stepped out the A-TEC building and walked over to the commissary.

The first tinges of sunset were painting the western horizon. His car was in the lot; Sarah must have driven it over. But she wasn't in it.

Inside the canteen, a few airmen from other units were scattered around the tables. He spotted Sarah sitting at a table alone.

"Hey," she said, moving towards him. She looked worried.

"It's fine. I think they're going to take me."

"What?" Sarah gaped at him. "To Russia?"

"Shhh . . ." He pulled her to a table in the corner, far from prying ears. "It's my only chance of saving him. Of bringing him back."

She couldn't hide the shocked expression. "Why on earth would they take you? And why in God's name would you want to go?" She suddenly looked on the edge of tears. "Red, I'll never see you again."

"Baby, baby. It's fine."

She stared at him as if he were a child. "Nothing about this is fine."

"This thing. It'll be the world's fastest stopover. They'll throw some grenades or something at Daedalus, and I'll grab Brandon."

Teardrops leaked from her eyes. Red rested his hand on hers and glanced around the room. A couple of airmen gave them a sideways glance, but went back to their chow.

"He's not even Brandon, Red. He's not who he said he was. Let them deal with it. There's nothing for you there. Baby, you've got to move on." She shook her head. "I can't believe they'll even take you. Why would they do that?"

"Because I can find him. They need someone who knows what he looks like."

She threw her hands up. "Half the base knows what he looks like."

"Half the base is drunk in Maggie's. It's basically me and Colonel Tucker, and I can't see the old man climbing into the back of a C-130."

The sound of trays clattering echoed around the largely empty canteen. Red looked across to see a couple of diners scraping their plates and depositing dirty cutlery.

When he looked back to Sarah, her expression had changed. "You've got to let him go, Red." She hesitated. "He's not your father."

"I never said he was."

She sat down and pulled out a chair for Red.

He nervously glanced around the room again.

She picked up his hands and stared into his eyes. "I think maybe he replaced your father for you, baby. And that was great for you. He was kind and wise and you needed him. But—"

"But what? Now I've got a chance to pay him back. To offer him a life in America. To give him freedom."

She shook her head. "But it was all an act, Red. He was putting it on to get what he wanted. I'm sorry this sounds harsh, but you fell for it. And now, this loyalty of yours, it's misplaced. And it's going to get you killed."

Her eyes filled with tears. She stared at him. "I can't believe they would go along with this. You're a test pilot, not a damn soldier. Don't go, baby."

She sobbed.

"Sarah, no one knew him better than me."

She shook her head, but he didn't let her speak. "No one. I got to know the real person, I'm sure of it. And he belongs here. He had to do what he had to do, but now we can give him a chance for a life of freedom."

"Listen to you, Red. You don't even know his real name."

"Vasil. Vasil Demichev."

"Christ."

He shrugged. "Of course, he has a Russian name. He's Russian! But he's also a damn fine test pilot, and he'll be a star back here."

Sarah sat back up in her chair and folded her arms across her chest.

"What makes you think he wants to come here? Russia's his home. He stole the goddamn airplane, Red. You think he's loyal to you? The only loyalty he's shown is to the USSR. Our enemy."

"He had to do that. He was probably being watched this whole time."

She shook her head. "You've been brainwashed by him. That's what's happened. Maybe he even wants you to go on this stupid mission. Maybe it's all part of his plan."

Red hesitated. "This discussion's going nowhere. I need to get back to it."

She didn't move.

He stood up. "He's not my father, Sarah. He's my friend. I'll see you later."

She remained in her seat. Red hesitated and then walked out.

The other side of the commissary door, he stopped again and thought about going back in, before shaking his head. "I don't have time for this."

Outside A-TEC, a new security cordon was being put in place. He glanced at the nearby buildings to see workers being led away. Edwards, a place of research with a large contingent of civilians, was apparently being put on a military footing.

Red approached the entrance and was forced to show his ID. A guard ran a finger down a long list on a clipboard, before standing aside for him.

As he entered the main office, men were moving tables and chairs to turn it into a briefing room.

Doyle appeared in front of him. The six-foot-tall CIA deputy director put a hand on his arm, and drew him to the wall.

"Now, listen up, Brunson. I don't like this, but here's the deal. You lead us to him. You get one minute. If it's clear he's not coming back, you will be dismissed back to the C-130. Understood?"

Red nodded.

"Coming along for this ride is the worst decision you'll ever make," Doyle continued saying, "and you've made some bad decisions lately. But Gabriel wants your eyes on the ground, and that's why you've got a place on the Herc." He leaned in close. "You can never talk about this. If you die out there, and you might, no one will ever know the circumstances. You're in our world now. You think you know what a dark flight is? You have no idea how dark this shit gets. And respect the men. Your life depends on them."

Red swallowed. "Yes, sir."

"We brief in ten minutes. Pay close attention."

Doyle turned and marched to the front of the room.

The men in black fatigues lined the back, guns slung across their shoulders, sidearms in holsters. In front of them, a line of agents in the familiar civilian uniform of pressed white shirts and black-framed glasses. The older, more senior government representatives lined up along the side walls. A mix of soldiers and agents sat in the chairs in the centre.

"Attention," Doyle began. "This is a Dark Operation. There will be no record of it anywhere. You do not discuss it with anyone outside this room, and once we're back, you do not discuss it again in your lifetime. Is that understood?"

"Yes, sir!" the combat men shouted. The others mumbled.

"We have men from the NRO, CIA, and Special Activities here. That's a lot of ears and eyes for an operation that doesn't exist. Don't for one second believe we won't know it's you if you talk. You'll find yourself in a military prison for a long time. I'll hand over to Gabriel for the brief. Listen, understand your role, and obey."

The bearded, bald Gabriel flipped over a blackboard. It was littered with lists. He pointed to the timing panel on the left.

"Wheels up tomorrow morning. 0450. We get out of here before anyone else is up. It's a long haul. How far?" Gabriel looked across to the corner of the room. Red turned and for the first time noticed two men in dark flight suits. Presumably the C-130 crew. He didn't recognise either of them.

"Ten hours to Wainwright," one of them said. "One refuel stop."

The other pilot caught Red staring and give him a little nod of the head.

"Okay," Gabriel continued. "As usual, the flight crew will brief separately. You have a spare pair of hands on board if you need them." He pointed at Red. A few heads turned, and he caught some confused looks. "Captain Brunson flew the Daedalus. He also recruited Vasil Demichev to work here at Edwards." The room laughed. "So, he wants to make amends and help us out. He will act as the ID agent for this op.

"I suggest you sleep on the flight. Everything will happen overnight tomorrow, and we need you alert and awake. Wheels up from Wainwright at 2200. Estimated time on target is 0200." He tapped the time on the blackboard to emphasise his point. "The run is a little over one thousand miles. We transition to low-level five hundred miles out, so it's going to be rough. The boys will pick out the route based on terrain, so we can't be precise with the times, but it won't be earlier than 0200.

"You have two objectives." He tacked a picture of Daedalus to the blackboard. "Number one, our priority mission. Destroy this aircraft. Purple and Yellow teams. We've chosen ten half-kilo blocks of C4."

A ripple went through the men at the back.

"That should do it," one of them said.

"As you can tell, we're not taking any chances. The aim is to make any reverse engineering impossible. Collateral damage is not an issue. Now, if the missile is no longer attached to the aircraft, it becomes a secondary target. Yellow, that will be your priority to locate it and destroy with your allocated C4.

"Wilson's in charge of detonation for both teams. You obey him precisely, or people get hurt. What's the situation, Ed?"

A soldier at the back stepped forward. He was short, with wiry black hair.

He looked down at his notes. "We need to be five hundred yards away for detonation. The missile has two thousand pounds of HE, in addition to five kilos of C4. That's a lot of fireworks going up at the same time.

"For det, we'll have four-minute timers on two of the blocks. Those are our timer blocks, TB-1 and TB-2. All the other blocks will be wired to these by me. Four minutes gives us enough time to get clear. I'll give those orders. The shout will be 'TB-1 DET.' When you hear it, repeat it loudly and start running in a straight line to the Herc. My advice is to run like hell."

"Why two TBs?" said a soldier next to him. "Doesn't that complicate it?"

"If the missile's no longer attached to Daedalus, we'll need a TB on that. In that case, Milligan will oversee TB-2 with Yellow." He ran a finger down his notes, apparently checking he hadn't missed anything. "That's it."

"Silencers on," Gabriel said.

The soldiers groaned.

"Until it gets busy, and the surprise element is gone. Then your team leaders will advise." Gabriel turned back to the blackboard. Next to Daedalus, he pinned the ancient picture of Dupont.

"Objective two. This is Vasil Demichev. Or at least it was, twenty-five years ago. Captain Brunson will help us locate and ID him. Mr Demichev will be offered the chance to accompany us back to the US of A. After that fails . . ." Laughter from the back. "Rounder and Chubbs, you are in charge of Brunson's movements. He's back to the C-130 and out of the way. Understood?"

Two men among the crowd at the back nodded.

Red stared at his handlers. They were both the size of small houses.

"Finally. Green, you're on point. You have your own double objective. Keep the C-130 safe. It's our only way out. And keep the Reds off the det charges until they go. The Herc will reposition on the eastern side of the airfield as soon as Yellow, Red, and Blue are on the ground. Green, you can set up your perimeter once it's repositioned. So, everybody else, expect the bird to be on the taxiway beyond the control tower. We have no idea if the field will be lit, so keep your wits about you. I really would hate to leave you behind on this one." More laughter at the back. "So, what can go wrong?"

"Everything," the soldiers shouted in unison from the back of the room.

"Correct. We don't know where Daedalus is or even if it's there at all. We don't know if the missile is still on the underbelly or already dismantled. We don't know if Demichev is there, whether he's a prisoner and chained up, or back in fucking Moscow. We don't know anything. So be ready to react. Ideally, we use surprise and minimum force, with the C4 det taking place as we reach the Herc. But that's probably not going to happen. Listen to your team leaders. They will be the only ones to make the extraction call. When they do so, you react instantly, or you learn to speak Russian."

Sarah drove home alone.

She cranked a window open and let her small car cruise slowly along the desert road back to Rosamond.

At home, she pushed the door open, but it caught on the mail.

She leaned down and picked up a couple of envelopes. Too exhausted to open them, she dropped her keys on the counter walked into the bedroom, and fell onto the bed.

She drew her knees up to her chest, closed her eyes, and thought about Red, in the middle of Russia, in a firefight.

Unwanted images flashed into her head of him lying on the ground, blood pooling underneath his flight suit.

She shook her head, trying to physically dislodge the pictures.

The house was dark and cool.

Sarah couldn't find the energy to get up and put the lights on.

CHAPTER FIFTEEN

IT WAS EARLY when she woke. The drapes were open, and first light filled the room.

She rolled onto her back and stared at a familiar stain on the ceiling.

Her mouth felt horrible. She dragged herself off the bed and brushed her teeth, before stepping into the shower, discarding the clothes she'd been wearing for twenty hours.

Wrapped in a dressing gown, Sarah tramped into the kitchen.

Next to her keys was yesterday's mail. She flipped over an envelope.

It was addressed to *Captain Red Brunson*.

"What the heck?"

She turned it over; it was a handwritten envelope.

Who thinks he lives here?

She studied the writing. There was something about it. Foreign?

She toyed with it for a moment longer, then tore it open.

Inside was a sheet of paper that looked as if it had been ripped out of a notepad.

Her eyes went straight to the bottom of the short message.

Your friend,
Brandon.

Ten minutes later, she was speeding to Edwards, cursing her underpowered car.

The journey took an age, but when she reached the gate, she could see there was an issue. A long line of vehicles backed up. Security men buzzing around the lead car.

She pulled onto the side of the road, and leaped out, running to the front of the line.

"Ma'am?" one of the gate guards said, holding up the palm of his hand. "Get back into your car, please. We're going as fast as we can."

"I don't have time. I need to get to A-TEC urgently."

The soldier looked her up and down. "A-TEC is closed."

Sarah scrambled into her pockets for her base pass, thrusting it into the soldier's hands. He studied it briefly and handed it back.

"Essential personnel only."

"What?"

"That's our orders. Edwards is closed to nonessential personnel, just for a couple of days. You'll get a call from your unit commanders or boss later today."

"No! I must—"

"You need to get back in your car, ma'am."

"Please, sergeant. Let me in."

"Lady, he said get back in your car." A voice came from

behind, and Sarah swivelled to see an impatient-looking driver in the car at the top of the line.

She pushed the sergeant away from the other driver's earshot. The soldier looked surprised, but moved a few steps.

"Sergeant, you need to get a message to Captain Red Brunson."

"Ma'am, I'm not in a position to do that. You can call him."

Sarah shook her head. "No time. You've got to tell him he mustn't go." She stood waiting for a response. "It's urgent. He's in danger."

"I'm sorry, ma'am. This will have to wait until you're allowed access again. Maybe tomorrow."

Sarah began to cry. "No, no. You don't understand. They're all in great danger. I need to get a message to them."

"Lady, I do not know what you're talking about, but I'm getting close to arresting you for obstruction. You need to leave here and go home. Like I said, make a phone call."

The soldier walked off. Sarah looked beyond him to the gate area, but it was crowded with other guards. The idea of making a run for it briefly crossed her mind, but so did the image of being shot in the back.

Slowly, she turned and trudged back to her car.

She didn't even have the A-TEC number with her. She'd need to get home and try. But it was now gone 0900, and she feared it was too late.

CHAPTER SIXTEEN

RED LAY on a bare metal bench that ran along the inside of the Hercules. He shuffled himself along, attempting to make it more comfortable, his head resting on a camouflage jacket they'd provided for him.

As they'd boarded the transport aircraft in the predawn darkness, there was a rush to the few webbing hammocks by those experienced in similar long trips.

Unable to get comfortable, he stood up and wandered to the steps that led to the cockpit.

The pilots, Hank and JD, had been welcoming during their side brief. Red hadn't asked them who exactly they worked for or where they did their training. He sensed questions such as that were not appropriate.

He sat on a jump seat between the two crewmen and looked out on the greenery of Oregon as they slowly ploughed their way north.

The ASI read two hundred ten knots, and Red winced. His last flight to Wainwright had been in Daedalus, at two thousand knots.

"What's the ground speed?" he asked over the intercom.

One of the men looked at his notes. "We're making three thirty."

Better, but still painful.

He understood the need for the Hercules. It was the world's most versatile military transport. They'd be grateful for its ability to transit under the radar and land on whatever strip was presented to them at Omolon and then get out.

He thought back to the first trip north with their own Hercules. And who had flown it up? Brandon Dupont.

Vasil Demichev.

Red imagined him plodding north for ten hours, plotting his audacious act.

Man, he must have been nervous.

They refuelled in Canada. It was the middle of the day at a busy military airfield: Comox in BC. The crew jumped out to oversee the operation. Red looked out the side door, and wondered if anyone at the base had the slightest idea what was inside this nondescript cargo aircraft.

He eventually got comfortable on the Herc, using all the clothing he'd been issued as a makeshift blanket. But sleep was fitful.

In his mind, over and over, he rehearsed the moment he would meet Vasil.

It would have to be a quick conversation. They'd allocated him sixty seconds, and he assumed they meant it.

But it wouldn't take long.

He would offer this talented test pilot a place in the free world.

Doing what he loved.

It was what he deserved. Friendship needed rewarding.

.   .   .

He was woken by a loadmaster shouting orders to strap in for landing.

Red propped himself up and yawned. He fumbled underneath his flattened clothes. A man next to him grabbed his straps and offered him a harness latch.

"Thank you," Red shouted.

Like most of the team, his neighbour had a thick beard and sun-beaten face.

The aircraft landed firmly, and within minutes, they spilled out the cargo door at the rear.

It was grey, but just about light. Red looked at his watch.

"We're one hour behind," Gabriel shouted over the chatter of men checking kit around him. "It's 1510 local. We ship out in seven hours. Go get some sleep."

Some men stayed in the back of the aircraft, rearranging equipment, readying it for its next flight deep into the Soviet Union.

Others quickly made their way through the freezing air to the small buildings around the control tower. Red followed them in, feeling lost without his usual colleagues around him.

Once inside the communal room, he wandered along the corridor and entered the dark underbelly of the control tower. He climbed the stairs, following the sound of voices above.

Inside the tower a US Air Force airmen sat with headphones on, in front of a controller's station. Behind him a major loitered with a clipboard.

They looked surprised to see someone. The major nodded but didn't challenge him.

"Hi. I'm Red Brunson from Edwards."

"Hello, Mr Brunson!" the major said. "Sorry, didn't mean to ignore you, but we're under instruction not to ask anyone anything."

Red smiled. "I understand. Listen, I need a place to crash for a few hours, and I seemed to remember you have some comfy benches in the radar room."

The major nodded. "Be our guest."

Red looked out. The weather was considerably better than the last time he was here. But, standing in the same place, it was hard not to think about him.

Vasil. He still couldn't get used to it.

Vasil.

Not Brandon Dupont.

And this is where it all had come to fruition. All his planning, all his subterfuge.

He had been up here an hour or so before. Monitoring the security men, most likely.

An image flashed into Red's mind. The two bodies. The shocking sight of blood spreading in the snow.

Sarah had argued with him about Vasil's true nature, but she didn't even know the worst of it. The man had killed.

Because he had to. Under orders from a brutal dictatorship.

Red made his way back down to the intermediate level in the tower: the radar room.

It was a perpetually dark place, and empty now. Just him and the gentle hum of equipment.

A telephone sat on a table next to the comfy bench. He paused for a moment, then picked up the receiver and dialled Sarah's number.

It rang for a long time.

He hung up, and settled down for a few hours of sleepless rest.

. . .

Colonel Montgomery Tucker sighed on the other end of the line.

"I'm sorry, Sarah, you have no idea how big this thing is. There's nothing I can do."

"Please, Tucker. He thinks he's on a rescue mission."

"Whichever way you look at this, and I understand your interpretation, it doesn't change anything for the mission—"

"But Red—"

"Red is your concern, and mine." He paused. "But it's not the CIA's."

The reloading of the C-130 took place in near silence. Nerves and tension filled the air.

Under cover of darkness, they climbed out of Wainwright and headed across the international dateline into tomorrow.

Red looked at his watch and decided he'd prefer the low-level run-in, from a more comfortable seat. He unstrapped and moved to the front of the cargo hold, emerging a moment later into the flight deck.

He got the merest of acknowledgments from the two pilots as he strapped into the centre jump seat and donned a headset. They were just concluding their low-level checklist.

Moments later, they adjusted the throttle and the nose lowered.

The ride became bumpy as they passed through thin layers of cloud. The descent from twenty thousand feet was slow. Red could just about make out the VSI, which read one thousand feet per minute. They had twenty minutes of plunging towards the cold sea.

Red didn't blame them for taking it slowly. He dreaded to think what the water temperature was this far north.

At one thousand feet, the pilot in the left-hand seat inched the yoke back and edged the four throttles forward. The descent slowed to a couple of hundred feet per minute.

At five hundred feet, he levelled out. Both men sat up, rigid with concentration.

Outside, he could make out the odd whitecap beneath them. It was a gentle swell. Not that anyone would survive more than a few minutes if they ended up ditching.

They settled into a pattern, with just the occasional course correction. Red had learned in the brief they were getting helpful radio beams from a source known only as "Osprey" on the sheets. He knew better than to ask how the US military was using a radio beam that ran across the ocean and deep into the Soviet Union.

He imagined a submarine, just under the surface of the cold northern sea, with a long antenna protruding high into the air. As he thought about it, he realised it was probably two subs, a hundred or so miles apart, with separate beams they could use to precisely locate themselves. Classic triangulation, in a land where the navigation aids spoke a different language.

"Four minutes to landfall," the copilot called.

Ahead, a black mass rose from the sea.

The USSR.

The copilot lifted a small pair of binoculars to his eyes and described what he could see.

"River inlet. Come five right."

The pilot nudged the Hercules a few degrees to the right.

Red was impressed. Although they had some moonlight, he could barely see a thing.

The copilot glanced back at him and waved the binoculars.

"They're night vision. Not perfect, but they help. You can have a go on the way back if we're still alive."

"I heard rumours about those things, but had no idea they're in use."

"Shipping to Nam as we speak," the copilot replied.

"They need all the help they can get," the pilot added. "Poor bastards."

The coast loomed above them as they got closer. The aircraft jumped a couple of times, hitting air pockets.

"Here we go. Left two. Drop one hundred. Come right one. Level . . ."

For the next twenty minutes, the copilot was glued to the night-vision device and gave a stream of instructions, which the pilot blindly followed. Red was in awe at the trust.

"Pop-up when you're ready. We need to get a fix," the copilot called after thirty minutes.

The pilot used the throttles and yoke to lift them a thousand feet into the air, as the copilot studied a small box welded onto the panel to his right and made notes.

"Back down," he called as he marked the map with the new distances. After a couple of seconds, he had an X on the chart. "Got it. Slight heading change. Come left two-eight-two."

A lake appeared on the nose, and Red listened and watched as the crew took the C-130 down the left-hand side, hugging the rising ground.

They've done this before.

For another thirty minutes, they settled into a routine of valley-seeking or treetop-skirting when the ground opened up.

After an hour or so, they carried out a second pop-up to reacquire a fix, then came back down with an adjustment for their heading. A stopwatch on the right-hand panel showed time to target approaching.

"You better head back. Give them a ten-minute warning," the pilot called over the intercom, without taking his eyes off the terrain ahead.

Red felt the knot in his stomach tighten.

He replaced his ear defenders and headed down to the cargo area. It was busy. The men grabbed their guns and ammunition from an open pallet of kit at the far end, and, around the edge on the webbed seats, soldiers smeared black camo paint across their faces.

He felt a hand land on his shoulder and jumped.

Gabriel lifted one of Red's ear defenders. "You stick to me like glue. Understood?"

The C-130 rolled and banked; the men put hands out to steady themselves.

An aggressive late correction. They were lining up.

A few minutes later, amid the roar of the aircraft, the wheels thudded down onto Russian soil.

Red shook his head, willing his mind to catch up with events.

He felt the aircraft roll out and turn sharply off the runway. The engines wound up again, and for a second time, the men steadied themselves as she was brought around. It was a fast taxi.

The aircraft was still slowing under brakes as the rear cargo ramp began to lower. The moment the Hercules stopped, men dressed in black disappeared into the night.

Gabriel's hand was on Red's shoulder again, and they edged to the ramp as more men left the aircraft in front of them.

Eventually, they stepped off the ramp.

The airfield was dark; the only lights came from a block of buildings in the distance to their left. The C-130 had parked on the main runway, unlit.

Gabriel jogged, and Red kept up with him. Around them were a dozen other men. Blue Team, he assumed.

"This is going to be a lot of running," Red panted.

"Keep quiet," Gabriel said in a hiss.

It was quickly clear how Red's fitness was nowhere near the other soldiers. Luckily, it was a slow jog, just above walking pace. Some men, silhouetted around him, were carrying a lot of gear.

They crossed a taxiway with white lines and studs for lights. Just like a US field.

The nearest buildings were single storey, with a traditional-looking control tower in the centre. Opposite, across a large expanse of apron, lit by orange floodlights, were three large hangars and smaller office buildings.

As they passed the block next to the control tower, they entered the lit apron.

Three Russian fighter jets stood in a neat row outside the farthest hangar.

Red stopped and stared.

"Move!" Gabriel barked.

"MiG-21s," Red said, his mouth open. "These are brand new."

"We're not here to sightsee."

Red jogged again and turned his attention to where Vasil might be.

Through a gap between two hangars, he could see a larger building that marked the domestic side of the military site.

They had some way to go.

As they crossed the apron, he spotted a team attempting to open a hangar door ahead. It wouldn't budge.

They ushered through a man with a black bag and, just before Red, Gabriel and Blue Team disappeared behind the building, he saw what looked like a block of explosive being wired.

So far, no opposition.

But that wouldn't last. Especially if they were about to start using C4 bricks to loosen the hangar doors.

Behind the hangar, Red spotted the first of the airfield's accommodation blocks. It was a long, two-storey affair, with a large central hub. He tried to count as they jogged. Fourteen windows on each level; that made at least fifty-six rooms.

As they got closer, he started to pant heavily.

Gabriel pulled up into a fast walk. "You okay, Mr Test Pilot?"

Red nodded, trying to steady his breaths, cursing his lack of fitness.

Suddenly, Gabriel grabbed him by the shoulders and ran, slamming him into the side of the hangar.

Shocked, Red looked up, but Gabriel put a hand over his mouth and stared out.

"Here they come."

He turned to see headlights on a road that led into the main base. The vehicles were moving quickly towards them.

"Right, they're going to contact Blue Team in ten seconds. When they do, we need to hoof it over the apron to the buildings."

As predicted, the vehicles sped through a gap between the hangars to their left. Shouting in Russian followed, and immediately the sound of *wap-wap* as the Americans' silenced weapons unloaded.

Louder *thud-thud* sounds replied from the Soviets. But Gabriel prodded Red, and they were on the move.

As they approached the nearest and largest accommodation block, Red studied the rooms again. The windows were bigger than he thought. A light came on, and he saw the bed arrangement.

"He's not in there."

"What?" Gabriel turned and stared at him. "Why? How do you know?"

"That's junior ranks. Bunks."

Red's eyes scanned left and right down the road from where the vehicles had emerged. But the only other buildings were single storey and obviously not accommodation.

Cracks echoed around the airfield.

Gabriel shoved him to the ground, and the entire team dropped as a small car appeared. It stopped at the open gate that led to the airfield side of the site.

For the first time in his life, Red saw an actual Soviet soldier. An officer. He emerged from the vehicle looking confused, scanning the area.

He was just about to get back in his car, when his body jerked, and he stumbled. A moment later, his head exploded.

Red felt sick. Adrenaline burst into his veins at the sight of a body dropping in a heap of blood and brain. Shot by one of the soldiers around the hangar. They must have already disposed of the first vehicle of Russians.

How many men would die tonight?

"Come on!" Gabriel shouted and grabbed him, propping him upright, manipulated like a child's action figure.

They ran, keeping in the shadows, avoiding the lit gate area. More shots rang out. Red didn't dare turn to see if they were the target; he just ran.

They reached the fence that ran along from the airfield gate.

"Everyone okay?" Gabriel asked. The team grunted.

Red shook his head in amazement. "Somehow."

"Being shot at focuses attention. They wouldn't have noticed us, as long as Blue kept them busy."

Red turned his attention to the buildings beyond the wire. Most looked like offices of some sort, but the nearest was a smaller, two-storey block of accommodation.

"Let's explore."

"We haven't got time for a fucking expedition, Brunson. You said you'd know where he is."

"He's not in there," he said, motioning to the largest building they'd now passed. "I guarantee it." He looked at the team and caught the doubtful expressions on their faces. "Can you cut through this fence?"

The sound of an explosion behind made the men whip their heads around.

"Grenade," Gabriel said with reassurance.

If it were the main detonation, they'd be in danger of missing the flight home.

"We need to do this quickly. Talk to me, Brunson."

"He was used to better accommodation. Maybe that place." Red pointed at the building on the other side of the fence. The surrounding men moved quickly and set to work on the wire.

Cracks of gunfire rang out from some way behind them.

A siren went off. The noise came from tinny speakers attached to lampposts along the main road that led into the site.

Lights flickered on around them.

"We're running out of time," Gabriel said in a low voice.

"We're through," one of the men at the fence shouted.

Gabriel pushed Red in the back, and they ran towards the gap. The other men were already on the other side.

They approached the building, just as the outside lights came on.

As they got to the door, a Russian airman stumbled out, still buttoning his jacket.

No weapon, as far as Red could see.

Two soldiers moved in front of Gabriel and Red, levelling their guns at the terrified junior officer. Two more soldiers swept past them into the building.

The soldier stumbled backward and raised his arms in surrender, disbelief etched across his face.

Gabriel stepped forward. He shouted something in Russian that ended ". . . Vasil Demichev."

The Russian froze.

Gabriel shouted it again, but all the Russian did was slowly shake his head. Red scrutinised him. The look of shock was subsiding.

He must have recognised the name.

"He's an officer," Red whispered to Gabriel. "He knows why we're here."

"Yes, he does." Gabriel pulled a pistol from his holster and walked up to the man. He whipped the gun across the man's head. As he hit the ground, Gabriel shouted again in Russian and pointed at the building, but the man curled up into a ball.

Gunfire erupted next to them and Red jumped back, just in time to see one of the soldiers in the dark lobby opening fire.

"We've got company," he shouted, followed by "Clear!"

Gabriel led Red into the building.

On the ground, he saw a twitching leg. His eyes followed the shape. A Soviet soldier, slumped on the bottom step ahead of them. His head arched back, mouth open in a silenced scream. Brain and gore seeped out from the missing part of the back of his skull.

Despite being in the military, the only body he'd seen before the two guards at Wainwright was his father's. So far tonight, he'd seen three men killed.

Gabriel grabbed the lapels of another half-dressed Soviet officer, who emerged blinking from a room to their right.

In the dim light of the corridor, he thrust a pistol under his chin.

"Vasil Demichev?"

The Soviet said nothing, but slowly, his eyes swivelled to the corridor ahead of them.

"He's here somewhere," Gabriel said. "You three stay here and give us time." He pointed at three of the men. "The rest, with me. Spearmint and Tackle, take the rear." Two of the men moved behind Red, and again, Gabriel pushed him to get going. He followed the lead two soldiers, then Gabriel into the lightless corridor.

As Red put his foot down on the hard tiled floor, it gave way beneath him, and he fell sprawling, landing on something soft. He realised with horror, he'd slipped on a pool of fresh, warm blood and used a dead Soviet officer to break his fall.

"Christ," he said to himself. He was shaking.

Gabriel marched back, wedged his fingers under Red's armpits, and hoisted him up.

"This is no time to go flaky on me, test pilot. Get it together."

The lights came on.

Ahead of them, the leading soldiers opened fire.

The silencers were off, and the sound was deafening. Red clamped his hands over his ears.

"Clear!"

They shouted in unison, and Gabriel shoved Red forward again.

As they turned into the walkway, Red ran past three more bodies on the floor, machine guns next to them.

"I'm having one of those AKs," he heard a soldier ahead say.

They kicked the doors down, one by one.

"Demichev?" they shouted.

In a room directly above, Vasil Demichev slowly pulled the covers back on his bed and sat up. He rubbed his eyes and cocked his head, listening carefully to the shouts of the men who were coming for him.

He got to his feet and opened a small officers wardrobe, before lifting his neatly pressed uniform off its hangers.

Gabriel shoved Red forward. "Get over there and do your job."

He peered into the first two rooms to see frightened twenty-something pilots staring wide eyed at him.

"No," he said.

They moved on.

Gunfire erupted outside once more.

"Get down!" Gabriel screamed. His call sounded wild and high pitched for such a big man.

He pushed Red into one of the rooms.

The Americans returned sustained fire back down the corridor. Shouts went up between bursts.

"Two more!"

"One down!"

Eventually, the shooting ceased.

"Clear!"

Red exchanged a look with the terrified Russian on his bed.

In the corridor, Gabriel was on the floor pulling a white bandage tightly around his arm.

"You're hit," Red said.

"It's nothing. Keep going."

Behind them, more shouts and gunfire.

"We are seriously short on time," Gabriel shouted. "Move the fuck on!"

More doors kicked down. The rooms were empty or filled with bewildered Russians, none of whom was Vasil Demichev.

The soldiers ran through a connecting door at the end of the corridor. One of the front men pulled it shut and jammed it using a dead Russian's AK-47.

"That should give us a short breather," Gabriel said.

They had both entrances covered now.

This wasn't the sort of tactical situation Red was trained for, but he was getting the hang of it.

The adrenaline had taken over, replacing the shock of the first kills with a surreal feeling that none of this was real.

Gabriel appeared behind Red, clutching his arm; the white bandage was soaked in blood.

"Up!" he shouted, and Red climbed a short staircase to the second level.

It revealed an identical corridor.

One of the front soldiers waited at the top of the stairs.

"This is the only way up," he said to Gabriel. "I'll stand point."

They kicked in the first door. Red moved behind the soldier as he levelled his weapon at a figure sitting on a small bed.

Vasil Demichev gave Red a warm smile.

Red stared at his face. Etched with experience and wisdom. Calm in the storm.

What else did he expect?

He was midway through dressing, buttoning a shirt over a white, pressed T-shirt.

"I told you not to come. For once, you didn't listen to me!"

"What?" Red stepped forward into the room, past the soldier with his barrel still aimed at Vasil. "We're here to bring you back."

Vasil stood up. "Do I get a hug?"

Red stared for a moment longer. Vasil did not hide his Russian accent. Gone was the faux Mississippi drawl.

He stepped forward and embraced his friend. Vasil patted his back a couple of times and then pulled back.

"I'm impressed. But somehow I knew you'd figure it out."

"The lake."

Vasil nodded. "The one mistake I made."

"Clock's ticking." Gabriel said, calling from behind.

"We need to go," Red said, urgingly. He looked around for any belongings Vasil might want to take with him.

"Go where?" the Russian said calmly.

"Home, of course. Your new home. In America. I've organised it for you. It's all sorted. You'll join us at A-TEC. Where you belong. A new life in a free country!"

Vasil slowly sat back down on the bed. He patted the mattress. Red looked uncertainly at Gabriel, who shook his head.

Red sat down, anyway.

"How's Sarah?" Vasil asked.

"We don't have time for this, Brunson," Gabriel said.

"She's fine."

"She's a good woman. A good person. Don't lose her."

"Vasil. We need to go."

Vasil looked around his small room. On the desk next to the bed was a black-and-white picture of a family. Red studied it for a moment. Four children. The tallest boy must be Vasil. Taller than him, though, was a girl.

Vasil took the picture off the top and pointed at her. "Taisa. My sister. She lives in Rostok with my father." His finger moved to the older man in the picture. He wore a large-rimmed dark hat and stood with a straight back. He looked too old to have young children.

"Papa," Vasil said. "You would have liked him. He was the lead in the technical drawing team at Ilyushin, for a while."

"He designed the fighters we go up against?" Red asked.

Vasil laughed. "No, he was strictly on airliners. He was amazing. He turned the designers' ideas into drawings for the engineers. He had a hell of an eye for aerodynamics. He thought I would follow him, but of course, for me, it was always about the military jets."

"Time's up," Gabriel called from behind.

Before Red could say anything, Vasil put his hand on his shoulder. "You want me to go home, but I am home."

"But we're here to help you escape."

Vasil smiled and looked over his shoulder at the soldiers. He shook his head. "I don't think they're here to help me."

"Yes, they are." Red's voice cracked. Vasil looked at him, a slight smile on his face and sympathy in his eyes. Vasil then clasped his hands together and stared at the floor.

"Vasil?" Red said weakly.

The Russian raised his head slowly. He looked past Red to Gabriel beyond him.

"How does it work?" he asked.

"How does what—" Red began saying, but Gabriel cut him off.

"He gets removed first." Gabriel nodded at Red.

Red wanted to stand up, but he didn't trust his legs. Nausea churned in his core. "Vasil, you don't understand. You don't know what they're going to do."

Vasil looked around the room.

"Okay Maybe I'll come. But Red, you must go ahead with them."

"What? No. I'm here to get you to the Herc. We need to stick together."

"I'll do what I can," Gabriel said. "Let's go."

The soldiers began to move.

Red stood up quickly and turned his head between the two men. "What's happening? Are you coming?"

Vasil stood up slowly. "Yes. I'm coming. But it's best you go ahead."

For the first time since they had entered the building, Red noticed the firing outside. He'd tuned it out. Distant thuds marked grenade explosions, mixed with the pulsing cracks of machine guns.

Gabriel led Red and Vasil down the corridor to the stairs. The two other soldiers waited for Red to move before following him, cutting Vasil off, somewhere behind.

When they got to the stairs, Gabriel met the man they'd put on guard. He leaned in and said something, before moving off. The line of soldiers followed him down. The guard waited for Red to pass before taking station behind him.

Downstairs, they moved quickly to the main entrance.

As he arrived, Gabriel stopped and waved for them to halt, then slipped around the corner into the foyer. In an eerie silence, they heard his conversation.

"Situation?"

"One truck to our right. Maybe six grunts. They're not engaging or moving, probably waiting for backup."

"Where, exactly?" Gabriel asked.

"Two hundred yards that way, just beyond the line of trees."

"You need to give us cover. Enough to get six of us away."

"Roger."

A moment later, Gabriel's head appeared. "Follow!"

They gathered in the foyer. Gabriel flicked a switch on his rifle.

"Full auto," he whispered to the other two, who made the same adjustment.

Without further words, the three soldiers and Gabriel moved as one through the front door. Each of them opened fire, facing right.

Gabriel screamed. "Run!"

Red felt a shove and he set off, covering his ears from the roar of the unloading weapons.

They ran full steam over the road until they reached the shadows on the far side. They were a hundred yards down the fence from where they entered, but the soldier at the front had found a small gate. He booted it twice, but it failed to give. He stepped back, aimed his rifle, and released two rounds into the lock mechanism. Sparks flew in all directions, and Red covered his eyes.

The group moved through the new gap.

Red tried to catch his breath, his head pounding from the noise of the guns and the adrenaline filling his system.

He looked back for Vasil and glimpsed him, closely

escorted by the two soldiers. His friend looked back and smiled weakly.

He looked like a prisoner, not a man being liberated.

Red thought there was something he was missing, something important.

Once through the fence, they ran to the back of the main accommodation block and again, Gabriel ran to the corner first and ordered everyone to pin himself against the wall.

"Where's the aircraft?" Vasil called from along the line.

"A half klick from the tower."

Vasil looked confused. "Why so far away?"

"Shut up," one of the soldiers barked.

Red didn't answer.

Gabriel appeared. "Okay. The main group is in a hangar opposite, to the right. Looks like they're ready to leave. Probably waiting for us."

They heard a muffled shout from the other side of the apron, followed by an unholy cacophony of gunfire. Men sprinted from the dark recess of the large hangar, emerging from a ragged hole in the large metal doors, which must have been the work of an explosive a few minutes earlier.

"We're off."

It was quite an operation to witness. Men stood bold in the open, unleashing a stream of machine-gun fire. Red was not a gun expert, but he knew these were large-calibre weapons unloading on the Soviet defenders.

A soldier grabbed his arm.

"Now, run!"

They took off. He tried to look back, desperate to see Vasil. Something was happening, and he felt out of control.

"Go, my friend!"

He heard Vasil's voice! Where is he?

Red stopped.

"Hey, move!" a soldier shouted from ahead.

Red saw him. Fifty yards back, flanked by his guards.

Their eyes locked. Vasil shook his head. "Don't look back, my friend. We need to move forward," he shouted.

Was he crying?

Red felt his arm gripped again; he was yanked away.

"We need to move—" The soldier was cut off by a thud sound. His grip went limp, and he fell to the ground with a scream.

Red immediately crouched next to him. Panicking at the sight of a burly soldier's face screwed up in pain. He was gripping his side.

"I'm fine," he said through clenched teeth.

"What?" Red said. "No you're not—"

He was cut off by two other soldiers who arrived and scooped him up.

"Out of the way!" one of them shouted.

Red stood up and looked back for Vasil. They had to stick together. That was the whole point of being here.

His eyes went to the jagged opening of a hangar two hundred yards to his right. Sitting inside, in the dark, was the unmistakable shape of Daedalus. In the shadows, in its element. Its last few seconds of existence.

His eyes searched back. Finally he saw Vasil. His group had taken cover when the soldier was shot, but now they got back to their feet.

They took off, but Vasil stood still. He looked directly at Red.

Why wasn't he running?

"Vasil! Please!" Red cried.

"Run! Go! Go home to Sarah. She needs you."

He was in pain. His face white, as if he were facing a firing squad.

His escorts took a moment to realise he'd stayed behind; they turned back.

As they did so, Vasil Demichev took off, running across the apron towards his Soviet colleagues on the other side of the lines.

"No!" Red screamed. He instinctively leaped after him, but on his second stride, he felt a heavy boot to his legs and fell sprawling on the ground.

He tried to scramble back up. As he spun over, Gabriel appeared over him, his eyes obviously following Vasil's run. He calmly raised his rifle to his shoulder and flicked the auto-switch back to semi.

Thud. Thud. Thud.

Three rhythmic shots. The gun pulsed into his shoulder.

Red snapped his head around, in time to see Vasil collapse, fifty yards away.

"No!" he shouted again.

Vasil's legs shifted on the ground as blood spread out beneath him.

The cover-fire team looked to its right, surprised to see a Soviet behind the lines, but perhaps relieved to see him cut down.

They continued to lay down fire, while the last of the men escaped from the hangar.

Red rolled away from his own captor and scrambled to his feet. But the man grabbed him again.

"Let me go!" Red shouted, staring the man down.

The soldier glanced at Gabriel, then released his grip.

Red ran full ahead and slid down next to Vasil.

He was on his back, his stomach a bloody mess.

Red could only stare at his friend.

But Vasil looked calm, the pain that was etched on his face replaced by a warm smile.

"Thank you for coming for me," he said with a croak before coughing up blood.

Red's eyes filled with tears at the sound of his friend's voice, weak and fading. "Why, Vasil? Why did you run?"

But there was too much blood in his mouth for him to talk now. Red looked down to his wounds. Was there any way to save him?

Red grabbed his hand.

Bubbles appeared in the blood around his mouth. Was he trying to speak?

Red leaned in closer, but heard only a stomach-churning gurgle. He lifted his head away and stared at Vasil's lifeless eyes.

A hand grabbed Red, and hauled him away. He didn't resist, and found himself breaking into a run assisted by the soldier.

Behind them, vehicles began to move.

They reached the side of the control tower and entered the shadows. In front, a small team carrying a large gun set it down and mounted it on a tripod.

It unleashed its first rounds. Deep thuds.

He glanced back to see the Soviet vehicles abruptly stop. Two of them sped towards cover provided by the tower, while the other burst into flames.

"Keep going!" someone shouted.

They still had three hundred yards to the C-130. It sat on the far side of a long grass area, props turning.

Gunshots again from behind. Red looked over his shoulder; the final cover-fire team were on the move, pursued by the Russian vehicles.

Rounds fizzed past.

He couldn't think straight; shock and confusion had taken over.

Vasil was dead.

A thump smacked into his back, throwing him forward.

Red crashed to the ground, rolling onto his back; a searing pain spread from his shoulder.

He screamed.

Hands appeared either side of him and yanked him back up, causing another shooting pain across his back.

"Can you walk?"

His heart was pounding. He felt as if he might faint.

"How bad is it?" he managed to ask.

"Can you walk?" came the impatient shout from the soldier on his right.

Tentatively he stepped forward. A numbness was descending. He began a lopsided gait, supported by the two men.

Despite the help, he fell again.

"Fuck. Come on, man!" one of them shouted, while the other turned and loosed off a few rounds at their pursuers. The sound deafened Red in one ear. A strong smell of discharged weapons filled his nostrils.

He'd avoided Vietnam so far and, as a test pilot, he thought the risk of being sent to war had passed.

But here he was, on a secret front line, buried deep inside enemy territory.

Vasil was dead.

He considered giving up.

Then an image filled his mind.

Sarah.

Beautiful Sarah. The image was detailed. The sun streaming through his kitchen blinds lighting up her face. She was laughing, smiling, at him.

He had to get home for her.

She was his, and he was hers.

It was his duty. His promise.

He wanted to be with her more than anything in the world.

Those stupid conversations he'd had with the men when drunk, *what does love feel like? How do you know?*

This is what it feels like.

He was woozy. His hand went to his back. His clothes were sodden. The mix of blood from the dead Russian he'd fallen on in the lobby, and now his own.

"Get up!" one of the soldiers shouted. "Last chance, pilot man."

Two hands hoisted him into the air.

Red stared at the soldier for a moment and then looked across to the waiting aircraft.

Sanctuary.

Sarah.

"Let's go," he said.

The soldier nodded. "Good." He seemed relieved to see some sign of life from Red.

He felt his feet skipping across the concrete as he was hauled over a taxiway.

More shots passed them. He heard a *clunk-clunk* ahead as sparks flew from the C-130. The aircraft was hit.

Fifty yards to go.

A single bullet could suddenly end it all.

Red wanted to close his eyes. The pain from his shoulder was pulsating.

He kept a vision of Sarah in his mind.

Finding the strength to stay upright.

He talked to himself to force out the confusion.

You're on an airfield.

You need to keep moving.

Stay upright.

The soldier screamed at him. "Come on, for fuck's sake. Work!"

Somehow, he found some more energy and pressed his feet down to help propel them.

Twenty yards to go.

A grinding mechanical sound suddenly filled the air. They looked up in time to see the nearest engine splintering. Shards of propeller flew into the night sky.

The prospect of a Soviet jail loomed.

They reached the aircraft and swerved around to the ramp at the rear.

The C-130 was instantly bathed in bright light.

Red thought he must be hallucinating, delirious from blood loss.

He tried to turn, seeking a logical explanation for the ethereal glow, but as he did so, he was punched to the ground, along with the two soldiers. An invisible shock wave had knocked them off their feet, five yards short of the ramp.

The explosion.

Daedalus was dead.

After the thundercrack noise of the blast, all they heard now was the sound of debris falling onto the concrete nearby.

The guns were silent.

Red finally looked back in time to see a huge orange fireball rise high into the night, before burning itself out.

As he stared, he was hoisted to his feet one final time and shoved into the cargo bay of the Hercules.

Chaos and shouting around him as men and equipment spilled in. Shouts went up, checking no one had been left behind. At least, no one alive.

The C-130 began its takeoff roll with the ramp just starting to close.

Dull thuds suggested the surviving Soviet soldiers had got back on their feet.

The aircraft seemed to be running fine, albeit on three engines.

Red was upended by his handlers and laid flat on a stretcher.

Hands felt under him as the C-130 lifted into the air.

"Shift over, man," someone called, and he was turned, fingers exerting pressure just below his shoulder. He yelped in agony again.

As Red rolled back, he looked at the man on the stretcher next to him.

Lifeless eyes stared back.

Someone drew a sheet over the body.

A needle slipped into his arm; Red closed his eyes.

The morphine eased the pain.

Images appeared before him.

Dupont smiling in his yellow Stearman.

Sarah in Maggie's at the bar, beaming as she read his note.

The three of them laughing by the lake.

Vasil, bleeding out on a concrete apron.

Gabriel's precision shooting.

Thud, thud, thud.

CHAPTER SEVENTEEN

THE WOUND WAS NOT SERIOUS. He'd been lucky, according to the medic at Wainwright. Maybe some ligament damage at most. But they'd check when he got back to California.

He was patched up, his arm put in a sling. Back on the C-130, he got his own stretcher for the long haul back to Edwards.

They gave him more painkillers, and the flight back passed in a haze.

At Edwards, the ramp lowered, and he was escorted off as walking wounded.

He looked around for Gabriel. He needed answers. But the commander was dealing with his own dead and injured.

They delivered him directly to the base medical centre.

He sat on a gurney in a small room with a basin and no windows.

A doctor prodded his wounds, making him wince.

No one asked what happened. No one raised an eyebrow at a test pilot presenting with a bullet wound to his shoulder.

"Looks like flesh for the main part," the doctor said.

"That bit of pressure pain means the round may have clipped your collarbone, so we'll send you for an X-ray. But otherwise, it's a case of a few stitches and some rest."

"Will I lose any use of my arm?" Red asked weakly.

The doctor shook his head. "Nah. Gladys will look after you now."

The doc swivelled and left Red alone with a middle-aged staff nurse. She dabbed a cold liquid on his bare flesh, and stuck a needle into him.

"Just to numb the pain while I stitch you up, Captain."

An uncomfortable silence hung in the room as the nurse worked. The medical staff would be under instructions not to ask questions, but Red wanted to talk.

The door opened again, and Gabriel stepped in.

"How you doing?"

"Fine," Red lied. He spotted the bulge on the commander's own arm. "And you?"

Gabriel shrugged. "Told you at the time. Just a graze."

Red shook his head slowly. Crazy images of a fierce fire-fight floated around his mind.

"I'd forgotten you were hit," he said quietly.

Gabriel raised an eyebrow and looked at the nurse. "Would you give us a couple of minutes, honey?"

"I'm in the middle of stitching him up!"

"Just a couple of minutes, I promise."

Reluctantly, she put down the tool she was using into a metal bowl. "Well, if the anesthetic wears off, he's not getting anymore."

"He's a big boy," Gabriel said, as the nurse left the room and closed the door behind her.

He moved to the only chair, against the wall opposite the gurney, and sat down.

"What the hell happened?" Red said. "I thought he was coming with us?"

"From the moment I saw that family picture, I knew he wasn't going anywhere."

Red thought about the faded photograph: the sister towering over Vasil, the father aged years before his time.

"Couldn't we have sent them a message, so they knew where he was?"

"You're being naive about our Soviet friends. Stalin may be long gone, but traitors are treated the same. The fact we were there meant he'd made a serious mistake, or he had deliberately given up the information. Either way, our arrival landed him in a whole heap of torture trouble."

"So, why didn't he come back?"

"If he escaped the Soviet Union, they would have come for his family. Then his friends, then his friends' families and their friends. One by one, they'd find themselves under interrogation in the Lubyanka and then either shot in the head or sent to the gulags."

Images of blood spurting from a gaping head wound from the first soldier he'd seen killed filled his mind. Now that he'd witnessed such death firsthand, there was nothing abstract about the threat to Vasil's family.

"I'm sorry, kid. But the moment we arrived, his fate was sealed."

Red stared down at his knees. "He seemed so calm." A memory of the conversation came back to him; he looked up. "Wait a second. Why did he agree to come with us?"

Gabriel shook his head. "To choose the circumstances of his own death."

Red stared at the huge soldier, calmly relaying the awful realities of the world to which he had briefly been exposed.

"He knew you were going to shoot him?"

Gabriel nodded. "Better to be shot a hero trying to escape your captors. He probably hoped it would help the story when they came to examine his motives. Not that they're a subtle bunch, of course. I suspect they've already rubbed him out of the photographs."

CHAPTER EIGHTEEN

A-TEC WAS QUIET. Red gathered his belongings. He looked up, noticing an old F-86 Sabre on the taxiway. It was used for refresher training.

So A-TEC was back in action.

As he watched through the planning room windows, the replacement B-57 taxied out, while a Talon was shutting down in front of the hangar.

Back to normal. As if the events of the past week had never happened.

He found his car keys, and had to think for a moment about where it had been left. The commissary. That felt like a month ago, not three days.

He looked up to the airfield door, at the sound of laughter as Johnny Clifford and another pilot walked in. They stopped their chat when they saw Red.

Clifford made his way over. "You okay?"

Red nodded.

Clifford lingered, but said nothing. Eventually, he reached out and gave Red's good shoulder a light pat.

. . .

Red's car was right there in the lot.

Life with one usable arm was taking some adaptation. He put his bag down and opened the door, before slinging the bag in the back.

He closed the door with his leg and looked up to the BX.

There was a figure at the cash register. But it wasn't her.

He walked over and stuck his head inside.

"Hi, hon," one of the girls nearby called. He couldn't remember her name.

"Is Sarah here?"

She shook her head. "No, hon." She glanced at the clock. "Her shift ended an hour ago."

"Thanks," Red said and started to back out.

The woman stopped what she was doing and walked towards him. "You'll be a sight for sore eyes, I can tell you that. She's not been right these past few days. They don't have telephones where you been?" Red's eyes went to his sling. "Where *have* you been, anyway?"

"Out of town."

The woman looked doubtful. "Well, don't let me keep you. Honestly, I think she thinks you're dead or something. I guess it'll be a nice surprise."

Driving was awkward. Red had to use his left hand to operate the gearshift, which was on the right-hand side of the steering wheel. But once moving, he believed he was moderately safe.

The road to Rosamond stretched out ahead, and he entered a trancelike state, as the images and sounds of death and blood continued to drift in and out of his mind.

It was hard to move on. These were images that left a stain.

He forced himself to think methodically through the events, obeying some inner voice that said it would help.

The dark interior of a special operations forces C-130.

Men shouting as they ran from chasing Soviet soldiers.

Vasil, smiling and asking him about Sarah.

Vasil cut down by Gabriel's shots.

Thud, thud, thud.

Those final words. *Thank you for coming for me.*

But that's how I killed you, my friend.

The way Vasil behaved. Almost serene. Or was that resignation?

He had known. That was for sure. He had known what was coming. The way he spoke to Gabriel when he was sitting on his bed. Red hadn't cottoned on, but everyone else understood. Vasil was planning a death that would inflict the least amount of trauma on Red.

As he made sense of the events, the dark feeling of dread began to lift.

He drove slowly, using the time to let the thoughts flow, making no attempt to keep them out.

Eventually, the images of violence faded, to be replaced by the moments that led him to that remote backwater of the Soviet Union.

The farm, in a remote backwater of Mississippi.

He went over the conversations, again and again.

How many times had he missed a chance to see the truth?

Every moment Dupont acted oddly. Each time he asked for more information before disappearing for a day to magically reappear with a fully formed solution.

His reluctance to join them in the bar, after his clumsy episode in his first week at Edwards.

Signs he should have seen.

Instead, he made excuses for him. He had a wise, older friend when he needed one.

His father had let him down. Absent at his son's most vulnerable time.

And so Dupont had stepped in.

One person knew. One person saw.

Sarah.

Three days ago, it angered him. Her ability to cut through his life with her all-seeing eyes.

How did she know?

She didn't need Dupont to be something else. To her, he was always an interloper.

To Red, he was much more, and his judgment had been clouded by emotion.

The sort of weakness that can kill an unwary pilot.

Of course, not even Sarah knew just how much of an interloper Dupont really was. But she was smart, her instincts strong.

He smiled as he visualised his smart, confident girl.

Red coasted into Rosamond. Sarah's car was at his house.

The front door opened, and she appeared, running as he drew to a stop.

She arrived at the car and pulled open the driver's-side door. She leaned in to hug him, stopping when she saw his arm.

"Are you okay?" She helped him out. "Red. What happened?" Sarah placed a gentle hand on his injured shoulder.

"You know, you're the first person with the audacity to ask me that."

She paused. "I guess I don't really need to ask, do I?"

"It's a light wound. A few stitches. I'll be fine."

A car drove past. Silence hung between them for a few seconds.

He could always change the subject, as he was expected to do.

But standing in the afternoon sunlight, outside his shabby, single-storey home, gazing at the vision in front of him, Red decided there would be no more secrets between them.

In that moment, he made another decision.

But that would have to wait.

"Brandon's dead. It's over."

Sarah rested a hand on his cheek and wiped away a tear. She didn't look surprised, just sympathetic.

"I'm sorry," she whispered.

Red pushed the car door shut with his hip.

As they got to the house, he stopped. Sarah's strawberry-blonde hair was almost red in the angled sunlight. Her brown eyes wide, twinkling.

He hoped his eyes conveyed as much as hers.

"Let's sit in the sun," he said, and he brushed down the tatty bench next to his front door. It was those few weeks as the seasons changed when the desert temperature was perfect.

They sat. She put a hand on his thigh. He closed his eyes.

His life at Edwards started to melt away. Smelly and noisy experimental aircraft. Tasking sheets for risky flight profiles. Blood and guts in Omolon. The images fading to black and white.

He was in the right place, and he wanted to be here with her, forever.

"I need to tell you something," she said. "He warned you not to come for him."

Red opened his eyes. "What do you mean?"

"He wrote you a letter. He sent it to my house. I guess he needed to be sure that only you would get it. He knew he'd given away his location. Or at least he thought you would work it out. It was a personal plea for you to keep quiet."

Red recalled Gabriel's frank assessment of Dupont's predicament. "He knew if we came for him, his life was over. I told them where he was. I killed him."

"You killed him?" Sarah gripped his arm.

"Not literally."

She brushed his hair with her fingertips, waiting for more.

He let out a slow breath. "But I was there. It was all horrible."

"Red, are you okay?"

"I think so."

There would be no more tears. Not for Brandon.

The light of the sun was rapidly turning into a deep orange. Sunsets moved quickly in the desert.

"Red, you weren't to know. You went with them to save him."

"Which you thought was stupid of me."

"I was worried about you. I thought I'd lose you."

"You also wondered whose side I was on."

She leaned forward, into his eyeline. "So, what would you have done? If you knew? If you'd read the letter?"

Red looked away. The yard needed tidying. A half oil drum roughly cut into a barbeque grill lay lopsided on the bare desert sand.

"I don't know."

"Don't you? If you'd kept that information to yourself,

the aircraft would still be in Soviet hands. You'd have saved Brandon. A spy who you'll never see again. But you would have given up your own country's secrets."

He smiled at her, unable to reconcile the image of her carefree bouncing around the tables in Maggie's, and on the register at the BX, with this smart, insightful woman who wouldn't be out of place in a meeting at A-TEC.

"I didn't see things as clearly as you, Sarah." He placed his good left hand on hers. "You were right. I had a hole in my life. I was easy pickings."

"Don't be hard on yourself."

He glanced up at the water tower. He never did get Brandon up there. "But I needed to go. I think you were wrong about that. I needed to find out for myself."

"And what did you find out?"

Red paused and looked at the bare ground, where once there had been well watered lush greenery and flowers. His mother's labour of love.

"I watched my father die." As he spoke a tear rolled down his cheek. Sarah squeezed his arm.

"I know," she said.

"It sounds strange, but I think it helped me."

"Really? I think it must have left you in pieces."

Red took a long breath. Fighting off the images that began their usual intrusion into his mind.

"Yeah. It did. But at the same time, I knew he was gone. There was no mystery, no uncertainty. When my mother died, six years later, I wasn't there. I came home expecting to find her in the house, even though I'd been told. But I went to see her."

"At the funeral home?"

"Yeah. I remember as clear as yesterday. This guy says 'she's in there, waiting for you'. I push open this door, see her and immediately know, she's not there. That's not her. Just her old body. She's gone. I think it must be what animals do."

Sarah didn't say anything but she held onto his arm, tightly.

"I think it was the same with Brandon. It took a little longer to sink in, but the moment he escaped from us and started running at the Russians, I knew."

"That Brandon was gone?" She asked.

He turned to face her. "That he never existed."

She raised an eyebrow. "And you're okay about everything now? About him dying?"

"I'm okay that Vasil Demichev died. I'm sorry for him, but he understood the risks. He didn't seem surprised when we arrived in his room. You should have seen him. He was so calm."

The sun disappeared behind the house opposite. The evening chill immediately made its presence known.

"Let's get inside," she said.

The house was warm with trapped daytime heat.

In the kitchen, Sarah poured a glass of water. The ingredients of a decent-looking meal sat on the tabletop. Corn, steaks, and potatoes. He realised how hungry he was.

"Don't suppose there's a beer in the fridge?"

She tipped the water away, opened a cold Budweiser, and handed it to him.

"You have one, too."

They clinked bottles and took a drink. She placed hers on the counter and Red watched the condensation running down the side of the bottle. Just like the billboard images.

"I'm sorry about what I said before you left," Sarah said. "In the commissary."

Red's lower back ached. He moved to the table and took a seat. Sarah remained standing, leaning against the sink.

"You don't have to be sorry. You were right." He smiled at her. "I think maybe some of it was genuine. I think he liked having me as a project. Maybe he was looking for a kind of son. There's an irony."

Sarah toyed with her bottle. "But, maybe it was all calculated? Remember how big the prize was for him?"

Red smiled. "Maybe."

He set his bottle down and stood up, moving over to her. He stared into her eyes. She looked unsettled for a moment and laughed nervously.

"What is it?"

"I've been offered an exchange tour to England."

Her face fell. "I see."

"Come with me."

She furrowed her brow. "How would that work—"

"As my wife."

For a beat, there was no sound in the house. Sarah carefully reached for her beer and took a long drink, not breaking eye contact.

"Well?" he asked.

"Don't joke with me," she whispered.

"Will you marry me, Sarah MacLean?"

She continued to watch Red closely, not moving from her spot, leaning against the sink. "Is this the shock talking? Have you really recovered from what happened over there?"

He smiled. "This is me talking."

"You want us to get married?" She spoke slowly.

"I think one of the reasons you didn't trust Brandon is because you thought I didn't need him. I didn't need a father figure. You believed in me, and you wanted me to believe in myself."

"Everyone wants that for you, Red."

"I know that now. Or at least I'm starting to believe it. I got America into a big mess, but I wasn't the only one fooled by a pretty sophisticated ruse."

She stood upright. "But you were the one who got us out of it."

"I was. I played my part. Brandon played his. I think we ended up equal."

"I'd say you ended up the winner."

Red paused. He looked down at his feet, then back up at Sarah. "There was a moment, in between the bullets and explosions. We were running. Brandon was ahead. He shouted back at me to keep going and don't look back. Then they shot him. At the time I think he didn't want me to witness it."

"Understandable."

"But I think he meant it about me as well. It was his way of releasing me from the guilt."

"Do you feel guilty?

Red shook his head. "I don't think so. Thanks to Vasil. And thanks to you."

She set down her beer and draped her arms around him. He moved his left arm around her.

"Now, Captain. Where's the ring? Please tell me you have a ring?"

He laughed. "Let's go to LA this weekend."

Their foreheads touched.

"So?" Red tilted his head and pressed his nose against hers. "You have to say it out loud."

Their lips drifted together, and just as they met, she whispered.

"Yes."

They both grinned as they pulled back after the kiss.

"I'd like to get you something, too," Sarah said. "I know it's not traditional for the girl, but I've been saving the rent from Brandon, and it seems like the right thing to do."

"Thank you."

"So what would you like, Captain Brunson?"

Red looked at his wrist on Sarah's shoulder. His fire-damaged Omega told him it was 1130.

"I think it's time for a new watch."

The End.

ALSO BY JAMES BLATCH

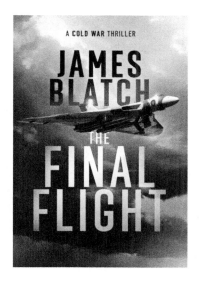

Turn the page for a free preview of The Final Flight.

THE FINAL FLIGHT BY JAMES BLATCH

It begins with nothing.

A space in the sky, silence on a radio channel.

A turn of the head in a control tower; a first inkling that something, somewhere, is not right.

There could be a range of benign explanations.

But old squadron hands sense death quickly.

Events unfold with their own momentum and a predictable narrative.

Somewhere in the countryside, a puzzled farmer stares at a plume of rising black smoke.

Within an hour of the missed radio call, a man in uniform knocks on the door of a married quarter.

He stands in silence, hoping his presence alone will convey the gravity of his message.

It always does.

Families mourn, but the men in flying coveralls must go back into the air.

They bury their friend, then bury their grief.

Away from public view, serious men with clipboards pore over the debris and piece together the sequence of events.

Arguments and compromise precede the publication of an official document on flimsy government paper.

It invariably contains two words. A final insult to young men who had so much of their lives to live but who died in the blink of an eye on a weekday afternoon.

Pilot error.

THE FINAL FLIGHT - CHAPTER 1
TUESDAY 7TH JUNE, 1966

The peace of Blethwyn Valley was shattered for thirteen seconds.

The rabbits sensed the man-made thunder first and bolted for their burrows. The sheep, slow to react, scattered only as it arrived overhead, briefly blotting out the June sun. Invisible vortexes sent a buzzard tumbling in the air.

The four engines left a trail of black smoke in the disturbed wake and a deep rumble that quickly faded.

There were no witnesses.

The RAF Avro Vulcan bomber had come and gone on a sleepy weekday in a remote part of Wales.

The Welsh were at work.

And that's how the men of the Royal Air Force Test Flying Unit liked it.

To be unobserved.

Had there been a witness—maybe a farmer turning his head at the sudden and loud intrusion to his otherwise tranquil surroundings—it's doubtful he would have noticed anything unusual about this particular flight.

He may have been able to identify the Vulcan, perhaps

because of its distinctive delta wing, but it's less likely he would have spotted the bulge of white casing with a glass-panelled front, nestled under the nose of the bomber.

Although unremarkable in appearance, it was the most secret and significant item of military equipment on the planet.

Inside the white casing, behind the glass, was a laser.

As far as the outside world was concerned, laser was a rudimentary and far from mobile technology.

But then the world doesn't know what the world doesn't know, and the men of the TFU were under threat of arrest to keep it that way.

As the Vulcan exited the far end of the valley, the wings rolled left, and the throttles edged up to eighty-five per cent of maximum to sustain the target speed through the turn. The stick eased back, the rudder deflected left—just a little —as the nose heaved thirty degrees and the jet rolled out on a new heading.

On board, not a single member of the crew had touched a flying control.

In fact, they were discussing the football.

Chris Milford tried to ignore the navigator's drone regarding the England squad for the forthcoming World Cup. He didn't share Steve Bright's concern that there were too many West Ham players in the side. He understood the point about the Hammers being a pedestrian, unglamorous side that didn't produce the type of flair players needed to win a World Cup, but Millie had work to do.

He concentrated on inserting a reel of magnetic tape into a brown cardboard sleeve. A simple enough task on the ground, but difficult when your seat is being hauled through the bumpy, low-level air at three hundred and fifty knots.

After a successful struggle, he scribbled a serial number

on the cardboard and dipped into a pocket on his flying coveralls to pull out a small notepad. Millie adjusted the light that hung down on a pipe from the panel in front of him and added the tape serial number to a list. He had to pause as the jet rose and fell, weaving its way through the Welsh hills.

Alongside the serial number, he noted the date, flight number and time. He paused, casting his eye up the list of previous entries, noting the accumulation of flying hours.

So far, so good for project Guiding Light.

Millie tucked the notebook back into his pocket and turned his attention to the switches, dials and readouts in front of him.

Sitting in a well below the cockpit, facing backwards, he studied the converted navigator-radar station.

The Guiding Light panel sparkled orange, electronically generated numbers pulsing as they changed in a rhythm directly linked to the aircraft's proximity to the ground in feet.

Millie watched them carefully.

The display went from 307, to 312 and a moment later 305.

They had asked Guiding Light to fly the jet as close to, but not below, three hundred feet. It was doing a good job of the task.

The veteran engineering officer was still getting used to the marvel of it all. Somewhere behind the switches and dials that surrounded him, electronic wizardry connected the laser's range-finding data to the Vulcan autopilot.

Two pieces of technology in direct communication. Millie hoped they didn't fall out..

To his relief, the captain Brian Hill, interrupted Steve

Bright's football monologue with a clipped question over the intercom.

"How many more tapes?"

Millie pulled his oxygen mask over his face.

"That was the last one. I'm out now."

"OK, we'll stay at low-level until we get to the estuary as planned," Hill replied.

With the recorder no longer capturing data from the laser, Millie wondered why they would continue at low-level. But he remained silent on the matter. It would only be a few minutes.

His hand went up to a small black rotary dial beneath the main height readout. He turned it, clicking it through its eleven stops, each a pre-defined position around the nose of the Vulcan.

In fact the system scanned twenty-seven separate locations sweeping from thirty degrees left and eighty degrees down all the way across to the same position on the right, taking in the view up to forty degrees above the nose.

A design engineer at DF Blackton once told him they began by mimicking how much a pilot's eyes absorbed from the picture in front of him, and improved on that.

Millie noted the twelve hundred feet or so of space to their left and imagined the rocky side of a Welsh hill. He turned the dial back to the number one position, more or less straight down.

Two hundred and sixty-one feet to the unforgiving ground beneath them.

"Do you ever take your eyes off those numbers?"

Millie glanced across to Steve Bright and shrugged.

"Our lives in the hands of a computer with this aircraft's flaky electrical system? Yes, I like to keep an eye on them."

Millie tried to be an amiable crewmate, but it was no

secret he no longer enjoyed these trips. Squashed into a flying dungeon with the ever present threat of a sudden end to everything.

He looked back at Brighty; the nav looked bored. A consequence of his job being replaced by a flying computer.

"Hungry?"

Brighty perked up as Millie passed over a sandwich from his flight case.

He unlatched his seat, swivelled it around to face the empty middle position and stretched his legs. They ached from being squeezed under the workstation.

With his oxygen mask dangling under his chin, he muttered to himself, "This is a young man's game." But his words were lost in the perpetual roar as the jet thundered its way across Wales.

He looked up the short ladder to the cockpit, where Brian Hill craned his neck, looking down toward him.

"Getting ready for your afternoon nap, Millie?"

Millie smiled and pulled his mask across his face so his words would be heard on the intercom.

"Would be lovely. Try and fly smoothly."

Hill laughed and turned back.

A third voice piped up on the loop. Rob May, in the co-pilot's seat.

"We're not here for smoothness, my old friend."

Millie noted tension in Rob's voice; the young test pilot was technically in control of the aircraft, although much of the decision making had been ceded to Guiding Light.

Hill drew the curtain back across to cut out the light glare from the windshield, allowing Millie and Bright to see their dials and displays clearly.

Millie turned his chair back to the workstation and again kept a close eye on the height data as it ticked over.

The numbers updated every three quarters of a second. It was hypnotic. He fought the urge to close his eyes.

He reached forward and rotated the black dial once again. Position two showed 1,021 feet, position three showed 314 feet. They were hugging a valley, just three hundred feet from one side.

The computer was showing them what good tactical flying looked like.

He rotated it back to position one. Nine hundred and fourteen feet directly below them.

Nine hundred and fourteen feet. Really?

Suddenly Millie was lifted in his seat.

He felt the aircraft plummeting.

Must be trying to get back to three hundred feet above the ground.

He called into the intercom. "Why are we so high?"

"We're not," Rob May's clipped voice responded.

The aircraft continued down.

Millie grabbed the desk to steady himself.

"What?" he shouted, urgently needing clarification. If they weren't really at nine hundred feet but the jet thought they were, it would try and descend into the...

"What's happening, Rob?" Millie shouted. He glanced at Steve Bright, who stared back at him.

Millie's eyes darted back to the range reading.

803.

"What's going on, Rob? How high are we, for god's sake?"

He needed to know what the picture looked like outside.

"Rob?"

Eventually, Rob replied. "About one hundred feet."

Millie looked back at the reading.

749.

"*Talk to me, Millie.*" Rob shouted.

"Christ, it's gone wrong. Cancel. *CANCEL.*"

They were under instruction not to intervene with Guiding Light unless absolutely necessary. But surely they were about to die unless they took control?

Sweat dripped from Millie's forehead. Why was Guiding Light suddenly blind? Why was the laser looking straight through solid rock?

In the back, they felt a lurch as the autopilot disengaged.

Millie sensed the angle change as the nose raised, but he knew the momentum of the heavy aircraft was still downward.

He looked over his shoulder and stared up into the cockpit; the curtain was pulled open by the g-force.

Millie saw Brian Hill's hands move down to the yellow and black ejection seat cord.

"Oh, shit."

Ejection was only an option for the two pilots. Millie and Bright had no chance of getting out alive at this height.

He closed his eyes and braced for death.

The aircraft continued to sink.

Is this it?

He thought of Georgina, beautiful Georgina. And Charlie. Where was he right now? In a maths lecture, probably. Oblivious to the enormity of the moment.

The aircraft shuddered.

It was almost imperceptible, but the plane's momentum switched from a descending path to a climbing one.

He opened his eyes and looked around again, in time to see Hill release his grip on the cord.

Hill suddenly pointed forward and shouted. "*Trees.*"

The aircraft rolled right and Millie was pinned to his

seat as the engines surged to full throttle and Rob May threw them into a spectacular powered, turning climb.

Vibrations rumbled through the fuselage as the engines screamed; the aircraft complaining and creaking under the stress.

Millie groaned as the g-force gripped him, pushing him down into his seat.

They held the gravity-defying manoeuvre for a few seconds, until the wings levelled.

Millie let out a long breath he hadn't realised he'd been holding in.

He looked across at Steve Bright, the nav's eyes bulging wide above his mask.

The throttles eased back and the aircraft settled.

It seemed like a full minute before anyone spoke.

Eventually, the silence was broken by the normally unflappable Brian Hill.

"Jesus Christ."

Millie's eyes rested on the tape data recorder.

It was switched off and empty. Whatever just happened, it had happened after he'd stopped recording the height readings from Guiding Light.

He realised he needed to write down what he'd seen with his own eyes, but he couldn't move.

Too much adrenaline in his system.

He settled his breathing and eventually fished out a pencil.

The system had taken them to within a whisker of a catastrophic crash. The all-singing, all-dancing laser had seen straight through solid earth and told the onboard computer to descend.

How it had happened was beyond him.

It was someone else's problem now. One of those clever

boffins at DF Blackton in Cambridge would have some explaining to do.

He added a note to the end of his description of the event.

Guiding Light evaluation suspended.

———

Wing Commander Mark Kilton struggled with the acetate sheet. The image in the overhead projector was either upside down or back to front, and now it was out of focus and too large to fit the screen.

The tall and wide American lieutenant general took his seat at the table. "You fly jets better than you operate a projector, Kilton?"

Kilton offered Eugene Leivers III a thin smile and gave up with the projector. He took his own seat at the repurposed dining room table that had somehow found its way into the side office he'd commandeered for the meeting in the station headquarters building.

Paint peeled from the walls of the 1930s construction and the unseasonable heat of an English June made life uncomfortable for the five men in the room.

Leivers removed his jacket, replete with three rows of medal ribbons, and hung it on the back of his chair. He made a dismissive gesture with his hand toward the white screen intended to display Kilton's diagrams, and spoke with a Louisianan drawl.

"Forget it, Kilton. I know what Guiding Light does. What I need to know is, does it work?"

Kilton glared at him. "It works."

"Outstanding."

RAF Air Vice Marshal Richard Mannington stood up

and opened the curtains. Kilton winced as daylight flooded in.

"Sunshine," said Mannington, "to illuminate a moment of British engineering triumph."

Kilton turned to the general. "Guiding Light is working and it will change everything."

A broad grin spread across Leivers's face. "Damn straight it will, Kilton." The general leaned forward and banged the table. "Gentlemen, I have to tell you, we've carried out some theoretical simulations using the information you've provided about Guiding Light, and the results have been phenomenal. *Phenomenal*."

He took a deep breath, lowered his voice.

"What I'm about to tell you will never leave this room. Understood?"

The general's eyes darted between Kilton, Mannington and the two other men sitting at the table. They each gave a nod of acknowledgement.

"Terrain-following radar, the new technology we're both rushing to fit to our new jets, is dead."

"Dead?" Mannington asked.

"Dead, Dickie. The Russkies can detect it."

Kilton tried not to show his shock.

"But we're planning to fit TFR to everything," Mannington said. "The laser... Guiding Light. It's supposed to be a backup."

Leivers continued. "It just got promoted. Instead of helping our boys get in and out of the badlands, TFR will do the opposite. Every Russkie SAM from Berlin to Vladivostok will lock on and blow them out of the sky. They may as well be flying with floodlights and a big arrow that says *SHOOT HERE*. Damn shame."

Kilton inhaled. "Do the Russians know we know this?"

Leivers smiled at him. "No, Kilton. They do not. And neither do they know about Guiding Light. Your silent laser solves a very big headache at just the right time. This goes all the way up the line. And I mean all the way. This is not about winning World War Three. It's about preventing it. Once we have an unassailable advantage over the Reds, it's game over for them." He leaned back and spoke a little more slowly. "And that's why I've got POTUS's attention on this one."

Mannington turned a pencil over in his hands. "What's *Potus*?"

"POTUS is the President of the United States, Dickie."

Minister of State David Buttler cleared his throat. "General. The United Kingdom is not putting Guiding Light on a shelf for sale to all comers."

Leivers balked. "All comers? I thought we had a special relationship, Mr Buttler."

"Of course we have a special relationship, General. But we must remember that Guiding Light is a system that gives us all an advantage only so long as the enemy remains oblivious to its existence. At least until it's fitted to the fleets."

"You don't trust the US to keep a secret?"

"Britain trusts America implicitly. It's just that the chances of the secret getting out are simply higher the more people know about it. How many aircraft are you considering it for?"

The general shrugged. "Two thousand to start with."

Ewan Stafford appeared nonchalant, but Kilton knew him of old and knew damn well the short, tubby managing director was doing cartwheels inside.

"And what else?"

"Excuse me?" said Leivers, tilting his head to one side.

Buttler spoke with patient clarity. "The order for

Guiding Light would be substantial, and I'm sure our colleague here from DF Blackton is doing his best not to burst into song. But we'd like to know that our most secret military breakthroughs can be shared both ways."

The general shrugged again. "Well, that's a little beyond my powers, Minister."

"But not beyond the powers of POTUS, I assume?"

"Well, no—"

"And you have POTUS's attention on this?"

The general thought for a moment. "Yes, sir. I do. And I dare say there will be some good deals for both of us in the pipeline. But this is something to discuss when we're ready to talk turkey. So far, we haven't seen this thing working."

Kilton felt the eyes swing back to him.

Stafford spoke up. "Perhaps Mark could give us all an update on the trial work his team have been carrying out for a while now. A very long while."

"As you're aware, Mr Stafford, the Royal Air Force Test Flying Unit will be the sole and final arbiter of Guiding Light's operational effectiveness. We have a detailed trial timetable and it is being executed even as we speak. The two working Guiding Light systems have been fitted to a Vulcan and a Canberra. The Vulcan is airborne at this moment with a TFU crew." He glanced at his RAF issue pilot's watch. "We've flown one hundred and ninety-four hours as of this morning."

"And no problems?" said Leivers.

"No. We're still a few weeks from sign-off. We did agree three hundred hours of intensive airborne time. You want to fit this to two thousand jets and we want to equip more or less our entire Bomber Command fleet. I think it's in all our interests that it's working as advertised."

"Fine," said Stafford. "But I need not remind the room

that the longer we wait, the more chance there is of a leak."

Kilton ignored him and turned to General Leivers. "You're sitting in the United Kingdom's most secure RAF station. As long as the project remains under wraps here, there is no scenario where it's rendered ineffective. The Soviets will have no clue what it is or how to defend against it. And when it's operational, and it will become operational soon, NATO jets will for the first time be able to operate deep into Russian territory without giving off any radar energy whatsoever. At low-level we will be invisible."

Leivers clapped his hands together and beamed. "That's what we're doing this for. Kilton, you deliver this system and it's not just Mr Stafford's accountant you're gonna make happy. We are gonna be friends for a long time."

"Excellent, Mark," said Buttler. "Very good work from TFU. This won't be forgotten."

General Leivers' hand appeared at Kilton's shoulder. The man from Baton Rouge leaned in close and whispered loud enough for all to hear. "I've dedicated my life to defeating communism, boy. It's a nasty, lethal plague and you, my friend, have its final demise in your hands. Don't let me down."

Kilton nodded. "General Leivers, you have my word."

———

The meeting broke up. Kilton reminded the room that they allowed no papers relating to Guiding Light to leave West Porton. The men obliged by pooling their briefing notes into a single pile for him to deliver to TFU's secure cabinets.

Leivers looked suitably impressed with the emphasis on security. "You really do run a secret operation here, don't you, Kilton?"

The air vice marshal cut in before Kilton could answer. "You'd be forgiven for thinking there's no station here at all. At Group we call West Porton RAF Hidden."

"Then I'd suggest we're doing our job properly," said Kilton.

Leivers disappeared out of the room.

Mannington turned to Kilton. "What's that American expression you used once, Mark? *Need to know*. I suppose you think your superiors don't need to know anything."

Kilton continued to shuffle the papers into a brown folder.

"We do need to know something, Mark," Mannington continued. "There is still a chain of command. Just keep that in mind, please."

He walked out of the room; Ewan Stafford followed close behind, offering a tip of his hat before he placed it on his head.

The minister paused for a moment, allowing the others to move out of earshot.

"That was impressive, Mark."

"I thought the same of you, sir. Quite the card player."

The minister smiled and clicked his briefcase shut.

"You realise this project cannot fail. After the mess of TSR-2, we need this victory. Having to cancel a high profile fighter-bomber project was embarrassing to say the least. Guiding Light needs to be a success. As I said, it won't go unrewarded. The PM's always on the lookout for reliable men in the upper echelons of the military. You deliver Guiding Light, we authorise Blackton's sale to the Americans. That's an extremely welcome injection of cash just when we need it. A winning scenario for all of us."

Kilton looked out of the window where Mannington was helping Leivers into his staff car. Buttler followed his gaze.

"And we'll make sure the Americans know who it was who delivered this project. But Mark, if we have another debacle, particularly a leak from TFU, then it's going to be very hard to justify the existence of this unit you've created. You're already ruffling feathers with the RAF brass as it is."

"There will be no leak from here, but I don't like information going up the line to Group." He nodded toward the receding staff car outside. "I start to lose control of who knows what, and that's when it can get leaky."

"I understand. So, how can I help?"

Kilton looked at him. "Allow me to report direct to you, direct to the Air Ministry and cut out Group and the RAF Main Building."

"You realise what you're asking? The men with gold braid on their shoulders won't be happy."

Kilton thought for a moment and shrugged.

Buttler smiled. "I can talk to the PM. I think he'll see the benefit of such an arrangement. Between you and me, he believes most of the RAF now hate him for ending TSR-2."

"They do," Kilton answered quickly. "But then they're mostly old romantics who think we're stuck in the 1940s. Some of us exist in the real world."

"They're a powerful bunch, those old romantics as you call them. Your head's above the parapet now Mark." The minister walked to the door. "You'll find your life was a lot less complex in 1940, shooting down the Luftwaffe and staying alive for another day. I'll talk to the PM. I think we can probably agree you report direct to the Ministry for now. Keeping in tight in the name of secrecy. It would be a tragedy for all if this project failed before that deal was signed."

The minister's heels made a clicking noise on the hard

floor as he disappeared, leaving Kilton alone with a brown envelope filled with papers and stamped *TOP SECRET*.

―――――

Millie reached forward and flipped a switch marked *DATA PANEL ELEC*. The orange numbers presented by the Guiding Light system went dark as the electrical supply was cut off.

He tucked his flight case back under the navigator station and secured it with a bungee cord. Inside were the four reels of magnetic tape he had filled with height data, recording the flight at low-level. He thought four would be enough to cover the run, but he missed the last couple of minutes, which included the moment when the system went haywire.

But it wouldn't matter, since there were four men on board, and they could describe what happened accurately between them.

The aircraft's wings rolled and he felt the g-force increase, pressing him into his seat. But it was gentle; Rob was guiding the delta-winged jet smoothly onto finals for RAF West Porton. It was a flying style that matched his nature.

A moment later, with a squeal of rubber beneath them, they were down.

Once the aircraft came to a stop at the end of a brief taxi, Steve Bright was quickly out of his seat and opening the hatch. Millie stayed put, but watched as the nav extended the yellow ladder.

It was a warm June day. Millie removed his helmet and oxygen mask, and ran a gloved hand through what was left of his sweaty grey hair, now matted to his head.

Eventually, Brian Hill pulled aside the curtain, looking haggard. He nodded at Millie but said nothing as he descended the steps.

Rob was behind him. Millie winced at the sight of his reddened face with pronounced stress lines, squashed into the helmet.

He looked like a man in his forties, rather than a fresh faced twenty-nine-year-old.

"You OK?"

Rob looked serious. He nodded and continued down the ladder. Millie picked up his case and followed him out, feeling for the metal rungs below him. Everything seemed to take more time these days.

He felt Rob's hand on his back, giving him some help as he concentrated on jumping backwards the last couple of feet below the bottom rung. He landed and wobbled in his cumbersome flying boots, grateful for the support of his friend.

"They didn't make this thing with fifty-four-year-olds in mind," he said, relieved to see Rob smile back at him.

As they turned and walked toward the TFU hangar and offices, Millie instinctively rested a hand on Rob's shoulder.

"You did well. You saved us and the jet."

"I don't know if I did do well, Millie. I was slow to react. You had to shout at me." Rob paused and glanced back at the Vulcan: pristine white, hunched on its landing gear. "I nearly lost it."

"We've been told not to interfere unless absolutely necessary and we've logged, what, nearly two hundred hours? All your experience was working against you. But you got there."

Rob kept glancing back at the aircraft. "It can be overwhelming if I stop to think about it. The jets are large, new, colossally expensive. Three crew members I'm responsible for."

"It's a lot for a youngster, isn't it?" Millie smiled at him. "Look. You did well today. You acted in time, and frankly that's all that matters. Think it through. If you feel you could have done better, work out why and learn. But it's always going to feel messy when things go wrong, Rob. And boy did they go wrong."

"It did go wrong, didn't it? What happened?"

"The laser saw straight through the ground, or at least the computer misinterpreted the feed. Either way, it commanded the autopilot to descend as if we were nine hundred feet not three hundred."

"Can we ever trust it again?"

Millie scoffed. "Not until what happened today is completely and utterly understood and the problem solved."

They carried on into TFU, where they drank tea and didn't discuss the incident with anyone. That was the TFU way. Mark Kilton had made it clear that you only discussed projects with those who needed to know.

But Millie could tell by their colleagues' glances that they knew something was up.

It was such an odd way of operating. In any normal squadron they would be sharing their tale, getting it off their chest, drawing comfort from the looks of horror and empathy from their friends.

But not at Mark Kilton's Test Flying Unit.

After handing in their flying equipment and coveralls, Millie ushered the crew into a side office to debrief.

Once the door was shut, Brian Hill led the questions, all aimed at Millie as the project leader and the man most familiar with the inner workings of Guiding Light.

Millie looked at his hastily scrawled notes.

"I happened to be rotating the selector, checking our general position. When I switched it back to number one position, it showed nine hundred odd feet below us."

"Nine hundred? Christ, Millie, we were still at three hundred," Hill said. "So that's why Guiding Light dived us toward the ground. It couldn't see it."

Millie shook his head in bewilderment. "I suppose it was doing what we asked it to do. Fly us at three hundred feet. It was just trying to get us back down."

"It chose a perfect time to go blind," said Brian Hill. "A state of the art, one hundred thousand-pound system descending a four engine Vulcan jet bomber with four people on board into the Welsh rock? Someone, somewhere better get the sack."

Millie took out the chart and with Steve Bright's help, they did their best to draw the aircraft's track along the valley, marking the spot with an *X* where it had all gone wrong.

"And you definitely didn't have a tape running?" Rob asked Millie.

"No. I brought four tapes based on the low-level run time and I'd just finished the last one."

"Damn shame," Hill said. "The tapes record everything, don't they?"

"Erm, I think so," said Millie. "I've never seen what they do or don't record. They all go off to Cambridge for a main-frame computer to read. But it doesn't matter, does it? If we'd been in a standard fit Vulcan and the autopilot had misbehaved, we'd report it just like this." He motioned to the chart and notes on the table. "Just everyone write it down now while it's fresh and I'll speak with Kilton."

Hill laughed. "Good luck with that, old boy."

"He won't have a choice, Brian. We have to shut it down."

"I agree, chap. But all the same, good luck."

Millie folded up the chart and gathered the notes.

Hill stood up to his full six feet four inches and put his arms around Rob and Steve Bright.

"You know what I need?"

Rob tilted his head. "Does it have something to do with the mess bar?"

"Exactly. Beer. I need beer and I need drinking companions. I've had enough of this malarkey for one day." He led the two younger men out of the room.

"I'll secure the paperwork," Millie said to the empty room.

————

There was a short queue at the NAAFI shop as Millie picked up a packet of John Player No. 6. Five minutes later, he pushed open the door to the mess bar to discover the usual crowd of men, back in uniform but looking a little dishevelled from the day's airborne activities.

Beers in hand, cigarettes in mouth; tales of flying and smoke filled the air.

Brian Hill, Steve Bright and another TFU pilot, Jock MacLeish, stood by one of the pillars in the middle of the room. Millie went to the bar first, where the white-coated steward was already pouring a scotch.

"I've been here too long," he said as he took the tumbler.

When he arrived at the pillar, Hill was speaking, and he caught the tail-end.

"... anyway, it was damn close."

Millie opened his new packet of cigarettes and screwed up the flap of silver paper folded over the filter ends. He offered the pack around, and Hill leaned forward to take one. When they were close, Millie spoke quietly.

"I hope you're not being indiscreet, Brian?"

Hill shrugged, and tapped his cigarette on the drinks shelf surrounding the pillar.

"We can trust old MacLeish. He's Scottish. The most trustworthy of the Celts, I believe."

"That may be," Millie continued, more quietly than Hill, "but he doesn't need to know."

Hill snorted at the incongruous use of Kilton's new buzz phrase, but Millie continued to look at him, waiting. Eventually, Hill gave a resigned look and nodded in acknowledgement.

In the awkward silence that followed, Millie drained half the measure of scotch, savouring the smoky flavour. The alcohol dulled his senses; it felt good.

He scanned the room, looking for Rob. The bar was filling up quickly as officers came off duty from various parts of the station: air traffickers in one corner, station adminners in another.

An ageing man with sunken eyes raised his glass. Millie lifted his tumbler in return, nodding at JR, a pilot with 206 Maintenance Unit, an unglamorous outfit nestled in the far corner of the airfield.

The rest of the room was TFU. Loud, brash, elite. His colleagues occupied the bar and most tables. What would it have been like thirteen months ago, with 206 MU as the sole flying unit? Rather nice, he suspected, and he suddenly felt a pang of jealousy for aircrew whose only task was the final flight of retired aircraft.

Finally his eyes landed on Rob. He was nestled among the elite of the elite: the chosen few senior test pilots, grouped at one end of the bar.

Millie raised an eyebrow and looked at Brian Hill.

"How did Rob end up over there?"

Hill glanced over. "Ah, the big boys came and took him before you got here, I'm afraid".

Millie studied Rob. On one side of him was Red Brunson, an American on exchange from Edwards. Glamorous and larger than life, he flew with his own grey 'flight suit' as he called it, and a fancy helmet complete with mirrored visor. He looked like an Apollo astronaut.

At the other side was Speedy Johnson, a legend to every schoolboy in the 1940s and 1950s. Kept breaking speed records for the RAF as the jet age blossomed.

"You can't blame him," Hill said and it took Millie a moment to notice he was being spoken to.

"Huh?"

"You can't blame Rob, having his head turned by that lot. He's a promising test pilot."

"Let's hope they don't corrupt him," Millie eventually said.

A round of drinks arrived; as Millie reached for his next glass of scotch, he noticed a ripple of movement across the room.

Mark Kilton had arrived.

This precipitated a stiffening of backs and subconscious opening of groups, hoping he would join them.

Kilton inevitably moved in to drink with the set crowded at the bar. Rob smiled at Kilton, who slapped him on the back.

The room was now heaving. Thick smoke hung in the air, and the heat of the day was making it uncomfortable.

Millie glanced at his watch. Six already. Georgina and Mary would be waiting for him and Rob, impatient to eat and get on with the card game.

He drained his glass, said his goodbyes, and approached the group at the bar. Red Brunson gave him a friendly slap on the shoulder as he arrived. Speedy Johnson exclaimed, "Ah, Milford. Come to talk to us about data?"

The group laughed.

"Well, someone has to look after the computers that are replacing you lot."

This provoked some mock booing from the pilots.

On a whim, he turned to Kilton.

"Boss, can I have a word, please?"

Kilton nodded and they moved off to a corner near the mess piano.

"I was going to brief you tomorrow, and I will, but I thought I should let you know. Guiding Light failed today."

Kilton's expression didn't change at first. Then he looked puzzled.

"What do you mean, 'failed'?"

"It went blind, at three hundred feet and three hundred knots, in Wales."

"Blind?"

"Suddenly we were descending. I happened to be looking at the panel at the time. The laser thought there was nine hundred below us. In reality we were still at three hundred."

"So you cancelled?"

"It took a moment for us all to adjust to what was happening, but yes, Rob did a good job and intervened in time. Just."

"Just? How close did you get?"

Millie paused and took a breath. "The tape wasn't running, so I can't be certain."

"You don't have any record of it?"

"I made some notes, but no, the tapes were used up at

that point. It was the end of the run."

Kilton stayed silent, studying Millie, making him shift on his feet.

"Anyway, we've no option, boss, but to ground Guiding Light until Blackton can identify the issue and see if they can rectify it. If they can rectify it, I'd suggest we start the trial from scratch."

A flash of anger crossed Kilton's face and Millie took half a step back.

"And you don't think you're making too much of this, Millie, as usual?"

"I'm sorry? With respect, boss, it nearly killed us."

Kilton shook his head. "Put it all in writing and drop it on my desk tomorrow morning." He made to leave, but then turned. "And no discussion with anyone."

Millie nodded. "Of course, boss."

He watched as Kilton joined Brian Hill and Jock MacLeish, rather than go back to the bar group.

Millie went back to the bar and tugged Rob on the shoulder.

"We'd best be getting back, young man. The wives will be waiting for their card game."

"Oh no! Rob's dad's here to pick him up," said Johnson. "Ooh, please, Rob's dad. Can he stay for just one more drink?"

Rob looked at his newly presented pint.

"I might just have this first, Millie. I'll see you at yours later."

———

The rusting wheels of Millie's ten-year-old Rover complained as he scraped the kerb outside his married quarter.

"And that's why I'm not a pilot," he reminded himself, clambering out and into the warm June evening.

The sound of laughing women drifted from the back garden as he made his way down the side passage.

Georgina and Mary sat in two tatty garden chairs. Summer dresses, floppy hats, and what looked like gin and tonics in hand. Georgina in her favoured red, Mary in yellow. Millie stood and watched for a moment.

"Darling!" Georgina shouted when she spotted him. "Whatever are you doing lurking in the shadows?"

Millie set down his flight case just inside the open French doors and picked up a third garden chair.

"Just admiring the local beauty."

"Peeping Tom, more like." Georgina lifted herself and kissed him hello. "Drink? scotch?"

"Do we have any ice?"

Georgina thought for a moment. "I don't think so, but I'll see if I can pull something off the inside of the freezer if you like."

"Needs must."

Millie's relief at being home must have shown in his eyes, as Georgina loitered for a moment.

"Everything OK?"

He tried not to glance at Mary; this wasn't the time to say anything about the incident. It was up to Rob and every member of aircrew what they shared with their wives.

"Yes, fine. Just tired."

Georgina looked unconvinced, but then disappeared into the house.

"Well," Millie said turning to Mary, "I thought you might be missing us, but apparently not."

Mary laughed. "The heatwave is so gorgeous. It's just nice to be in the sun."

"No cards tonight?"

"Well, we need four for cards. Did Rob go home to change?"

"Actually, he was still in the bar when I left. I expect he'll be along later."

"Fine, well we can enjoy the evening sun, the three of us." She leant back in her chair and closed her eyes, her shoulder-length brown hair gently shifting in the breeze. Millie smiled at her; so young and pretty and with an up and coming test pilot by her side.

He felt a twinge of jealousy as he recalled the time after the war when he was promoted, and he and Georgina were considered the young ones.

The three of them ate outdoors and remained there in the last of the warmth; it was unusual for it to last so long into the evening.

The Milfords' grandfather clock tolled, its gentle clangs seeping out of the house through the open doors and windows. Ten bells. It was apparent Rob would not be appearing that evening. He was either still in the mess or had headed home, worse for wear.

Millie walked Mary back to their married quarter, two streets away in Trenchard Close.

The house was dark.

"Not here, either." She turned to Millie. "Has my husband forgone us for some new drinking pals?"

"I fear so. We all need to let our hair down every now and again."

She looked thoughtful for a moment. "Yes, of course. A bit rude as we had cards planned. Sorry, Millie."

"Think nothing of it," he said and they kissed their goodbyes on the cheek. "I'm sure he'll be back presently."

Millie sauntered home. Had he missed anything important in the bar of the officers' mess?

It was nagging at him, the brief exchange with Kilton.

Making a bit much of this... Bloody silly thing to say.

He thought of Kilton going over to Brian Hill as he was leaving.

Were they discussing the Guiding Light situation without him?

He looked up as he approached the house and saw Georgina in the kitchen looking at him. He gave a little wave and pushed open the front door.

She was at the sink, apron on, finishing the washing up.

"Let me help you," he said, and he picked up a drying up cloth.

"Thanks. You know what I thought watching you waddle back home?"

"How handsome I look?"

"Yes, obviously, but also how porky you look. You need to lose some weight, mister." She poked him in his side.

"I know, but it's so tedious exercising and, god forbid, dieting."

Georgina stopped washing up. "What happened today?"

Millie smiled. "I can't hide anything from you, can I?"

"Nope."

Millie shrugged and spoke as casually as he could.

"We had a little moment in the air."

"Oh, god." Georgina pulled off her yellow rubber gloves. "Tell me."

"It's fine, it's fine. Everyone's OK. It was just a moment. Briefly scary, but we got out of it and that's all that matters. Actually, Rob was flying and did a sterling job."

"Rob was flying? Is that why he isn't here tonight."

"I think so. Letting off some steam in the mess."

"Fair enough. Did you say anything to Mary?"

"No. That's up to Rob. Everyone's different."

"Can you tell me what happened?"

Millie thought for a moment. "Not really. Sorry."

She reached forward and put her hands on his cheeks. "It doesn't matter. I'm glad you're safe, Squadron Leader Milford."

They kissed and he welled up, the near-death experience catching up with him.

He'd seen it in others: a delayed reaction.

Georgina didn't seem to notice. She released him and walked over to their wall calendar, pinned to a cork board over the table.

"I nearly counted the days today. It's something like one hundred and twenty. She lifted the pages until October showed.

"I'm sorry, what?"

Her finger rested on October 19th. "This is the day, isn't it? October 19th. Your last day in the RAF."

"Ah. Yes."

She let the pages of the calendar fall back down.

"One hundred and twenty days, Millie, that's it. All I ask is that you remain in one piece. OK?"

He laughed. "I promise. Believe me, I'm looking forward to it as much as you are."

"Are you?"

"Yes, of course. I'm going to take up sailing, remember? I'm sure the RAF pension can stretch to the Lee-on-Solent place we saw. Just."

She tilted her head, appraising him. "Good. It'll be fine, Millie. We'll still see all our friends, wherever they get posted."

Millie finished the drying up. Georgina disappeared and reappeared with a tumbler of whisky.

He sat down at the kitchen table and lifted it to his nose.

"Ah, the Glenfiddich."

"Well, I think you need a treat. And it's the posh tumbler, the wedding set. Last one standing."

"The last one? We started with eight."

She smiled. "All things must pass, Millie. Anyway, the attrition rate for glasses in married quarter is pretty high. We've had some pretty wild nights over the years. I think we must have lost three of them in Hong Kong playing that silly game with the cricket ball."

Millie laughed at the memory. "Test Match Sofa was a brilliant game. I was quite the slip catcher when positioned correctly near the piano."

"I'm sure you were, I'm sure you were."

She kissed him on the head and whispered, "I'm glad you're home, Squadron Leader Milford."

He squeezed her hand and smiled up at her.

"Don't worry, our retirement is safe. I'll be getting under your feet every day before you know it."

"Good." She smiled back and headed upstairs, turning off the hall light.

The kitchen light was dim; the midsummer sun had finally set. Orange sodium light from the street lamps filled the window. Millie turned the tumbler over in his hand and let the light glint off it. A beautiful piece of crystal. Such a shame they'd lost the others. But maybe it was a price worth paying for the fun they'd had.

He made a mental note to ensure this tumbler survived into retirement. Something to drink from and remember the glory days.

He drained the glass, suddenly remembering his

morning appointment. Nobody came away from a Mark Kilton encounter without bruises.

———

A drunken test pilot played the piano, badly. Rob laughed, still huddled in among the senior pilots.

Kilton watched from the bar, as the pianist beckoned the men around Rob to join in with the song. Most of them sprung up, but Rob remained in his seat, enjoying the show.

The TFU boss picked up his drink and made his way over, choosing the vacant space next to his young prodigy.

"I've been thinking about this nonsense in the Vulcan. I don't think we can let a single uncorroborated incident derail an internationally important project."

He studied Rob, who nodded slowly.

"Its strategic importance cannot be underestimated, you understand that don't you, May?"

The music grew raucous as the men sang a bad version of Cliff Richard's 'Livin' Doll'.

Rob nodded again, staying silent.

Kilton had to raise his voice above the singing.

"Don't you think there was a chance you could have overridden the autopilot with the stick?" Rob furrowed his brow, but Kilton continued. "It won't disengage if you touch the stick. The computer will fight you for a bit until you let go."

"I didn't grab the stick until we cancelled," he finally said.

"Maybe not grabbed it, but it's a tight space, and you may have gently leaned on it or subconsciously pushed it forward while monitoring the flight. You wouldn't have been the first to do that, May."

Rob pondered.

"I mean," Kilton continued, "it would be enormously helpful to me personally to hear that there might be some other explanation. And it's possible. Isn't it, May? You might have accidentally nudged it. That's all it would take at that speed and height to cause a scare."

Rob bowed his head.

"You're not in trouble, May. This is what testing is all about. Now we know how she'll react." He paused and spoke slowly. "It's important you agree that you may have nudged it."

Rob's head came back up and he turned to look at the boss. Kilton gave a small nod of encouragement.

"I suppose it's always possible."

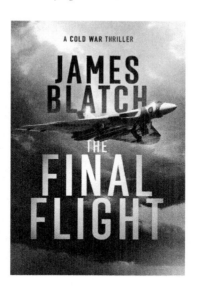

The Final Flight is available now at the Amazon store

FROM JAMES BLATCH

Please join my occasional newsletter. This is best place to keep up to date with future releases.

jamesblatch.com

If you enjoyed Dark Flight, please consider leaving a review.

Reviews are hugely important to authors as they help the book gain additional promotion in the online stores.

ACKNOWLEDGMENTS

As with The Final Flight, my father, a former Royal Air Force test pilot provided the most valuable help while I wrote this book.

Despite being in his nineties, he remains sharp and speaks with a clarity about military flying operations. And he pulls no punches, for which I am grateful!

As this book was set in the United States, I was lucky enough to be able to call on military veterans from the US armed forces to help with the inevitable Britishisms and other less authentic observations I may have made.

I would particularly like to thank Chris Burnett, a former US Marine aviator, who now flies 777s for United Airlines, for his invaluable help and more importantly, his enthusiastic support for my writing.

In addition, Tom Milkie, who worked in the aviation industry at Edwards Air Force Base, also provided valuable feedback on an earlier draft of the novel.

My advanced reader team is a growing force of writers and readers who have very kindly given me their time. I am grateful to you all!

I'm lucky to be part of a writing community where mutual help and support are par for the course.

Andrew Lowe is my UK based story editor. He asks the hard questions about why characters behave in a certain way and between us the story becomes more than just a series of events to describe.

Leighton Wingate is my US based copy editor. His work in correcting my Britishness was invaluable. Leighton turned out to be a perfect pick, with many personal connections to the locations in the book. I hope we will work together again soon.

As with my previous novel, I strive for authenticity, but of course, it is a novel and I have therefore stretched some aspects of reality. 'OpSec' or Operational Security, enforced to the strict degree that it was in the 1960s would have meant a much less interesting story, and so the characters in Dark Flight are a little more relaxed about such an important issue than their real-life counterparts were!

Any inaccuracies are entirely my fault. If you spot something or would like to feedback, I would love to hear from you.

James.

james@jamesblatch.com

ABOUT THE AUTHOR

James Blatch is a former BBC defence reporter and a former BBFC film examiner.

James covered British military matters around the world including stints on the aircraft carrier, HMS Invincible, as well as reporting from Ali Al Salem (Kuwait), Gioa Del Colle (Italy) and Bardufoss (Arctic Circle, Norway).

He was lucky enough to fly twice with 1 (Fighter) Squadron in a Harrier MkT.10 as well as with 41 Squadron in a Sepecat Jaguar.

Today James lives near Huntingdon in the UK with his wife, two children and two dogs. He works in publishing and other ventures.

The author, after a flight in a Jaguar, Royal Air Force Coltishall, 2003.

© Crown Copyright

facebook.com/jamesblatchauthor

twitter.com/jamesblatch

instagram.com/james_blatch

Printed in Great Britain
by Amazon

82325902R00210